FINDING MY FOREVER

S. DREAMS

1

Now

The world outside the tinted window blurred as a jet-black hatchback drove in the rain down the motorway. It was evening and getting darker as the car drove down the quiet roads towards their destination which was a quiet town. The wind pushing the grass, forcing it to lie down and submit to its power. Birds were trying to fight against the wind but would soon give up and go with the flow.

"I know this is all new to you sweetheart but please be good." A soft hesitant voice broke the silence from the driver's seat.

Please let this one work, Paige Fields thought with a worried and tired sigh. Being a social worker was difficult. Her profession consisted of seeing different families and children, often helping them solve problems or helping them in a crisis. Her work had always been challenging but she wouldn't change it for the world. It helped her to see the difficulties children and adults faced behind closed doors and it opened her eyes. Paige was always taught to not grow attached to her clients, but Elisa Fayers was different.

They had heard of the girl's name more than once within social services. Social workers who had worked with her in the past would say how impossible she was to work with, how cold she was, how she hardly spoke, and when she did it was sarcastic as anything. No social worker had stayed with Elisa and her case for more than a month, giving up on the child and deeming her hopeless. Stories of her circulated the workplace which made others shy away from ever having to meet her. The day Paige was called in to meet said little girl, she was ready to turn down her case without even knowing anything about the child, she was ready to say no to her boss who insisted she was the only person for the job. But the moment Paige laid eyes on the little girl who looked small and vulnerable in the metal chair holding onto a little teddy bear, all her negative thoughts flew out the window. How could she leave this child with lifeless eyes to the jaws of the world?

Elisa Fayers was a special case and a special little girl who needed love. Who needed a family who loved her despite her odd character, who simply needed to be a child. Reading through her file tugged at Paige's' heart as she read the papers which spoke of the little girls' life. The many families she had passed through. She swore to always be there for the lost girl, and 8 years later she knew exactly how she functioned. Elisa was like a lot of little 16-year-old girls. But at the same time, she was not. Paige knew exactly what made the child sad, what sent off triggers, what made her angry, what made her hurt, she knows that the child was patient but if she wanted something then she would do anything to get it. Paige called this arrogance and stubbornness. But Elisa called it determination. Despite her little trouble making ways and little tricks she loved to play especially on Paige, she could not help but love the girl and praise her to her family every time Elisa had done something amazing. Whether it was speaking more than yes or no or just smiling at her, Paige was there for it all and was proud of every small achievement.

Finding a family for Elisa was the hardest. She had lived with her mother Delilah happily until she was murdered in cold blood.

They never found the killer and Elisa never saw the incident as she was out cold when they found her and so they closed the case; helping the child move on and hoping they could give her a life she deserved. They had an inkling that Elisa knew or saw something as she would tense at the mere mention of her mother. But to help her heal from the loss, they simply put her into therapy and tried to help her focus on the future, something that didn't work for a girl who didn't want to speak.

She was only 8 at the time- desperately needing a family. They had gotten in touch with her father only for him to refuse in taking her in. Paige could not understand what parent wouldn't want their own child but knew it would break the little girls heart; and so instead of telling Elisa that her own father didn't want her, she told her that her father wasn't in a position to look after her.

The girl had accepted it with no questions and did not seem to be too worried, and so the topic of her father was never mentioned again. From then on, she was put into foster home after foster home, only ever staying for about 4 months before the foster family begged for her to be taken back. The longest stay she had ever had in a foster home was 8 months. But even that eventually turned to ruins and Elisa came crawling back into Paige's car. She could never understand the problem and the foster families always refused to explain their reasons for giving up on the girl. Paige eventually gave up demanding an explanation and would just drive over, thank the family, and take Elisa to a new family. She could not tell how the little girl ever felt most of the time as she hid her feelings well. But when she could tell how she was feeling, which was rare, it was mostly anger at something she could not control.

"They really are nice. I promise. The eldest is Alexander. He's 26. Your other brothers range from 25 down to 18. You're the youngest." Paige had been in the process of finding a new home for the girl when she stumbled across her father's file and found that Elisa not only had 1 sibling but 4 of them. All older than her in fact and all boys. They had been living with their father in England while Elisa had been living with her mother in California. What confused the social worker was that there was no paperwork sating a divorce between the mother Delilah Fayers and the father William West. They had been happily married with their 5 children but at some point, during their marriage, they had separated with no hard feelings and seemed to not want to end their marriage despite not having any contact. It was strange and made her a bit angry that William had been looking after his sons but refused his daughter. Paige had immediately tried to get in contact with the West family and when she did, it wasn't William she spoke to. But Alexander West- the eldest of the West siblings. She found that Alexander had guardianship of his siblings as their father had gone missing and that he was more than willing to take in his little sister. She recalled the conversation they had over the phone and how shocked he was, she could hear the emotion in his voice and felt a wave of pity for the man who was parent to all his younger siblings.

Rubbing at her forehead slightly she looked into the rear-view mirror and her eyes landed on the girl who had her cheek pressed against the window and held her phone tightly to her chest. Again, Elisa did not seem shocked at the news that she had siblings. Perhaps shocked at the amount but not shocked that she had siblings at all, which lead her to believe that perhaps she had lived with her brothers for a while before her mother took her away. Paige didn't know what her brothers were like but wanted to put her at ease. She just needed stability, god knows what else she hides and refuses to talk about with her therapist.

"We're nearly there sweetheart.... how are you feeling?" Her eyes met the smaller humans' eyes in the mirror. Her cold hazel eyes meeting Paige's bright green ones, emotion non-existent and hidden behind that mask she has grown with over the years. How could hazel look so cold?

"How should I feel?" Her soft voice was monotone and empty, it's how she always spoke. With no expression in her voice, as if she were a robot that hadn't been programmed to feel. Paige pushed back the heavy sigh that was threatening to escape her lips like it normally does when she was being difficult. Her lips twitched letting Paige know that she knew she was pushing her social worker but honestly did not know how to feel. She was confused and dare say worried, but she wouldn't tell her social worker that, no, she would keep it to herself.

"I don't know darling, only you will know." She spoke in a calm voice and she nodded after a moment before returning her gaze back outside and watching as the sky grew darker. Deep down the older woman knew she was nervous. But she had this way of hiding everything behind a mask. The social worker did not know whether it was a gift or a curse.

They turned onto a side street that went through a small field before there was a lone house with deep woods surrounding the home. It nerved Paige how hidden from the world it seemed to be, how isolated and cut off it was. The house was lovely, it looked cosy and well-lived in. There was a swing on the side of the house and on the other side seemed to be football posts set up. Small daisies and dandelions spread out and hidden amongst the grass, honeysuckle and Boston ivy climbing up the side of the house with small fruits and soft sweet scent permanently staining the air around the house. This was a complete change to what Elisa was used to. She had been in many homes but most of them lacked a unique feeling and seemed quite bland. This was the home that she lived in as a baby, this was different. Paige felt worry build up in her chest like it usually does whenever she must drop Elisa off at a new home. She never knew how it would turn out and she hoped each time it would go well. Elisa was like her own child and she knew that she would do whatever she could to make sure she found her forever home.

Paige parked up in the driveway hearing the gravel crunch beneath the tires before turning to look at the girl. For a moment, all they could hear was the heavy fain pelting against the window and he wind whistling.

"You ready sweetheart?" Paige asked gently not wanting to rush her. Elisa looked at her with a blank look before nodding stiffly, grabbing her rucksack and a small suitcase. She watched Elisa's every move, noting how she kept her eyes on her shoes and her shoulders tensed. Her small hands clenching, digging her nails into her palm. Paige frowned in concern; she had never seen the girl act like this. This was a lot of emotion from an emotionless girl, and she worried about how coming to her birth home would affect her.

Elisa walked silently feeling as if she was walking into danger, which in her mind, she was. She was moving in with men she had to call brothers but knew hardly anything about. That's what made her twitch. She hated being unaware, in the dark. Elisa looked up at the woman who was the only constant figure in her life and watched as an encouraging smile was directed at her. Assuring her she would be safe. Happy. She didn't believe her. Happiness was scarce in her life, something she hadn't felt in a long while.

"You sure?" Paige asked the little girl once more making Elisa shrug. Nothing she could do now but face whatever lied ahead for her. She looked up at the double oak doors letting out an annoyed sigh, as if being there was a mere inconvenience. *Say hello to Elisa West.*

2

Now

Elisa had gone through many things in her life, different situations that have moulded her personality. She had grown up to be a brave girl, one who will take on any situation head-on. But even she will admit that this moment was daunting, she was nervous as anything. The people she was about to meet were her blood, which was even more dangerous than the past families she had been with. She had a bond with these people who she hardly remembered. Her social worker would never understand despite being the only one who knew enough about her.

The oak door opened quickly and a boy- maybe a year or two older- poked his head out like a meercat. Paige smiled gently at the young man who had answered the door and made sure she was relaxed. If she were tense, then so would Elisa and then it would take forever to make her understand she was safe. A reason, unbeknownst to her, meant that she always had to reassure Elisa that each new home was safe. That she could lower her guard and get to know the people she was living with.

The boy who answered the door was one of the West siblings, Preston West, who was the youngest in the household. He was also the only West boy who could not care less about his future which normally meant his older brothers had to steer him to do things. He was the baby of the family and never had to worry much about anything. Something which would change the moment he opened the door. Preston had been in the middle of a video game with one of his friends from his 6th form when the door knocked. Of course, he assumed it was one of his brothers so he ignored it knowing they would eventually go through the back door or open the door with a key. But when neither of those two happened and another soft knock was heard, he abandoned his game in resignation ready to yell at whichever idiot had dared to stop his game.

He just was not expecting to see two unfamiliar people when he quickly pulled the door open. A woman in her mid-thirties holding a clipboard with a young girl holding a suitcase. His eyes lingered on the short girl with light caramel hair who was staring down at her feet like they were the only thing interesting in her life.

Who on earth were these people? Why would they even be out here in the pouring rain at this time? He stared at them completely confused. They didn't look familiar in any way and he was left stumped and unsure whether or not to let them in. Despite them looking harmless, he had been taught to never judge a book by its cover.

Had he missed something in the family meeting yesterday? Was he supposed to do something? The woman smiled gently at him and he straightened; aware that these two people had come out of their way to find this house. The West house wasn't exactly easy to find. You had to drive down quite a few back streets before going down a narrow road through a large field. They knew exactly where they were going and that sent the alarms in his head ringing. Although Preston wasn't the smartest of the siblings, in his opinion, he knew that random people shouldn't know where they lived unless they had been shown. This caused the boy to be on edge and narrow his eyes at the two.

"Hi. How may I help you?" Paige wanted to chuckle at the boy who obviously wasn't aware of their arrival and was cautious, if his tense body was any indication. His voice was polite and sounded bored, but she knew he was suspicious.

"Hello dear. I'm Paige Fields. I've been in contact with someone named Alexander West?" Paige knew who the boy was of course as Alexander had told her the names of his brothers. But judging on his reaction, she didn't want to scare him and make him slam the door in her face. His brown eyes lit up slightly at the mention of his older brother and nodded vigorously whilst relaxing, yet he kept his guard up. The older woman smiled in pride that the young boy knew to not trust anyone straight away.

"Please wait here. I'll go grab him!" Preston called to the two women who stood under the porch roof before quickly running up the stairs to his brothers' room. Paige chuckled as she heard his thundering steps echoed through the house while Elisa clenched her jaw. She faced the other way just wanting to be shown her room and sleep. Preston barged through the bedroom door ignoring the fact that he had broken one of the West rules of knocking before entering and looked around the large room for his eldest brother.

Alexander didn't have the largest room in the house despite the stereotype of the eldest sibling having the biggest bedroom. The walls were a dark navy blue with light grey carpets, there were a lot of white and navy trinkets surrounding the room including the shelf of trophies from his high school and college years. Across one wall was a family picture. It included the boys with their father. That had been their family for the past 13 years, but Alexander knew he would be changing that photo soon.

"Yo Alex?" Alexander sighed heavily from his bathroom at the sound of his youngest brother. His shoulders slumping and eyes briefly closing before he lifted his chin. He looked at himself in the mirror making sure he looked presentable enough to meet the social worker. That's probably what Preston was hollering about. He ran a hand through his chocolate brown hair and straightened the collar on his white shirt feeling the nerves running across his skin.

Alexander was guardian over his three brothers. Their father went missing 8 years ago and nobody knew what happened. Their father wasn't unhappy or in trouble or anything. He had a good life with his sons' but he just... disappeared one day. Their father never came home from work. Soon enough the police dropped the case saying it was a dead-end and there were no leads or clues, leaving Alexander as his brother's guardians. He didn't mind; he loved them to bits. But sometimes he finds it hard to balance parenting and being a brother. Even if his brothers were old enough. They still needed to be kept an eye on. He had become a parent at such a young age and didn't have time to mess about with his brothers, he had to be the responsible one and make sure they lived together safely and happily.

The eldest West sibling worked as a police detective in their little village. Robin Hoods Bay which was in the District of Scarborough. Their home was closer to the wooded area of their village but every now and then the brothers would venture to the coastline, less now that they were all adults. Although their village was small and it seemed that there would be hardly any trouble, surprisingly there was quite a few troublemakers, thieving and sometimes runaways he needed to look for. But Alexander was amazing at his job and always finished the case within a day or two. As he straightened his shirt, he could see the tattoo on his collarbone peeking out from under the fabric, a smile touched his lips as his finger rubbed at the ink permanently etched into his skin. 5 birds. He had gotten the tattoo when he turned 18, a tribute for Her. Elisa.

Alexander remembered the most about their little sister. He remembers her giggles, her contagious smile, her adorable button nose, her bright sparkly hazel eyes. His memories of their little sister faded year by year until she was simply a fleeting thought in his day-to-day life. He missed her of course. But.... he could not help that childish thought that always echoed in his head, that their little sister had taken away their mother from them. Now, adult, he knew that she was only a little three-year-old baby. How could it ever be her fault? But the child in him needed a reason to explain his mother's absence and Elisa was that reason.

Sighing heavily in anticipation, Alexander ran a hand through his brown hair that needed a good trim and walked into his bedroom where Preston was leaning against the bed, absentmindedly chewing his lip. A nervous habit he had required over the years.

"C'mon. Out." Alexander gave a light shove to his brother who whined and sent him a glare to which he only glared back and ruffled his hair. The brothers walked down the stairs together; Preston wondering if his friends had carried the game without him while the other brother began to sweat. He was going to see his little sister for the first time in years, 13 years to be precise. How much had she changed? He couldn't wait to hug her. He wanted to see if she still gave her big bear hugs, if her eyes still twinkled when she was planning something, if her dimples showed when she smiled brightly. He couldn't wait to see the little sister who left them. But he also didn't want to see her. A small part of him wanted to shun her and make sure she felt the pain the brothers felt when their mother left with her.

When their mother chose one sibling over the rest of them and let without a simple goodbye or reason.

Preston paused in the living room doorway as he saw his older brother stop in the middle of the hallway. He saw him tapping his fingers on his thigh. Just as Preston had a nervous habit, so did Alexander. It was rare for the siblings to see the eldest anything but confident. So, this nervous action caught Prestons' attention as Alexander breathed in and out slowly as if he was preparing himself for an upcoming war.

Paige watched the man in the house; she watched as he struggled to compose himself and felt her heart reach out to him in sympathy. She understood this must be hardest on him as he was old enough to remember young Elisa the most. What she didn't realize was that his anxiety and fear was for another reason completely. That Elisa being here wasn't scaring him the most, nor was the responsibility of having to look after his long 'lost' sister. No, Alexander wasn't struggling for those reasons.

Elisa peeked from beneath her long lashes to study the man just inside the house. His fingers drumming against his leg, the sheen of sweat above his brow and the aura of nerves was practically suffocating her. She noted his emotions and understood immediately what nobody else could sense, the realisation made her want to either laugh at his predicament or sigh in annoyance.

Alexander had not told his younger siblings that Elisa was coming home.

She's beautiful, is all Alexander could think as he stared into the girls' cold, hazel eyes, eyes that were nearly identical to their fathers. She avoided his gaze refusing to look him directly in the eye. He noted the way her brown hair cascaded over her shoulders in chocolate waves, the way it covered one of her eyes and the white ribbon that tied two locks of her hair back. Alexanders breathe caught as he realized that he was looking at a young lady- no longer a baby or a child. He was not seeing the Elisa West they once knew; he was looking at Elisa Fayers who had been in a whole different world compared to her brothers. He swallowed his nerves and plastered on a smile.

"Mrs. Fields I presume?" The false confidence practically dripping from his voice as he turned his eyes to the social worker who stood patiently. The woman smiled at him and Alexander slumped at the warm feeling her smile gave, the motherly feeling she gave off making him relax.

"That's right! It's lovely to meet you, Mr West." She nudged the girl forward gently and his eyes went back to the little human who was now clenching her fists tightly. Suddenly as if realizing that it was still pouring with rain and the two were probably wet and getting unbelievably cold, Alexander flushed and opened the door wider in embarrassment.

"Oh, I apologize. Please come in!" Paige chuckled and nudged Elisa into the house before she walked in and closed the door behind her. The house smelt like vanilla cupcakes and Elisa felt herself stiffen; it smelt like her mother once did. Alexander led the two into the living room and noticed Preston was pulling on a black jacket while talking on the phone to someone. His eyes met his older brother who was looking at him questioningly.

"I'm off to stop the night over at Andres. That cool?" Preston asked already knowing Alex wouldn't mind and so grabbed his backpack not paying attention to the two females behind Alexander.

"Sure, just make sure all your coursework is done or I'm dragging you back here." The threat clear in his tone and Preston huffed knowing he would do that if he did not complete his coursework. He picked up his binder and waved it in Alexanders' direction before walking out the back door, throwing a quick bye over his shoulder.

The eldest sibling sighed in relief, that was one less thing to worry about. Now all he had to worry about was his other two brothers who had no idea about their newest housemate. It's not that he was ashamed of her or anything, he was worried about their reactions. Like him, his brothers had become rather spiteful towards their sister for 'taking' their mother which then also grew into hatred for their mother taking away their sister. All in all, it was not looking great. Needing time to gather his thoughts and compose himself, he offered them a seat on the soft white sofas before excusing himself to make some tea for them all. He hadn't even spoken to Elisa and he already felt like he had failed in some way.

Elisa finally looked up from her lap and observed her surroundings once the man had left the room. They were in what looked to be a living room. A large tv screen on the opposite wall to where she sat, with shelves of books and pictures on either side of the screen. The wall to her left was complete glass; a large glass window that filled the entirety of what would have been a wall. She could not help the awe and wonder that flashed through her body as she looked out over the fields that were covered in purple flowers. Perhaps lavender? The sofa she sat on was soft and she stopped herself from stroking the velvety fabric. Comfort and luxury were foreign to her and she did not want to get used to it. She felt Paige's eyes on her and sighed in frustration as she heard the unspoken questions. Without even looking at her Elisa spoke.

"I'm fine." Paige's eyes softened at the two softly spoken words from the teenager. Two words she used on a daily occurrence. It was always 'I'm fine'. She hummed in disbelief and looked around the room just as Elisa had. Part of Paige's job was to make sure that the house would be suitable for a child to live in, and the environment was safe to her mental and physical wellbeing. She had already done background checks on all the boys and checked the history of the town; without a doubt, she knew Elisa would be safe and possibly happy here. It would just take time for her to adjust and settle in a life where people will not leave her.

Alexander walked back into the room with two steaming hot cups of tea and one hot chocolate with two marshmallows and just a bit of whipped cream. A drink his mother used to love, and his baby sister used to love stealing from his mother and siblings. He wondered if she liked it now. He placed the tray on the table in front of the sofa they sat on and handed them their cups. He lifted the hot chocolate to the girl and watched as she simply looked out the window, not once looking at him. His eye twitched slightly and he placed the cup in front of her before sitting down in the other sofa. He smiled softly trying to ignore the sting of rejection from his sister.

"So..." He started but realised he did not know what to say making Paige smile and look at Elisa. She saw the way the 16-year-old stiffened on the sofa and clutches her phone tighter. Clearly, she would have to instigate the conversation. Like she normally does.

"Well Mr west-"

"Oh, please call me Alex." Alexander interrupted the woman.

"Alex. It is lovely to be able to meet you in person. I'm Paige Fields. I have been Elisa's social worker ever since she.... since she was 10 years old." Alexander watched how Elisa sucked in a breath before letting go slowly. He also felt his heart stutter as he realised what Paige had said. Elisa, his little sister, had been alone for years. Why she had not come home was beyond him and he suddenly felt the urge to know exactly what his sister had to live through. He wanted to know about the woman who left them, what happened to her? But he knew he could not ask those questions just yet no matter how badly he wanted to know.

"Elisa. This is your eldest brother, Alexander. He's exactly 10 years older than you and knew you when you were a baby." Paige said to Elisa who only tensed more. The silence stretched as they waited for Elisa to say something, to look up, to react, something. But she simply stared out the window as if this situation did not affect her in the least, as if the man across from her was nothing to her. Paige felt the frustration bubble up in her chest but kept calm. This was the worst she's ever seen Elisa and she knew it was because there was an actual bond between the two people in the room. A blood bond.

Alexander did not know what to say. He wanted her to look at him, he wanted to know this girl who was supposedly his little sister. But she would not even look at him. He sighed and looked at Paige who looked back at him, she needed to talk to him alone. Alexander smiled tightly and stood up smacking his hands together before rubbing them.

"Right then... Elisa? I'll show you to your room so you can relax before dinner tonight." Elisa stood and grabbed her things. He offered to help carry her suitcase or rucksack, but she backed away from him not wanting him to touch any of her belongings. Sighing heavily, Alex took the hint and showed her out of the living room and up the staircase with his shoulders sagged. Elisa felt a twinge of guilt in her heart as she saw Alexander tapping his fingers against his thigh. He was nervous; she was making him nervous. She wanted to reach out and introduce herself, to tell him what made her Elisa. But she denied her right to be his sister and simply followed him like an omega wolf following their alpha leader.

Alexander led her down the hallway and stood in front of a door at the end, his head tilting sightly as he tried to catch her eyes.

"This is your room. I'll give you a proper tour either later today or tomorrow. Take your time and relax. I'll call you down when dinners ready." Elisa said nothing and whizzed past him into the bedroom before closing the door quickly; leaving Alexander wondering what his life was now going to entail. Was there always going to be this invisible barrier between them? Was there any hope to repair their forgotten sibling bond?

The two stood on either side of the door. One was a confused and hopeful man, longing to be able to hold his little sister and find out exactly who she was. The other was an empty and cold girl, searching for answers to questions she never asked.

Alexander raised a hand to knock, wanting to demand her to talk to him, but instead laid a hand on the wooden door; thoughts of shunning her left his mind and all he wanted to do was know her. He was her big brother and he had to be there for her, figure out how to make her smile, how to bring back the twinkle in her eyes.

"Um.... yeah.... you have to come down for dinner when I call you Elisa. I'd like to get to know you." He called out to her but once again she did not reply making his hope dash out the front door. He nodded and pulled his hand away in resignation, his fingers going back to beating a tune on his thigh.

"Welcome home little sister." He whispered lowly before walking back down the stairs.

Elisa stood in the darkness of the bedroom with only a lamp shining in the corner and the sounding of retreating footsteps being the only sound she could hear other than her breathing and the words he had mumbled; a small smile gracing her face.

3

Now

The library in the small village was his home away from home, the books that lined every shelf was an opportunity of escaping reality. Dust never settled as he was constantly cleaning; showing his love of books and the millions of stories that were printed in ink. Owen loved his job at the library and did not care about the thoughts of other men his age. His passion was writing and what better way than surrounding yourself with millions of authors? It was his haven when he wasn't home or working at his second job at a café.

The other young man who had been hunched over a table all evening stretched with a groan. His pencil rolled across the surface and was suddenly stopped by Owen's quick reflexes. He paused in his cleaning and studied the man who rubbed his eyes aggressively.

"You're not sleeping again." Owen did not question but stated in a knowing voice as his eyes lingered on the dark circles under the younger man's eyes. He groaned and began packing his belongings away sluggishly, giving away his tiredness.

"Leave me alone man." He grumbled wearily with his eyes half-closed, his long eyelashes brushing his cheeks. Owen shook his head, determined to push his little brother to tell him the truth.

"Why? What's going on?" Once again Owen states in his soft and calm voice, the voice that always managed to relax people no matter the situation. The man sighed knowing he was not pestering to be annoying- it was just his nature to care for everyone and worry about them. It was just who Owen West was. Roman threw his bag over his shoulder and barely looked at Owen who was studying him like a doctor would their patient.

"I've had a lot of orders for personal paintings and I'm so behind schedule." Owen eyed his younger brother with a knowing smile completely ignoring the excuse Roman had given him.

"Nightmares. Have you been taking your pills?" He asked as he locked up the register, turned off the scanning machines and printers. Roman sent his older brother an exasperated look who completely saw through his lie.

"Can you not reach out to your motherly instincts?" He scoffed annoyed while Owen simply smiled unoffended. It was true that Owen's personality was very motherly since their mother left and his brothers often commented and complained about his consistent questioning and making sure they were okay. His caring and loving nature made up for all the affection they missed out in the past few years; and although he was overbearing, Roman and the others were grateful for his thoughtful ways.

Owen shrugged and made sure the library was locked up before the two made their way through the backdoor of the building and into the cold crisp air. Roman sucked in the fresh air and looked up into the clear night sky; he smiled slightly as he caught sight of a few stars that were normally hidden behind dark clouds. The two brothers were the complete opposite yet seemed to be the closest out of the four brothers. When Roman was sad Owen was there to console him, when Owen was distant Roman would be there to shake him back to reality.

The two brothers walked through the empty streets of their village in comfortable silence. The waves crashed against the cliffs and the wind blew gently- ruffling the boys' hair fondly. The cobblestone paths were lit only by the warm glow of the streetlamps; the village deserted of life and activity. Their car was parked just outside the small village. They lived in the field nearer the woods where nobody would disturb them. Why their father had them live there, they will never understand, but they never complained about the peace they got from living away from other people.

As they neared the house, Owen noticed the living room light on along with one of the bedrooms upstairs. He furrowed his brows in concentration as he tried to figure out which room it was. Certainly not his, nor Alex. It could have been Preston, but he could have sworn Preston's bedroom was the left window. Roman was not as curious as Owen was and thought nothing of the light on the second floor. The brothers unlocked the door to their home and went to search for the others. They paused when they saw their eldest brother and Owen felt that familiar ghost of concern peeking out from his heart.

Alexander sat in the kitchen with his face buried in his hands, dinner had been uncomfortable, to say the least. He had tried and tried multiple times to engage Elisa into a conversation of getting to know each other. But all he received was a blank look. He did notice a few things about her behaviour however which had him questioning her past life with both their mother and her life in the system.

The moment he mentioned their mother she tensed up and her eyes would flicker to stare at her hands, when he asked her about the foster families, she had stayed with she would have a sad look on her face, and whenever she did look at him when he spoke, he noted how she never looked him in the eye but rather looked past his head slightly or at his chest. She never made eye contact; she did not want to know him, and he cursed his earlier thoughts of wanting her to feel pain. She wasn't what he expected, and he wanted to know everything. He sighed in frustration and lifted his head, only to let out a small yelp when he came face to face with Owens curious one.

"What have we said about the personal bubble Owen? To not touch the bubble. You just obliterated mine!" Alexander snapped. Owen frowned as he studied him before speaking his opinions; not at all affected by Alexanders words and tone.

"First Roman isn't getting sleep and now you're stressing about something. No, wait you are frustrated because something is not going your way. What is it?" He asked his brother who looked at him incredulously. Alexander mentally wrote down that he would have to chat with his brother yet again about his tendencies to read people out loud. Sometimes it got on people's nerves and he didn't blame them, not everyone wanted their feelings being spoken about openly.

"It's nothing. Dinner is in the microwave if you want it." Owen watched his brother leave the room and go upstairs with his head hung low and his hand running through his hair, tugging slightly. Roman heated their food and set it in front of Owen before digging into his own plate.

"Where's Pres?" Roman shouted out knowing their brother could hear.

"At Andres!" Alexander yelled back.

Owen furrowed his brows and stopped chewing his food. So, Alexander was home alone. They had a rule of not leaving the lights on if you were not in the room, and they never broke it.

So, who was upstairs? Which room was it? He stood up, leaving his food unattended, and walked up the stairs to figure out why this issue was bugging him. His gut was telling him that something was different; something was amiss, and his gut was never wrong.

Alexander was just coming out of the bathroom when he detected movement on the far side of the hallway. He thought for a hopeful moment that Elisa had left the room to come talk to him. But his hope diminished when he realised there was a person about to enter the room- not leave it. Before he could stop his brother, the door was opened.

Owen stared in complete confusion at the figure sat on the window seat. Their legs hugged to their chest and their eyes which had been previously looking out the window was now staring at him expressionlessly. Hazel eyes that should have been lively and warm, were cold and empty. A deep dark hole of nothingness which could suck in any person staring directly into her eyes. Her hair covered her face mysteriously as if protecting her. Owen could not read this little girl; he could read every one, he could always see through their facades. But this girl whose eyes seemed to be hollow had no story to tell. Not one that he could read anyways.

Alexander rushed to his side breathless and investigated the room. Owen turned to his brother wordlessly, searching his face for an explanation.

"Look at her properly Owen." Alexander finally let out. Elisa watched Alexander struggle until he finally gave in, her eyes went back to observing the new man who was her other older brother. Owen- The second eldest. Narrowing her eyes, Elisa took note that this man was one to watch out for. The way he had been studying her intently earlier suggested that he could normally pick out lies and would know if someone was hiding something. That is someone she needed to avoid.

Owen looked back at the small 'child'. Her hollow hazel eyes narrowed at him and glinted with a knowing spark, her hair looked like flowing chocolate, almost like caramel even. He saw the way her clothes practically swallowed her and how she curled into herself. But not out of fear; it was like she was protecting herself in that position. His eyes scanned her features which seemed childlike, but he could see that she was in her middle teens. Maybe 17? Alexander told him to look at her. To look at her. It was not until he focused on her face that he noticed something under her left eye. A small beauty mark. Any person could have a beauty mark under their eye, but it wasn't that specific feature that caught his attention. He knew her. He knew those hazel eyes, the eyes that were missing the sparkle.

Owen's lips parted in astonishment as he finally realised who the little girl in front of him was.

"Lissy?" He breathed as memories breached his mind of a small giggly baby girl who he adored with all his heart. A baby girl he had dreamed of one-day meeting again and holding her close, but his dreams were put on hold as she rolled her eyes and looked away from him. Alexander shut the door abruptly and grabbed Owens's arm, breaking him from his daze.

"We are going to leave her while we talk. I have not had the chance to talk to her or find out everything from the past years she has been with mum and in the system. I need to find that stuff out, but I do not need nor want your guys hassling her. This is my job to handle understand. Don't even think of telling Roman-"

"I'm not a kid Alex. I am also right here. You do realise I could hear you all." Roman scoffed as he leaned against the bannister rail with a look of unconcern- his eyes, however, portrayed his curiosity. Alexander groaned in annoyance. He had hoped to let her settle in for at least two days and get more information on her from Paige before he told his brothers. But it would seem the universe wanted him to introduce all his brothers to their sister immediately. He grabbed both of his brothers' arms and dragged them to his room, ignoring Romans annoyed protests of being manhandled and Owens confused questions.

Elisa sat on the window seat that she knew would become her favourite place, the breeze from the open window soothing her warm skin and teasing her hair. She pressed her small fingers to her cold and slightly chapped lips as a heavy emotion set deep in her heart. She pulled out her phone and rang the number- her eyes closing as she listened to the familiar ringing as she waited.

"Why didn't you tell me they were persistent in knowing who I am?" She whispered as she recognised the emotion rising in her chest, her ears picking up the faint talking from her brothers. Her eyes darted towards the closed door as she focused on the emotion leaking out from her mask.

Worry.

Roman had his arms crossed on the table with his head leaning on them, tiredness eating him up and sleep trying to pull him back into its arm's. Once again, he had another restless night of nightmares and he had resorted to just staying awake to finish off some paintings. He wasn't one to talk about his feelings or any of his problems, so the nightmares were kept between him and his pillows. He would rather suffer alone then worry his brothers.

Alexander stood by the kitchen window sipping his coffee and looking out across the fields. Simply enjoying the peace, he currently had knowing it wouldn't last very long. Peace never lasted in the West household and so he learnt to take advantage of those moments and enjoy it. How his parents kept their sanity, he had no clue.

Owen stood by the stove making fried eggs for his siblings; his eyes flickering between Alexander and Roman in concern. He knew Roman's nightmares were getting worse and that even though he took his sleeping pills, he would somehow wake up in the night drenched in sweat. He wanted to help his brother but how could he help someone who did not want it? The only thing he could do was constantly checking up on him and making sure he knows Owen was there for him no matter what.

Elisa observed the scene from the doorway, partially hidden and away from their eyesight. She was never one to hesitate or wait. She would dive headfirst into any situation especially if it were a situation that possibly scared her. If she waited, she would never do it; a saying her mother would tell her. Taking a breath, she stepped into the room and immediately all eyes were on her small form that stood confidently. She noted her brothers' different reactions to seeing her.

Owen had a soft and welcoming smile on his face no doubt glad to see her, Alexander watched her with a curious expression, not quite sure how to act around her, whilst Roman glared at her heatedly showing her exactly what he thought of her presence in the house. *Great*, she thought bitterly, *another enemy.*

"Morning Lissy! I am making a fried egg for everyone. You okay with that?" Owen asked cheerily completely ignoring his idiot brothers who were acting as if she was a stranger. She was not a stranger, at least not in Owen's eyes. She was his little sister and although they had not been in each other's lives for 13 years, she would never be a stranger to him. They just had a bit of catching up to do is all.

Elisa peeked at her brother under lashes and saw a ball of sunshine, literally. She wanted to smile at how he tried to ease the obvious tension in the room but remained her blank mask. Completely ignoring his attempts at conversations, she sauntered over to the coffee maker and poured herself a cup. Alexander wrinkled his nose as he watched his youngest sibling drink pure black coffee, no sugar, or any milk; Elisa saw his look and raise a single brow, her eyes growing colder, daring him to comment on her choice. Alexander flushed slightly and cleared his throat as he returned his gaze to the lavender fields. *She is one scary kid*, he thought.

When Alexander had dragged both Roman and Owen into his room, Owen had immediately began throwing questions at the eldest sibling. Roman was confused at the fuss that was being made over this random girl. He had let his mind wander as he tuned out everything being said, exhaustion pulling at his eyes, begging him to give in. Until his ears perked at the sound of a familiar name and shock ran through his system, Lissy. A nickname that was given to their baby sister 13 years ago.

He remembered feeling confusion and hope when he realised that their newest housemate was their little sister. But his emotions flipped abruptly, and he couldn't help but feel the rage and hatred leak into his heart. The same little sister who had stolen their mother from them was back, the same little sister who had caused their father heartache. Now she had waltz back into his life for what reason? Where was his mother? How long had Alex been planning her return? What else was their brother hiding?

He stared at her, openly showing his resentment towards her. He did not trust her; sister or not, he didn't trust her around his family, he didn't trust this weird girl who showed no emotion. The room was tight with the uncomfortable atmosphere that had been created by the siblings. Owen huffed loudly knowing he would be the one who had to create the bridges. Always the peacekeeper.

"So Lissy! I do not think we've introduced ourselves! I'm-"

"Owen the ball of sunshine. Alexander the alpha wolf, Roman the one with staring problems, and my other brother Preston who isn't home right now. I'm Elisa, not Lissy and I'll be in my room." With that she was out of the room as quick as she had made her entrance, leaving the brothers stunned. Owen smiled at the little description of him, and Alexander tilted his head as he stared at the spot, she had been moments before. Roman simply scowled even more.

"Oh, my days, Andre has this cool game that he wants us all to play, we were up all-night playing. Don't worry I've done all my work but..." Preston paused in his ranting as he walked in through the back door and looked around the kitchen in confusion at the looks on his brothers' faces.

"Did I miss something? Was I supposed to do something? Wait I didn't do anything!" Roman was the first to snap out of it and scoffed as he stood up and walked out mumbling about bratty girls. Alexander rolled his eyes at Preston and followed Roman out of the room and upstairs to his bedroom. Preston frowned and looked at Owen for answers looking like a lost puppy.

"What I do?" Owen chuckled at his brothers' obliviousness and shook his head.

"Want some breakfast?" Preston nodded with bright eyes as he slipped into the chair Roman had been sat on previously and carried on rambling to Owen who listened with a fond smile.

Elisa changed into black denim jeans and an oversized t-shirt, her hair brushed out into her natural waves and she added a black ribbon that held back two locks of her hair. Her lips twitched as she tied the ribbon, her mother used to tie her hair up with ribbons and did the same for Elisa. It was the one familiarity she and with her mother. She applied Chapstick as normal and turned around when she heard someone at the door. Alexander waited for her to let him know he was okay to come in, but instead of hearing her quiet voice again, she opened the door harshly and peered at him blankly.

"I'm taking you shopping. You need things." He said half expecting her to say no to him, so he was pleasantly surprised when she nodded, grabbed her phone, and looked up at him expectedly. Roman passed the two and roughly pushed past Elisa who rolled her eyes and simply followed Alexander down the stairs to the navy-blue Ford Fiesta which was sat in the driveway.

Alexander buckled himself in and checked that Elisa had done the same before he set off for York; the hour drive long enough to get to know the person next to him. He tapped the steering wheel with his fingers, drumming to a beat only he could hear. Their surroundings whizzed past them as they drove down the long road Paige had driven down only a day before.

Elisa felt her patience grow thin as she knew her brother wanted to speak but was hesitant to do so.

"Yes?" She finally spoke, prompting him to speak and say whatever he needed to say. Alexander looked at her from the corner of his eye and knew she was not one to beat around the bush, just like their mother. He smiled slightly before nodding.

"What's your favourite colour and why?" Elisa looked at him dubiously; he shrugged at her look.

"Humour me." He said in response to the unimpressed look she made. Elisa rolled her eyes and thought about it. Do not get too close, that was the rule. She was not to get too attached to her brothers, that was the rule she had made for herself. But maybe she could answer some of his questions- if they weren't too personal.

"Green." She finally said. He raised a brow like she did, wanting her to continue.

"Because... it's the colour of life. Green is the colour of life and even though life isn't always so great. You can't help but find it beautiful." Elisa said wistfully and Alexander thought about her words that struck him deeply. It hit him that... this girl may not have had the best life while he and his brothers had a decently happy one. His eyes lingered on her wondering what had happened to her to make her sound so mature and grown up.

"Hmm ok. Your hobby?" Elisa thought about that question. *Hobby. What was her hobby? What did she like doing?* She liked drawing now and then, she used to write in a journal, but she abandoned that after a while. Maybe she would start writing again. *Did she like baking maybe?*

"I'm not too sure. Going from foster home to foster home made it hard to settle down. I was more concerned with my survival than a hobby." Alexander furrowed his brows at her choice in words but understood that she may not have had the luxury of having tried new things.

"I know that you've been in the foster system since you were 8 years old. I... how did you get there?" He asked hoping to find out more about their mother, more about her. He knew that she was probably not around anymore, hence why Elisa had been forced into the system. But he was not given details. This girl was the only one with those answers, she was the only one who knew why it took so long for her to be sent back here to her family, the one who knew everything. He looked over at her and saw her fists clenched tightly and her eyes staring straight ahead; glazed over as if she was watching something.

"Elisa?" Alexander called out to her hoping to snap her out of whatever trance she had fallen into, but his voice fell on deaf ears. His eyes went back to watching the road, his fingers drumming on the steering wheel once more, and the niggling feeling that he may have messed up before they even began to form a bond. Alexander was so absorbed in his thoughts, that he did not realise Elisa was struggling herself.

Elisa could not hear Alexander calling for her, she could not feel the vibrations of the car or smell the citrus car freshener. Her mind stuck somewhere else, another place, another time. It was as if the mention of her being in the foster system had triggered all the pain she had to suffer through. She smelt the heavy smoke from the burning flames that surrounded the room and felt the warm blood dripping down the side of her head. She heard the dripping of liquid falling onto the ground next to her. She felt the branches of twigs and leave scratch her as she ran deeper into the woods. Her mind flashed with images and memories from her past that she would much rather forget. A simple question that seemed innocent was a key to opening one of the memory chests of horror.

"C'mon Lissy, talk to me." Alexander called out, gently touching her arm making her blink from her dark memories and focus on her hands.

She was so out of touch with reality that she didn't correct him on the name, nor did she glare at him for touching her. She did not respond to him still and let the silence envelop them. Her mind focused on the last image her mind conjured up for her. A black rose with blood dripping from the velvet petals.

Soon.

4

Now

Preston never missed the woman known as Delilah West, his mother. He was too young to miss what his elder siblings had. He never knew the affection of a mother, the hug of safety, the kiss of love. He had never had his hair stroked away from his forehead or his tears wiped from his cheeks. Never had he experienced a Mother's Day. None that he could remember anyway.

Whilst he showed no care for the issue, he hated how he missed out on having a mother. There were no motherly figures in his life; except Owen who would show him daily how their mother would have cared for them. But Owen was Owen, and he could never be a mother, as much as he thought he was.

"Hey, bud." Owen walked into Prestons' room, a nervous look on his face. Preston looked up from his laptop and looked at the crease between his brothers' brows.

"Sup with you?" Preston asked without skipping a beat. Owen sucked in a breath and climbed onto the green bed in front of Preston. Alexander always left Owen to break the news to the younger boys; said he could handle it better and explain things clearly. Normally Owen was proud to have that role. But he would do anything to not be the one to tell Preston about his sister. A sister he probably had no recollection of.

"How's college?" Owen asked instead of his original question. He was testing the waters of his brothers' mood. Preston looked at him with a brow raised knowing Owen was there for something else.

"Great. So, what's up?" Owen examined his little brother. His hair messy from running his hand through it and his eyes were curious. Hazel eyes that were almost identical to Elisa. The difference being that while Prestons' eyes were bright with childish energy and mischief, Elisa's were empty and had an almost sinister look to it. Eyes that had seen far too much of the world and knew it's true face. He sighed in nervousness and nodded his head as he got ready to say what needed to be said.

"What do you remember about mum?" The question caught Preston off guard, and he looked at Owen who looked curiously at him. They never talked about their mother, something he was both glad about but also disappointed over. He used to ask as a child but as he slowly grew older, he realised their mother was a taboo subject and it was best to avoid asking questions.

"Nothing? I don't know anything about that woman. Why?" Owen scratches the back of his neck realising this was going to be much harder to explain. He pursed his lips as he tried to figure out what he could say that may trigger a memory from their childhood.

"What do you remember about our childhood?" Preston gave Owen a weird look and laughed slightly at all the random questions.

"What's with all the questions teach?" Owen just stared at him, begging him to comply with his somewhat strange behaviour and he rolled his eyes as he thought about his past, giving into Owens's strangeness.

"I remember going to the beach with you, Roman and Alex. I remember playing hide in seek in the woods with Andre, hiding while you guys, Finley and Karson would look for us. I remember stupid things and ooooh remember the forts we used to build in-"

"YES, but do you remember anyone else? Like a little girl?" Owen interrupted desperately. He hoped that he had some sort of memory of their baby sister, some sort of remembrance that there was a fifth West sibling. Preston chewed his lip out of habit as he tried to figure out what his brother was trying to get out of him, what his brother was wanting- no needing to hear from him.

"I don't know man I don't remember. What girl? Is she an old childhood friend that I don't remember? I'm really confused about why this is so important."

"She's important in our lives Pres. Don't you remember her? The small baby that would sit on the picnic blanket giggling when you would make faces at her. A little girl who would cling to me or the others? Think please?" Owen was pleading now, he needed Preston to remember their sibling on his own- he didn't want to throw it right at him. Preston thought and thought until a memory flashes through his mind something very faint and blurry. He was sat under the table with a little girl younger than him, sitting in his lap giggling as they tried to stay quiet. The memory faded as quickly as it came, and he wondered if this was the girl Owen was trying to hint at. But who was she? Why was she in his memories?

"What dunderhead is trying to say is that you have a sister," Roman called out from the doorway making Owen shoot him an incredulous look and Preston look on with furrowed brows. His head turned to look at his other brother who had an angry sneer on his face.

"You what?" Preston asked looking between his older siblings who were glaring each other down. Surely, he heard wrong.

A sister? Where did she pop out from? Where was she? How old was she? The little girl in his memories was his sister? He was so confused, and Owen felt sympathy as he watched the emotions cross his younger brothers face. Preston couldn't recall a sister; he wasn't aware they even had one! Why had they never mentioned her before? Was he the only one that didn't know about her?

"You aren't the baby no more bro!" Roman snickered as he walked over to the window seat and sank into the soft cushioned seat. Owen wasn't a violent person but at that moment in time, he wanted to strangle his brother for his words.

"Wait, wait, wait... we have a little sister.... it wasn't the girl I saw yesterday, was it?" When his brothers said nothing, he had his answer. A little sister. Someone younger than him, someone who would look up to him. He thought back to the girl he saw but could not remember much about her except the fact that she seemed to be shy? He wanted to know who she was and why she was here... his mind paused as he realised something.

"Where has she been? Like why didn't I know about her?" Roman chuckled coldly as he prepared to tell his brother exactly what he thought about their so-called sister. Owen shook his head in warning but Roman was never one to reign in his anger, he embraced his anger like an old friend and introduced it to his brothers.

"Our little sister took mummy away from us. She is the reason we haven't had a mother and the reason dad was always so down. Now she's come back, without our mum, with a social worker. It's obvious to see that mum isn't around anymore. It's all her fault." This time Owen didn't hold in his annoyance and threw a pillow at Roman who simply glared at the offending object before throwing the heated look at Owen.

At his words, Preston stiffened, and his eyes grew angry. He could have had a mother, but his sister had taken her away. He didn't know what to think. But the child in him who always yearned for a mother, blamed the person who prevented him from having one, his sister.

"She was only 3 for crying out loud. What would she have done that would make mum leave? Elisa is innocent in all that happened. Mothers' absence was her own doing and choices and simply dragged our baby sister along with her. It isn't. Her. Fault."

Owen was livid at the words Roman spoke as he knew that Preston would always listen to the words that made sense in his head, which didn't always mean the truth. In this case, Preston's eyes darkened considerably, and Owen knew that Elisa now had two brothers who didn't appreciate her presence in the West household. He knew that she would find it hard what with two brothers practically hating her and shunning her existence. He felt sorry for the girl who had not had the chance to tell her side of the story, what she knew about their mother. She was already being pushed aside and isolated.

What Owen and the boys didn't realise, is that Elisa had been invisible her whole life; and it was the only way of living she knew. In the dark, alone, and independent. Nobody could disappoint her that way. Her brothers' feelings for her would not affect her in any way.

Elisa observed her surroundings and took note of everything around her from the shops to the different kinds of people walking past her. Alexander had taken her to different shops trying to get her to pick out everything she needs. But to his annoyance and confusion, he watched her pick out jogging bottoms, jeans, and large oversized jumpers. She did not even glance at the skirts or dresses and when asked she simply told him that that type of clothing wasn't practical. Again, her weird choice of words made him pause and look at her. He did not know her, and no matter how many questions he asked her, she wasn't going to open up. He would have to take a different approach, maybe telling her one of his secrets would make her comfortable, show her that he was willing to trust her with something he hadn't told his brothers.

"I hate being the eldest." He blurted out making her head snap to him. Somehow despite all the noise, she was able to hear his words and focused on him only.

"I guess that sounds bad, but I want to be able to not have that responsibility. I want to be childish too and I want to be able to joke around with my brothers and friends. But I've constantly got to watch the boys and make sure they are behaving themselves; I just want to not have to be responsible you know?" Alexander didn't realise he was blurting out his masked thoughts out loud, nor did he realise that his little sister was listening attentively to every word. Her arm brushing his as she shifted closer to him.

"When you were born, I was so happy, so excited. Finally, a little angel and no more beasts running around me. I wanted to spoil you, to become your best friend. I will never understand why mum took you away. I do not blame you, Lissy, you were a child and still are. I don't know what you've been through in your life, but we are here now."

Elisa bristled at his words. 'We are here now', he said. As if that fixed every past problem she had in her life. As if it fixed all the tears and sleepless nights. We are here now. But where were they back then? She could not blame them for anything she knew that, but she also knew she could not count on them. It was easy for him to say that they could just put the past behind them and move forward. But she couldn't, not after what she had been through. The moment past and she felt the animosity between them grow once more as she distanced herself. Her eyes strayed away from her brother and wandered around until they landed on a mother and daughter.

The daughter was huffing with her arms crossed angrily as her mother tried to get her to eat a sandwich, the mother gave up and sighed angrily going on her phone. Once the daughter realised, she didn't have her mother's attention anymore, she spun and catapulted herself at the woman who chuckled and hugged her daughter back, smoothing down her hair and pressing a kiss on her head. Oh, how she missed her mother and those perfect moments. Elisa let her lips tilt up ever so slightly at the sight before looking forward again, missing the look of sympathy on Alexander's face.

"You're lucky you know. You got to have mum all to yourself. The boys and I were constantly fighting for her attention." He chuckled at the memories but cleared his throat once realising that the subject of their mother was very sore. She didn't feel very lucky at all, despite having their mother all to herself.

"Anyways, is there anything you want to ask me?" He asked her as they carried on walking through the crowded building, nothing catching her attention or interest.

"Like what?" Elisa replied monotonously, clenching her fists as she resisted the urge to facepalm at the uselessness of the conversation.

"I don't know. Maybe if I work? Do I have a job? Do I have friends?"

"Oh.... Where do you work?" She repeated his words back to him making him give her a deadpanned look and roll his eyes at the lack of interest in her voice. He wouldn't give up yet.

"Well, I'm our villages very own Police Detective." He said proudly; a fact that he knew would have impressed his parents. Elisa, however, froze in her steps and stared at him in pure fear; an expression that had him stop in his steps and wonder what terrified her so much.

"You're a what?" She breathed shakily hoping she misheard whatever he had said. But when he repeated the words and it was exactly what she heard the first time, she quickly excused herself to go to the toilets. Once in there she pulled out her phone and dialled a number, the familiar ringing sound putting her at ease. Her walls reinforcing themselves with more blocks of steel.

"You told me to avoid the police. What do I do now that I know my brother is a detective?"

Roman West was not always mean and, how people say, detached. He was the softest and most passionate towards other people, he trusted too easily and now that he thought about it, he was naive thinking the best in everyone. He was popular in school and the person everyone looked up to; he was the golden boy.

When Elisa was born, like his brothers, Roman was entranced by the little bundle of happiness in their mothers' arms. He remembered being too shy and too scared to even go near his mother until finally he gathered enough strength to hold his youngest sibling. He remembered how he held baby Elisa's hand only for her to wrap her small fragile fingers around his pinkie finger. From that moment on, pinkie promises were their thing; Roman was no doubt her favourite brother. But life happened, and she was gone before he knew it.

He sat in his room staring up at his ceiling while listening to the soft piano music playing from his phone. As much as he claimed to be the typical bad boy, everyone in the West household knew he was just an undercover nerd who adored classical music and art. He thought back to the moment he first saw Elisa. 13 years later and she wasn't the same little baby-faced angel who would giggle at anything. She was a little lady with hard eyes and a blank face; someone who did not want to be noticed or seen through, this Elisa was a stranger wearing his father's eyes. She was hiding something he knew it, and he was determined to find out who this girl was.

Roman did not always hate his little sister, it was a feeling that gradually grew and stabbed his heart as time went on. He would wait on their swings, watching the driveway and hoping he would see his mother come back with Elisa. He would jump and grab the phone whenever he heard it ring. But as time went by, the hope faded and the resentment set in; resentment for his mother for taking away his best friend, resentment for the girl who wasn't as affected as him.

He swallowed and sat up in his bed running a hand through his messy hair, his eyes heavy from the lack of sleep and his body feeling sluggish. He wanted nothing more than to fall asleep in his bed, but the nightmares of the past kept him awake. The glass, the screaming, the blood, and the pain. So much pain that he still felt it, like a phantom pressing cold kisses to his skin.

Shaking his head, he stood up and walked over to his unfinished painting. Why he started to paint the picture he will never understand. It was chiselled into his brain, so detailed that he couldn't ignore his artistic side and painted it. At the moment all he had painted was a hand open, shards of glass surrounding the hand and some pieces were embedded into the skin.

"I don't know what to do."

His head snapped up when he heard the softly spoken voice, faint and vague. A voice that was trying so hard to stay quiet and hidden, Elisa. He slowly walked over to his wall; trying to hear what his sister was saying. He couldn't hear much and so he looked around his room in desperation until he found it, an empty glass. He pressed it against the wall and sighed slightly when he could hear her much clearer than before.

"He's a detective! What if he finds out everything? What if he tries to get involved? I don't know what to do here!"

Distress leaking from her tone. Alex. She was talking about Alex being a detective. Who was she talking to? Why was she feeling so... lost?

"I don't know what I'm doing here... I don't belong here. I want.... I want a home-"

Her voice cracked and she stopped talking as she sucked in a breath and released it shakily. Roman felt a twinge of emotion as he listened to her weak voice, the only bit of emotion he had heard from her since they met. He hadn't heard her speak this much since she's been here, and it hurt him a bit that she could talk freely to this other person. But who was it? Why was she telling them about Alex? Roman pulled away from the wall as more and more questions piled up in his head. As he moved from the wall, he forgot about the glass which now fell to the floor and he squeezed his eyes shut.

Idiot, he thought angrily as he heard all movement from her room cease, the talking had stopped. He knew she wasn't dumb, but he hoped she didn't click on that he was listening and could hear what she was saying.

Elisa stared at the wall that stood between her and Romans' room. He had been listening.

What had he heard? she decided that the best thing to do was to ignore it and hope he didn't ask. If he brings the moment up and asks who she was talking to, she'll be truthful. She was talking to a friend. Elisa sighed and slid the phone under her pillow before quickly changing into her new bedclothes. After the phone call in the toilets, she had returned to her brother pretending as though she hadn't freaked out at his words. They had then returned home with limited conversation and Elisa quickly ran to her room to hide until dinner time. She knew her brothers could be patient for only a small amount of time before they began demanding answers. She had a feeling they were going to be asking soon, but she was willing to put it off as long as she could.

"Hey Lissy! We have a few guests coming over tonight who really want to meet you." Owen said from outside her door.

Meet me? she ran her hand down her face in frustration not really wanting to spend unnecessary time with them. But the part of her, the part that longed to be loved and accepted urged her to comply.

"Do I need to be there?" She asked flatly, Owen chuckled at the frustration lining her voice.

"They're here to meet you Lissy." She groaned under her breathe at the nickname and his cheery singing voice that made her want to gauge her eyes out. Too much happiness in one person.

"It's Elisa, Owen, its Elisa!" She snapped angrily while he simply grinned from the other side of the door, enjoying the anger seeping out of her.

"Oh, I know Lissy. I know." His grin widened as he heard her muffled scream. He would never stop calling her Lissy. It was his only connection to the little sister he lost, and he knew that by time she would get used to the name. Alexander stopped next to Owen and shook his head in amusement.

"Do you need to aggravate her like that?" He asked Owen who nodded vigorously with a large grin; the opposite facial expression was hardly ever seen on his face.

"Of course! It's a brother's job! Besides, it's the only time she shows emotion and I'd rather see that then the robotic look she has normally." Alexander went to say something when her voice sounded close to the door.

"You do know your still stood next to my door, right?" She asked coolly and the two brothers spluttered out apologises before rushing down the stairs; they didn't want her to hate them even more then she already seemed to. She shook her head in irritation and opened her door, tying two locks of her hair back into a white satin ribbon, at the same time Roman left his room. They locked eyes, cold and empty staring back at curious and guarded eyes. He scowled at her and stormed down the stairs while she simply rolled her eyes at his retreating back. She didn't want to care about his hatred towards her, but she was only human, and it hurt. She would have to hide it behind her mask, alongside every other emotion she had successfully managed to hide.

Preston sat in the living room on the sofa, Owen finished setting up the floor cushions and blankets, ready for the movie night they had planned on having to ease Elisa into her new home. They were hoping she would relax more when she realised, they were her family, and they were willing to try. Well, Owen and Alexander at least.

Preston felt both unbothered but also curious about the sister he never really knew. A girl who was only two years younger than him. He had noted the different reactions of his brothers and it made him curious. Roman was angry, Alex was scared and seemed to be doubting himself and his skills around her while Owen seemed overjoyed to have her home. However, he could still see the wariness whenever he spoke of Elisa, meaning he wasn't sure what to make out of the girl. Something Owen was a professional at doing, seeing through peoples' facades.

He looked up as the girl who had already tipped the balance of their household, walked into the room. She had her arms crossed over her chest, empty eyes and a blank face, her eyes roamed the room before stopping on him. He saw the flash of surprise before it vanished quickly, and she studied him in complete boredom.

"I'm-"

"Preston. I'm aware." She interrupted him making him clench his jaw. He hated it when people interrupted him, and he didn't like the way she was acting. As if this was routine, as if none of this was a big deal for any of them when really, it was.

"And your-"

"Elisa your sister." She stated looking away from him as if his existence was nothing worthy of interest. He went to say something else, but a figure ran into the room with a yell.

"AND HE'S HERE. YOU CAN ALL STOP PANICKING COZ THE KING IS-" The newcomer stopped his ranting and stared at Elisa who looked up at him. He stared with his sea green eyes swimming with confusion and astonishment. He observed the way she held herself and the cold look she gave him. She was unfamiliar but at the same time, familiar. He could never forget those eyes.

"Lissy?" He breathed. She rolled her eyes and stormed up to him angrily; ready to put this man with unruly copper hair in his place.

"My name." She poked him in the chest harshly as she carried on walking towards him making him back up.

"Is not." She stood on tiptoes glaring at him while he peeked down at her feeling surprised at the turn of events.

"LISSY!" He rubbed his chest pouting as the small human glared up at him with her slender finger stabbing him; he found it quite cute how she thought she was scary when she really looked like a mouse.

"Ok, ok separate you two. Elisa this is Finley. He's one of our close family friends and knew you growing up. You two always had this love hate relationship. Picking on you was his favourite thing." Owen chuckled in remembrance not seeing the small glitter of curiosity in her eyes as she looked back at Finley.

"And Finley. This is Lissy." Owen quickly hid behind another new person just as Elisa threw a pillow hitting the new person square in the face making him whine.

"I didn't even say anything!" She sent him a look that made a shiver go down his spine. Who was this mini demon glaring him down?

"It's a warning for you to stay quiet and not even think about calling me that stupid name." She sneered and he frowned while Owen and Finley laughed, Roman rolled his eyes and Preston looked on not knowing whether to laugh or copy his brothers lead. Alexander walked into the room with two more people. An older man and another person who looked to be the same age as Roman.

"Ok let us get to introductions. This is Andre, Finley, and Karson. They grew up with us and we are all practically siblings. And this is Harrison....dads' best friend." The man looked over at Elisa with a shocked and fond expression. She was getting pretty fed up with these shocked expressions and held in the sigh that was bubbling its way up. Harrison was an older man with grey hairs mixed in his black hair like salt and pepper, he had laugh lines.

"You look just like your mother... but you have your fathers' eyes." He smiled, but the West boys tensed looking at her reaction. She nodded politely and looked away, she was glad she shared something in common with her father and it warmed her heart knowing that she had a piece of her father with her, his eyes.

A calmer reaction, Alexander noted.

"It's so nice to see you again Elisa. How have you been?" He asked her.

"Fine." Short and simple. She did not want to talk to just anyone if she could avoid it. Harrison understood that she didn't want to talk and immediately switched the subject to Alexander's job. Everyone settled down and Elisa looked over at Harrison in gratitude, he looked at her and winked as he carried on with his conversation, keeping the attention off her.

Huh. He was in her good books.

The boys all settled down ready to watch a movie, pizza boxes surrounding the room and the scent of cheese and garlic filled the air. They refrained from putting too much attention on Elisa but kept an eye on the girl who seemed much more relaxed. She sank to the floor and held her knees to her chest as she listened to the boyish chatter and watched the movie, she didn't even know the name of.

Was this what family was? Her lips twitched as she felt a smile threatening to take over her face. But then reality hit her, and an emotion filled her chest. Not anger. Not annoyance. Not frustration.

Pure sadness.

Because no matter what happens, she could never truly be part of their family.

5

Now

Elisa gasped for breath when a cold calloused hand slid around her throat, squeezing, cutting off her air supply. As the seconds passed the hand grew tighter and tighter making her lungs gasp and her heart pound uncontrollably. Her hands frantically clutched at the large hand trying to pry it off her throat. A low chuckle sounded above her, and the person ran their finger down the side of her cheek making her shiver in disgust and fear, the feel of cold metal from a ring scratched her skin.

The cold bit at her skin and the twigs stabbed into her back. Raindrops soaked her to the bone with her hair plastered to her forehead and covering her eyes. She could not see much of her attacker, and black dots began covering her vision. She could see the rain around them, the stars shining brightly while her attacker with the skeleton mask glared down at her.

Get away.

Get away.

Get away!

Her eyes snapped open hastily and scanned her surroundings with wild eyes, searching for the threat. Her eyes adjusted to the darkness of the room and she realised that it must have been early morning. Motionless bodies littered the floor, and she felt her breathing pick up in confusion and fear.

How did she get here? What had she... what had happened? Elisa shook her head trying to shake away the daze the dream had left her in. She was not there. She could not be there.

She quickly checked herself; no hand around her neck, no pain in her body, no blood on herself, no evil towering shadow; she was safe as could be. Her hand rubbed against her neck as if she could still feel the hand cutting off her air supply. She calmed down as she saw the familiar face of Alexander on the floor opposite her. His lips pouting slightly and his face clear of stress, Preston had his head leaning on the sofa behind him with Andre laying on his legs. Finley was curled up in a bean bag, the remote in his limp hand. Roman, Owen and Karson were on the other sofa leaning against each other snoring gently.

She took notice of her own position and realised they had given her a whole sofa as she had fallen asleep earlier than them. She didn't know how to feel about the fact that they had picked her up without her knowledge but brushed it aside as they had given her space whilst still making sure she felt included.

Was she really that tired that she didn't feel herself being moved? The thought nerved her as she was always a light sleeper when she did manage to drift off. Elisa hardly slept in general for reasons her past foster families and Paige never knew and could never understand. Reasons she wouldn't willingly offer to them or anyone else.

She silently stood and stepped over the sleeping bodies on the floor to get to the kitchen, careful to not jostle them in any way. But she had a feeling that these boys could sleep through anything, the complete opposite to how she functioned. Running a hand through her knotty hair she sighed tiredly at the boys who slept with not a care nor worry in the world. How could they sleep without feeling vulnerable? She would wake up at the smallest of sounds. She felt a cool breeze and lifted her head towards the darkened kitchen which must have had the windows open. Elisa wasn't fond of the dark, but her eyes had adjusted, and she didn't feel scared, so she carried on ahead with the intention of grabbing a cup of water.

However, Elisa froze when she saw a figure sat at the dining table; a figure that had its back to her and sipped from a cup calmly. Her mind immediately calculated different plans, but the one that stuck out to her told her to protect her brothers and the boys. She reached for the living room door behind her and silently shut it, she then slipped into the kitchen further and closed the door.

No way out.

"You just closed your only escape. Why?" His low gruff voice asked in the silence quizzically, not even bothering to turn around. She clenched her jaw looking around for something to use as a weapon to protect herself.

"My brothers are in there. I won't let you hurt them." She stated coolly not giving away anything as she tried to figure out who she was dealing with, protection mode activated; no fear allowed.

The man turned around slowly to face her and turned on the light making her blink from the harsh brightness before setting her glare on the man. She froze when their eyes met, and her stance relaxed. He smiled softly, curiously studying the way she stood in a defensive position before she realised who she was looking at. Elisa mentally facepalmed and looked at her fathers supposed best friend Harrison. He smiled at her warmly and calmly brushed off her reaction to seeing him before speaking.

"Its late child. Why are you awake?" Elisa watched his movements as he walked around the kitchen cleaning plates away while she slipped into one of the bar stools. She didn't respond and looked down at her hands which seemed a sickly pale in the light of the kitchen. He hummed and chuckled at her stillness.

"Alexander said you weren't a chatty kid. What happened?" He teased, but his words caught her attention and she looked at him curiously. Harrison caught her expression and couldn't help but smile at her look. She looked like a lost puppy with her hazel eyes slightly sparkling and her lips pouted, adorable. He knew she wouldn't ask her questions and simply carried on talking.

"When you were younger, you were this bouncy and hyper little monkey who would run around after her brothers and the boys. They would play tag with you and you would turn it into a game of hide and seek. You would find the best places to hide, and it would take ages for anyone to find you. Owen would be the first one panicking after the first ten minutes." He paused letting out another laugh.

"They were your knights in shiny armour and you were their little princess. The little girl they would bend over backwards and jump off a cliff if she asked them to. You were only three when... but you were the chattiest baby out of the lot. Always gurgling in another language and ordering us about with your hands on your hips, your pout and puppy dog eyes."

He grinned at the memory of watching a little angel-faced Elisa babbling to her siblings, her brows furrowed and arms flailing about as if she were talking about something serious. Her brothers watching her with wide eyes, their attention focused on her only and taking in everything she was babbling about. Almost as if they knew what she was talking about. They were typical siblings, they fought, insult, and tease each other. But when it came to Elisa, it was like they were her subjects and they watched her every move to make sure she was always safe.

Elisa frowned at the happy expression on his face as he recalled a time that she didn't remember living. She so wanted to remember those times of rainbows and flowers that seemed to be almost a dream. But her brain was tainted with nightmares that would never go away. He was describing the life of a girl who was lost long ago, a girl who could never be found.

She blinked out of her bleak thoughts as a white mug was settled in front of her. Hot chocolate filled her senses and she sighed deeply in contentment at the warm chocolate that sat mockingly in front of her. Harrison chuckled as she relaxed and lost some of her tenseness.

"Still love hot chocolate, huh kid? The marshmallows are in that bowl next to you. Get some sleep kiddo." She waited until she heard Harrison retreat upstairs, no doubt to a guest room, then she reached over the table to grab a few of the small soft clouds which she dropped into her drink.

Her weary eyes looked over the warm mug and noticed something that warmed her heart, something that made her ache as she looked at the design on the mug.

Our little miracle. It said in calligraphy. It could have belonged to anyone this mug, but deep down she knew this mug was hers. It was a phrase her mother always used to say to her when she would tuck Elisa in bed every night.

You are my little miracle. I love you; she would always whisper in her soft and loving voice that would always make her feel at home. Her eyes misted over but she blinked the moisture away, not allowing herself to grieve.

Crying does not solve the past, she had learnt, and so never thought about her mother again after her death. Elisa banished all thoughts from her mind and pushed the memories back into the box they had started leaking out from. There were chests in her mind that were locked shut and should never be opened, she had to remain clear minded and that meant not focusing on certain things including the past.

She walked out of the kitchen and through the back door onto a porch, a single hammock swing swayed gently in the breeze. She settled into the fabric and watched the sky turn from a dark navy blue to soft peach and orange, the stars blending into the light sky; her cold hands nursing the warm mug.

Crying doesn't solve anything.

When Alexander woke up that morning, he immediately sought out his sister. The sister who had fallen asleep in the middle of the movie and had ended up leaning against Karson who slipped an arm around her shoulder, the little sister who mumbled in her sleep and held her arms and legs close to her body.

The little sister who was nowhere to be seen! His eyes widened in realisation when he noticed the blanket she had been using, on the floor.

He stood up abruptly knocking into the beanbag where Finley was curled up like a baby. His eyes scanned the room desperately looking for the little girl who had been asleep on the sofa a few hours ago. Preston let out a sudden snore and Alexander whirled round to slap him around the back of the head to wake him up.

Preston woke up to a flash of pain in his head and let out a loud groan of pain before glaring at his attacker who didn't pay him any mind.

"What was that for?!" He shouted, alerting the other boys. Andre sat up banging his head on Roman's knee, Roman hissed and threw his arms out, hitting Karson in the stomach and Owen in the face. Alexander waited in irritation as the boys yelled at each other and stood up grumbling.

"Right ok SHUT IT!" They turned to look at an annoyed Alexander and raised a brow at his agitation.

"Elisa is missing!" Various expressions crossed the boys' faces, but Owens was the most comical. His eyes widened in horror and his face paled, he slapped his hands to his cheeks looking awfully like the screaming man from that painting he saw once in a museum.

"MY BABY! WHERES MY INNOCENT LITTLE LISSY?!" Owen screeched like a banshee making the boys wince. They heard a tired yawn and turned to the source which had caught their attention. Finley sat up in the beanbag and grinned at the other boys, unaware of anything going on in the world like normal.

"Lovely morning isn't it guys?" Finley smiled, Roman whacked the back of his head harshly making Finley topple to the ground at Alexanders feet.

"FOR CRYING OUT LOUD GORILLA HANDS WHAT HAVE I DONE NOW?!" Finley yelled rubbing his head in pain, a common occurrence within the friendship group. Roman took a threatening step towards Finley with a murderous expression. Karson and Preston stood in front of Roman trying to prevent him from going near Finley.

"He didn't call you anything man. We have better things to do." Andre tried to interfere and save Finley from being pummelled. But Finley being Finley frowned in confusion and opened his mouth again.

"Yes, I did. I called him a gorilla." Andre facepalmed and backed off in surrender while the other boys shook their head at Finley's obliviousness and moved out of Romans way. Roman's eye twitched and he tackled Finley to the ground eliciting a cry of fear from the latter.

"IM NOT A GORILLA YA FRENCH FRY!"

"OY IM NOT FRENCH WHAT YOU ON OTHER THAN STEROIDS?"

"IM NOT ON STEROIDS EITHER YOU SCRAWNY LITTLE-"

"LANGUAGE WOMAN! GET OFF ME!"

Alexander ripped Roman away from Finley who was helped up by Karson.

"Back to the matter at hand which is so much more important than you two squabbling little girls." Owen said glaring coldly at the two boys making them shift; Mama Owen was terrifying, and they knew from experience to never cross his path when he had something in mind. Right now, it was finding Elisa.

"I'll talk to you later Roman, but for now... WHERE'S MY BABY, CUTIE-PIE, PUMPKIN, SWEETHEART, ANGELIC, LITTLE LISSY?!" Owen carried on shrieking until Alexander punched his arm to pull it together.

"Calm down. She's probably in the bathroom or something." Karson suggested being the only one thinking rationally and the boys spread out around the house trying to figure out where she was just in case, she wasn't in the bathroom.

Owen's voice was heard continuously as he panicked every time, he discovered an empty room, Roman sighed tiredly and frustrated as he thought his sister was just an attention seeker, Preston and Andre were in the kitchen getting breakfast ready for them as they weren't as worried as the older boys and

Alexander were checking the downstairs rooms with Karson, muttering under his breathe about how he's already lost his sister.

Harrison casually moved into the kitchen to watch and listen to the idiots wandering around the house looking for their princess. Just like old times except this time she wasn't even hiding, and the boys were just blind bats. He wondered how long it took until-

"You guys stress too much. She's in the hammock." Finley snickered as Owen pushed past everyone to yank the door open roughly and search the porch area for his sweet baby sister.

"LISSY!" He cried loudly in relief and happiness making Elisa looked at him wide-eyed and horrified at his approaching figure. Alexander walked over to the doorway and watched his brother take the mug off Elisa, hand it over to Finley, and then proceed to lift Elisa into his arms. He chuckled as Owen squished her cheeks together making her look like a fish and cooed to her saying how much he loved her.

'Get off!" She muttered trying to get out of Owens vice-like grip, but he simply hugged the life out of her and ignored the biting insults she was throwing his way. Alexander let a small smile cross his face at the scene; he just loved to rile her up.

'I was so worried!" Owen cried throwing his head back dramatically making Elisa wrinkle her nose in revulsion.

God he is such a drama queen, imagine what he's like if I actually go missing, she mused to her mental self.

"Are you CRYING?" She asked incredulously noticing the silver gems rolling down his cheeks to which he wailed even louder and held onto her tighter. She scoffed as she managed to push him off of her and stormed off inside to get some quiet in her room before she faced them again. Thoughts flying in her head faster than she could interpret them. But the main thoughts that repeated, stuck in her mind.

One, her brothers were dramatic.

Two, her brothers were idiots.

Three, they were too soft and vulnerable.

She sighed as she listened to her brothers and the boys laughing downstairs in the kitchen where she had left them. She wanted to open up to them, she did. She wanted to be able to joke around with them and stress them out as a little sister should.

But she needed to hold back; needed to stick to herself. It was like a slap to her face as she remembered her role in life, a role that was forced onto her without her permission or acceptance.

Do not cry Elisa, she thought as she tugged her hair frustrated.

Crying doesn't solve anything.

Growing up as the second eldest West sibling, Owen made it his responsibility to be the one his siblings could turn to whenever they needed a shoulder to cry on. He wanted to be the one that his younger siblings could look up to. Although Alexander was the eldest, he knew he was already holding so many responsibilities with keeping their siblings safe physically; Owen would keep them sane mentally and emotionally.

He remembered the day their mother left home. How his brothers and friends were all playing in the garden while their mother put Lissy to sleep. He thought back to how he had gone inside for a water break but instead heard his mum sobbing softly; a sound that would break any child's heart. Owen had abandoned his cup of water and followed the soft cries into the living room where he saw his parents holding onto each other like they were each other's lifeline.

His parents were so in love; what had happened?

To this day Owen never understood why his mother left with their sister, he never understood why she never said goodbye to him. He guessed it hurt less that way as their mothers' presence just slowly faded by time and became a distant memory. It still hurt; it was just more bearable.

Owen smiled at the last family photo they had which included their mother and Lissy. Smiles shining brightly at the camera. How he wished his family were complete. How he wished Lissy grew up with them and stayed the giggly girl she was. He ran a hand through his hair with a sigh of sadness, he would make sure she was happy here. He would fix his broken family.

It had been over 2 weeks since Lissy had first come home, and they had gotten nowhere with her. She would hole herself up in her room and avoid any interaction. She would roll her eyes whenever Owen or Alex tried to involve her in family game night, she would refuse to eat dinner with the rest of them, she would avoid them in the hallway and wouldn't stay for more than 1 second in the same room as them.

It's like she didn't want to be anywhere near them, and that fact hurt him more than it should. But at the same time, he had a feeling that she wanted to talk to them, she wanted to laugh and joke with them. There were small quick moments of hesitation before she always rejected them, and that was enough to keep his hope rising. She must be feeling lonely within the household even if they tried with her. He had to try even harder.

Owen pulled on a denim jacket and grabbed a rucksack before barging into her room without notifying her. She quickly put something in her bag and looked up at him with a glare that made him shiver but wonder what she was hiding.

It probably isn't important, he mused.

"Seriously?! Ever heard of knocking? What do you want now?!" She snapped angrily as Owen grinned down at her completely ignoring her bad mood. He loved messing with her.

"We're going on an adventure! It's going to be a great one. WHAT A BEAUTIFUL DAY! We're-"

Owens loud and merry singing was cut off by a pillow that hit him from behind. Roman smirked in victory whilst still looking half asleep, his hair was messy, and Owen wouldn't be surprised if there was a bird nesting in there. Roman put his silver tongue piercing between his teeth and Owen screwed up his face. Why Roman decided to get a tongue piercing he will never understand and Roman would always stick his tongue out at Owen as he knew it made him uncomfortable. The joys of having a brother!

"It's too early for your happiness man. Go to sleep!" Preston whined as he walked into the room sleepily and leaning against Roman who simply rolled his eyes and pushed against Prestons' heavy head.

"Oh, sure! Let's have a meeting in my room! Who has the presentation?" Elisa spoke sarcastically and glared at the intruders in her room. Roman sneered back at her and Preston waved her off while Owen chuckled. She went to get back into her bed, but Owen made a tutting sound and stopped her.

"Nuh-uh. We're going to the beach!" He cheered making his siblings groan, despite being the second oldest, Owen was probably the most childish.

Wow, that's rude.

"Must we?" Roman mumbled not wanting to spend unnecessary time with the stranger in the house. As if hearing his thoughts, Owen sent him a look, now he was determined to fix their sibling bond!

"Yup! So, I suggest you get changed, grab a bag with whatever you need and get downstairs before I drag you by the hair and drown you in the sea!" Roman and Preston blinked at Owens words and how he said it with a beaming innocent smile. They rushed to their room not wanting Owens' threat to come true and Owen smirked at the power he still had over them before turning to the girl. He studied her face and his smirk slipped at what he saw. Her eyes flickered to him and she glared again; her mask back in place and the walls in her eyes had been rebuilt.

"Well? GET OUT!" She shouted and he whimpered as he ran out of the room to escape her rage; she was still a scary kid. The door slammed shut behind him and Owen thought back to what he saw.

In that one moment, that one fleeting glance, he saw many emotions. Not the stone-cold Elisa he had come to know. He saw the hesitance, the panic, worry, fear. But she hid it all and her guard came up when she saw him watching her.

She was hiding something, something that was scaring her.

Owen waited for his siblings and smiled when Lissy finally came down wearing light blue denim shorts and a white floral kaftan. Her hair was in its usual messy waves and a cream-coloured rucksack on her back. Her hands were clenched, and her eyes focused on her feet as she refused to look at her siblings.

Alexander walked down the stairs yawning and raised a brow when he saw all his siblings in beachwear while he was in his uniform with his phone in his hand. Preston looked at him with wide eyes and looked at him in hope.

"You coming with us Alex?" Alexander smiled and ruffled his hair fondly. Preston had always secretly looked up to Alexander and loved the times they hung out, the admiration that shone in his eyes was always a relief to Alexander and reassured him that he had raised him the best he possibly could.

"Nah. Sorry bud. I've got work. Have fun though, okay? We can go for a picnic another day if you want?" Preston nodded in acceptance and walked out the door whistling happily. Roman fist bumped him and Owen high fived him before they strolled out after Preston. Alex looked at Elisa who was hesitating, she looked torn, and he wanted to get rid of whatever was worrying her. Before he could ask her if she was ok, she looked up at him and... Smiled? Alex blinked in surprise but smiled back at her warmly. He memorised the smile she gave him, the way it made her look younger, free. It's funny how a small tilt of the lips could change the way a person looked.

"Have fun, Dove." Alex spoke softly to her using the nickname he gave her when she was younger. Her eyes softened and she nodded before giving him a timid wave and running after the boys who had already started walking. He stood there for a moment with a warm feeling, she was trying! Maybe there was hope for the siblings after all?

Owen laughed as Roman tackled Preston and dunked him into the sea. Preston managed to kick Romans legs out from under him and they both tumbled into the water wrestling and laughing at their childishness.

He turned to look at Elisa and his smile slipped slightly. She sat in the grainy warm sand watching the waves hit against the rocks that lay at the bottom of a cliff, her knees pulled up against her chest and her hair flying gently around her with the wind. He walked over and sat next to her, ignoring the way she tensed.

Elisa sat there silently, and Owen didn't push her to talk. He had a feeling that she was working up the courage to ask him something and so he wasn't going to interrupt her now. She finally made up her mind and looked over at her brother, her eyes lingering on the ink on his wrist.

"Does your tattoo have a meaning?" Owen blinked, that wasn't what he thought she would ask but he smiled anyway at her interest.

"Why do you think it means something?"

"Because you seem like the kind of guy whose really sentimental." She shrugged as if it was nothing and he grinned at her answer, she was more perceptive than he thought.

"Yeah. I guess I am... It does mean something I'll admit. Five birds... five West siblings." Owen watched her eyes soften into pools of honey as she looked at his wrist, her brows furrowed, and she lifted her small fingers to the tattoo. She lifted his wrist closer to her face and he could feel her warm breath and his skin. He knew what she had seen and swallowed feeling a sense of vulnerability.

"The bird... the small one at the end... It says-"

"Lissy. It says Lissy." Owen finished for her knowing she was in too much shock and surprise to put together a proper sentence. Elisa felt her heart warm as she stared at the tattoo with her nickname on his skin, her heart waging a war with her mind and she didn't know how to feel.

"Why would you do that Owen?" She asked confused. Her name, she had mentally accepted that she was Lissy to Owen, was inked on his skin. Practically permanent.

"We thought we would never see you again Lissy. You were our little sister, the one that completed our sibling bond. When you left, it ripped the bond, and we had no means of connection. This tattoo was the only reminder we had of you. Alex got his first, and then when we all hit 18, we all got the same tattoo. Just in different areas. Even Preston, although he doesn't exactly have the same sentiment to his tattoo like the rest of us. We never told him what it meant, and he just wanted one since we all had one."

Her eyes widened at his answer and she felt it hard to ingest his words. She looked over to the crystal water where Roman and Preston were seeing how long they could stay underwater. They had the same tattoo somewhere.

"Of course, Alex and Roman have their own nicknames that they gave you when you were little so instead of theirs saying Lissy above your bird, it'll say whatever they used to call you." Owen finished and they sat in silence. Her brothers had always had her in their mind. Even Roman who seems to hate her. She didn't know what to feel, what to think, what to do. Owen decided to change the subject to get her mind off the tattoo. Her face was scrunched up in what looked to be pain and he wanted to take that pain away.

"You're starting school next week. It's a boarding school as well so there will be kids from all over. Preston will be in the 6th form, which is attached to the school, so you'll have a familiar face." Elisa jumped at the thought. School? Why on earth is she going to school?

"Owen I've never been to school. Mum home-schooled me after kindergarten." Owen pursed his lips at the word kindergarten.

"I forgot you lived in America." He mumbled and frowned as he realised how far his mother had taken his sister. Did she really want to forget her whole family that bad? Then he backtracked on what she said.

"Hold up. You've been home-schooled since you were... what... 5?"

"6 actually. Mum felt better knowing I was always in her reach and home-schooled me until I was in 3rd Grade. I had online tutors, so I kept up with my studies as I moved from home to home. I'm currently doing 10th-grade work and prepping for exams." She shrugged and Owen thought about it.

"You're going to be in Year 11 here which is the last year of high school. You can then either stay on till 6th form or you can go to a college. We all went to this 6th form and then carried on to University. It's your choice then. But Alex and Paige thought it best for you to have at least one year of school. And hey, its September. You have a few months till your final exams and I'm sure you'll do great!" He encouraged her.

Elisa didn't get scared. Growing up her mother always told her to never show fear. Fear was an obstacle that she had to quickly bypass to survive. She was never scared about moving from home to home, she was never scared when she first broke her arm when she was 11. She wasn't even scared when her mother died.

But coming to England, to live with brothers her mother had taken her away from, that was scaring her. Her new life was terrifying, and she didn't know how to handle the things being thrown her way whilst still trying to keep up her guard. She wasn't worried about keeping up her grades because she knew and believed in herself that she could get amazing results.

What terrified her, was the people she knew she was going to meet. People who would no doubt try to become her friend. She already had a hard time battling off her stupid brothers. But what about people in school? Kids her own age? How was she going to survive high school? She pressed her fingernails into her palm and finally asked the question she had been wanting to ask one of her brothers since she arrived.

"Owen?"

"Yeah, Lissy?"

"Where's... Where's our father?" Owen froze at her question. She didn't know. But in all fairness, he didn't know where their mother was or why Elisa was here.

"Well, where's our mother?" He shot back calmly, she swallowed knowing that her answer would break them.

"I asked first." His lip curved and he sighed sadly.

"We don't know. Dad has been missing for years. They assume he's..." She knew what he was insinuating, and her heart pounded against her chest. Her brow furrowed as she tried to make sense of what she was hearing.

"When did he go missing?" Owen closed his eyes as he tried to calculate the years that had passed since they last saw their father.

"Well... Alex was 22 when he got his job... he was 18 when he got his tattoo and I think it was a few months later so... Roughly 8 years ago dad went missing?" Elisa felt her eyes widen, her breath caught in her throat, her skin pale and she could practically hear her heart throbbing.

8 years ago, their dad went missing he said.

Could it just be a coincidence that their father went missing at roughly the same time their mother was murdered...? Maybe it was not linked and there wasn't a connection. But deep-down Elisa knew.

It wasn't just a coincidence at all.

6

Then

There is an answer to every question, to every problem, there is a solution, to every secret there is the truth. Secrets were the whispers of stories floating around within the shadows, never clear enough for a person to catch.

The West family had always had secrets surrounding them. Secrets which started off with the right intention, to protect people and help them. But one small mistake, one miscalculation changed everything. That miscalculation cost the West family to go their separate ways and although they weren't together, there was some happiness in their dark lives. Trust is an important thing and if it's placed with the wrong people, it can be used against a person, that trust you gifted to someone can become the most lethal weapon.

Delilah West hummed softly to a tune only she could hear; her feet glided gracefully across the cool kitchen floor as she mixed the soft gooey chocolate ganache. She listened to the waves crashing unforgivingly against the beach outside their home and smiled softly as she heard the mischievous giggles echoing in the house. The evening was perfect and felt like a dream.

"Your little one is full of energy isn't she." Her best friend Audrey grinned as she strolled into the kitchen with her hands cupping a mug of lukewarm coffee. Delilah followed her friends' amused gaze, and they watched their children running about with oddly coloured hands, their feet slapping against the laminate floor. It took Delilah only a moment until she realised what their hands were covered in.

"Kids! Be careful! I don't want you to get paint on-" She stopped as she watched her daughter and her daughters' best friends bump into the wall; their rainbow hands had pressed against the white walls and transferred the colours making her shake her head and kiss her teeth. Children were absolute blessing but sometimes, all Delilah wanted to do was keep her daughter in one room so she couldn't make a mess in the rest of the rooms.

"Oh... sorry mummy." Delilah couldn't help but chuckle at the pout on her daughter's face and swept her into her arms, blowing a raspberry on her neck; a squeal ripping from her lips. She cuddled her daughter closely and pressed a kiss to her rosy cheeks.

"Would you like some chocolate cake?" She whispered into her 8-year-olds ear making her eyes light up and her head bop up and down excitedly. Audrey's children, Leah who was 4 and Levi who was 10, slipped into their own chairs and grinned up at Delilah awaiting their cake patiently.

Elisa climbed up onto the chair next to Levi, her tongue stuck out in concentration as she lifted one leg onto the chair and struggled to pull her body up. Levi grabbed her arms and helped Elisa into her chair making sure she was settled and wouldn't fall.

Audrey hid her smile behind her coffee cup as she watched the two children who began to make faces at each other and tried to make each other laugh.

Delilah poured the dark chocolate ganache over the warm cake she had baked and cut everyone a slice before finally sitting down. She watched the children's eyes sparkle as they quickly devoured their dessert messily and got ready to leave the table to play more games. They never sat down long enough. She looked over at her little girl and grinned when she saw the chocolate crumbs sitting on her chin, she reached over to wipe the crumbs away, but Levi beat her to it. He gently wiped her chin clean before they both sent each other matching grins. They then left the table, Levi lifting his 4-year-old sister into his arms before they ran off giggling to no doubt play with the finger paints, they had found.

Delilah was proud of her little miracle, the little girl who woke her up with a smile every day. She was happy that her daughter was living a good life, even if it wasn't the life, she had wished for her. Elisa was happy, she had friends, she was a smart little one who knew right from wrong and knew things that many teenagers would just be learning. She was growing up into a strong girl who would be able to take on the world.

"You doing ok Lila?" Audrey broke through her happy thoughts and her smile slipped at Audrey's question. She thought back to the problems she tried her best to hide from everyone and their dangerous lives. Although Elisa was happy and seemed to be excelling through life, she wasn't in the dark about the truth. Delilah had made sure she was aware of her four older brothers; her four knights who she would one day meet again.

Alexander her Alpha leader, the brother who would lead her the way and would guide her when she was lost. Owen her rock, the brother who would lend her a shoulder to cry on and make sure that she was always smiling and happy. Roman her guardian angel, the brother who would hold her when she was scared and protect her from any harm. Preston her partner in crime, the brother who would play pranks with her and help cause mischief.

Elisa had heard stories of her brothers and what they were like, how much they loved her and how they couldn't wait to see her again. She wanted to know who these brothers were and have a happy family. Delilah told Elisa about her father, how she was his little princess, and she would listen to her mothers' stories with her eyes wide in amazement. She had her own knights who loved her more than life itself, and she could not wait to meet them.

However, Delilah had also informed her of the dangers that surrounded their family, the monsters that stood in the dark just waiting to pounce and take away all they hold dear. Delilah made sure that she bought her daughter up to be a strong and independent individual and to always stay aware of her surroundings, to never let her guard down. It was tough for her to watch her daughter's carefree nature being influenced with the knowledge of the darkness in the world.

"I'm fine... I'm happy she has Levi, Leah and she has you! Her aunt Dree Dree." The two friends chuckled at the nickname Elisa had dubbed Audrey with when she was younger.

"But I... I wish she knew her brothers. Not from the stories I tell her. I wish she knew them personally, remembered how it felt to have older siblings who would go to the ends of the earth for her. I want to see my boys again and tell them how sorry I am for leaving them... abandoning them..."

She trailed off as she realised exactly what she had done all those years ago. She had abandoned her children and took off with their sister, she had left them with no clue as to why she left. She knew they held resentment towards her, and she didn't blame them. In fact, it comforted her that her boys held something against her because it meant they still cared, she just hoped that resentment wasn't against Elisa too.

Audrey looked over at her friend in sympathy; she saw the tiredness in her eyes and the pain from not seeing her whole family. Delilah was a strong woman, but there's a limit to how much weight a woman can hold without the help from anyone else. There was a limit to how much she could keep in and Audrey wondered when her breaking point would be.

"I may not know the extent of your past or anything that you are going through. But I admire you for how hard you are trying to protect your family and look! You've raised a beautiful daughter while doing whatever you're hiding from me and everyone." Delilah rolled her eyes but looked over at said girl who was putting paint on Levi's face with a bright smile; Leah giggling at the faces Levi was making to entertain the girls.

"I'm protecting her now... but.... how long-" Delilah stopped talking and sent her best friend a sad look which was reciprocated. Audrey stood up offering her arms out in comfort and the two women held each other, one offering support and the other clinging on.

"Whatever you have to do Delilah West. Do it. You're both strong enough to handle whatever is being thrown at you. She.... is strong enough." She nodded and tilted her lips at her neighbour who had quickly become her other half.

"Come on little monsters! Home time!" Leah ran into her mother's awaiting arms and held onto her shirt with her thumb in her mouth.

"I tired mama." She whined and Audrey rolled her eyes at her dramatic child who squeezed her eyes shut and pretended to fall asleep.

"You seemed perfectly fine a minute ago you little faker." She tickled the 4-year-old making her giggle loudly. Levi walked in with Elisa. He tugged her blue ribbon out of her hair and ducked behind his mother before she could swat him away, he giggled at her pout and waved as he skipped out the door with his mother and sister following.

"Bye Levy!"

"Bye-bye Eli!"

Being a West was hard, something the children would slowly grow up to realise; something Elisa had already been taught. She knew the consequences that came with the name and she learnt how to survive. She has just never had to implement those skills and her mother hoped she never would.

She changed into one of her mothers' shirts that were practically a dress on her, her hair braided back into a loose plait while she talked endlessly about her day; Delilah humming and ahhing at the right moments. They sat on the balcony in their huge cosy grey beanbag with a large fluffy blanket cocooning them; mugs of hot chocolate clutched in their hands as they stared up at the dark blue sky. They watch the stars blinking at them above, both thinking different things.

Elisa hoping that one day she could stand on the beach with her mummy and her missing family and look up at the stars together. Delilah smiling and staring at the stars knowing somewhere, her boys and her love would be staring at the same ones, miles apart but the same world.

"Mummy?"

"Yes, love?"

"Can we see daddy and my knights soon? Then we can all be happy and look at stars together!" she chuckled and brushed her lips on her daughter soft hair, the innocence her child radiated warmed her heart.

"Of course, my love. One day we will all be together, and we can all be happy. But remember what I said?" Elisa turned in her mothers' lap and looked up at her with a serious look.

"Monsters don't stop hunting. So, we can't stop hiding." The look on her daughters' face made her sigh sadly. She hated that she had to teach her daughter certain things that no 8-year-old should know or even think about, but she knew her daughter needed to know these things to protect herself. Hopefully, she would not be alone, and she wouldn't have to bear all the knowledge for long.

"What do you do if the police talk to you?"

"I don't know anything."

"What do you do if... if mummy isn't here anymore?"

"I run! I run and don't stay still and don't stop until its safe." She nodded and pressed her forehead against her daughters, she pressed a soft kiss to her small button nose before she peppered kisses all over her face making her giggle, the sweet giggle that always made her smile. She felt something coming; like something bad was going to happen and change everything she had worked for.

"Good girl." She whispered and soon felt her daughters breathing even out as she ran her fingers up and down her back. She wrapped the blanket around them tighter as the cold wind blew over them and pressed her cheek against Elisa's head, her hair fluffy and strands flying in the soft breeze. Her phone rang and Delilah quickly answered it with a smile knowing who was on the other end.

"Hello, stranger." A deep voice said, and she giggled like a schoolgirl talking to her crush, just his voice made her feel safe and at home. It made her feel like everything happening was nothing but a nightmare.

"Why hello there. How are you doing fine sir?" She replied in a teasing tone and his answering chuckle made her smile, her heart warming.

"I miss you. They miss you. They are stubborn ole fools but... they miss their mother and their little sister. How is my munchkin?" He asked longingly wanting to hear everything their daughter was getting up to. Those monthly 5-minute calls weren't enough to catch up everything the other parent had missed on their children's lives. The separation was hard on them all, especially the boys as they had no idea what was happening. Elisa was aware that they had to hide from the bad men, but she didn't know the exact reason why, something her mother would soon regret.

"Our little miracle is growing up too fast... she misses her father and her knights. She wants to see you all again soon. We both do."

William walked into the living room and stared down at his sons who were sprawled about on the sofas asleep. He walked over and pulled a blanket over Preston who was snuggled up to Owen, Alex had his own blanket wrapped around him and Roman had his legs over his lap. He smoothed down Roman's hair and kissed his head knowing he wouldn't have that chance if his third eldest was awake.

"Soon Lils. Hopefully, soon we can see each other again and the children can live their normal lives." His dreams of their happy family were shattering day by day, but still, he hoped, still he smiled for his boys despite knowing the truth of their future. He was an adult and knew the consequences of their actions, but he prayed that their children wouldn't have to pay for their mistakes.

"Oh Will... we both know how this will end... Elisa is aware of everything. I gave her everything she needs to know and remember." Elisa stirred in her sleep and clutched her mother tighter as if knowing what fate had in store for them, Delilah tightened the blanket around them both.

"I'm planning on telling the boys tomorrow after work. Alex is old enough to understand and they can all protect each other if anything did happen." William closed the living room door and went to check all the other doors in the house when he heard a bang. He paused for a moment wondering if one of his boys had woken up; he walked over to check and saw that Roman had been pushed onto the floor and was now snoring loudly. He chuckled.

"Your sons are pigs, Lils."

"Oh, leave my babies alone!" She giggled and sniffed, she tasted salt on her lips and quickly wiped away the tears rolling down her cheeks like they do every time she spoke to her husband. William heard her sniff and closed his eyes wishing he could hold her as he did 5 years ago before their mistake. His jaw clenched and his head leaned back against the wall, he hated this.

"Together soon." He reminded her softly and she nodded on the other side of the phone looking up at the stars. Hope was the only thing they had left, the only thing they could cling to; a bright light that shone in their darkness.

"Together soon." She repeated but this time they could both hear the defeat in her tone. They both knew deep down in their hearts that they may never see each other again and as they both finally accepted the inevitable, it seemed as though the universe finally put their destiny into action.

Delilah tensed as she saw a car coming to a halt at the bottom of her driveway and a man getting out. She sucked in a breath and quickly but silently walked inside with Elisa wrapped up in the warmth unaware, she held her daughter close to her not willing to waste the precious minutes they had left.

"Will he's here!" She gasped into the phone but instead heard static, she cursed and quickly dropped her phone inside the backpack. Elisa's backpack. The backpack that contained everything and anything her daughter needed to survive and protect herself.

"My love wake up. I need you right now my miracle." Delilah whispered into Elisa's ear over and over and her eyes snapped open alert. She understood immediately that they were in trouble and sat on the ground watching her mother, awaiting instructions. They heard their front door open slowly; the intruder not rushing knowing that his prey was trapped. They could not go anywhere. But what the intruder did not know was that the moment he had opened the door, he had set off a timer. If Delilah didn't input a passcode within two minutes, William West would be notified that something had gone wrong. They did not trust the police, but it also sent a notification to a friend Delilah had made on the force that she could rely on. She needed to get hr daughter to safety and hidden away in the system.

Elisa watched her mother rush around the room putting items into the backpack. She heard the footsteps leisurely walk up the stairs towards them; a low whistling could be heard. Delilah quickly shoved the backpack under the bed and pointed at it, Elisa had to have the bag with her no matter what.

"Lay down my miracle." She whispered to her daughter, her brave daughter whose eyes shone with childish innocence. Delilah knew what was going to happen next, she knew what the future possibly held for her baby girl. By the time the police got there, it would be too late for her, but at least her daughter would be safe. Their back up plan was now in progress and there was nothing she do to change her daughter's unforgiving fate.

At least her daughter would be somewhere where he would never find her, or at least it will take him quite a while to find her. Although the pain in her heart overpowered her logic as she realised, she would now be abandoning her daughter and children forever. She quickly knelt and pressed her shaking lips to her forehead, trying to convey how much she loved her baby girl.

"Look away." She whispered, pleaded. Elisa laid her head on the soft carpeted floor, but she peeked through her arms at her mother who wiped her tears and steeled her features.

The door opened and the whistling grew louder. Delilah's eyes landed on the person standing idly in the doorway, a black hoodie covering his head and keeping his face shrouded in shadows. He did not speak, she didn't either. She knew what he wanted but she wouldn't do it, wouldn't give it. He wouldn't hurt her daughter she knew; they didn't kill kids without a good enough reason; he only believed Delilah and William had the knowledge. But Elisa knew everything too, Elisa was their computer backup that had all the escape plans and data.

She was their hidden file.

She stared at him with a cold smirk, emotion draining from her face as she refused to show weakness in front of her killer to be. Her eyes brightly shining with unshed tears knowing her daughter would be a witness and her innocence would be shattered. Her hand slyly stroked her daughters' small hand on the floor and Elisa closed her eyes remembering her mothers' words before peeking once more.

"Do it!" She hissed at him, he tilted his head and walked over wordlessly to Delilah who was kneeling on the ground. Her body partially protecting the child he could see hiding; the child he was not interested in. He waited for Delilah to give him what he had been searching for the past few years. But as anyone who had met the Wests knew, they were stubborn human beings. She wasn't going to speak, and she wasn't going to hand him what he wanted, he had no use for her. Delilah smiled one last time at her baby girl.

"I love you so much my little miracle." She breathed out, her voice cracking as her throat clogged with emotion. The bit of hope she had been holding onto crumbling as she accepted her ending.

"I love you, mummy." Elisa whispered back with her voice just as shaky and scared, her words muffled slightly by her arms.

"Together soon my love." The intruder chuckled at the words exchanged and raised his hand in the air, Elisa saw a glint of metal in his hand that was suddenly bought down to her mother. There was a slash of flesh being torn and a burst of dark red. Delilah's body slipped to the ground in slow motion as she choked on the thick liquid that pooled in her throat, the liquid that began dripping from her pink lips and onto the carpeted floor. Her hand reaching out towards Elisa who lay on the ground with wide eyes and her lips parted in a silent scream, their eyes locked as they showed each other everything they were feeling, their fingertips brushing. The fragility of innocence shattered in the silence and the darkness of the world planted the seed of fear in the back of her mind.

Green eyes full of love and adoration sent waves of sadness, regret and heartbreak for not being able to watch her daughter grow up. She wanted to apologise but she felt her heart grow weak, her brain shutting down quickly but felt like years. Her lips turned up into a weak smile as she tried to reassure her daughter that it was okay, everything will be okay, they will see each other again.

Hazel eyes screaming with agony and pain, her heart crying out for the loss of a mother. She wanted to crawl into the arms of the woman who gave her nothing but love, the woman who did everything to make her smile. Her whimpers quiet and her arm still outstretched towards her dying mother.

Sirens were heard in the distance and as quick as he had arrived, the killer was gone, leaving behind devastation and pain. Like all monsters do.

William sank to the ground as he listened to the static finally disappear as the signal jammer was out of distance. He listened to the police sirens on the other end of the phone and quickly cut the call off knowing what had happened. He felt empty and he closed his eyes as the dam broke, she was all alone, she would be alone for a while and he knew that a certain call was no doubt going to come. Their backup plan would hurt their children a lot, he knew that, but if this plan worked, then it would mean they were free. She could do it, he had faith in their daughter, as much as it pained him to let her do this alone, he knew she could do this.

Elisa stared at the eyes that no longer sparkled, her own eyes blurring as her mind forced her body to shut down, to protect whatever innocence she had left. The first chest being built in her mind and quickly pulling the last memory of her mother inside, the pain, the fear, the heartbreak sucked into the chest and locked away.

The doors burst open downstairs and she heard her Aunt Dree Dree calling out their names, the worry evident in her tone and Elisa relaxed knowing that the monster had made itself known.

She had to keep running, that is what her mother told her and that is what she must do.

A single tear rolled down her cheek as she finally closed her eyes and gave in to the darkness that called out her name softly. The last thing she saw was a black rose laying in the pool of blood next to her mother's face, the velvet petals stroking the pale skin of her cheek.

"Together soon mummy."

7

Now

Alexander sighed tiredly as he turned his car into the driveway of his home, it was early in the morning at around 2 am. He had been given a new case that had him confused and lost on how to go about it. Throughout his career within the police force of their little village, his case files included small incidents that he could solve within a week, less if it was simple. He had always loved the idea of investigating different crimes and being a hero. A child's dream that became a reality except there was hardly any crime.

That was until the body showed up.

He remembered how he received a call over a week ago from Sargent Jonathan informing him of a body that had been found washed up on the beach. It had shocked all officers including Alexander; washed-up bodies were something they had never dealt with before. To make their matters worse, after the post mortem examination they had found out that the body hadn't died from natural causes, there were multiple stab wounds and a jagged slit across the throat. They were possibly looking at a murder case and Alexander had become the detective he had always wanted to be as a child, but now was quite terrified.

The body had been killed recently which unnerved him, he had a little sister, and they had a possible murderer on the loose. His protective instincts were going haywire and every day after work when he came home, he would check in on all his siblings and watch them sleep for a moment. Reassuring himself that they were okay and breathing. Alive.

Alexander locked the house door behind him and let out an exhausted sigh. He heard a clatter and suddenly stood up straight with his head snapping towards the kitchen, a soft light pulsing like a heartbeat. Grabbing an umbrella that was propped up next to the door, he slowly walked towards the room with his heart pounding. He walked in with his chosen weapon pointed out but paused when he met blank eyes that looked between him and the object.

"Wow. An umbrella. Threatening much? What ya going to do? Open it indoors and give me bad luck for the rest of my life?" Elisa drawled with a hint of amusement lacing her tone, Alexander chuckled and ran a hand down his face in relief. An action that didn't go unnoticed by the youngest West who immediately began making them warm drinks.

"I thought you were..." He shook his head not finishing his sentence and sank into one of the chairs next to the island in the middle of the kitchen.

"Thought I was?" She prompted not liking an unfinished sentence; it made her anxious and they were normally unfinished because they carried upsetting truths.

"Don't worry about it. Why are you awake? It's way past your bedtime." He asked sternly with disapproval. She rolled her eyes as she stirred two cups full of warm liquid before passing him one and sitting opposite to her brother. Alexander smiled inwardly as he smelt the hot chocolate and sent her a grateful smile to which she shrugged off.

"Couldn't sleep. Why are you home late? Owen is getting worried because you are hardly home anymore." He knew he was worrying his brothers; Owen being worried is an understatement and he knew that his other siblings were having to deal with an overbearing 'mother' who hated to see them out of his sight for longer than a minute. He was probably demanding that their doors were open at all times and that they checked in with him at least 5 times a day.

"Are you worried?" He asked her instead and watched her huff and turn away. But the tips of her ears were red, adorable. His little sister cared; he grinned at her turned head and sipped the hot liquid. She was slowly showing signs of being comfortable around them and it made him smile when she would catch herself nearly smiling or getting to relaxed around them, she was unconsciously beginning to let her guard down.

"How was school?" Alexander hadn't really had the chance to sit down and ask her about her school life. She had started her new school a week ago and he was curious about how she'd settled in, if it was hard or if she was uncomfortable. He didn't realise until Owen told him that she had been home-schooled most of her life. He wondered why their mother chose that option and why she sounded to be overprotective. He didn't remember her like that, she was always the type of mother to encourage them to do things out of their comfort zone.

Elisa furrowed her brows at the question and thought. High school in England wasn't what she thought. When she had walked in, people were milling about in the hallway talking and catching up with each other. It wasn't like how she had read in books or seen in movies, nobody turned to look at her weirdly or start gossiping about her, nobody had eyed her up and down trying to find a fault to tease her about. Everyone was in their own world smiling and laughing with their friends or talking animatedly about something. She had pouted and wondered what else movies and books had lied about.

Preston had walked alongside her watching her face for any hint of her nervousness. But he was met with a blank look that simply observed her surroundings. She didn't even look worried or ask him anything. He was confused. He didn't hate her like Roman, but he didn't necessarily love her as Owen did. He was like Alex. Unsure of what to make of her. He had shown her to her classes and as soon as the warning bell rang, he was off to go find his own friends. She would be fine on her own.

Elisa had walked into her first class and talked to her teacher who had welcomed her quietly and said that there was no seating plan. She walked to a desk that was closer to the door so that when the bell rang, she could leave quickly. Her day was decent for her first experience in school. She didn't make friends, but she smiled politely at anyone who smiled at her. That's how her first three days went, until she met Sasha.

Sasha was bubbly and sweet, the opposite of Elisa and she loved it. She felt at complete ease with Sasha who didn't care that Elisa was distant, who didn't mind that she was a girl of few words, she didn't poke her for information. She had bouncy auburn hair that was normally pulled back into a messy bun or a ponytail, green eyes that shone like emeralds and glittered with mischief. She simply accepted her with a grin and announced that they were soulmates as soulmates didn't have to be two people who fall in love but simply two people who shared the same soul and were destined to care and understand each other. A notion that moved the West girl and made her embrace this newfound friendship.

Elisa's interaction with other people didn't stop at Sasha, in fact, she was then attacked by a human-sized Labrador. Not an actual dog, but rather the human version of one, named Cyrus,

Sasha's boyfriend. He had ashy blonde hair and oceans in his eyes, his personality soft yet hyper. She learned that they had been friends from childhood and soon became a couple in year 9, and they then met Quinton who was their resident bad boy. Quinton held the typical appearance of one with his black hair and eyes that glittered like stars in the midnight blue sky, a single ear-piercing in his left ear which was a dare by Cyrus.

She remembered how he glared her down upon meeting but shrivelled under her icy gaze once he realised she wasn't going to back down. His appearances contradicted his true personality and although he was partially hostile towards her, he was secretly a soft and quiet boy who observed everyone around him. One thing her mother taught her was to never cower under another human being, they were nothing different to herself and if they could act all big and strong, then she could act even stronger. Elisa had been sucked into their little group and no matter where she was in the school, they would always find her. It was borderline creepy in her view but knew they were harmless.

"Its.... high school?" She replied back to Alexander who smiled at her confused tone.

"Any friends? How's classes? Do you need help with work? Is there anything you need me to buy you?" He rattled off question after question making her eyes roll and lips twitch as she fought against the smile that wanted to appear.

"I have three friends, classes are fine some easy some hard, I don't need help with work and no I don't need anything. Now, what's going on with you? You seem real shaken for some reason." She leaned forward and studied her eldest brother in curiosity. Although she had sworn not to get close to her brothers, she couldn't help but worry about her brothers' sudden absence at home.

"Pft shaken? What are you talking about? Are you okay? What's wrong? Did something-"

"Yeah, I can clearly see that your stable right now and have no worry in the world. But I swear to all things holy, if you walk into my room and sit on my bed watching me like you have been doing every night, AGAIN, I will honest to god punch you in the face." Her tone was innocent as she sipped her hot chocolate, waiting for him to give in which she knew he would. She had sussed her brothers out and knew most of their triggers while they were still at the bottom of the ladder figuring out how to climb and avoid the obstacles that would set them back. Alexander flushed slightly as he realised she had been awake whenever he went to check in on them and sighed making her inwardly chuckle.

"It's just a case. I've never had one this hard and challenging before and to be frank, I'm a bit scared." He admitted.

"Rant."

"What?" He asked her incredulously to which she simply raised a single brow, he had begun to hate how she would look down at him like he was stupid.

"Rant. Tell me what's stressing you out exactly, what's annoying you, what's scaring you. I used to listen to mu-" Alexander looked at her with a sympathetic look as she paused and looked down at her mug with a small frown. Although they were siblings and shared the same mother, Elisa had their mother and nobody else whereas he had his father and brothers. She lost the only family she was aware of before being placed under his care. He knew that even though she didn't show it, she was hurting. She cleared her throat hiding any evidence of pain from her voice and face before carrying on.

"Mum used to rant to me nearly every day, telling me what she missed and loved, what she hated and the smallest things that would annoy her. Most of the time I wasn't even listening. I was just sat playing with my toys or falling asleep. But by the end of it, she would kiss my nose and thank me for listening. It helps... maybe you should try it." Elisa shrugged as if sharing a memory wasn't a big deal, but to Alex, it meant the world. His sister had opened up to him, shared a piece of her life back when their mother was alive and happy. He had been shown a glimpse of what their mother used to do, and he felt thankful that she had told him that piece of information.

"Okay but... let's get this straight, I never tell the boys about my cases because I'm not even allowed to. My job is always going to be stressful and scary but that's just something I have to deal with. I'll rant once. This one time. You never bring it up again understand?" She nodded and pointed to the living room, they took their mugs and sat on different sofas. Elisa curled up and sipped the last bit of her drink before setting it on the table next to her. She then focused her attention on her eldest sibling who leaned his head back.

"I've always dreamed of being an amazing detective. You know. Like Sherlock Holmes. I wanted to solve crimes and connect clues. Our small village didn't have many crimes but when there were, I could solve them easily. Last week.... there was... an incident?" He frowned as he thought of how to rant without letting out too much information.

"We found something. Something that shouldn't there, and it was fresh... it set off alarm bells in the station because we've never dealt with something like this. I haven't. I'm scared that I can't do my job properly. Not only do I need to protect you guys, but I have a village who counts on me to protect them. I can do it. But. I can't at the same time. I'm just so scared all the time. Paranoid that I'm going to come home one day, and my younger siblings aren't breathing. I'm scared. So scared."

He squeezes his eyes shut as he confessed his fear. He was scared of losing any more family. His brothers, his little sister, they were all he had left. He continued to tell Elisa about his fears of losing them. How he was scared that Owen was going to crack under pressure, that Roman would one day shut them out for good and that Preston will stop looking up to him. He was petrified that he would fail his brothers and now that he had his sister back, he was scared he would ruin any chance of a normal sibling bond with her. He admitted that growing up he hated the thought of her but now loved her so much. He told her that he was proud to be a police detective and although their parents would be proud of him, he knew their father would have fought him against becoming one. Their parents had this weird thing against the police force, and the government in general. But he knew that his parents would smile at him knowing he took the job to protect his family.

Alexander didn't realise how much he kept from his siblings until he finally let it all out. All the worries, stress and frustrations had poured from his lips and he could feel his shoulders relax, as if he had been holding the weight of the world on his shoulders and finally allowed himself to rest. His eyes fluttered open as he let out a heavy sigh.

"Your right. It does help." Alexander frowned when he didn't hear a reply and lifted his head. A smile touched his lips when he saw his little sister curled up on the sofa with her eyes closed and soft slow breathing. Walking over to her, he chuckled, she looked so much like a little baby with her fist crushed against her cheek and her lips parted. He lifted a blanket and gently laid it over her. She sighed and shifted slightly before relaxing back into the sofa. Alexander hesitated before lifting his hand and brushing her hair away from her face. His palm lingered on her cheek and he leaned down to press a soft feathery kiss on her nose like their mother did. She leaned into his touch slightly making his heart warm.

"Thank you for listening, goodnight dove." He whispered into the silence before he walked out of the room and upstairs to the bathroom to get ready for bed.

Elisa's eyes fluttered open as soon as she heard the bathroom door close. She pulled out her phone, her free hand creating crescent moons in her palm as she dug her fingers into her skin, the line rang like always before she finally spoke.

"I need you! It's going to happen all over again I can feel it. I don't want to lose them! Please! Give me a sign or something! Please tell me how to protect them!" She begged softly into the phone. She turned her phone off after ending the call and lifted her fingers to her nose where she could feel the remnants of soft kiss her brother placed on her. She smiled and felt her eyes water, he listened to what she told him. Elisa laid her head back on the arm rest completely unaware of the shadow that separated its self from the darkness in the hallway. The person made sure the little girl settled and succumbed to sleep before he walked into the room. She was asleep for real this time and so he wasn't worried about walking in. He leaned against the opposite wall so he could study the small girl without making any noise, his eyes ran over the peaceful look on her face.

Roman stared down at his little sister with a suspicious and curious look, his eyes darting between her unconscious self, to the phone she always carried around. Looking at her now he saw a little girl adjusting to her new life, his shoulders lost its tension as he slowly covered her upper body with the blanket when she shivered slightly.

"What are you hiding?"

Driving.
Rain.
Music blasting.

Roman smiled brightly as he drove down the long silent road, he looked over at the girl occupying the passenger seat. A girl who taught him that anger, hatred, pain, was temporary; that life was meant to be full of love and happiness. She was the one person he could talk to about his emotions. His conflicting thoughts about his mother and sister.

She made him smile in the two years he had known her. She looked back at him with a bright smile as she sang along to the music, her platinum blonde hair flying due to the open window. But like all things in the West family's history, his cause for happiness was short-lived.

"ROMAN LOOK OUT!" She screamed. He looked back at the road and tried to swerve the car away from the black car that had appeared out of nowhere.

Screams.
Screeching.
Yelling.
Crashing.
Silence.

"ROMAN!"

Roman woke with a start and his fist flew blindly at the dark shadow hovering over him. The figure grabbed his flailing arms and pinned them back; forcing him to calm down. He pushed back for a few minutes until he heard the familiar calm and collected voice that bought him back to reality.

"Breathe.." Owen sighed in relief as his younger brother stopped thrashing and blinked away his nightmare, the dazed look fading.

"I'm-"

"You're not fine! Stop saying that! God..... stop pushing me away please!" Roman paused and stared at his brother who was close to breaking down, his older brother who never frowned for too long or let out a tear. It tugged at Romans heart and he swallowed as he felt guilt biting at him for always being harsh towards him. The two brothers sat in silence for a moment. Waiting for the other to talk.

"It's the same. Every night. I see her smile. Her laugh. I see happiness and light. And in a blink... it's gone.... she's gone." Owen flinched as he remembered an accident that occurred about 3 years ago, an accident which made the already cracked Roman, shatter. They didn't know much about the girl except the fact that she was Romans best friend and gave him a reason to smile.

"She's in a better place Ro you can't keep-"

"Blaming myself? Haven't you got anything new to say? Besides. It was my fault. I couldn't protect her. How can I protect..." He trailed off clenching his jaw and pressing his knuckles to his eyes as the self-hatred pushed through the exhaustion.

Owen stared down at his lap feeling a wave of hopelessness drowning him. Was he losing his brother to the past? He wanted to hug him and hold him like he did when they were younger. He wanted to protect him from the invisible threat that kept attacking his mind.

But Owen knew deep down that this was a battle Roman had to fight alone.

When morning came, Alexander noted the bags under Romans eyes and saw the way Owen's shoulders were slumped. He felt helpless and his insecurities were forcing their way to the front of his mind. He looked over at Preston and couldn't help but smile when he saw Preston talking animatedly on the phone like he normally does every morning before school. He finally glanced over at his last sibling and frowned, she looked exhausted.

"You ok Lissy?" Owen asked softly, noticing his usual cold and distant sister, had worry and pain in her eyes. She nodded as she slowly ate her cereal. Her lack of words worried the elder brothers more and they exchanged looks. They had to fix this somehow, Alexander had to fix this. Owen nodded his head in Romans and Elisa's direction. Alexander hesitated before nodding at his brother who had told him his plan through eye contact.

"Preston, Karson is going to pick you up. Roman will pick you up, Elisa." Roman and Elisa looked up with wide eyes, both horrified at the oldest Wests instruction.

"Are you MAD?! I don't want to be anywhere near this freak!" Roman spat and hurt flashed in her eyes before fading into numbness, Alexander glared at him and Roman shrunk into his chair.

"She's not a FREAK, and as her older brother, you are going to get to know her! You too Elisa, I'm not letting you slide your way out of this one." Elisa's shoulders slumped further. Great, time with the brother who hated her the most.

Throughout the entire day, Elisa's mind was buzzing wildly with different thoughts, memories and worries. She was scared for multiple reasons and didn't know what to do, her mother was counting on her to protect herself and her brothers from a threat she can't see. A threat they had never seen the true face of. Anyone around her could be the one she had to protect her family from. But how would she know, when all the threat leaves is a calling card after they've pulled their crime? Nothing could pull her from her thoughts, not even a bubbly Sasha who decided that they shared a personal bubble.

"Turn that frown upside down!" She sang in Elisa's ear making her wince and gently push Sasha away.

"C'mon Sash leave the girl be." Cyrus laughed at the girl who simply waved him off.

"No no, she needs to smileeeeee! Earth to Elisaaaaaaa! I miss youuuuu!" Quinton shook his head at Sasha and studied Elisa who seemed more detached than normal, the mask cracking slightly as he saw emotions he had never seen her express before. He frowned before grabbing her wrist and yanking her not so gently out of her seat and out of the school cafeteria, ignoring her yells of protest and insults.

"Get off you brute!" She snapped at him making him raise a brow and simply drag the girl behind him towards the picnic tables that had been situated neatly in a semicircle.

"What's with the silence?" He finally asked her as he laid down on the grass next to the bench she sat on, she scoffed and looked away from him.

"Oh sorry! Didn't realise I'd have to talk 24/7 to appease your school life." Quinton smirked and peeked over at the sassy little girl who was frowning angrily at nothing in particular.

"Oh, don't get me wrong. I'm enjoying the silence. I just want you to go back to normal so Sasha will stop singing for your attention." Elisa quickly turned her head to glare at him making him immediately shut his eyes. She didn't say anything for a few moments and Quinton opened his eyes to look at her. His smirk faded when he saw the trouble look on her face and her hazel eyes getting darker, he sat up to watch her carefully.

"My brother hates me, and our older brother wants us to talk it out." She mumbled. Quinton blinked confused; she was telling him her life story. Something he usually detested from people but was willing to listen to hers.

"I... I can't talk to my brothers freely. Like this. So, you're the next best thing. I'm scared of talking to my brother. Because I don't want to sit there and listen to how much he hates me."

"Do you hate him?"

"What?! Don't be absurd he's my brother how could I-"

"You're his sister, so how could he hate you?" Elisa blinked at his reply but sighed shaking her head.

"You don't get it. Ever since I walked into their lives, he's shown me how much he hates me-"

"Have you asked why he hates you?"

"Well, no but it's quite obvious. I got mum and he got dad. Not to say he doesn't love our father but... I stole our mother." She shrugged and Quinton nodded as if he understood.

"Why don't you open up to him. If you're like this with us, I imagine your exactly the same with your brothers. Closed up. Talk to them. Help them understand who you are." Elisa shook her head closing her eyes in frustration.

"But.... what if when I tell them my past, they get rid of me. What if me telling them the truth puts them in danger?" Quinton watched the girl he had come to accept as a good friend struggle to explain her feelings. She was worried about something much more than her brothers feelings towards her, there was a slither of fear in the way she spoke and he wanted to know what could possibly be scaring her.

"Will it put them in danger?" She turned to look at him dead in the eye; her voice a mere whisper and made his blood run cold.

"So much danger."

Elisa stood in the car park wondering if Roman was going to stand her up, part of her hoped he had so that she wouldn't have to endure a car ride of tension and hatred. But the other part of her hoped he came because he realised he wanted to know her. Quinton had offered to wait with her but she quickly assured him that she would rather face her brother alone. He had hesitated before shrugging and walking off making her smile slightly at the care he was beginning to show.

Soon enough she saw a familiar car come to a screeching stop in front of her. He rolled down the passenger window and didn't even spare her a look as he spoke through his teeth.

"Get in or I'm leaving you." She hurried down the steps and jump into the passenger seat. As soon as her door closed he drove off, not bothering to wait for her to put her seatbelt on making her squeak and hold onto her seat. They sat in silence as they drove to their home which was just outside the village. However, she frowned when she realised they had turned a different corner and were, in fact, driving away from the village and their home.

"You missed the turn..."

"Yup." She swallowed at his nonchalant tone and sank back in her seat while making sure she was buckled up; she felt her gut clench in weariness.

"Hand it over."

"Hand what over?"

"Your phone." She furrowed her brows, and her feet subtly nudged her bag between her legs.

"Why are we not going home?" She shot back at her older brother who gritted his teeth.

"Believe me I don't want to be anywhere near you! But Alex told Owen to lock us out and if we don't spend at least an hour together, he'll ban me from seeing my friends. Now. Phone." One of his hands left the steering wheel and was held in front of her.

"What? No!" She snapped. She wasn't a bratty teen, not in any way. But that phone, that phone is the one thing she couldn't part with. Ever. His head snapped to look at her; eyes blazing in hot uncontrollable anger that she matched with her own cold and icy temper.

"Give me the stupid phone Elisa!" His voice louder and had a biting edge to it making her eye twitch.

"Why? Why do you want my phone? If you want to make a call use your own."

"I want your phone so I can find out who on earth you've been speaking to."

"My friends? Duh." She said absolutely confused. But his next words made her freeze and pale.

"No. The person you were speaking to before you even started school. Who were you talking to?" She scoffed as she tried to play it off; he had heard her speak. He had heard her worries and begs. He had heard her vulnerable moments of crying for help. Although she didn't say anything vital or anything that could possibly get her in trouble or put him in danger, she didn't like the fact that he was listening out for her.

"Did it not hit you that I may have some friends from my past homes?" He sneered and shook his head.

"You're hiding something. Something I know that will hurt MY family. So, I HAVE to know what you're hiding." She felt a stab to the heart when he spoke but tried to brush it off. It was her family too; she just couldn't get close to them.

"I'm not hiding anything, and you can't have it." Roman tsked at her disobedience and looked over at her feeling the rage build up. Her phone was peeking out from her bag and his hand shot over to grab it, her hands grabbed his wrist as she tried to pull the phone away from him.

"LET GO!" They both yelled at each other, neither one realising that Romans foot had pressed harder on the accelerator and they were now driving fast down the long empty road.

Elisa didn't want him to find out this way. She wanted to be able to protect them from the truth as long as possible and save them herself. She didn't want them to carry the burden their parents had accidentally left her with. They just wanted to prepare her. But after her mother's death, she simply became the next bearer of knowledge, the next target.

"Please Roman stop!" She begged over the roaring of the car and the pounding in her chest. He ignored the little girl wanting to find out everything she was keeping hidden, he needed to protect his brothers from the girl who had infiltrated their home. Elisa remembered where they were, and her eyes shot to the window in front of her. A car drove out of nowhere and her eyes widened.

"LOOK OUT!" She screamed making Roman break out of his angry haze and look to the road. His own eyes enlarged, and both of his hands tightened around the steering wheel as he turned to avoid a collision. But for a reason Roman didn't understand yet, the car purposely drove into their path to throw them off. Roman cursed and turned the steering wheel once more, the car swerved and went off-road into the bumpy fields that went downhill. He struggled to gain control of his car and could vaguely hear Elisa screaming in pure fear over the beating of his own heart.

Driving.
Rain.
Music blasting.

Tears sprang to his eyes as memories flashed through his mind, blinding him in the process. Time slowed around them as he saw their car hurtling towards a large tree. I'm so sorry, he thought weakly. He looked over to the little girl next to him. Her screams muted, tears streaming down her red cheeks, hands clutching her seat. I'm so sorry, he wanted to tell her; the little sister he had shunned for no reason. His past was coming back to haunt him, and he wondered whether this was his punishment for hurting his only sister ever since she came back, he wondered if this was the consequence of his anger and hatred throughout the years. Having his sister back only to have her ripped away from him again.

Screams.
Screeching
Yelling.
Crashing.
Silence.

"ROMAN!"

Roman blinked and coughed; he rubbed his chest which was sore from the seatbelt pulling back on him. Something warm dripped down from his forehead and he winced, lifting a hand to the sudden pain, his ears were ringing and his movements sluggish. Time not following its laws and played games on his mind as he saw double, everything partially blurry and too bright for his eyes.

"ROMAN PLEASE!" The familiar voice echoed panicking and his heart tugged. He shook his head slowly and rubbed at his ears trying to get rid of the annoying ringing.

"ROMAN!" The person sobbed and he finally had enough strength to look at his door, his side of the car had taken most of the damage and his car door was pushed in. Probably how he received his head injury. He looked to the passenger side and through his slightly blurry vision, he could make out Elisa taking off his seatbelt and cupping his face with her warm hands.

"Can you hear me?" She asked worried and he nodded and swallowed as he tried to move about, glass shards falling around them. He winced and she watched him carefully to see if he had any major injuries others than the cuts they both received around their bodies.

"I'm ok, we'll have to get out from your side though." She nodded and they both slowly and carefully edged out of the car through her broken door, avoiding the glass that had smashed from the windows. Elisa quickly grabbed her phone and held onto it before turning to look at Roman who kneeled on the floor; hands gripping his hair in an almost painful way. She hesitated before kneeling in front of him, she felt the urge to hug him and reassure him that everything was okay.

"Roman?" She asked softly, unsure of her brothers' current mood.

"I almost killed you..." he murmured so quietly it was hard to miss, but Elisa heard it and she immediately shook her head knowing it wasn't his fault in any way.

"No, you didn't. It was my fault. I... I should have explained my reasoning." She tried to switch the blame, but he shook his head.

"It wasn't your fault. You're just a kid. I'm the adult here. I should have... talked to you. Not treated you like a stranger." He looked up at her and lowered his guard. Elisa finally saw who he was. A broken boy lost, looking for a purpose. Searching for someone to blame for all his pain and losses. She saw a man who had to grow up without his mother and his father, never truly understanding why they had left him behind. She clenched her fists tightly making crescent moons in her palm, she looked away from his piercing eyes and stood up holding a hand out. He took it and she helped him stand up before putting distance between them, ignoring the anger and hurt on his face as she moved away from him.

"We'll have to walk back; I don't have service out here." Elisa had a slight limp as her ankle had twisted slightly but her determination pushed her to walk and ignore the pain. They walked up the grassy hill back to the road, the black car nowhere in sight. They began their trek along the narrow long road hoping for a car to drive past them, the silence between them tense.

"Just.... before we go back.... tell me. Who do you talk to on the phone? Why is the phone so important to you?" She stopped in her tracks; her eyes closed as she realised she would have to tell him. She had to, after all, she knows that this accident wasn't an accident. That car had been waiting for them. She walked back over to her older brother and hesitated before giving him the phone, her hand shaking slightly.

"What are you-"

"You wanted to know who the person I always talk to is. Call it." Roman studied his younger sibling who he now noticed looked exhausted, more tired than he's ever seen her. She looked clueless as if she didn't completely understand what she was doing but knew that it was the only thing she could do. They had service now and he could finally do what he had wanted to do since he first heard her secretive phone calls. He looked through her call history noticing that one unnamed number was consistent, she nodded as he pressed the number and put the phone on speaker. They listened to the familiar ringing as Elisa's phone tried to connect. She swallowed as the call dialled out after five rings; Roman frowned and he went to end the call. She shook her head making him open his mouth to speak but the voicemail greeting stopped him, Elisa lowered her head and closed her eyes at the answering machine.

"Hi! This is Delilah West. I'm sorry I couldn't pick up your call. Please leave a message and I'll get back to you as soon as I can by-"

"Mummy I want to say bye!"

"Ok let's say it together my love."

"BYE!" Beeeeeeeeep.

Elisa smiled up at her brother who stared at her with teary eyes.

"Hi, mummy. I'm, I'm ok. Everything's ok. I'm still really worried because I know I have to tell them everything." She peeked up at her brother who closed his eyes letting more tears roll down his cheeks, realisation slapping him in the face.

"I'm sorry I failed you mum, but I promise I won't let anything bad happen. Roman loves and misses you, so do the other boys." His eyes opened to look down at his baby sister an emotion dancing in her honey eyes as she watched his reaction.

"Love you." She said softly and there was another beep to announce the end of the voice recording. She gently took the phone back from Roman who kept opening and closing his mouth, not knowing what to say. She smiled weakly at him and cleared her throat, her hair pressing against the blood on her forehead and her clothes were also ripped up with spots of blood.

"After mum died I had nobody. Nobody who understood me or knew what I was going through." She looked down at her phone and held it to her chest.

"She left me multiple videos for different occasions, my birthday, for when I'm sad or I've accomplished something amazing! She left me voice notes so I could listen to her voice before I went to bed. I don't really look at them because it hurts too much... but they exist on this phone." She smiled sadly, vaguely remembering the days her mum would make the short videos on the phone and when she had asked why she was making those videos, her mother had simply told her that they were so Elisa will never go a day without hearing her mother's voice or seeing her face.

But it wasn't the same.

"Leaving my own messages when I was scared or sad made it feel like she was still here, and that she would get back to me as soon as she could. It helped." Roman let out a shuddering breath as he berated himself for thinking so harshly of a little girl who was mourning. A little girl who was hurting and didn't feel comfortable enough to talk to her own brothers. Roman had been taught that anger, hatred and pain were temporary, that life was meant to be full of love and happiness. Looking at the girl in front of him, he finally felt relief. The last puzzle in his life had fit into place. His sister. He wasn't amazing at expressing his emotions and knew that he had a whole lot to apologise for. If there was one thing he knew about Elisa, was that she was as stubborn as him. He would have to apologise for the rest of his life for the way he treated her! But at that moment the least he could do was kneel in front of her with his back facing her.

"What are you doing?" She asked, perplexed at his sudden change.

"Piggyback. Get on." She waited for a moment but did what he said knowing that this was his first step to mending their long-forgotten bond. She took her own first step and wrapped her arms around his neck. She clung onto him and quickly wrapped her legs around his waist as soon as he was standing again, her cheek pressed against his surprisingly soft hair and she heard him let out a sigh.

"Am I heavy?" Her voice was meek and timid, something he hadn't heard from her. He chuckled and began walking, her feet slightly kicking against his thighs.

"Your light as anything Shadow."

"Shadow?" She questioned him making him falter in his steps before nodding with a soft smile as memories of a little girl shuffling after him flooded his mind.

"When we were younger you followed me everywhere. You would copy whatever I did and listened to whatever I told you to do. You were my Shadow." He explained and her heart warmed at the memory he shared with her. She leaned her cheek on his shoulder letting out a content smile when something caught her eyes. Ink under his right ear, 5 black birds with a name under the smallest bird, Shadow.

"Shadow?"

"Yeah, Ro?"

"No more secrets promise?"

She let a single tear loose as she closed her eyes and gave a thin smile. As much as she hated what she knew was going to happen, she knew it was the only way and she didn't want to let her brothers down anymore. She wanted to let them in, she wanted her knights back. She nodded in agreement and he let out a relieved sigh.

"No more secrets. Promise."

8

Then

William West sighed tiredly as he locked his cupboard. He made sure no files or equipment was out before switching off the light and finally making his way out of the room he had been cooped up inside for days. He whistled as he spun his keys on his finger and made his way down the long dimly lit corridor his brown hair pulled back into a bun and he brushed the fallen strands behind his ear.

"Dr West! May I have a quick word?" A grating voice called out from behind him, and William inwardly sighed in frustration. He just wanted to get home and hide in his blankets, away from any other human. But he had to paste on a polite smile and turned around to face the people walking towards him.

"Ah hello, Dr Lawrence! How can I help you?" Dr Lawrence was a man in his late 20s, just a few years older than William himself. He was a lovely man who enjoyed getting to know each of his colleagues; a man who although got on his nerves for his incessant chirpy talking was a man William could trust wholeheartedly. The older man came to a stop in front of William and gave him a triumphant smile and a strange glimmer in his eyes.

"I'm doing amazing kid. Your work is absolutely ASTOUNDING! Scientists from other countries and labs are wanting to simply meet you because of your research!" William blinked at the sudden praise but grinned, nonetheless.

"Thank you, Sir." Dr Lawrence chuckled at the younger man before looking at his fellow colleagues. They nodded back at him before they walked off, leaving the two scientists to talk.

"So, Dr West. You're a scientist who is very qualified in your chosen area. You've managed to find possible treatments for certain diseases and it's amazing what you can find! We, the board has talked about you proudly and they would like to offer you a private assignment of sorts." William perked up and raised a brow in curiosity.

"What is it, sir?" Dr Lawrence sighed with a smile that hid his worries and doubts about the sudden assignment he was told to offer to William West. He liked the young man, he really did, but he had his orders to follow from above.

"They would like you to participate in a study with a small set of scientists who are qualified in their own areas. Equipment and any materials you may need will be provided along with workspace. Your assignment is to actually use your research and make a cure for the diseases around the world."

"Any specific disease?" William asked completely serious.

"No. You have the opportunity to put your mind with other gifted scientists and hopefully create treatments and cures for illnesses." William felt an unbelievable amount of pride and excitement. He was within the small group of scientists who had been chosen to take this assignment on. He couldn't wait to get started and see how their minds could create something that could help the world.

He had told his best friend all about his new assignment and Harrison couldn't contain the excitement he had for William.

They had celebrated with drinks and looked forward to the new chapter William was about to begin. The West man had grown up always pining after his parents' love, trying to make them proud of him for anything he did. But nothing was ever good enough for his parents and it wasn't until his parents sadly passed away did he realise he has to start living a life that he was happy with. He loved his parents with all his heart but was ready to move onto his next chapter.

It's funny how words could sway a person, a few sweet nothings could seduce a person into falling into a trap. The moment William and the other scientists agreed to the private assignment, their fates were sealed, their lives would never be the same and there was no way out of the grave they had dug themselves in. They had picked the forbidden fruit not caring about the consequences, simply hearing the praise and adoration they received from people they didn't know. Humans crave the love and praise from others, its written in our DNA, like peacocks shaking out our feathers whenever someone notices one of our talents. We bathe in compliments, taking the words into our heart and consume our thoughts and actions. Who would have thought that a few small words, a single compliment and interest in our skills and qualities could make us blind to a person's intentions? Words were a dangerous thing and could easily influence the mind, persuade us into a false sense of security and it would be too late to get away. William West was trapped, and like all victims, he didn't even know it yet.

He began his new assignment in a private compound that contained his new team and extra workers who were there only when they needed them, they had unlimited resources and shared their knowledge with each other. He himself was a Ph. D Epidemiologist; someone who studied the spread of diseases and travelled to any research facility when he was needed. He loved his job and loved discovering new ways to help the people of the world in anyways he possibly could.

William walked down the empty hallway towards his office, his footsteps echoing in the silence. They hadn't settled on finding a treatment or cure for a specific disease; they had started by researching different viruses and figuring out their cell structure. It took a lot of work to find out exactly what they needed to know, and they were mostly up to the late hours of the morning; sometimes not even sleeping because they were desperate to find something they could start with.

The moment they finally had a breakthrough was a moment of celebration within their small team. There were 6 of them in total who led their own mini teams to aid in their research. But the main 6 always got together to help each other out and explain theories. They had finally had one that could possibly work. Using gene therapy to treat unhealthy human cells. They believed the most they could do was possibly find a long-term treatment, but they now had hopes of creating a cure that would get rid of viruses and diseases forever. They were going to create a serum that would program the cells in the hosts body to fight any disease and infection, it would change the way of living and would mean that so many young people would actually get to start their life. It was like a mini computer that hijacked the cells into doing what it wants. They began experimenting more and more on different cells and animal cells, creating new possible results and failures. Dr Lawrence checked on their progress and was pleasantly surprised to see that the 6 scientists he had chosen, had managed to put all their knowledge together and start working on cures. He was amazed at their skills and knew that with more time, they would probably be able to create vaccines for people to take.

He sighed as he turned a corner and saw someone in a lab coat like him hiding behind a wall. His lips turned down in confusion and he walked over to ask the person what they were doing. He gently laid his hand on the person's shoulder making them hiss and whirl around wide-eyed.

William West was star struck.

He stared into moss green eyes that stared back into his dark brown ones in frustration, her red painted lips turned down into a frown and her brows knitted together as she stared at him.

"What are you-" She slapped a hand over his mouth and pulled him against the wall next to her, he gave her a confused look to which she simply lifted a finger and pressed it against her own lips. He then heard what she was listening to.

"It's possible but that's not our purpose he-"

"You better start re-evaluating your answer. I'll be back for a final decision and if you haven't decided to comply, then we have no choice but to take over." A low angry voice snapped. They heard more mumbling before William realised someone was walking towards the door, he grabbed the woman's hand and quickly hid around another corner. They heard the people saying their goodbyes and waited for Dr Lawrence to also leave, the man in question left the room with a heavy sigh and headed away from the pair.

"What was that?" William asked referring to the discussion they had heard.

"I saw these guys all dressed in black suits walk in with briefcases. When I asked Dr Lawrence about it he told me to stay in my office and stay out of it." She said crossing her arms in annoyance, her gut was telling her to do the opposite and to find out what the head scientist was hiding. Despite the fact she agreed to the private assignment, she was still hesitant to put her effort into it. Something didn't add up, their cause, she didn't trust the man and she needed to know what he was hiding before she helped.

"I'm guessing you don't like to be told what to do?" He mused and she scoffed as she looked up at the man she had seen working in one of the labs near her.

"Of course, I don't! I hate men who are like that. Think they're so superior and that women are weak and someone to be pushed around." He chuckled at the pout on her heart-shaped face, and she sent him an icy glare.

"Luckily for you, I'm not that kind of guy. Though we need to work on your scary face.... you look like a kitten." He whispered the last part, and she swatted his arm playfully. He chuckled and held out a hand towards her.

"William West. It's lovely to meet you...?"

She grinned up at him and slid her dainty smaller hand into his larger one. Sure, they worked together but she was the quietest out of the 6 chosen scientists, he didn't know her really and she didn't know him. Yet there was a sense of familiarity between the two, as if their souls understood one another, knew each other, and they were reuniting after centuries of being apart.

"Delilah. I'm Delilah Fayers."

The two scientists grew closer and even began their own side project together, working on making their own treatments for diseases. Dr Lawrence approved of their project and kept a close watch on them which bothered Delilah to no end. She would notice him sometimes walking out of their lab whenever they weren't in there or how he would casually look over their notes. She swore she saw him swap a vile of chemicals for something else. Her gut kept trying to tell her something was wrong. But she didn't listen, something she regretted one day.

That day started like it normally did for the two scientists. They had been working on their project for a year; working on a drug that could be consumed by an individual and heal them of any illnesses big or small, once a year. It would balance out vitamins and minerals, erase any cancer cells or viruses. They would call it the Miracle Pill, the medicine of the future, one that would give a second life to those who had barely seen the world and its beauties. She didn't see the negative side of their project; all she saw was the hope that they could give the world.

Delilah rubbed at her eyes tiredly and sipped her bitter coffee, her heels clacking against the floors of the empty hallways. She turned a corner into their lab and smiled when she saw William. He looked up from his computer and sent her a cheeky grin as he saw his favourite girl approach him.

"Hey, stranger." He said with a mischievous glint in his eyes. She smiled back warmly and stood next to him handing over his own hot drink, a pumpkin spice latte. Her nose wrinkled in disgust as he sipped it and shivered at his strange drink choice.

"I don't understand how you could drink that." She mumbled and he chuckled slipping an arm around her waist as she stood. The two were inseparable and she knew in her heart that she had found a one in a million man, someone who was both selfish and thoughtful. He wanted to help the world, his part of serving humanity, but he wanted to do it for himself too. He wanted to prove to himself that he could be happy doing something his parents never paid attention to. She admired him and he in turn admired the woman who stood by him, learned about him and became his whole world without him even realising it. She leaned against him and they stood in peaceful silence as they looked at the numerous piles of paperwork, vials and the machines that contained their final result. The Miracle Pill.

"I can't wait to present this to Lawrence. We could help save so many people with this Lils." William said excitedly. She hesitated and set down her drink as she turned to him her eyes scanning his familiar features.

"He gives me bad vibes Will. I'm telling you something is wrong about all of this. Ever since the beginning, he's been.... weird." William sighed at his best friend and held her shoulders making her face him.

"Lils what is he going to do huh? He's a scientist in the medical field. His whole life is dedicated to helping the world and fighting off diseases."

He tried to reason with her, but ever since he met her, he knew that once she had an idea in her mind, she wouldn't let it go. Sure, enough ever since they were first recruited for this project nearly two years ago, she's always avoided Lawrence. Delilah shook her head and moved away from the idiot who was so blind to the secrets she knew were being kept from them. The whispers that echoed within the walls. She wasn't as subdued as the rest of them, and the whispers of doubt would grow louder the longer they stayed there.

Something else was going on.

They worked in silence to finish the last of their work, they mixed in the correct amounts of chemicals and wrote down the measurements in their book they kept specially for their project. A red leather-bound book that held all their experiments and failed ones. Delilah yawned as she poured in a vial only to frown as she watched the clear liquid turn a neon purple. William abruptly stood up as they examined the liquid.

"What did you pour in?" He asked slowly, utterly confused at the reaction. She checked and sniffed the vial only to freeze. She rushed towards their equipment and began to figure out what the unknown solution she poured in was. After a few minutes, their equipment beeped, and she paled.

"What is it Lils?"

"It's a mixture of the most dangerous poisons... there's Botulinum and Ricin present. Where... where did this come from Will?" She asked in complete fear. They didn't work with poisons, so how did a vial of them appear in their lab? Her eyes widened in realisation and she let out a scowl.

"Lawrence. He's been hanging around here a lot more. Always looking over our shoulders and asking us questions about our work."

"That's his job Lils you can't-"

"But it's not though is it! He was simply given the order to recruit 6 scientists and give us free reign to put our heads together and create treatments and possible cures. He wasn't given the task to babysit us William don't you see it?!" She snapped back at the man she had grown to care about. She needed him to understand, to believe her. She stepped closer to him and almost begged.

"I need you to be on my side." She whispered. Looking into her eyes he saw her determination, the pleading for him to understand what she was saying and trust in her words. He hugged her to his chest and rested his chin on her head. This woman was his everything, she had never been wrong, and she always made sense in her ramblings. He trusted her.

"I am on your side Lils. Always okay?" She nodded against his chest and sighed out in relief, her arms tightening around his waist as she pressed her face into the white sure he wore beneath the lab coat. It was them against whatever was happening, they were a team. Delilah suddenly realised something. Something she should have realised a long while back.

"Those men in suits. They came here to speak to Dr Lawrence about something. There's a connection there. We need to find out what they talked about." William didn't hesitate. He knew she had been right the whole time, that something perhaps more sinister was at work. How could they find out more information? They hadn't really seen those men again and they couldn't ask Dr Lawrence outright in case Delilah was right; that he was up to something.

"Cameras maybe?" She asked, and a smirk came to William's face as he thought about a certain someone who had always had his back in everything since their college days.

"Harrison. He's great at all things technology. He could hack into the system without being traced back."

Harrison walked up to the back entrance of the building his best friend worked at, why he was here he had no clue but knew it must have been an emergency. The door opened and William pulled his surprised and confused friend through the door. Harrison listened in rapt attention as William explained their theories and concerns and agreed with their plan.

"I'll do whatever but.... whose Lils?" Delilah popped out from one of the adjoined rooms and sent a gentle wave at the man who gawked at her. He never imagined his best friend would meet someone just yet and judging by the way his eyes followed her in awe and adoration, neither did he.

"That'll be me! I'm Delilah. It's lovely to meet you, Harrison, I've heard so much about you!" Harrison stared wide-eyed before he made the connection and punched William hard in the chest causing the latter to wince.

"Are you serious?" William groaned and rubbed at his chest.

"Deadly. No offence but are you blind miss?" Delilah blinked confused then let out a soft chuckle as William huffed.

"He's an ugly little goblin. You can do so much better." He teased his best friend but really was glad that he had someone to call his own.

"Yeah, yeah anyways. Can you hack into the cameras?"

"Sure. I need the room, day and time if possible."

"What if we don't know the day or time?" Harrison groaned and mentally throttled his idiot of a best friend.

"It'll take me ages to find what you need then." Delilah thought and smiled.

"I remember the date. Here..." She typed it into the keyboard and Harrison began searching the timings while William looked up at the woman confused.

"How did you remember?" He asked curiously setting off a bright blush on the young woman's cheeks. She looked down at her hands avoiding his gaze as she became shy, an emotion that was rare of her to show.

"It was the first day we met... What can I say? I'm a sentimental person." She shrugged as if it wasn't a big deal but to William, it meant the world.

"Oh here, men in black. You sure you're not part of some coverup?" Harrison joked with the two others in the room but paused when he saw the looks on their faces. The looks of fear and sudden concern, as if the thought had hardly occurred to them and they were now realising how deep their situation may be.

"I sure hope not." William mumbled as they began to listen. They watched as Dr Lawrence sat at a desk with three men in front of him. They each held a briefcase and were stone-faced.

"What you're asking for is the opposite of what I stand for. I don't make drugs, not the ones you're looking for." Lawrence scoffed. The man in the middle nodded.

"The world is at its peak. Population pollution at its highest. Natural selection used to do the job for us by ridding of the weak and unable. But you scientists nowadays work to make sure that people don't die from their weaknesses. And the population is expanding. What can we do but.... play executioner?" Delilah tightened her hold on William's shoulder. Dr Lawrence looked horrified.

"What is it you're asking me to do really?" He asked in a mere whisper.

"I want your little sheep to make a... medicine let's call it. One that will immediately kill off the consumer. Obviously, we know that your sheep are loyal followers and probably have the same principles so... give them free reign. I'm sure they'll have many spill ups and failures in their experimenting. We have our own scientists, and they can put together the remains of what your scientists have made. Don't tell them about this meeting. Let them think they will be heroes of the world." He chuckled coldly.

"It's possible but that's not our purpose he-"

"You better start re-evaluating your answer. I'll be back for a final decision and if you Haven't decided to comply, then we have no choice but to take over."

William felt cold and internally screamed. Delilah was right from the beginning but his pride and willingness to follow the orders of Lawrence had clouded his own judgement. Harrison felt sick; his fingers danced along the keyboard as he tried to find out who those men were through a facial recognition system.

"Guys we're screwed," Harrison called out getting the attention from William and Delilah who had fallen into their own thoughts.

"What is it?"

"He's Scotland Yard."

"Why is Scotland Yard interested in our research?" Delilah asked baffled at their discovery. Harrison dug further.

"He's got criminal links... There's a schism. The majority of Scotland Yard are doing their job but there are some who have links to criminal activity, international dealings... the black market- what trouble are you two in?" Harrison turned to the pale scientists who looked absolutely petrified. Their work was meant for good, but any good enough scientist who knew exactly what they were doing could easily change the purpose of Project Miracle. Instead of healing and curing, the serum could be used to kill and destroy once inside the host.

"A lot of trouble." They spun to see Dr Lawrence closing the door to their lab. Immediately Harrison deleted any trace of him on the computer and William stood in front of Delilah; Delilah huffed and stood right next to him, not liking being shielded.

"You used us for what? What do you get out of this?" William asked in disgust. Lawrence lowered his head and pulled out a small remote from his pocket. Immediately all the cameras went down and their shoulders dropped, not sure whether to hear him out or run.

"Listen carefully. We've been watched since the very beginning by Them. What you saw and heard is correct. They wanted a 'medicine' that can kill off a human once consumed. Your project was the one they were most interested in... I... I put the poison in the vial because I knew they were watching. I wanted them to believe that we could have made what they wanted but they will never get it." Delilah caught onto what he was saying.

"You played them... you wanted to have the upper hand." Her voice gentle and understanding.

"You need to get rid of all your data and research. Burn it all. I've set everything into place I've erased all of your names including all the other scientists, from the Project. They won't know who you are, and you'll be safe. Away from all this trouble. I've got cash ready for you to take and disappear to start a whole life, but you need to hurry. They'll know that I've done something and will be here soon!"

William and Delilah didn't waste a second, they began to delete their backup data while Harrison burned extra papers. Delilah shoved their red book into her bag earning a raised brow from William. It didn't just contain their data, it contained their memories, her moments and letters between William and herself. That book was her story and she refused to part with it. They then turned towards their project. The Miracle Pill. One small mistake, and it could be the end of choice, it could be the end of humans living a fulfilling life. Delilah let out a heavy sigh and they began to dispose of their project, wincing as she watched their years' work go down the drain.

"Lils look..." She turned and remembered that she had taken a bit of their project out a day earlier and had placed it in a container. If they wanted to carry on with their project they could! She placed the vial that contained the Miracle Pill that had not been contaminated by poison, into her bag with the red journal ignoring the worried look on her best friends' face. Within minutes the lab looked as good as new, and all trace of the Miracle Pill was non-existent. Lawrence nodded at the three young adults and sighed.

"The government aren't to be trusted; you've seen first-hand proof of that. Scotland Yard isn't to blame, it's the group who decided to drop all their morals and create their own rules. But they are still hidden, unknown, and they still have resources. Nobody is to be trusted and I'm afraid you are going to have to lay low for a while. Especially if they find out that you two were the scientists who came close to creating what they wanted. Even if it was by mistake and my own fault for swapping those vials." Harrison stood forward.

"I'll help keep an eye out when I can. We need to hide you two far under the radar." Lawrence nodded in approval and looked at the two scientists who gazed at each other in fear. Their eyes full of concern for each other and what lay ahead of them. He smiled sadly knowing he had ultimately chosen their life for them, a life of hiding, running.

"I'm sorry you two were dragged into this. The initial goal was to gather 6 gifted scientists to help create a better world... but nothing life-changing would go unnoticed by the government. I'm so sorry." Delilah hugged the older gentlemen and sent him a smile.

"To each their own Dr Lawrence. I wish you the best of luck." She whispered. William shook hands with the scientist and said their last goodbyes. The other scientists had one by one left the facility in the hope that they could find a new life away from the game they had started.

"Don't let them find you, because once they do. They'll never stop searching. They don't know your names or faces for now. But their technological skills are far more advanced than ours. It'll only be a matter of time."

Delilah felt fear creep into her heart, and she clutched onto William's hand making him look down at her in concern. She didn't show fear, she was the bravest woman he knew. But there's only so much a human can pretend before they finally let the fear show and take over.

"Lils..." William whispered her name making her moss green eyes look up into his dark chocolate ones.

"We're going to be ok. We're going to get through this. Together."

"Together." She repeated and held onto him tighter. They would do this together and would be okay. They were stuck with each other forever, but neither of them were repulsed by the idea. It was them against the world, together.

Black SUVs skidded to a halt outside of the research facility, men poured out like ants from an anthill. The man who had talked to Dr Lawrence a year ago stormed through the hallways; ready to rain hell down on the Head scientist of the Project. He fixed his wrist cuff as his feet pounded against the floor, the sounds of his men shouting and searching the building, echoing.

"LAWRENCE!" He boomed making the man shake to his core, he hadn't been a very religious man but now he prayed for his life to be spared. The man slammed the doors open to the very room Lawrence stood quaking in. He took in the bareness of the room, the same cameras that they had been watching through were turned off, and the building had no sign of other life except Lawrence. Realisation punched him in the gut, and he towered over the frightened man.

"Where are the scientists you recruited?" He asked slowly, death lacing his tone.

"Sir? I don't know what you're talking about." Although Lawrence was scared, he spoke with a tone of indifference. The man sucked his teeth and nodded slowly with a scowl.

"So that's the game you want to play? Fine." He spat. He spun on his heel ordering his men to search the building for anything he could use to find the scientists.

"Sir there's nobody other than that scientist. Everything seems to have been burned up and computers have been erased." A man told his boss.

"Burn the building."

"But sir what about the scientist?"

The man turned to smirk.

"What scientist?"

The news of a research facility burning by an unknown cause, spread through the news like wildfire. Anyone who knew the scientists affiliated with the building was silenced, anyone who questioned what the building held was ignored.

One by one the 4 of the 6 scientists were found.

All but William West and Delilah Fayers.

9

Now

Preston was used to being alone. He was used to coming home to an empty house, used to eating breakfast in silence, used to not seeing his brothers for sometimes more than two days. He saw Owen the most since he was the mother hen however even he would be in the library for hours just reading or walking around.

He didn't blame his brothers. Nor did he hate them for it; it was just how their lives worked. But with his sister coming home, he couldn't help but be thankful that she had made such a huge impact on their life. He saw his brothers more. Owen was full of life, Alex was making more of an effort and even though Roman was still Roman, he knew that her being here still affected him. Preston just didn't know if that was good or bad yet. He sat in his room on his bed playing a video game; he could hear Andre shouting through his headset and would make a few comments every now and then. His mind completely focused on the graphics on his TV and Andre who was yelling and cursing anytime they were killed. After a while, Preston realised someone was knocking on his door and he sighed in annoyance.

"Yeah?" He called out loudly to whoever was trying to interrupt his alone time. He didn't peel his eyes away from the game as he assumed it was one of his brothers come to either complain about the noise he was making or telling him to come and eat something.

"Hi." A small voice spoke making Preston snap his head towards the door in surprise. Elisa leaned against the doorway rubbing her foot against the back of her ankle. He hadn't seen her around much, so it was a surprise that she was in his room.

"Hello..." Preston said kindly; slightly awkwardly. She had been here for weeks, but they hadn't really had a one to one. He couldn't blame that entirely on her as he knows he had also been avoiding her. Not because he didn't like her but because he wasn't used to this. Having someone younger in the house which meant he had responsibility. Preston cleared his throat as he realised they both hadn't said anything.

"So, you need anything?" He asked her bluntly and she blanched for a moment before shaking her head and mumbling an apology as she turned to leave, his eyes widened, and he paused his game properly.

"Hey wait! Come sit." Preston found himself saying and after a minute or so Elisa shut the door and shuffled over to the bed where she perched herself on the end. The two youngest West siblings sat in silence; Preston playing the game whilst looking at her every now and then and Elisa stuck deep in her thoughts. Just talk to her Preston, he yelled at himself. He peeked at her from the corner of his eyes and swallowed before finally letting words slip past his lips.

"I don't remember much about you, you know..." He mumbled making her smile that he was even attempting to talk at all.

"I know... you were 5 when mum took me away." Preston nodded feeling his heart harden slightly at her mention of their mother. Out of all the siblings, he spent the least amount of time with her. He didn't even remember much of her. Yes, he had his father, however, he was soon missing from their lives too. He was 10 when their father went missing so his only father figure was Alexander. Sometimes the West boys forget how little time and memories Preston had with their parents, too stuck in their own lives and grief. It was the reason Preston spent more time out of the house then in it, and when he was home he spent it alone in his room. It's not that he didn't love his family or favoured his friends more than his siblings. He just hadn't had much time to experience the family life; his mother gone, his father working and although he spent time with them it was like his mind and attention was elsewhere sometimes. Alex had tried to hold the parent role but didn't realise that giving his siblings attention and making sure that acted their age when they were younger, was important. No matter what Preston thought and said about his parents, his heart still yearned for what he didn't remember.

"What was she like?" Elisa looked at her brother and sent him a soft smile as she heard the desperation and longing in his voice. She kicked off the black fluffy slippers that Owen had gifted her, he had gifted them all a pair and insisted they wear them around the house at all times. Elisa pulled out her phone and opened up the photo gallery. Instead of answering Preston's question, she gave him her phone which had a video open, ready to play. Preston pressed the play button and his eyes widened as he saw a beautiful woman with bright green eyes, a smile as bright as the sun and light brown wavy hair. A woman who shared similar characteristics to all of his siblings.

"So, I'm assuming if you're seeing this, I didn't get to see you again, Preston? I recorded videos for you and all your brothers, birthday videos, Christmas wishes and even videos for when you hopefully one day start your own family." Preston felt his heart thunder as he stared at the woman who was his mother.

"I love you Preston my littlest knight. When you were younger you were such a cheeky little monkey. Always hiding when it was bath-time, waking us up at early hours in the morning and your pranks! Oh, your pranks made me laugh for hours! How you got such funny ideas never fails to amaze me and I know that you've grown up to be the same mischievous and prank-loving boy you were when you were younger." Delilah West giggled slightly making a small smile come to Elisa's lips, she missed that giggle.

"I want you to know sweetheart that I'm sorry for leaving you. I'm sorry for not explaining to you or... or reassuring you that I was coming home, but baby please understand that whatever has happened in our lives was never planned and your father and I did everything we could to keep you and your siblings safe and happy. I will try my very hardest to come home to you love." Preston frowned at her words confused but knew that Elisa would help him understand. Delilah wipes away a tear on camera and smiled brightly.

"I love you, Preston. So much my darling. One day we will meet again, we'll be together." She paused and chuckled slightly, remembering a memory her children were not privy to.

"Together." The video ended and Preston felt a small hand wipe his cheek. He looked at Elisa who gave a sad look as she took the phone back.

"I'll let you keep the phone later tonight so you can watch and listen to all the messages and videos she left for your past birthdays." Preston nodded at her; his own hands wiping away the tears that had slipped down his face.

"Mum never let me forget you. She reminded me of every memory, everything about you and the others. Although I did not know who you really were, I couldn't remember knowing you so maybe that's why I wasn't as affected as you all. I didn't really know you." Preston listened intently as Elisa began to tell him of all the stories their mother told her. How Elisa and Preston would hide from their brothers for hours until everyone got worried, how Elisa would be a distraction while Preston smuggled sweets into his pockets for them to eat later. Elisa told him story after story. Memory after memory, her smile wide as she recalled sitting in her mother's arms watching the stars, listening to the tales of the West siblings. Preston found himself smiling with tears rolling down his cheeks as he listened to his baby sister, he could feel the love his mother had for them all through the stories and his heart warmed.

"What happened to mum Eli?" She did not think much of the new nickname but froze at his question. She had not told any of her brothers what had truly happened to their mother. Sitting up straight, she turned to face the doorway. Preston frowned as she stayed quiet.

"What happened with you and Roman anyways? I haven't seen him since you guys came back, and he normally comes in here to bully me about something." Elisa winced knowing that Roman was currently fixing his injuries. As soon as they had got in, he had wrapped Elisa's ankle and told her to ice it before he went to shower and get rid of all the glass. She had then proceeded to change into fluffy pyjamas and decided to talk to Preston, she had to come clean to them all.

It was time to let them in.

Elisa stood up and nearly fell when she put too much pressure on her ankle. Preston quickly steadied her, slipping an arm around her waist and pulling her arm around his neck.

"You, ok?!"

"Downstairs. I need to talk to you all." He nodded and together they made their way down the stairs and into the living room.

She realised that Alexander and Owen were also home and were currently snapping at Roman who was sat on one sofa ignoring their questions. When Alexander had come home from a stressful shift at work, he expected to hear yelling between Roman and Elisa with Owen trying to defuse the situation. What he didn't expect was to see his brother sprawled out on the sofa with a bandage around his head, wrist and scratches on his cheek and arm; Owen nearly having a fit as he was throwing question after question at him.

"What on Earth happened to you?!" Roman rolled his eyes as he kept his focus on the movie that was playing, not wanting to hear the concerns his brothers were spewing out.

"Why are you bleeding?"
"What happened?"
"Do I need to take you to the hospital?"
"What hurts?!"
"Where's Lissy?"
"Oh god, what did you do?"
"How did this happen?"

Roman let out a loud groan and buried his face into his arms.

"Hey, pass me that cushion over there so I can suffocate myself and pass away peacefully." He said and his older brothers glared at him unimpressed. Elisa giggled at Romans words making everyone turn to look at her. Owen smiled brightly, Alexander looked down at her in adoration and Roman looked at her partly in guilt and relief. A screech made them all wince.

"WHY IS MY BABY LIMPING?! WHAT HAPPENED TO YOU BOTH?!" Owen yelled as Preston helped her over to the sofa where Roman was.

"Just please calm down Owen. I think it's time we talk." Alexander saw the look on her face, and they all settled down.

"What do we need to talk about Dove?" Elisa sighed heavily, her fears coming back full force. She let down her guard and looked down at her hands that she had just noticed were trembling. This was it. She played with her fingers, pinching her skin, and picking at the dried blood. No doubt she was going to have a few more scars added to the collection of nearly invisible ones. Roman took pity on his sister and started the conversation to help her out.

"Start from the beginning Shadow." She sent him a grateful smile whilst Owen and Alexander exchanged a surprised look. Something clearly happened for them to sort out their attitude with one another.

"What do you know about mum and dads' jobs?" She asked her brothers who looked confused at her question but turned to the eldest. He frowned slightly at the odd question not understanding why their parents had anything to do with the injuries his two siblings had acquired.

"I think mum worked in a cafe and dad was... I can't remember what dad did. I think he worked in the doctors' surgery?" She shook her head and sighed, they knew nothing. If only their father was here, it was his job to tell them but clearly, he vanished before he could tell them anything.

"Well, there's no easy way to say this so long story short.... mum and dad were scientists who made a mistake with a project they were recruited for and had to hide from the government who wanted their project for bad reasons."

Silence.

"You what?" Preston blurted out and she huffed knowing that she was going to have a hard time trying to explain the story. Roman screwed up his face in disbelief but didn't speak up.

"Mum and dad were research scientists working on a project. I only remember the basics. They were working on a medicine that would treat unhealthy cells in the host's body. I was too young for mum to tell me everything and, I later realised she didn't want me to know everything right then and there." Preston let out a sigh of relief.

"So, they weren't crazy scientists!" They gave him a weird look to which he raised his arms in surrender and gestured for her to carry on.

"They were being watched by the government who wanted to use their research and make it do the opposite of what our parents intended to use it for." Alexander studied his sister, his mind full of questions. They were trying to act calm so she wouldn't stop talking, but their minds were filled with confusion at what she was telling them.

"What happened to mum."

For a moment nobody said anything, they simply watched their sister who had a million emotions crossing her face. The most prominent emotions being heartbreak and fear.

"We were at home with aunt Dree Dree, Levi and Leah. It was a normal day with me playing with my two friends.... they went home and mum and I went to stargaze on her balcony like we did every night... I asked about you guys and she said we would one-day star gaze together. Then.... she said monsters never stop hunting..." She paused and an expression crossed her face; one that Alexander didn't like. Her words weren't making sense and the chest in her mind that she had locked shut, was fighting to open. She slowly looked at her eldest brother not knowing whether she should carry on. Her mother told her to avoid the police for obvious reasons. This unknown group had people everywhere, especially uncover as police officers. They were not to be trusted...

But this was her brother, her knight in shining armour, her alpha leader. Him being a police officer was something their parents had never thought of, which threw a spanner into the plans. The people he worked with could be watching them, could be using him. She was told to always trust her family and that didn't stop just because of his career.

"She told me not to trust any governmental figure, including the police." Alexander's eyes lit up in understanding.

"That's why you reacted that way when I told you what my job was..." Embarrassment painted her cheeks.

"You're making this sound like it isn't a big deal. What happened to mum?" Roman asked tightly through clenched teeth as he clicked on that she was stalling.

"I fell asleep after we talked and... I could hear her talking to someone. I honestly think she was talking to dad." Owens's brows raised while Alexander and Roman shook their heads.

"Impossible, they didn't talk. They separated for a reason Dove so-"

"Maybe not the reason we grew up to believe." Owen blurted out and eyes were on him. With furrowed brows, Alex concentrated on his baby sister.

"Someone came. Mum was rushing about waking me up, throwing stuff in a backpack and- she looked so scared. But so determined and worried and... I was laying on the floor when the door opened and there he was." Roman slowly sat up straight as he noticed the shift in her body language and voice. This was something new. Her voice shaking, her hands trembling. The boys noticed how her eyes glazed over as if she were watching something they couldn't see.

"I couldn't see him- it was dark- I can't remember- I think- no he wore blue- wait he wore a hood- she was in front of me- he was tall- but I was smaller then so maybe he was the normal height and- I-" Roman gently moved to kneel in front of the shaking girl and took her small hands into his own.

"Shadow..." His voice was soft and calming but she couldn't hear over the pounding in her heart.

"It happened so fast- I could have stopped her- why didn't I call someone? - she was brave, so brave-" Alex gently nudged his younger brother out of the way and cupped the side of her face. He watched her eyes darting around wildly, her breathing coming in harsh pants and her hands clenching.

"Dove I need you to calm down for me, okay? Can you do that?" She focused on her eldest brother's voice and nodded through her trembling. She followed his breathing instructions while Owen wrapped a blanket over her shoulders. They had never seen her like this and in all honesty, they were petrified.

"Xander?" She whispered and he paused at the name she gave him. He hid his smile, not the time Alex!

"Yes, Dove?" She held her arms out like a baby and he lifted her small body into his arms. She hugged him tight as she worked up the courage to say what she needed to say, his hand rubbing her back comfortingly.

"He... he killed mummy. He- there was a knife and he- on her throat and she- she fell and said together soon and I- it was dark, I think I passed out!"

It's a strange thing, hearing about the death of a loved one. It's like your mind halts all thoughts, breathing becomes a chore and a ring echoes in your ears. Your eyes unfocused as your mind tries to remember the last time you saw that person smiling. Murder. You hear about it on the news and media, yet it seems like a faraway thought like it's not real; that no human would willingly take the lives of another.

The West boys grew up with an absent mother and a missing father. The thought that their mother had died when Elisa was bought to them, never actually registered in their minds. For some reason, they believed that maybe their mother had given her up too. Never in their wildest dreams would they have believed that their mother had been murdered, but deep down they knew it was true.

This was way bigger than any of them thought. Alex tightened his hold on his baby sister as he started to understand her. She had witnessed a murder at such a young age, and clearly, it had affected her view of life and people in general. She was just a scared little girl who had associated secrets and death together. He stroked her hair as she sobbed into his shoulder like a child, her little hands clutching at his shirt.

Preston stood in the doorway with eyes squinted, staring at the ground as he processed what they were told. Owen had a hand pressed to his mouth and his other hand was rubbing Romans back. Roman didn't know what to do with himself, his eyes looking everywhere but at the small princess who broke down in his brothers' arms.

Alex pressed a kiss to his sister's head and held back his tears, he had to be strong for the girl who had been brave for far too long. Owen raised his head as a thought occurred to him, he swallowed the lump in his throat wondering if she had the answer to the question the boys had been asking for 8 years.

"So, what happened to dad?"

10

Now

Owen had always been the most empathetic out of the West siblings. He had always tried to understand their feelings whether they were a small issue or not. He never wanted them to feel like their feelings weren't valid in any way. He knew exactly how to handle Roman's anger, how to handle Preston's detachment and how to handle Alex's cold personality. Growing up it got harder and harder to reach them, but he always managed to bring them back.

Lissy was a new case. He didn't know what triggered her, what made her smile or what made her cry. He didn't know how to bring the light in her eyes; he so desperately wanted to be the one to bring that spark back.

Preston was sat in the kitchen making hot chocolate for them all, thinking about what they had just learnt. Their mother had been murdered, their parents were scientists and made a huge mistake which ultimately decided their future, their father was missing. Elisa wasn't even aware that their father was missing. She had told them that he was supposed to be with them, she was shocked when she first found out and increased her ever-growing fear.

He traced the unfinished tattoo on the inside of his arm. When he was younger he always wanted the tattoo his older brothers had, he never understood the meaning behind it. Whenever he had asked, Roman would ignore him, Owen would smile and say he'll tell him one day and Alexander would look distant before changing the subject. They all got the tattoo on their 18th birthdays but unlike him, they would have a word over the smallest bird. He never understood why but now he did. It was the nickname of the littlest of the West siblings. Eli, that's what he wanted under the smallest bird.

"Hey, kiddo. You okay?" Owen spoke softly and picking up the tray of hot chocolate mugs while Preston picked up the marshmallow bowl.

"I dunno. I don't remember her... is it possible to miss someone you don't even know?" He was confused about his emotions. He couldn't really picture their mother, just faint flashes, distant laughter and phantom kisses. Elisa also lived in those faint flashes but at least he could get to know her. His mother, however, he would never meet, and nobody would be able to fill that spot. He didn't know whether he should be glad he doesn't remember her and her abandonment or cry knowing he will never meet her again.

Owen gave his brother a side look and didn't respond. Preston was the only one who had the less amount of time with their mother. None of them could relate to him as they had memories of their mother and his heart cracked at the lost look on his little brother's face. They walked into the living room and Owen met Alexander's worried red eyes. Elisa sat on the sofa staring out of the window. Her eyes were glassy from crying and cheeks rosy red, her hair messy and she looked as though she was protecting herself from any harm. Roman had his eyes closed but would look over at her from time to time.

Alexander didn't know what to do. His mother was murdered possibly by the government, the government for crying out loud! How was he supposed to protect his family from Them?! Were they still after his family? What were they after?? As if hearing his inner thoughts, Elisa looked over at him.

"Mum packed a bag when she left the lab with dad. She's protected that bag her entire life until... until she couldn't. She gave it to me, and I protected it, kept it with me through every home I went to. Never letting anyone search it."

"What's in it?" Roman asked her.

"The phone, a note saying to protect the contents of the bag with my life, a vial and a journal. There are some random photos and mums wedding ring too but.... the vial and journal are the most important."

"What do they contain?" Elisa made a face and sighed.

"From what I've read and know, it's mum and dads project. Whatever mum and dad were trying to make was somewhat perfected and mum put some of it aside while the rest of it was poisoned? I think mum said this was all that was left of their project." She yawned and rubbed her eyes. For a moment they all softened as they watched her shift her position to one more comfortable.

"Wait so it's possible that the same person who killed mum is after us?" Preston asked horrified. She nodded with a shrug.

"Yes and no. Whoever killed mum found out about me and after my first foster home, he made his first appearance, they didn't think I knew anything but wanted to make sure. I don't think they know about you... well, they probably do after that accident Ro." She said absentmindedly and Roman wanted to throttle her as soon as the words left her mouth.

"ACCIDENT?!" The eldest of the siblings yelled out while Prestons' brows furrowed.

"Is that why you were limping earlier?" He asked Lissy who flushed and looked at her hands timidly while Roman sent daggers into the side of her head for mentioning the accident.

"WHAT HAPPENED TO YOUR LEG?!" Owen shrieked as he caught sight of the bandage hidden under her clothes. She rolled her eyes in annoyance of his protectiveness and Prestons' lip twitched, at least her sass wasn't gone.

"It's just my ankle Owen. Besides Roman is worse than me." She winced in regret after the worlds left her mouth and felt holes burning into the side of her head. Since when did she talk this much to them?

"WHAT?! WHAT DO YOU ME-"

"OH, FOR THE LOVE OF GOD OWEN SHUT UP!" Roman and Alexander yelled making Owen pout; he was just worried...

"Fine.... we went for a drive after school and... we were arguing, and I wasn't paying attention to the road. A car drove in front of us and I swear it was on purpose because I tried to drive out of the way but... we went off-road and crashed into a tree or something." Without a word, Owen began checking over his younger brother and making sure his injuries weren't severe, Roman simply batting away Owens fussing hands with a scowl.

"I'm taking your paints away for a month. You jeopardized your life and your sisters' life. You can't let your anger always take over man." Elisa felt the guilt in her chest as Owen and Alexander reprimanded Roman for his mistake, to which the latter simply scowled and left the room. She let Owen fuss over her knowing it was more for his sake than hers. Preston looked sheepishly for opening his mouth and sipped at his warm drink.

"It wasn't his fault Xander. You can't blame him. The car came out of nowhere and-"

"He shouldn't have started a fight whilst driving! He could have killed you, Elisa!"

"But he didn't! It was my fault for keeping everything hidden and-"

"Don't take the blame for him! He is in the wrong, he-"

"HE WAS PROTECTING HIS FAMILY!" Elisa yelled back at her older brother who glared back down at her; knowing she was right. He was just beginning to realise how easy it was to lose his siblings. She swallowed and calmed herself before speaking again, wanting him to understand that it had been her fault. She had never needed to explain her actions and the reasons to all her secrets before and it was hard for her to open up and trust someone who was still technically a stranger, no matter the blood relation they shared.

"He was looking out for you. He didn't understand why I was acting weird around you. He didn't like it. He just wanted to understand Xander. You can't fault him for that... it was my fault for not telling you anything..."

"Did mum tell you to tell us?" Preston piped up.

"Well no... she told me dad was supposed to tell you guys everything so that one day when we reunited, I wouldn't have to deal with everything alone." Alexander nodded then furrowed his brows.

"What did mum think you could accomplish? Did she not think that people will be after you? Did she not think to destroy this research they had? Why just pass it onto you for us to worry about?" Elisa had thought that her entire life, she wondered why her mother had given her this burden to carry. Why she had insisted that, instead of getting rid of all the data, she was to protect it.

"I think... I think in mums mind she had hoped that it wouldn't come to this. That she would prepare me for the worst, but she didn't think I would have to protect her work. Maybe she was hoping that one day they could actually use their project for good? For the use they made it for?" That was the only explanation she could come up with. Owen cleared his throat and locked eyes with hazel eyes that looked slightly less cold than they were the first time he saw them.

"You said after your first foster home... he made an appearance? Who?" She rolled her eyes in frustration. She forgot about Owen the mother hen. The one who never let any small detail escape his eye and ears. For a moment she didn't speak, her eyes on her small hands. Preston stood up straight and walked over to his little sister immediately sensing her discomfort. He ruffled her hair affectionately making her blink and look at him in surprise, he grinned mischievously and tilted his head.

"It's been a long day huh? Why don't we question her tomorrow?" His eyes hardened slightly as he met his older brother's harsh glare. The younger west brother didn't wither and kept his stare on the man, determined to let his little sister rest before they picked at her brain again. Owen nudged Alexander with a subtle nod and after giving one last look to Elisa he sighed in resignation. He gave her a gentle look and nodded.

"Go get some sleep. I'll call your school tomorrow so you can sleep in a bit if you want." Immediately, Elisa gave Preston a beaming grin; thankful that her brother had gotten her out of another interrogation that could result in another panic attack. He gave her a cheeky wink back before he practically skipped out of the room, proud at being able to make the cold ice princess smile. Owen felt his heart warm when he saw the smile she sent Preston and he decided he may be able to push his luck.

"Hey, Lissy? Can I have a hug?" He asked sheepishly but instead of receiving the hug he had dreamed off from his baby sibling, she sent him a look of pure disgust before smiling up at Alexander and calling out a shy goodnight to the older brother. Owen spluttered and raised his arms confused while Alexander let out a low chuckle at his sisters' behaviour.

"But... but what did I do?" Owen whined; upset he hadn't gotten his hug.

"Maybe she's not that comfortable with that much affection yet. Give her time man." Alexander tried to reassure the mother hen who began mumbling profanities under his breath.

Elisa winced at the sharp pain in her ankle as she walked down the hallway and paused at Romans bedroom door that was cracked open slightly. She gathered her courage and peeked into the dimly lit room. She saw her brother laying on his bed staring up at the ceiling, an arm was thrown carelessly over his eyes and his other arm thrown across his stomach.

"You know it's creepy to stare at people in the dark." His voice drawled over the soft music playing in the room. Her cheeks darkened and she slipped into the bedroom. Roman didn't move or bother to acknowledge her and so Elisa took the time to observe his room.

The walls were white like most of the rooms in the house, however, she could hardly see the wall as there were paintings upon pictures, doodles and sketches pinned to the walls. Most black and white with random bursts of colour. Her eyes trailed across every sketch that Roman drew and her awe grew as she saw a painting of who must have been the boys and their father. Her breath caught as she looked at eyes that seemed to radiate life despite being stuck on the canvas. The father she could hardly remember. She looked away from the personal picture that stabbed her in the chest and saw the unfinished painting. Her heart stumbled. He had painted a hand laying on concrete. Glass surrounding it and although it was unfinished, she could clearly see the black rose that had been painted in the palm of the hand. Her jaw clenched and she turned away to look at her brother who hadn't moved.

"Why did you paint the rose?" She asked him. Roman frowned and peeked at the girl who stood with her arms crossed over her chest, eyes flickering from him and back to the painting.

"It's a memory. Today.... wasn't the first time I was responsible for a car accident. Except for last time, I was responsible for the loss of a life." Elisa flinched and felt sadness and guilt flow through her body. Guilt that her brother had to live with a consequence that wasn't really a cause of his actions.

"I wasn't paying attention to the road. I hit a car. I remember the screams, the pain, the glass and blood. I blacked out for a second. Or it could have been minutes. And when I opened my eyes." He sucked in a harsh breath as he remembered the lifeless eyes staring into his fearful ones.

"I never got to say goodbye or..." Elisa sat on the bed next to him and patted his leg understanding, not wanting to open one of the chests in his mind that he so clearly possessed to hide all his darkest memories.

"The rose was laying in her palm. Blood dripping from the tips of the black petals that were wilting. She was like that rose. Beautiful and unique.... ripped from life too quick." He roughly wiped his cheeks with the back of his hand and looked at Elisa who stared at her hands with her brows knitted together.

"It wasn't your fault-"

"Oh please, it was my fault and anything you or Owen say will-"

"They found you way before I came here..." Her nostrils flared, and her mouth felt dry. Roman sat up abruptly.

"It wasn't your fault Ro. You were being watched; you must have been. How they found you I don't really know. Our parents hid our existence really well. Were you ever in the public eye? Like were you ever known outside of Robin Hoods Bay?" He slowly nodded as he vaguely remembered one of the arts shows he had attended when he was in school.

"I had a painting that someone was interested in and they bought it. Turns out he was quite a famous artist from America, and I got a bit of publicity for it I guess."

"They must have heard your name. West. They linked it back to me and mum and they must have been watching you; they probably didn't know much about the others thank god, but you were their target. That car accident was planned. They planned on killing you, Ro." Roman shook his head; hearing the holes she stabbed in her story.

"How do you know they were planning on killing me?" She slowly turned to look at him and Roman saw the fear swimming in her hazel eyes. He understood her silence and felt his heart clench as he realised he may never have seen his sister again.

"They tried to kill you." He stated and she nodded as she tried to swallow the lump in her throat. He opened his arms out in a rare moment of vulnerability; wanting to hold his baby sister close. Within a blink of an eye, Elisa quickly got on the bed and threw her arms around her brother's waist. He hugged her tightly pressing his cheek against her soft hair, his hand rubbing her shoulder and the other holding her smaller hand. He felt the numerous scars on her knuckles and winced as he pieced together where they probably came from.

"My first foster home, they weren't nice people. They didn't hurt me or anything. They just... they kept saying I wasn't worth anything and that's why my father didn't want me to come home. They would constantly say mean things, Ro. Until one day they couldn't say anything." She shook slightly and clutched Roman's hand tightly.

"I came home from the library. It was my favourite place to be, and I refused to go to school. Social services allowed me to carry my studies on at home with online tutors. Anyways I got home waiting for the shouting to start but it didn't come. It was routine for me to let them yell at me until something caught their attention, and they would forget all about me. But it never came. My foster parents were sat at the dining table with their throats...cut open. My foster brother had red and purple bruises around his neck, his death caused by asphyxiation. According to the reports, my foster parents' vocal cords had been ripped out. Blood everywhere like a Banksy painting. I can still see it now... their cold, lifeless bodies sat at the table with their hands on the wood looking like they were about to eat." Roman wasn't a squeamish person but he winced when she casually spoke about another human's death as if it was something she normally witnessed.

"The killer was still there. In the house. Watching me, observing my reaction. Silently, in the corner. When I finally saw him, I ran. I ran through the back door and into the woods beyond our garden. I could hear him chasing me however where I was loud, he was silent. Almost flying through the trees. He caught me, Roman." Roman shifted and held his little sister closer to him. Her hand trailed up to her neck and stroked the small scar in the centre, his eyes following the action and freezing when he realised she could have suffered the same fate as her foster parents.

"I never really saw his face. He wore this mask that only covered the lower part of his face. It was shaped like a skull and he wore black goggles. I felt his hand on my throat, he was choking me. I couldn't breathe. He was all blurry and I could hear nothing but my breathing. It hurt so much but at the same time, it didn't hurt. Does that make sense? I saw the knife and felt the coldness of the metal on my neck. But I never felt the pain." Roman bit back a sob as he pressed his face into her hair, he stroked the wavy strands and pressed a kiss to her forehead. Elisa revelled in the love and attention he was giving her and felt the blanket of safety hug her tightly.

"I woke up a while later, I was on the floor near my foster brother. There was a note in my pocket." Elisa sniffed and breathed in the comforting peppermint her brother seemed to smell of.

"Let's play little West, this game of cat and mouse has begun. We will find you wherever you are, whoever you are with, I'll end them like we ended your mother. Till next time little mouse." She recited the note she had found that day.

"On their bodies was a single black rose. It's his signature, their signature. I don't know if it's one person who they send to kill people. Or if it's multiple people. But they leave a black rose over all their victims. I was watched, followed. I hated going outside. I convinced each of my foster families to give me up since I didn't want anything happening to them. I didn't want anyone else's eyes to go blank."

Tears rolled freely down his cheeks and she wiped them away with quivering lips.

"It isn't your fault big brother. We're just pawns in a much bigger game." She said softly in a small voice making him nod and give her a soft rare smile.

"Can I join the hug?" A quiet voice piped up and they turned to the doorway where Preston stood with a sheepish grin. Roman rolled his eyes while Elisa giggled and held an arm out. Prestons' eyes lit up as he rushed to his siblings on the bed and hugged Elisa to his chest. He didn't bother hiding that fact he had been listening and instead began sobbing into her shoulder. She held onto him tightly with her eyes clenched shut and Roman pulled his two younger siblings into his arms wanting to prevent them from anything that would make them cry again.

That was how Owen and Alexander found them just before they went to bed, the three youngest West siblings leaning against the headboard of the bed with their arms holding onto each other. Roman protecting them even in his sleep. A sorrowful expression grew on Alexander's face as his eyes landed on Elisa who was curled up between the two protective bears.

"Not comfortable with affection my butt. I want a Lissy cuddle!" Owen pouted at the scene in jealously but also smiled warmly. Alexander rolled his eyes at his childish brother but couldn't help but feel excited for his bonding time with his sister. However, his smile slipped as he remembered that his sister held more baggage then any of them and her troubles had not yet ended. He had a feeling it had just begun, and his sister would be the epicentre of it all.

"She's seen death. More death than we've ever seen, then I've seen. She shouldn't have had to deal with it alone." Alexander mumbled as he noticed the dried tear tracks on her cheeks.

"She's just a child... but she isn't alone anymore." Owen commented sadly before he sent a pleading look to the eldest West boy who simply shook his head.

"Leave them alone Owen. You'll get your hug soon enough." His tone filled with amusement as he dragged away a sulking Mama hen who wanted to shower his siblings in affection.

Elisa followed Sasha and Cyrus down the cobbled road. She looked around her in awe; houses and cottages tightly packed together, alleyways that weaved through some of the houses. A small smile graced her face as she watched shop owners encourage people to enter their shop. Different coloured flowers planted in nearly every doorstep and windowsill making her wonder if she had suddenly transported to another world. One which was more magical and serene. She listened to the soft idle chattering between customers and shop keepers, the giggling of children as they called out to their parents to hurry. Her eyes landed on each of the doors of the houses they passed. Each having a different name she found absolutely adorable with their brightly painted doors.

"Oh my god!" Sasha's shocked voice ripped Elisa out of her thoughts, and she immediately searched for the threat that caused her friend to shriek. But when she saw nothing worthy of fear, she turned to her friends confused at their reaction. Cyrus was grinning in amusement while his girlfriend was practically vibrating with happiness and glee. Her eyes wide and hands fanning her face.

"What?"

"YOU'RE SMILING AND I SWEAR YOU LOOK EVEN MORE LIKE AN ANGEL. SCRATCH THAT YOUR A GODDESS GIRL!" Sasha squealed. People looked over half in amusement and the other in exasperation. The thing about small villages is that people did know each other, so Sasha's little outburst didn't alarm anyone in the slightest. Elisa flushed slightly but rolled her eyes at the dramatic teen she had befriended her hands tightening the ribbon holding her hair together in a pony tail.

"I am a human Sash." Sasha looked like she was about to faint, and Elisa began to feel a little self-conscious. Just how badly did she treat people?

"A nickname too! Ugh! She just gave me a nickname Cy." Cyrus chuckled at his dramatic girlfriend and grinned at Elisa; happy that his new friend was relaxing and showing them a bit more of herself. Her hair out of her face showing that she was more confident than she was when she first arrived, her hands clasped behind her back. He could see a few small scars, one under her right eye which looked like it went in a straight line through her eyebrow, one on her lower lip and another on her jawline. Showing off her scars made a flicker of pride grow in their chests knowing she wasn't ashamed of them. The three friends carried on walking down the steep cobblestone path until they got to a beach. She tugged her cap further down so her face was partially hidden.

"Oh look! Hey man!" Quinton strolled up to the trio with a relaxed stride. He greeted Cyrus with the well-known dude hug where they shake each other's hand and then proceed to give each other a one-armed hug. Elisa and Sasha screwed up their noses.

"My two last brain cells were wasted on trying to figure out why guys have made this their thing," Elisa mumbled under her breath and Sasha huffed.

"I know right?! They won't even know the guy and yet they all suddenly know 'oh! It's a male human being! Let us do the pound, handshake hug!' Is there some secret book about men etiquette we don't know about?" Sasha asked shocked and Elisa's lips tilt up in amusement. The boys looked over at the two smiling girls with confused looks. Quinton studied Elisa blankly and tilted his head like he was examining something strange.

"Why is the zombie smiling?" Elisa's smile dropped and she sent him a deathly glare making him smile sarcastically at the girl.

"There she is." He sneered. Cyrus and Sasha rolled their eyes as they listened to the two idiots in their friendship group bickering and began the walk to an emptier area of the beach leaving the two to shuffle along behind in silence. Elisa felt eyes on her and finally turned to look up at Quinton's inquisitive blue eyes. Her brows knitted together as she stared back at him just as curiously. They didn't talk much. But when they did have their encounters, they were always trying to either outsmart each other or throw insults at one another. It was a strange friendship and yet Elisa enjoyed being around him. It was similar to Sasha. She hardly talked to the girl however she wouldn't mind listening to the girls' stories for hours on end if it meant they got to hang out. Cyrus was the calm patient one and Elisa admires him simply for being himself. The trio was everything she never thought she would want in friends, and yet she already loved them to bits.

"What happened?" He finally asked her, noticing the changes in her behaviour like the others but also picking up on something the other two hadn't. There was a slight sparkle in her usually dead eyes.

"I talked to my brother. We had a car accident-"

"Whoa, you good? Is that why you didn't come back to school for two days?" She nodded and carried on; ignoring the aghast look on his face and his searching eyes as he tried to find any indication that she was injured.

"We talked at home and I told them everything I've kept hidden from them. It... I feel lighter you know. I don't have to worry alone. But I'm still scared... that car accident is just the start of well everything." She chuckled but Quinton could hear the pain in her voice and wondered not for the first time, what this girl was going through. He swallowed as he looked towards the sea and pretended he knew exactly what she was talking about when in fact he was just trying to help her understand herself and her feelings.

"You're in trouble aren't you." She smiled slightly in confirmation at his statement.

"That's why you're like this huh. You push people away." She looked up at him and elbowed him teasingly making him give her a mock glare and rub his side.

"You in the same boat creeper?" He rolled his eyes at the nickname and ruffled his hair.

"Not really. I just know what it's like to push people away. From experience. Don't do it. You'll hurt a whole lot more when you look back and realise that there were people who understood you and wanted to share your pain so you wouldn't have to feel it alone." They trudged along the grainy sand listening to Sasha giggle as Cyrus talked to her. Elisa wondered what it was like to live a life Sasha did; where her only worry was if she studied enough for a test. She took Quintons words to heart and knew that the boy was right. She had been alone for so long and she just wanted someone to finally hold her and take away all her problems.

She looked around the beach and noticed how the number of people grew less and less until it was only the odd person walking along the waterline. Her eyes flickered towards the cliffs, marvelling in the height and the sort of reddish colour that appeared when the sun shone on the rocks. Elisa went to look back at the sea when a slight sparkle in the cliff face caught her attention. She turned to look at the spot but saw nothing out of the ordinary, nothing worthy of her time. However, her mind memorised the cliff as if storing the image away for a later date. The four made it to an empty spot on the beach closer to the cliffs. They sat down among gritty sand, pulled out the lunch they had all bought and ate in comfortable silence with the odd chatter. As the West girl sank into the sand, her finger brushed against something hard and cool. Her brows furrowed slightly as she saw something silver poking out of grains and she tilted her head back to the cliff behind her where she saw the sparkle.

"So, you used to live with your mum right?" Sasha asked slowly, catching her attention, and the boys tensed. Elisa smiled slightly as she realised they were all curious about her and had been waiting for her to tell them exactly who Elisa West was.

She briefly looked over at Quinton who was sipping on a bottle of Pepsi, he caught her gaze and she looked down at her hands before nodding to herself. Time to let them in.

"Hey. I'm Elisa West. I lived with my mother in Cali, and we lived near the beach." Sasha smiled brightly and began asking questions upon questions. Cyrus jumped in every now and then and Quinton smiled faintly at the younger girl who had taken his advice. She began to tell them about the games and adventures her and her mother had, the home-schooling, her friend and aunt Dree Dree. She told them all about a life that seemed almost perfect and happy. For a moment Elisa felt like she finally belonged somewhere.

But she knew never to hold her breath. She simply enjoyed the moment she was experiencing with people she could call friends.

Owen hummed as he mixed the cake mix in the kitchen of the coffee shop that was situated on one of the tightly packed streets in the village. The day was slow and quiet with the odd customer coming in to buy a pastry or dessert. The man smiled as he waved off a customer who ordered some coffee before throwing his attention to the person that walked through the door. His smile widened when his eyes met familiar sea-green eyes that shone with mischief.

"Hey, O-man!"

"Sup Fin." Finley slid into the stool in front of Owen and watched him work.

"How's muffin?" Owen raised a brow at the name he knew was meant for his little sister.

"And she thought I was bad at names? If she hears you call her that, she'll probably rip your hair out." They shared a laugh knowing that fact was true before they went quiet.

"But really. How is she? I didn't expect..." He trailed off as he thought of the angry little monster he had met, and Owen nodded sympathetically. He understood why she was like that now, but it still pained him knowing the past wasn't kind to her at all.

"She's just started opening up to us even though she's hesitant. She's scared about something Fin and for yours and the others safety I'm not going to go into detail. There are small, rare moments where she's this soft, talkative, kind girl but then she closes off and is quiet and hidden. We're working on it." He said and Finley nodded slowly.

"When can we come over?! I want to annoy her too man and she seems like a hoot to wind up." A playful smile lighting up his face as he thought of the many pranks he could play on the littlest West. Owen shook his head but shared the same mindset of teasing his little sister.

"Not any time soon. Well... I guess we could sort out a trip out of town maybe?" As the two boys chatted about future trips they could all go on, a voice Owen knew all too well caught his attention.

"What you doing here bro?" Owen asked in confusion as Alexander sighed heavily and sank into the chair next to Finley. He saw the stress painted across his face and quickly made a cup of steaming coffee for his brother.

"Another one." He said making the boys look at him confused.

"We ain't one of your police bros. What's going on?" Finley may be the clown of their group, but he also knew when it was time to be serious. Blood or not he saw Alexander as his older brother too and so when Alex was worried or stressed, it meant they should all be worried or stressed.

"They found another body washed up on the beach." The boys' eyes widened, and Owen immediately scanned the room making sure nobody could hear them.

"Dead?" Alexander gave him a look while Owen slapped him around the head at the stupidity their friend possessed.

"Well noooo the guy was sat there perfectly alive drinking a mocktail by the shore which immediately caused distress within the police force. Of course, he was dead you absolute idiot!" Roman's voice came hissing as he walked over with the others. Owen raised a brow at Alexander as he understood why Roman, and Preston was there. Alexander West was petrified and needed to make sure his family was safe.

"Yes, yes, he wasn't breathing. It's the second body to turn up in the same condition as the last... it's not a coincidence. They're beginning to suspect- wait. Where's Elisa?" Alexander took notice of the missing sibling and looked around wide-eyed. Roman frowned slightly and looked at Owen who looked at Preston. Preston raised a brow before panicking.

"Was I supposed to be babysitting her?!! Oh god, I didn't realise I'm so sorry, I can't remember maybe I left her at home??" The boys groaned. Owen checked his phone to see if she had texted him and smiled when he realised she had.

"She's with her friends at the... did you say the body was at the beach?" At Alexander's nod, Owen whistled and casually began taking off his gloves and apron as he prepared for what he knew was to come next.

"SHE'S AT THE BEACH?!?" The boys scrambled to their feet and rushed out of the coffee shop. They began bolting down the steep cobblestone hill throwing out profanities every time one of them tripped or nearly twisted their ankle. People watched them confused but moved out of their way immediately sensing they were men on a mission. Alexander hoped, he pleaded that Elisa was nowhere near the incident, he prayed that she would be blissfully unaware of the death that had stained part of the beach. Hopefully, she was on the opposite side away and happy and finally feeling safe. However, he knew that with their luck, she'll be right next to it.

Elisa heard the screaming, the yelling and shouting coming from around the rocks. They had watched people running past them and towards the screaming only for more yelling to erupt. The group found the whole thing bizarre and decided to up and leave the area so they could continue their chat. Despite their new plan, the teens found themselves stopping as soon as they heard what the shouting was about.

"SHES NOT BREATHING!"
"WHERE DID SHE COME FROM!"
"CALL THE POLICE!"
"THERE'S BLOOD ALL OVER HER!"
"HER THROAT!"

Elisa's ears perked up like a curious cat and she turned back to look at the growing crowd. Her heart thundered loudly, and her jaw clenched; eyes flickering over the panicked faces and she felt a lump form in her throat. She hesitated for a moment before walking towards the gathering, ignoring her friends calling her back. Quinton quickly grabbed her wrist to stop her from getting closer. A dark feeling in the pit of his stomach and his mind telling him to protect her from whatever was in the middle of the crowd.

"No." He told her firmly when she met his stern eyes. But Elisa was a West, the most stubborn of them all. Her nostrils flared and she sent him a glare rivalling that of his own.

"Yes." She snapped back. They glared each other down until finally, Quinton lowered his eyes. He sighed and slid his hand into hers before nodding in resignation. Elisa was surprised by his action but pulled him along behind her. They pushed their way through the herd, Quinton not willing to see whilst Elisa needed to see.

"OFFICER WEST! EVERYONE BACK AWAY!" Alexander yelled flashing his badge at the crowd making them calm slightly at the kind face. His eyes flashed to the body on the ground and his face twisted up in disgust and horror. He then searched the crowd for hazel eyes that he knew were studying what he saw. Owen quickly grabbed Elisa's free hand and dragged both teens away from the scene. Preston and Roman getting in between Quinton and Elisa, ripping apart their still tightly clasped hands.

In movies, whenever the character sees something traumatic or perhaps sees something that becomes the highlight of their life, the world seems to go in slow motion. Sounds become slow. Every action going through frame by frame slowly. It wasn't like that for Elisa, she didn't see everything suddenly slow down or pause. It was like the world was muted. She could see her brothers' lips moving. She could see the rushing around though it seemed a lot more blurred as if she was running past them at lightning speed. Her heart was beating faster than humanly possible, and she felt as though she had a fever, ears ringing.

Alexander held her face between his hands and shook her small form, trying to erase the glazed over look in her eyes. They had pulled her away quickly, but unfortunately, they hadn't pulled her away quick enough.

Elisa had seen the body of a woman with blood-red hair and tattoos on her arm.

Elisa had seen the bright green eyes staring blankly at the sky and water soaking her entire being.

Elisa had seen the blood dripping from the wound on the neck; a clear indication that the body was fresh.

"Dove? Sweetheart come on. Let's go home yeah. Let's-" She grabbed Alexander's wrists and looked him dead in the eyes. This was it. It was happening. What could she do? Nothing. It was happening and there was nothing she could do.

"Eli come on let's-" She shook her head immediately stopping Preston in his attempt to reassure her. Owen closed his eyes and slowly held her to his chest in an attempt to lend her some of his strength.

They hadn't pulled her away fast enough. She had seen it already. Elisa wouldn't have been bothered by the dead body or the blood, no. It was the cause of death that scared her and it was the signature left behind that petrified her.

A single slit across the neck.

A black rose sitting on the body.

"They're back."

11

Then

"Stop eating like that!"
"C'mon man close your mouth."
"Stop it!! You absolute donkey!"
"Look.. ahhhhh."
"CLOSE IT PRESTON!"
"GOOD GOD MAN THAT LOOKS NASTY!"
"I'm officially full. Thanks for that."

The West brothers argued over the dinner table and sent murderous glares to a 10-year-old Preston who found fun in annoying his brothers. Roman was his target as always and he knew just how irritated the temperamental West boy got when anyone did the smallest of things. Owen snickered and whispered other pranks and ideas to get on Roman's nerves; also, one of Owens favourite past times. Alexander rolled his eyes and huffed in his seat, he already had a headache from partying the night before with his school friends and listening to his brothers shouting was not helping the pounding in his head. He could feel his heartbeat beckoning in his ear and it sounded like endlessly playing drums.

"Don't you need to change Pres?" Alexander asked the small human softly, trying to be the big responsible brother he should be. Preston shook his head as he ate his jam and toast with his mouth wide open making Roman shudder in disgust.

"Nope! I have decided not to go to school no more!" He said confidently and proud of his statement. Owen chuckled and leaned forward in fake intrigue as he listened for his brothers arguing point.

"Oh really? What ya going to do then?" He asked his littlest brother in amusement.

"I'm going to stay home with Daddy and Uncle Harry!" William West walking into the kitchen with a single brow raised as he heard the declaration. He scratched the back of his neck and let out a low humorous chuckle.

"Oh, really pal? I guess you could stay at home... help me and Uncle Harry clean the house, wash the dishes, hang the clothes on the washing line. There's a lot too-"

"Hey, I just remembered I really love school daddy, so I'll help you after I come home okay? Okay, I'm going to get changed now!" Preston blurted out rushing out of the kitchen. Owen and William let out a laugh as they listened to the feet thundering away and the little shouts filled with the indignation of how cleaning shouldn't exist, and school should be optional. Roman let out another moody huff and William ruffled his hair earning a whine and a hand slapping his away.

"Why are you so moody today huh?" Roman let out another indecipherable mumble and stormed out of the kitchen, shoving his earphones in his ears. William smiled faintly as Owen gave him a huge hug and called out to Preston to hurry. Alexander stood up and hesitated.

"Sooooo you said you wanted to talk to me right?" William eyed his oldest child with a blank look; he watched Alexander's eyes flicker around nervously. A clear indication he knew he had done something wrong. He stood silent as he watched Alex fidget on the spot, letting him stress over what his father could say to him. He finally sighed and shook his head in disappointment.

"Your 18. You're in your last year of 6th form man. These exams are important and-"

"I get it jeez can you just stop with the lectures. You're not exactly great at them it's boring." Alexander regretted the words as soon as they left his lips. He watched his fathers' shoulders slump in defeat and mentally kicked himself for his harsh words. He knew his father was doing all he can. He had always tried the hardest for his sons and they always made it hard for their father. Their poor sweet father.

"I'm sorry dad, I know you're trying your hardest. I'm sorry I'm making it hard I just hate studying. It doesn't stick in my head!" William threw an arm over his frustrated son and snickered making the boy relax at the sound. As much as he sometimes hated his father's nagging, he loved him with all his heart and was glad he had such an attentive parent.

"It's fine kid. I was worse than you in high school trust me. I just want the best for you... is that a cliche parent lecture?" He stage whispered the last part and Alexander grinned at his fathers who looked down at him feigning innocence and confusion.

"Very cliche." He whispered back and William shoved his sons head away from him playfully.

"ALEXX. MOVE YOUR FAT BUTT WE'RE GONNA BE LATE!" Owen's voice echoed through the house and Alexander scowled at the insult. He waved bye to his father before grabbing his rucksack and chasing Owen out of the house, evoking a rather high-pitched scream from the latter.

"AHHHH GETAWAY YOU MOLE RAT!"
"I SWEAR OWEN WHEN I GET MY HANDS ON YOU I'M GONNA DROWN YOU IN THE SEA!"
"HA I'VE HEARD THAT ONE BEFORE- OH JEEZ DAD HE'S GONNA- OOF!"

William strode calmly towards the door and watched Alex tackle Owen, tugging on his hair as Owen's hair was the most precious thing to him. He didn't stop the fight as he knew it would end soon and it was just another normal occurrence between the West brothers. He heard shuffling behind him and looked over to watch Preston pull on his jacket with his tongue sticking out in concentration as he zipped the coat up. Before he could run out the door, William pulled a black wool hat over his head and practically covered his eyes; Preston whined at the action and stomped his foot.

"But daaaaaad! It's not even that cold!" He pouted but William simply kissed his head and pushed him gently out the door. Preston huffed and wiped his forehead clear from the kiss his dad gave him, he wasn't a baby!

"Do you want me to pick you guys up?" William called out to his kids who waved him off and yelled out a goodbye. Roman shouldered past his dad but hesitated and turned around meeting Williams knowing gaze.

"Sorry for the mood... not with it today." He shrugged, lowering his head in shame; the guilt flooding like it always did whenever he was mean to his family, yet his father simply nodded understandingly giving him a hug.

"Come home today and we'll talk about it yeah? Love you kiddo." Roman gave half a smile at the man who he saw as his hero. The man who understood him and helped him when he felt like he was drowning in a sea of endless thoughts and emotions.

"Love you too dad." They shared a warm smile before Roman turned on his heel and walked over to a bored-looking Preston who was kicking the stones in their driveway and making funny little noises.

"Come on mini man." The second youngest West boy held his hand out to the youngest and began walking down the gravel path.

"Ro? Can we have ice cream when we finish school?" Roman shot his little brother an incredulous look.

"Are you having a laugh? It's bloody freezing."

William chuckled and closed the house door shutting off the outside world. He began his usual routine of cleaning the kitchen, getting rid of all the dishes, laughing at the mess his little boys had made in one hour. He checked all the rooms making sure there was no mess to clean up before he retired to his bedroom and sank into his bed. He stared at the lone photo on his nightstand and sighed sadly.

Delilah Fayers.

The wonderfully stubborn woman who he met in that horrid place; the place that although was the start of his nightmare, was also the beginning of his life. The woman he literally bumped into and glared at when he opened his mouth. The woman who became his science partner and the science nerd who always wanted to prove a point.

Delilah West.

His amazing and beautiful wife who became his whole world. The woman who supported him when he felt low, who encouraged him when he was about to give up. Who always found a way to make him smile by simply looking at him with her gorgeous sparkly eyes full of wonder and curiosity.

Lils.

His best ever friend in the whole world. The girl he promised together forever with. Their forever that was cut far too short.

He stroked the picture with the pad of his thumb, smiling ever so slightly at the happiness that radiated from the woman who was taken too soon. William had to be separate from his wife in order for their kids to be safe; they always planned to one day meet again. But after the phone call the night before... he knew that he would never see his lovely Lils again. He couldn't believe how much life had taken from them and it hurt so much. Were happiness and ease not a choice for the Wests'?

He couldn't tell his boys what happened, he just couldn't. As the boys grew up they slowly asked less and less for their mother and it became a normality. Alex and Owen assumed they had just split up and Roman had turned his anger on the world. Preston was too young to understand and so he would question the whereabouts of his mother; never to receive a proper answer.

He waited for god knows how long sitting in the silence of their room waiting for the call he knew would cause someone pain. The ring pulled him out of his dreary thoughts, and he sighed, gathering his strength and picking the call.

"Hello?"
"Hi! Is this Mr William West?"
"Yes, that's me. To whom am I speaking to?"
"Great, I'm Paige Fields and I'm a social worker working with a little girl whose birth certificate has your name as her father. Elisa Fayers?"

William stood up and cleared his throat, his heart clenching at the familiar name of a little girl he hadn't seen in around 5 years. His baby girl. When Delilah left with their only daughter, they agreed to spread themselves out, so they weren't all in the same spot. She didn't take the boys because they had started school. Taking them away would raise questions. Elisa was a 3-year-old that hardly anyone had heard of. Delilah could easily slip away with their youngest without anyone raising questions. She was their little secret.

They had agreed to hide Elisa away. To tell her the secrets and mistakes the West parents had made. They agreed to one day tell the boys when they were old enough and could protect each other from anyone who may wish them harm. They agreed to hide their children from the monster known as the world.

"Mr West?" He blinked out of his thoughts and forced his voice to come out even.

"Yes, I am Elisa's father however her mother and I haven't been in contact for years. I don't have any responsibility towards that child." His mouth burned at his words and he hated how he had to deny any love he had for the innocent darling.

On the other end of the receiver, Paige gritted her teeth at the man's words, instantly feeling hatred towards the male she had never met. She had never wanted to throttle a human in her entire life. But she didn't know William or the risks the family was surrounded with.

"Oh? Well, Mr West, it is my duty to notify you that your wife Delilah Fayers was found dead in her bedroom with your daughter, passed out. You are her only living family member and-" William pulled the phone away from his ear.

He was faced with a decision. Take his daughter in and put all his kids in danger, or let her live a life free from the mess? His sons will graduate and leave the small town, making a life for their own. Also, away from the mess. It started with William and

Delilah and they were determined to keep the secrets between them. For it to end with them. With him.

"Look I lead a very busy life one that's not suitable for a little girl. Just please give her to a loving family. Thanks."

He hung up. Not wanting to make any more excuses. Not wanting to hear her try to convince him because he knew he would give in and it would ruin their plans of protection for kids. He wanted to see his munchkin, oh how he missed her adorable babbling. However, he knew it was better for her to not be near them. She was aware that William loved her, and she knew the reason. It would be hard for her nevertheless, but he knew she was strong and would one day make it back into his arms again.

The rest of the day consisted of William ignoring his phone, cleaning up, ignoring his phone, making dinner, ignoring his phone. He heard a ping and sighed in absolute boredom before opening the message. He stopped mixing the cupcake batter and frowned down at the text. He typed out a response and put the phone down, only for it to ping again. This time William didn't disregard the message and his eyes widened at the response. He cursed and quickly ran to his room.

He grabbed any and all letters from Delilah into a box and shoved it into a safe. He then picked up photos he wanted to keep safe and locked them within the safe before hiding the metal cube in a hidden cupboard in the back of his closet.

He grabbed a pile of papers and rushed to the fireplace; dropping the papers into the scorching fire and watching as the papers began to shrivel up and burn.

He sighed when everything that needed to be kept hidden was burnt and walked out into the hallway. His shoulders set tightly, eyes narrowed, and fists clenched in anger. This was it. William West let out a breath as the door opened and men filled the house. He would have fought them off, but he knew they would overpower him.

This was it.

He scowled as they cuffed his wrists and dragged him out of the house, painfully yanking on his wrists which were no doubt starting to bruise. He didn't know exactly who they were but he knew what they were. They pushed him into a car, a man either side of him holding a gun. He stayed silent as the car started and they began to drive away from his family home. A blindfold tightly placed around his eyes. He heard shuffling in the front and a low malicious chuckle was heard.

"It's lovely to finally meet you, Dr West. I've heard amazing things about your work." He stated. William tried to pull a nasty face, to convey his hatred, despite the blindfold he was wearing.

"Go. To. Hell." He spat. Another cold laugh, although this was, was empty. Pure evil.

"I think you and I are going to get on just perfectly Mr west." He drawled. William West felt a sharp pinch in the side of his arm and his last thought strayed to his children.

Stay safe, daddy will come home soon. I promise.

This was it.

12

Now

The living room was heavy with tension, all eyes on a pacing Roman and a pale looking Elisa. Sasha, Quinton and Cyrus were squashed together on one of the sofas, Finley, Preston and Andre on another, Karson leaning against the doorway watching over the people younger than him, and Owen sat on a beanbag studying his little sister.

Elisa's thoughts jumped around manically. She couldn't believe this was happening. How did they find them? Have they always been watching? If so, why had they started to show up now? What had changed? Why was it even happening?

"When you say they're back, are you talking about the person who caused your accident?" Preston asked warily, immediately understanding the trouble they were in. At Elisa's grave look Owen rubbed his face feeling the stress get to him, they were literal magnets for danger!

"Wait someone caused your accident?" Andre suddenly realised what Preston said, not liking the fact that something as big as this was kept hidden from them. They were practically family for crying out loud. They never hid anything from each other and judging by the West siblings faces, they could tell it was a bad situation.

"Yes. No. I-I don't know man it all happened at once." Roman sounded exhausted and looking around at her brothers and friends, she felt guilt eating away at her. This was her fault. She bought the danger with them.

"I'm sorry I don't know if it's just me but... what's happening? I'm really confused." Sasha piped up softly, unsure whether she and her friends should even be present in the house, however whenever they made a move to leave Elisa would give them a glare which had them sitting back on the sofa. Owen gave them a gentle look.

"It's nothing please don't worry about it. You can leave if you'd like I'm sure your parents-"

"No! As much as I'd love for them to return to their normal lives, they've no doubt been targeted too." Elisa interrupted and looked back at her friends with an apologetic look.

"Our life is extremely dangerous and... people who get close to me normally die... I didn't want to get close to you guys but I..." Sasha stood up and walked up to the girl she considered her best friend. She poked her cheek making Elisa crack into a small smile at the strange girl.

"I mean life is pretty boring. So, a little bit of danger seems like the right medicine. Besides... this all feels like it's out of a book and I want to have some sort of adventure I can tell my kids in the future." Cyrus tensed at the word kids and cleared his throat.

"17 Sash. We're still 17." He reminded her making her pout and wave him off.

"Mate who said you were in my future?" Cyrus blushed bright red before tackling the girl, making her squeal and grin as she carried on talking.

"We're here for you. We wanted to be your friend. We wanted to have you in our lives and if that means being a target for whatever. Then so be it!.... however, I'd rather not die... I won't be able to find someone to cover my work shift." Chuckles erupted around the room.

"Sooooo do you want to tell us what's going on?" Quinton prompted, wanting to know how he could help protect the people he cared about. The front door opened on cue and they all turned to watch Alexander stride into the room. He immediately sought out Elisa and lifted her into his arms making her squeak in surprise and cling onto his neck. He hugged her tightly and she frowned, rubbing her big brothers back.

"Are you ok?" She asked him concerned as she tried to wiggle out of his hold. He shook his head and let her stand on her own two feet. He threw his arms around her shoulders and tugged her to his chest, still not content on letting her go. Elisa stood there silently, allowing her big brother to hold her, knowing the situation they were in was scaring him a whole lot more than he cared to admit.

"You're not safe here. None of you are I... I checked out the body. She was local. Nobody noticed any weird behaviour from her, she was just on her daily walk along the beach. There was a bit of a struggle as there were a few scratches and cuts, but the main injury was the cut to her throat. Choked on her blood-"

Elisa zones out for a moment as she heard his last sentence. Choked on her blood. Just like their mother had; a painful way to die. She remembered the spark of panic in her mothers' eyes when she tried to find air to breathe in but only found blood. She remembered the moment her mother finally gave in and her body jerk a few times as she tried to breath. The way her mothers' eyes stopped flickering about and went dull, empty.

Alexander felt his sister tense and stroked her back, hoping to offer her some comfort. Everything was going way too fast for his little sister to comprehend. The situation was horrifying to the West boys, but it must be worse for Elisa. She had held in all this knowledge for years, seen more death than he ever had and never let herself get attached. The poor girl had been protecting her brothers without them realising it. He swore to do better, to get them out of the mess their parents had accidentally put them in and give his siblings a life they deserve; a life she deserves.

"That's two bodies. Two bodies that have been found that have been killed in the same way... the same way our mother had." Everyone turned to look at Elisa who stiffened.

"Your mum was..." Cyrus trailed off horrified and Sasha and Quinton looked pained. The youngest West sibling smiled sadly and nodded slowly.

"I watched it happen." She practically whispered and her brothers were once again slapped in the face with the realisation that her mind had been tainted with nightmares; too young to understand their meaning.

"We don't know who it is, or if it's multiple people. But they have a signature. A black rose they leave on the bodies. Yeah... there was one on both bodies we found, and our mother had a rose on her too. It's the same person."

"It's a warning but... it's not. It's like they want to rub it in our faces; the things they can do and get away with unnoticed." Owen chimes in.

"You say 'they'. Now I feel like you have a vague idea who." Andre added and they looked at the West siblings curiously. Elisa sighed heavily.

"They are the government. This is much bigger than a simple serial killer. We're talking government corruption." Shock filled the veins of the people who weren't aware of the danger. Despite the fear that had now been installed into their minds, they were determined to protect the people they cared about.

"I'm assuming you have a plan?" Roman directed his question at Alexander who nodded slowly. He let go of Elisa and let her sink onto the floor, ignoring Owens open arms and childish pout as she knew he wanted to hug her. She internally smirked when he huffed and sent dangers her way; she loved annoying him. How does it feel big bro?

"I have an idea yes. But I don't know who wants to follow it. They know we're here. There's no doubt about that. Hell, they probably know where we live and watch us-" He was cut off by Preston who immediately threw his phone on the ground and stomped on it. Everyone stared at the shattered screen confused.

"Why?" Karson asked the teen. Preston screwed up his nose.

"Are you thick? Have you never seen spy movies or action movies? They can track you through any electronic device- mate this is common knowledge!" Andre snickered at the dumbfounded look on the boys' faces, Alex facepalmed.

"Ok but all you did was smash the screen bubs." Sasha piped up from her place on the sofa. Preston picked up the phone and wandered out of the room leaving his brothers confused.

"Don't tell me he's going to do what I think he's going to do," Quinton said with a hint of a smirk playing on his lips. They waited for a moment before hearing the whirring of a blender and Preston whooping. Owen's eyes widened comically, and he jumped over the beanbag, rushing to the kitchen to see what his brother had done.

"YOU MANIAC THAT WAS FOR MY MORNING SMOOTHIES!"

"LOOK AT THE SPARKS OWEN!"

"FOR GOD'S SAKE ITS SPARKING TURN IT OFF!"

"FIREEEEEEE!"

They heard the blender turn off, a heavy, painful sounding slap and a whine from Preston.

"Man, that hurt! Are your hands made of steel?!"

"Imagine what an iron will feel like you little rat..." Owen's voice came ominously.

"ALEX!" Alexander rolled his eyes and tuned out the shrieking of his littlest brother as Owen was no doubt stalking him around the house, the promise of death emanating from his body.

"The plan?" Finley prompted as they all ignored the two West boys.

"Right yes. They're aware of our settlement here. Like Preston pointed out, we will need to leave our phones here. No contact. So, you'll have to let your guardians know they won't be able to contact you. They shouldn't worry much as you're with me so... we should be ok. I'll buy a burner phone for emergencies. But. The plan is we leave Robins Hoods bay. Just for a little while. A getaway of sorts. Away from the danger." They exchanged looks and slowly nodded. The plan seemed like a great idea.

"When would we go?" Cyrus asked curiously.

"Half term is near the end of October and so we can leave as soon as schools have been let out. We can go to the city. Lose ourselves in a much crowded, populated area. We don't have to go too far but somewhere we can hide a bit or maybe just make them believe we are going longer than necessary. We just need a break." Elisa dug her nails into her palm as she thought about the plan. Not only would it put her mind at ease that everyone she cared about would be out of the danger zone. But it meant they could trick the people after them. Make them believe they had left town for a while. Her eyes lit up in thought.

"Are any of you particularly attached to your phones?" Sasha put her hand up sheepishly along with Karson, Andre and Cyrus. The others shrugged.

"I was supposed to change my phone anyway so it's at your disposal." Finley shifted in his seat and waved his phone in the air.

"Mine is my dad's old one. I'm due an upgrade so we can use mine." Quinton shrugged as if he wasn't being a massive help to the group. She nodded and clapped her hands as her mind created an idea.

"We can throw them off by putting our phones on different trains. Or leaving them in different places. That way when we turn them on and they're being tracked, it'll lead them, whoever is looking for us, to the wrong place. The phone will be there but not us. It'll throw them off track. They won't know where to look or when we are going to be back." Alexander felt pride as he listened to the words his little sister spoke. She was smarter than any of them realised, she had more understanding of the world and it's dangers. She understood the ways of surviving.

"Ok, so the best way is to drive down. We're going to London by the way-"

"YES!"
"BANGING!"
"OH, MY DAYS!"
"SICK!"

Everyone yelled excited making Alex roll his eyes.

"We're going to London to HIDE. Remember that fact HIDE! We're going to lay low, yes we can go walking and perhaps visit some places, but we are not going to be going all out. So don't get your hopes up understand?" But his speech went unheard as everyone in the room had already grown excited at the idea of going out of the village, somewhere new. Elisa looked up at her frustrated brother and grinned.

"This'll be fun." Her voice filled with amusement. He scowled and ruffled her hair making her slap his hands away with a groan.

"Xander!" She pouted and he chuckled holding out a hand. She jumped up and they walked into the kitchen to make food.... order food. Their eyes landed on the table and Elisa stifled a laugh whilst Alexander hit his forehead on the wall next to him. The blender sat in the middle of the counter, bits and pieces of metal sat inside the cracked container.

"Is there any way we can return that child?" Alex mused and she burst out laughing, he rolled his eyes and shoved her playfully before he began ordering food for everyone.

The evening went on calmly, each of them getting to know each other. Owen watched everyone from his perch on the armrest of one of the sofas. Roman, Quinton and Andre were discussing a topic of importance to them, Alexander and Karson on their laptops discussing travel plans, Preston and Cyrus playing a video game, Sasha, Finley and Lissy waving their hands about as they talked about a movie they had watched. Well, Lissy simply watched them with an amused tilt of her lips. Finley threw an arm around Lissy and he watched in horror as she hugged him with one arm. She looked over at Owen and winked with a smirk and he glared her down.

He would get that hug from her. He swore it.

He was hopeful that they could get away from the danger. It was a good plan, but temporary. They would run for now, but they would find them eventually; did Alexander truly think they would all stay on the run for the rest of their lives? Lissy wouldn't accept that, he knew that sooner or later she would put her foot down and layout her own rules.

Elisa West wasn't a coward. She would fight to protect who she loved. It was clear for them all to see; and that thought alone worried Owen. To what extent would she go to protect them?

One by one the teenagers and men fell asleep. Snoring peacefully as they slept away, except the teenage girl whose nightmares kept her awake. Elisa sat up in her cocoon of pillows and sighed sadly. She wished she could sleep peacefully like her friends, blissfully unaware of the treacherous world they lived in. She heard whispers and frowned confused. She counted the heads and realised one was missing. Roman. Slowly, quietly, she tiptoed over the bodies and out of the living room.

"Stupid, stupid, stupid." The voice mumbled and she immediately knew what had happened. Peeking through the kitchen doorway her eyes saddened at the sight. Her brother sat in the open back doorway, his legs bent at the knee and his elbows resting on them. She heard the soft mumbling and could see the water droplets running down his cheeks; she walked over slowly, knowing he had noticed her presence.

Elisa sat opposite her brother, leaning against the open door, her eyes trained on the picture in his hands. She gently took the picture from between his fingers and smiled slightly. It showed a time of a younger Roman sat on a field. There was a girl sat next to him with her arms wrapped around his neck with a bright grin, another two boys making funny faces and another two girls who looked like they had been laughing. They all wore their uniforms and looked happy. Roman looked happy.

"What was her name?" She broke the silence as she stared at the girl who she knew was unfortunately no more. Roman sniffed and looked out towards the field.

"Grace. She kind of forced her way into my small group of friends. Determined to find out who I was. We became best friends after a while, and she taught me that life may be difficult..." She looked up and met his watery eyes. He swallowed as she gave back the picture and he smiled down at the memory trapped in time.

"But there are people in life who make all the troubles and hardships worth it." They stayed silent for a moment. Before she could try and convince him once more that it wasn't his fault, he rubbed his cheeks and sighed.

"When it happened... when the crash happened, everything was blurry. I had hit my head, and nothing made sense. But I saw her laying there in a pool of blood and glass... and laying on her palm was a black rose." The blood drained from her face as she realised what he was saying.

"I should have died that night, Shadow. But her life was mistaken as mine... it sucks that she had to lose her future." They heard a phone ringing and looked at each other confused. Alexander roused from his slumber and clambered over the bodies to get to his phone sat on the kitchen counter. He saw his two siblings and groaned.

"And you couldn't have picked the thing up for me?" Roman raised a brow whilst Elisa shrugged. He grunted and picked up the phone listening to his boss. As he listened, his mind cleared and he stood up straighter.

"Yes. Understood. I'll be there bright and early." He hung up and looked at Elisa who already knew that the words her brother was about to speak, would not be in their favour.

"Seems as though we may need to leave a little earlier." Alex ran a hand through his messy hair, Roman looking at him confused and Elisa looked troubled.

"Why's that?" Roman asked his brother who was now looking through his phone, for what he had no clue.

"They found another body."

13

Now

"No."

"Stop it, man."

"For crying out loud I'll kick you Pres!"

"Shut up both of you!"

"Stop BREATHING ON ME!"

"WELL STOP LOOKING AT ME!"

Slap.

"THE HELL WAS THAT FOR?!?"

"YOU LOOKED AT ME WEIRD!"

Kick.

"YOU WORM!"

Alexander's knuckles turned white as he clenched the steering wheel tightly. His eyes flickered to the mirror and he scowled at the two brothers fighting in the back seat, Owen sat next to them wrapped up in a blanket and earplugs stuffed in his ears as he slept. He shook his head and prayed for a service station to come up soon.

Elisa sat in the passenger seat with her feet on the dashboard and the red leather journal in her hands. She wore leggings and he noted that the navy hoody she wore looked remarkably familiar; he smiled as he realised it was Preston's. He looked at her from the corner of his eyes and saw her tongue sticking out between her lips as she concentrated on writing, her head tilting slightly and little hums passing her lips. He tuned out his brothers yelling and focused on his little sister who sat in her world away from the rest of them.

"Is that mum's journal?" Alexander asked making her tense at the question before relaxing after a moment; she sat up straight and leaned against the car door slightly before peeking up at him. The pen twirling between her fingers in a dance. How she didn't feel sick from writing in the car was beyond him.

"Yeah... there was over half the book empty. The first half being mum writings on the project, and I thought that... I could write everything that's happened to me since mums..." Alexander nodded at the words she still found hard to speak without leaking with emotion. He patted her knee gently trying to offer some reassurance and she sent him a grateful smile, grateful that they had gotten to the point of understanding without saying words.

"Have you read mums part?" Her head shook before pausing and nodding hesitantly, she looked shy, almost as if she was ashamed of reading what wasn't hers.

"I've read bits of it, but it's mostly filled with words I don't understand because they're scientific chemicals. I haven't read it properly because I didn't want to know more than I do you know? I had to prepare for the worst. The journal is in my hands, but I don't know what to do with it. So, I decided to not read it unless I had to. But there are some pages that have pictures of mum and dad, letters between them that I refuse to read, a few pictures of me from when I was younger and... one of you guys." At her last sentence, Alexander looked over briefly with wide eyes. Elisa caught the surprise in his face and felt her heart reach out to the boy, it hurt her knowing her brothers were in pain thinking their mother didn't love them. Even though she hadn't seen her father in years and didn't remember how he sounded, she knew that he loved her and that she had loved him. She didn't feel the need to mourn someone she had hardly remembered which was the same case in Prestons' feelings towards their mother.

"You know she loved you guys. She told me stories about you all the time. She would kiss your picture goodnight before she slept. She loved you more than anything." The eldest West sibling felt his eyes water at her words and nodded with a trembling smile. The empty and cold girl he first met was soothing him with the warmth and love that passed her lips. He was beginning to see the lightness in her eyes return and he wondered if this was the start of the baby Elisa peeking through. He knew he would never have the Elisa he knew; she was older, wiser and he loved her for who she had become.

"I know Dove. I know." He did know, he was aware. His mother loved all her children, and he was glad he was given that reassurance. That their mother didn't abandon them picking the favourite child, she had left them to protect their family. He didn't realise he needed that reassurance until Elisa gave him it and he was grateful for her thoughtfulness. It saddened him that he couldn't return the favour by telling her things about their father because as sad as it was, their father didn't always talk about Elisa and their mother. He would mention them from time to time but not enough. Now he knew why; so, the boys wouldn't put attention on their mother and sister. The phone rang suddenly making Preston and Roman stop their fighting and go quiet as Alexander answered the call and put it on speaker. They had decided to use their normal phones on the way to their destination so that they weren't being suspicious.

"Talk to me." Karson chuckled lowly on the other end of the phone as he heard the exhaustion and desperation in his best friend's voice.

"There's a service station coming up now. We can get some food and freshen up before getting back on the road." Alexander thanked the gods above and nodded even though Karson couldn't see it which tickled a quiet giggle from Elisa.

"Sounds great. Alright, bro, I'll see you in a few minutes then." He hung up with a sigh and looked into his rear-view mirror briefly.

"I swear if you two start fighting again I'm going to leave you on the side of the motorway understand?!" The boys nodded reluctantly wanting to finish off their petty fight but not wanting Alexander to carry out his threat and sent each other one last piercing glare before turning their attention outside the windows. Owen sat up abruptly as the car slowed down quickly before going back to normal speed and looked around smacking his lips; Elisa cringing at the disgusting sound and sending him a repulsed look to which he completely overlooked.

"Did I miss something?" He asked innocently, confusion marring his features as his eyes danced from person to person. Alexander nodded and waved a hand encouragingly as he spoke gently and kindly to his brother.

"Lean forward for a minute bro, come here." Owen leaned between the seats to hear whatever Alexander was going to tell him. Except Alexander didn't speak. He simply raised his hand and smacked the back of Owens' head.

"OW! JEEZ WHAT WAS THAT FOR?!" He smirked at Owens pained cry and stayed silent leaving a complaining Owen, grinning Roman and Preston, and Elisa stifling her giggle behind her hands. Sometimes she couldn't hold on that laughter that wanted to escape, her brothers were hilarious, and she couldn't hold the amusement. The car came to a stop in the near-empty parking lot. Immediately Roman opened the door with Preston clambering after them.

"FRESH AIR! THANK YOU, LORD!" Preston shouted dramatically with Roman rolling his eyes at his youngest brothers' antics. Elisa slipped out of the car and a grunt escaped her lips when a pair of arms hugged her tightly around the waist.

"PLEASE LET ME STAY WITH YOU! I CAN'T STAND BEING IN A CAR WITH THOSE BEASTS!" Sasha cried out as she held onto an uncomfortable and awkward looking Elisa whose eyes pleaded for someone to help her, all of which simply smirked at her distress. She had come so far from the blank girl they had first met, but she was still uncomfortable with physical contact and receiving affection.

"Hey, we're not that bad." Cyrus raised his hands in surrender when Sasha spun round pinning her glare on him.

"Not. That. Bad?!? I was sat in the middle with you curled up next to me, Quinton had his feet resting on the centre console meaning his legs were on top of mine, Finley had fallen asleep with his hand in an open packet of cheese Doritos and Karson decided it was freezing in the car which it really wasn't and turned the heating all the way up. It stank of cheese and sweat in that car and ugh Andre was in the boot of the car in those seats laying down with his socks off and NO!" She finished her rant with a gag and Elisa tried not to laugh at the 'pain' her best friend had to go through. As if sensing her inner laughter, Sasha faced Elisa with wide eyes.

"Oh, you find this funny huh?" She asked the blank-faced Elisa who simply raised a brow not saying a word; she knew Sasha would most likely ignore whatever she had to say.

"Well then! How about YOU stay in that dreaded man cave! While I swap seats with-" She trailed off as she saw Roman and Preston bickering again.

"You know what no. We need to stick together and work through this monstrosity together." Elisa nodded going along with whatever her friend had decided. They all went into the service station and went to freshen up in the designated bathrooms. Karson and Alexander had instructed them to meet at the Costa as soon as they had finished up, the two finding a table as soon as they had finished with the boys slowly wandering around by one.

"So, we're having a switch yeah?" Karson chuckled when he saw the exhausted look at Alexander's face.

"Oh god yes please." He practically begged.

"I'll take Preston. Swap him for Sasha since she wants to be with Elisa, and I know you want Elisa to stay in your eyesight." Alexander nodded in agreement. He loved his siblings equally and even though he knew Elisa had been alone for most her life and could protect herself, he wanted to do any and all fighting for her. Maybe it was just the big brother part of him that wanted to lock her in a bubble far away from the dangers of the world.

"Ok, so I'm having Elisa, Sasha, Roman, and Finley? And you're having Preston, Andre, Cyrus, Quinton and Owen... man good luck to you." Karson winced but shrugged.

"Either they behave, or I'll knock them out. Simple."

Meanwhile, in the bathrooms, Sasha was fixing up her hair, braiding them into two French plaits. She wore black velvet leggings and an oversized grey shirt, a blue flannel around her waist. Her eyes flickered over to the girl beside her who seemed stuck in thought. She gently tugged on her sleeve, making the girl jump and her eyes widen in surprise, as if she had completely forgotten where she was.

"You ok babe?" Sasha asked her, eyes swimming with concern. Elisa's lip tilted slightly, and she licked her slightly chapped lips. Without saying anything, Sasha pulled out a vanilla scented Chapstick from her purse and handed it to Elisa who chuckled inwardly.

"I always wondered why you smelt so much of vanilla. You have the body scent too huh?" Sasha grinned and pulled out a vanilla-scented hair spray and body mist.

"You bet! It's not too strong either and it's such a soothing smell." She sprayed a couple of times over her clothes before doing the same to the girl who welcomed the scent like an old friend.

"My mother is super into aromatherapy. Says it helps with her moods when she's sad or stressed. Vanilla is her personal favourite, and she has little bottles in each room. Gave me my own." Elisa smiled and her eyes met the bright green eyes that twinkled like stars.

"My mum smelt like Vanilla cupcakes." At her words, Sasha felt guilt shoot through her and pain stabbing her heart. She took Elisa's hand into her own and gave her an encouraging smile; she knew the West girl was only just starting to mourn her mother properly, and she would be there for her every step of the way.

"You're right, it is soothing, and I guess my mum had a similar idea. She had this vanilla cupcake mist that she would spray every morning. When I first came home it smelt like vanilla cupcakes and I didn't understand why... until I realised nearly every candle in the house was vanilla. It's my comfort smell, it's home." She felt shy as she revealed a part of her memories and thoughts, but at the same time felt happy that she could talk about her mother whose memory had slowly been faded as time went on.

"Talking about her helps huh?" Sasha guessed when she saw the melancholy look on her face.

"It helps to remember her... that she did exist, and she was someone. That she wasn't just a story of a woman. It helps. Remembering that she was real, that she once was." They shared a sad but understanding smile before Sasha squeezed their still clasped hands.

"Come on Ellie! Let's go grab some things before we meet up with the boys yeah?" As Sasha weaved them through the semi-busy service station, a thought occurred to Elisa.

"You know hardly anyone ever calls me Elisa."

"Yeah? What else does everyone call you?"

"You call me Ellie, Owen calls me Lissy, Pres calls me Eli, Xander calls me Dove, Ro calls me Shadow, Andre, Finley and Karson call me Muffin which I despise, Quinton calls me any insulting name, particularly Zombie... I think Cyrus may be the only one to call me Elisa." Sasha beamed and shook her head.

"Nahhh I don't think he's said your name since we first met but whenever you're mentioned or he mentions you, he refers to you as El or Ellie like me." Elisa rolled her eyes but deep down her heart warmed at the fact everyone had a personal nickname for her. She felt loved and adored and it was a feeling she hadn't felt in years; her cheeks tingled as she blushed, and a smile grew on her lips.

"Thanks for being my friend Sash."

The two girls bought random sweets and chocolate bars along with water bottles knowing the boys were forgetful and probably didn't think of everything. They paid with cash remembering their situation and that they need to avoid using any electronic device. Even as they walked through the shops they avoided the cameras and had their heads down.

Sasha chatted on as they exited the shop and walked towards the Costa where they could see the boys waiting around holding trays of coffee and hot chocolate. Elisa nodded absentmindedly as she casually looked around when something caught her attention. She saw a man wearing a black suit walk out of the men's toilets, black sunglasses sitting on his nose. Maybe she would have looked away, but her well-trusted instincts told her to watch him, that he was... oddly placed. Not meant to be there. Sure enough, his fingers lifted to his ear and he began speaking while slowly looking around, alarm bells ringing in her head as she gently tightened her hold on Sasha and quickened their pace.

"Ellie what are you-"

"They're here." Sasha's eyes widened and she asked no other questions as they moved with the crowd, blending in. Elisa counted three more men and concluded that their house had indeed been under watch and they had noticed the absence of the West siblings. They walked over to the boys and she took Preston's hand in her own. Preston went to tease her but once he saw the serious and nervous look on her face he immediately squared his shoulders and tugged her small hand concerned.

"Time to go!" She said in a chirpy tone which was a complete contrast to her expression. The boys immediately understood that they had to leave and quickly but subtly left the station. They immediately jumped into their assigned cars and without a moment's hesitation, both drivers peeled out of the parking lot. There was silence for the first 20 minutes as Alexander and Karson consistently checked their rear-view mirrors to make sure there weren't any cars the seemed to be following them. When both men were sure they were in the clear, Alexander called Karson with the burner phone and gave the phone to Roman to hold for him.

"I don't know who they were but it's most likely Them. A man left the men's bathroom and started talking in what I assume was a radio earpiece."

"Which is what?" Sasha asked quietly.

"It's like a walkie talkie. People working in governmental agencies normally use them to communicate discreetly. Not a moment later I saw three other men wearing the same as the first man I saw, all wearing that earpiece. They won't know where we are, but they'll be scouting around close areas. The quicker we're in London, the better." They nodded in agreement and slight worry.

"Isn't Scotland Yard based in London?" Finley asked warily.

"Which is exactly why they won't expect us there. But we will take precautions ok? No running around. We're staying in a bed and breakfast which honestly doesn't look amazing so don't expect grand, it's simple and does its job. We can pay in cash so we will be much safer than we would in a hotel. I don't want you guys worrying too much. You just need to listen and help lookout for anything dodgy. Karson and I will sort everything else out, understand?" They mumbled their agreements, and the cars went quiet.

"You ok babe?" Sasha nudged the dazed-looking Elisa who gave a nod.

"She looks like she's in shock. Get some sleep muffin." She nodded and leaned her head on Sasha's shoulder, the latter began stroked her hair reassuringly and hugging the West girl to her body. Roman and Alexander exchanged a look, Elisa West wasn't in shock. She was planning something, and they weren't too sure if they were going to like her plan.

Karson hung up on the phone and rubbed his chin in thought.

"We're staying in two rooms. The girls in one and the rest of us in another." As he thought, protests filled the car.

"Man there's 2 of them rats! And there's 9 of us! How does that work?" Preston regretted his words as soon as Cyrus and Owen slapped his arm in unison and sent him glares.

"Honestly I agree. Can't we get three rooms? One of the girls and two for us guys. Me, Cyrus, Andre and Preston can stay in one room and you, Owen, Alexander, Finley and Roman can stay in the other." Karson pondered over Quintons suggestion.

"We'll see when we get there okay? Just relax... we have a long way yet."

"Surely we're nearly there? It's been like an hour since we left the village." Andre hated car rides. Normally boys loved having road trips with their mates, nowhere in mind, no plan to follow. But this particular group of boys hated car rides because as much as they loved and cared for each other. They loved their space more and stuck in the car for an hour with his boys, was more than he could handle. Karson nodded slowly as he popped a piece of peppermint gum in his mouth.

"Yeah, yeah... just 4 more hours to go." The boys nodded before Owen did a double-take and gave a nervous laugh.

"Sorry... Alex must have hit me harder than I thought, did you say 4 hours?" The boys' eyes widened, hoping they had all heard wrong. Instead of replying, Karson sunk into his seat with a heavy smile, his sunglasses perched back on his nose. He sipped at his coffee that burned down his throat and tuned out the world as he looked at the car in front of him.

Karson ran his tongue along his teeth and his knuckles flexed as thoughts flew around in his mind. All this mess surrounding one family, a mess that didn't seem to be visible until Elisa West showed up.

A little girl holding onto secrets so dark, so devious. He wondered what else she had kept hidden, what else her brothers were hiding for her. He wondered why this was all happening for they still didn't know the actual reason as to why their mother was murdered, why the government was after them. He stewed on the fact that Alex, his best friend since diapers, was keeping things hidden from him. He would move mountains for his best friend; why wasn't he telling him everything? What else was the littlest West hiding?

That thought alone intrigued him the most.

14

Then

The air was sticky like the sweet honey in a jar. Almost suffocating. Sweat coated her skin like a second layer that felt cold even though she felt like she was in a sauna. Elisa groaned softly and kicked off her duvet with one leg sticking out and the other under the duvet; she shifted around the bed hoping to find one cool spot to relax in. Her dream began to fade away along with the memory of her mother's soft kisses as the heat began to become unbearable. Her brows knitted together and her hand reached up to wipe away the sweat that was gathering on her forehead. She began hearing sounds.

Crackling.

Shouting.

"ELISA!" Her eyes shot open at the sound of her name and she looked around wildly, her nose picking up what she couldn't yet see. Immediately she pulled on a thick jumper and dived towards her backpack not once doubting herself; her body working on autopilot as it lunges for the one thing she couldn't part with. She quickly opened it and checked the contents; everything accounted for. She opened her doorway only to gasp in horror, it was worse than she could ever imagine, and she wondered if she was still dreaming.

The entirety of the staircase was up in flames; flames that were slowly but steadily making their way to her floor. Her throat felt tight, and she immediately knelt so she was away from the thick smoke that clouded the ceiling.

"ELISA! GEORGE WHERE IS SHE?!" Her foster mothers' hoarse voice was heard faintly from the floor below her and she remembered how her foster parents had fallen asleep after watching a movie. At least they were safe. Slamming the door to her bedroom shut, Elisa rushed to her window; her survival instincts kicking in like they normally did whenever she was facing such a situation. There was no time to be scared or second guess. If she waited, she would never do it, her mother's words echoing in her head. Think Elisa!

Thankfully there was a tree by her window that was strong enough to hold her weight and she worked quick to get out of her room that was beginning to fill with the heavy smoke. Opening the window, Elisa could now hear her foster parents calling her name out with their neighbours shouting and yelling as they tried to find a way in. As they tried to save the little girl trapped inside. The cold air made Elisa shiver and bite her lips, the wind pushing against her weightless body. The rucksack on her back and buckled across her chest so it wouldn't fall.

"GEORGE! LOTTIE! IM HERE!" The two adults rushed around the side of their house and saw a small leg sticking out of the window. Lottie began hyperventilating as thoughts of their 12-year-old foster daughter in the hospital with severe injuries, sprang to mind. George immediately jumped into action and with the help of his neighbours, guided a ladder just below Elisa's window. His worries pushed aside as his determination to save the girl he came to care for deeply, flooded his mind.

"SLOWLY! IM RIGHT HERE, I WON'T LET YOU FALL." He yelled up at the little girl who saw the help being offered. She slowly lowered her foot onto the wooden ladder, her other foot following; slowly she let her hand leave the window to hold onto the wooden bar of the ladder. Her bedroom door now on fire and spreading along her carpet quickly... too quickly. As soon as Elisa was halfway down the ladder, George reached up, held the small girl to his body and rushed to the ambulance which had pulled up.

He sighed and stroked her messy hair down to tame the wavy mane, his heart calmed down as he reassured himself that she was ok. That his foster daughter was safe from harm. Elisa was shivering from the cold and the slight horror that if she hadn't woken up, she would be long gone. Just like her mother. She tightened her hold on the backpack that held everything important.

Everything was a blur as Elisa was checked over and Lottie kept blubbering. The girl herself simply sat there unaffected which began to worry the paramedics and Lottie. Paige had been informed and despite the ungodly hour of the early morning, she looked as professional and neat as usual wearing a white blouse, black pencil skirt, black heels and her hair in a low bun. Her concern filled eyes looking over the little girl and trying to come up with her idea of what had happened. Elisa let Paige cup her face between her hands and hold her tightly in a hug of safety; she tried not to smile at the concern her social worker showed as she demanded answers off of the adults around them.

"Was there any electronics that could have caused the fire? An iron, oven..?" A policeman asked George as they walked away from the van where Elisa and Lottie sat huddled under bright orange blankets. Elisa shifted and sat closer to a shaken Lottie who looked more scared than Elisa was.

"Remember when you first decided to foster me? I told you that when I know it's time for me to go, you have to give me up?" Lottie frowned as she remembered the words Elisa had immediately made them agree to. They were to say nothing about Elisa and simply send her back, words that they had disregarded as simply a defence mechanism.

"I remember. What about it?" Even though she phrased it as a question, Lottie knew exactly why Elisa had bought it up and felt the dread building in her stomach. She looked over at the little girl whose hazel eyes were dark, mysterious, the little girl who clenched her fists tightly and was too small, too young to be so serious.

"Bad things happen Lottie, it happened to my past foster families. I protect people by moving away before they can get caught. Before they can get hurt badly... today was either a warning or an attempt. It's time to go Lottie." Although her tone sounded indifferent, Elisa felt a cut where a line was being drawn through the two names that had been engraved on her heart alongside many other names that had been scratched out. Lottie and George Jones were etched into her memories like the other names that had taken her in, cared for her, maybe even loved her.

Lottie swallowed the hard lump in her throat and looked up at the dark sky, stars fading away as the colours grew lighter and the birds began waking. Moisture in her eyes that threatened to spill. Elisa put a small hand on Lottie's and sent her an encouraging smile.

"Thank you for taking me in." Lottie could hardly speak and simply pulled her into a hug, trying to pour all the affection she had into the hug. She rubbed her back and closed her eyes praying that the young girl would one day find happiness.

"I hope you the absolute best sweetheart. I don't know what it is your running from. I know it's too dangerous to speak about. I know that... I need to stay quiet so..." Elisa nodded and the two pulled apart. The older women felt her heart reach out to the little girl who seemed years beyond her actual age. Paige walked over to Elisa and Lottie with the intent to comfort them. However, she was stopped short when Lottie spoke up with a surprising level voice.

"Mrs Fields I'm sorry that I have to tell you this now. I was planning on ringing you later on today, but I guess fate decided to have it over and done with." Paige looked at the woman confused.

"Is everything alright?"

"I'm afraid this isn't going to work." It took the social worker only a moment to understand what Lottie was saying and she looked over at Elisa with a heavy sigh.

"May I ask what the issue is?" Lottie repeated what she had said before walking off to George. George Jones listened to his wife before his eyes snapped to the little girl. He understood immediately that the child was in trouble, deep trouble and that staying with him and his wife would only dig her deeper. Her eyes met his and they shared a sad smile, his eyes watery as he looked over at the girl who he had slowly began to see as his own. Goodbye.

Paige immediately began the process, and her phone was pressed against her ear. Elisa paid no attention to her and simply listened to the firemen and policemen that had turned up. Like always, she was hesitant and stayed out of the policeman's eyes. She couldn't trust them.

"There was nothing on. No appliances. No already lit fires."

"It's odd how it spread. Almost in a line."

"The whole house didn't catch fire immediately."

"Sir we found a matchbox in the bushes outside."

"Sir, it's been confirmed that there was Kerosene all over the carpets from the bottom floor to the second, into one of the bedrooms. The rest caught fire after the spread but there was a trail. That's how it started quickly." She swallowed as one of the firemen produced a black rose that sat in a transparent evidence bag, she felt lightheaded as she stared at the flower that mocked her.

"This was sat on the doorstep, sir." Her breathing faltered as she pieced together what had happened. It wasn't a warning; it was a deliberate murder attempt. She looked around the area feeling eyes burning holes into her body, simmering and scorching her cold skin. She paused in her searching and suddenly whipped her body to face the park across the road from her house, the one that faced her window.

She didn't know how she knew it was him, how she knew that he was the culprit. She didn't know why she didn't scream and cry at the sight of the man wearing a lower face mask that looked like a skull and black goggles. She blinked rapidly as he raised his hand and waved menacingly, mockingly. Her nostrils flared and jaw clenched feeling nothing but hatred towards the unknown man, a sense of déjà vu as she stared at his mask.

"ELISA! C'mon honey!" She licked her dry lips and rubbed her tired eyes, giving one last look towards the park, only to realise there was nobody there. Was there anyone there to begin with? Her eyes fluttered to the ground and she shrugged off the blanket which still sat on her shoulders. Her feet took her towards a concerned Paige who was talking to a paramedic.

"She's ok. Just keep an eye on her, shock mostly. Make sure they check her over."

"I'm going to take her to the hospital first."

Soon enough Elisa was on the road again in the back of Paige Fields car. Her eyes stuck on the fire that was being put out and the couple that waved goodbye. A single tear rolled down her cheek and she sniffed before quickly wiping the moisture away with the back of her hand. She gave a little finger wave to the couple even though she knew they couldn't see her any longer and they never would see her again.

"Bye-bye." She whispered and sat facing the front of the car; Paige letting out a breath as she watched the younger girl curl into herself.

"What happened sweetheart?" But like always, Elisa didn't respond to the question Paige always asked her whenever she had come to take her away.

Time went on as Elisa sat in a little room waiting for the papers to be processed, Paige was once again looking around for possible foster families. The little room was too small for Elisa's liking. It was bland, too cold, too bright. Small enough so that her thoughts kept flying back to her when she tried to let them go. She shuffled and ignored the breakfast tray on the table; her hands reaching over to her rucksack and opening it up.

The journal.
The vial.

She patted them with her fingers, reassuring herself that they were still with her before she pulled out a notepad and pen. She immediately began writing down her thoughts and the events that had just occurred. She skipped out the man in the mask and the black rose pretending it was an accidental fire and her foster parents had given her away because they didn't want her. It made it so much easier to pretend that the world and its habitants were all against her and that she wasn't pushing people away herself.

One day she would stop protecting everyone. One day she could stop running.
One day she can be a little girl... a normal girl... a happy woman...? How long was she going to live the way she was?

The pen scratched lightly against the paper and her tongue stuck out slightly as she signed the page off with an E and a small heart. The door opened and Paige walked in with a soft smile as she knelt next to the bed, her arms crossed on the bed with her chin leaning on them.

"Hey, darling. I found a family who would like to meet you. That ok?" Elisa nodded and held up the page she had ripped from her notebook. She knew immediately what Elisa was silently asking and smiled softly.

"We'll grab an envelope on the way out and we can post it in the letterbox." The two stood and Elisa quickly freshened up in the joint bathroom, her hair pulled back into a bun and she changed out of her pyjamas and into jeans and a shirt. Her bag slung over her shoulder and the folded paper between her slightly sweaty hand. Paige led her out of the quiet building and snagged an envelope from one of the desks. She silently watched Elisa slide the page into the envelope before writing an address. Paige handed her a post stamp and Elisa then walked over to the letterbox that was a little way down the street before she rushed back to Paige and the awaiting car.

"Who do you send those to?" Paige mused out loud but knew that the girl wasn't going to answer.

"Here's a pad full of post stamps and I grabbed a few extra envelopes for you."

Elisa smiled slightly at how well Paige knew her and settled into her seat. She'll have to send another letter once she gets to her next home.

Another temporary home. Another temporary family. Elisa wondered when everything would stop being temporary.

Or IF anything would stop being temporary.

15

Now

Elisa West had never truly belonged anywhere.

Moving from town to town, city to city, family to family, prevented her from making connections with anyone. Her situation was a reminder that connections meant death and so she was partly grateful for the consistent moving. She found it difficult to socialise with people and making conversation was a chore, how she wished everything could be different. But she knew that wishing doesn't do anything no matter how much she wanted something to be real. She had learnt to accept and be grateful for any moment of peace in her life and treasure it forever.

Her brothers and friends decided to have a movie night together in one room and so they had laid blankets and pillows all over the brown carpeted floor, the lights turned off with only the small TV as their source of light. The night had consisted of laughter and joy, pillow fights which then turned to arguments that had them laughing even harder, she had witnessed another fight between Roman and Preston and remembered that they were normal brothers who fought over the silliest things with Owen shouting at them to stop, Alexander spectating, and the rest of the boys egging on the fight like the typical males they were. Sasha and Elisa giggling to each other and every so now and then whispering something the boys couldn't hear which annoyed the boys to no end as they wondered what they were whispering about. She had spent a night of fun, something she wasn't used to, and enjoyed every moment until the last person finally slipped away. Limbs sprawled across each other as they slept peacefully in their warm and soft cocoon.

Once again, Elisa was the only one awake, the only one who stayed awake. Her mind too full of thoughts and memories that kept her eyes from closing, she didn't want a nightmare or a memory, she just wanted the silence and she knew she wouldn't get that by sleeping. Gently, she lifted Sasha's head off her shoulder and moved her leg out from under Preston's body. Years of practice meant that she could leave the room without a sound, the door clicking shut behind her but too quiet for the others to hear. The hallway light flickered as it died and her black socks rubbed gently across the floor as she walked away from the room; her need to be away from everyone too strong. She was used to being alone and although she was relieved that she wasn't, she couldn't help but want her loneliness back. Her haven, the one where she knew nobody would get hurt and she couldn't disappoint anyone.

London was loud and busy. The stars were hidden behind angry clouds that travelled along the vast sea of navy blue, little tingles across her cheek and neck as the cold bit her skin teasingly, the wind pushing against her as if trying to force her back inside. The bed and breakfast itself looked like the rest of the buildings on the street, packed tightly together with their heads down as they remained inconspicuous to any passer-by. The street lamps burning brightly in the darkness like artificial stars. Trees stood tall and proud with their leaves rustling in conversation, birds beginning to sing as the sky began to lighten.

Elisa sat down on the doorstep with her chin resting on her cold palm for support. The odd car would pass by making her head duck until it was out of eyesight, her senses always on high alert so that she couldn't be caught by surprise. A small chirp was heard and a little bird landed on the gravel path in front of her. Its head tilted to the side as it began pecking as something in the grass, its curiosity urging it to find out what had caught its attention. Iridescent bluey-green wings fluttered as the magpie hopped around a specific area.

"Curious little thing aren't you." Elisa mused, quietly to not scare off the bird that had become her little distraction for the time being. Elisa had always loved birds, ever since she was young she was obsessed with the different species, the differences each bird held. Yet they all had one thing in common, freedom. Something Elisa hadn't had or felt in a long time; consistently trapped by secrets and held back by the shadows that followed her relentlessly. Freedom was foreign to the youngest West and probably one of the things she dreamed of, hoping that one day she would be able to feel it, see it.

Her body stiffened as she heard the door behind her open and shut, the hand resting on her lap clenched and she held her breath as she waited to see who was behind her. To her utter surprise, she felt a weight drop over her shoulders and her head snapped up to see the person who had gifted her with a warm blanket. She curiously watched him sit next to her with his eyes locked on the bird who seemed to ignore the two humans. For a moment, the two sat quietly, enjoying the cold breeze that enveloped them, the cars beeping in the distance and the sky gradually growing lighter. Elisa rubbed the blanket between her fingers and bit her lip.

"Thanks... for the blanket." Elisa finally mumbled breaking the quiet they had been comfortably sat in. He chuckled lowly knowing that the little girl found it difficult to talk to people.

"Something on your mind?" Karson asked her but instead of getting a reply, she kept her lips pressed together and her eyes on the hopping bird, her barriers up like they had been since he first met her after all these years. He wanted to know the littlest West sibling, he wanted to know what she kept hidden, who she had become. Elisa was a mystery that he wanted to solve simply because he could sense the secrets she hid, she was a puzzle and unlike her brothers, she wasn't an open book.

"When you were younger, you were obsessed with flying. Birds were your focus and you dragged us all around whenever you saw one. We used to run into the woods and make little dens out of fallen branches and twigs." Karson began and Elisa inwardly sighed. Half of her loved hearing about the 3 years she spent with her brothers, but the other half of her hated how she remembers nothing of that time. She also found it disconcerting when people she hardly remembered talking about her like they knew her, they didn't know her, they knew a little naive and innocent baby. That Elisa had slowly disappeared into the shadows, hidden away from the world.

"We used to sit under the branches pretending to hide from a monster in the woods. You would play along but giggle whenever we shushed you. Alex would be the monster outside the den and make growling sounds which would make you laugh loudly and hold onto Owen. You would play along with us until you heard or saw a bird and that would be it. You would slither out of our laps and wobble your way after the birds, the monster outside the den no longer your concern." He laughed and looked at Elisa whose brows were knitted together in concentration. She pulled the blanket around her shoulders and held them under her chin; his laughter trailed off at her expression and he sighed almost sadly at the expression she held.

"Do you still love birds?" She smiled slightly at his question and nodded, memories of her and a little boy running across the sandy beaches mimicking seagulls filled her mind. Their laughter childlike and pure, their smiles as radiant as the sun shining down on them.

"Did you see them much where you lived?" Her head shook not wanting to share her memories of the little boy and her mother, those were hers, her memories alone. She blinked rapidly and cleared her throat as she locked the little boy back in one of the wooden chests in her mind, his laughter fading away until she couldn't even remember what it sounded like.

"No birds at all? Come on! Where did you live?" Elisa lifted her head and looked over at Karson who was studying her with a piercing gaze as if he was trying to see the darkest parts of her mind and soul. She didn't like how his questions had become more forceful, more prying. Her eyes studied his features as she tried to make her deduction of the man. His marble grey eyes were hard and clear, large and honest, she could see the intelligence and wisdom swimming in the depth of colour. He had a single ear piercing, a small little black stud in his left ear, a small four-leaf clover tattoo under his ear. His hair was surprisingly neat for someone who had been asleep, his hair looked like it had been gelled back. Elisa felt her gut twist and she swallowed the suspicions that were now beginning to rise.

"Why are you awake?" Karson tilted his head innocently with a small smile painting his skin, he could see her beginning to tense and her mind running wild with thoughts.

"I heard you wake up and when you didn't come back, I got worried. We got to look after each other am I right?" Elisa blinked and looked back at the bird that was now playing with a worm it had managed to pull out of its hiding place.

She didn't know Karson, not really. She never felt comfortable with people in general, she didn't know how she knew when to accept someone into her life. Her brothers had been accepted by her heart the moment she began to let them in, Sasha, Cyrus and Quinton were accepted the moment she told them who Elisa West was, Finley was just too soft for her to not accept. Andre and Karson were strangers. However, even Andre didn't make her feel the way Karson did.

Off.

Her skin felt itchy as if she could physically feel the spiders of suspicion crawling across her skin, making its way to her mind rather than her heart. Her hands unconsciously held the blanket tighter as if it was a shield that would protect her if need be.

"Magpies are common in England. Did you see them much where you lived?" She shrugged which made him sighed regretfully, his shoulders dropping slightly in defeat and his hand came up to rub the back of his neck.

"Look Muffin, I'm not the bad one here. Alex warned me to not be too pushy because I know that sometimes I can be pushy, but I promise you I just want to know who that little 3-year-old princess became." She could hear the sincerity in his voice and her gut untwisted slowly making her relax. She wasn't amazing at deduction like her brother Owen was, but she liked to believe that she could trust herself and her feelings over any fact. Her mind was at war and her gut was pinching as if not knowing what to tell her.

The magpie hopped closer to her foot making her completely freeze so that she wouldn't scare the creature. Her curiosity at an all-time high like it usually was whenever she saw something that interested her. She wanted Karson to leave her be and as if he could hear her mental pleas, he stood up and stretched making the bird hop and fly away eliciting an annoyed huff from the girl. He chuckled lowly and patted her tense shoulder.

"Alright, kiddo come in soon ok? It's getting lighter and I don't want Owen to scream the building down when he can't see you." With that, the older man opened the door to go back to their room, Elisa turned to watch him leave and her brows lowered as she saw a phone sticking out of his pocket, a phone that she hadn't seen before.

They had accounted for all of their phones so they knew which ones they would send on trains and which ones they would leave at home. There should only be Quintons silver iPhone, Finley's mustard covered phone and the burner that Alexander kept with them for emergency use only. The rest of them had left their phones at home except Elisa whose phone was turned off and stuff in the backpack. She wasn't allowed to turn that phone on no matter what and that was fine with her. But the phone poking out of Karson's pocket wasn't a silver or yellow phone. It was a black phone with no cover. A phone they hadn't accounted for. She wanted to bring it up with her brothers but she knew that with everything going on she had to be careful. She would watch Karson until she had something to worry about, even though her mind was telling her something was up.

She wanted to believe that his intentions and questions were pure and innocent, but she could feel it deep down, Karson was hiding something too.

Owen had always been in tune with his sibling's emotions. He knew when to leave them be or when they needed the extra attention, he knew when they needed back up or when they were able to handle a situation. Elisa was a tricky one to read but he believed and hoped that one day soon he could read her as he did with his siblings and other people. He could already see cracks in her tough demeanour, and it made him ecstatic whenever he could see one of the many things she kept to herself. It made him feel worthy, useful that he could figure out what his sister could be thinking when she kept everything to herself. She had made progress with people and he felt pride bubbling whenever he saw a small show of emotion or a little smile growing on her cute little face.

Despite everything going on, she was still trying and he was glad to know that recent events and information hadn't made her cower into the shell she was stuck in when she first came to England, in fact, she seemed to be trying harder to make an effort with everyone whether that meant sitting with them and engaging every so now and then in conversation or simply initiating hugs; she hadn't hugged Owen yet which made him want to slap the smug smiles on his brothers whenever they saw Owens sullen look. However, he knew it wasn't because she hated him or felt any ill intention towards him, it was her humour coming out to play, a little joke that had been created between the two of them.

When Owen had woken up on the morning of the 4th of November, he immediately remembered the plans Alexander had put into place to surprise the littlest West, a small little surprise that wouldn't mean much to the rest of the group, but he knew would mean the world to her. His eyes searched for his sister, but his smile slowly began to dip when he couldn't see her figure anywhere among the other sleeping bodies. Panic began to cloud his mind as visions of men dressed in black suits dragging Elisa away in the dead of night, never to be seen again, entered his thoughts. They should have been more careful, they should have taken turns to keep, they shouldn't have let their guard down so quickly. Before Owen could scream, a hand slapped over his mouth and he looked up to meet unimpressed hazel eyes that studied him.

"Were you going to scream?" She asked bluntly as she sank onto the bed next to him; Owen being one of the lucky ones to steal a place on the bed along with Karson, everyone else piled away on the floor.

"No!" He squeaked out and she tilted her head in a 'really' gesture making his cheeks flush a dark colour and his eyes avert to the blank TV. Even though she was his little sister, she sometimes acted like the older one, she seemed way too mature for a 16-year-old which made him both delighted but also glum at the fact that life had forced her to become that way at such a young age and had thrown many obstacles at her to harden her once carefree personality.

She joked around but she was also too serious, a perfect mix of Alexander and Preston, she was indifferent towards other people but was caring and loving in her way, an ideal blend of Roman and Owen. She was exactly like her brothers and had their qualities way before she even met them, and even though Owen was young when his mother had left them he still remembered her loving and selfless personality; Elisa was a carbon copy of their mother with her brothers' qualities and her father's look. A finger hesitantly touched his wrist where his tattoo was, and he watched his sister pout slightly as she stared at the black ink which was etched into his skin.

Elisa didn't need to say anything for Owen to understand the question burning in her eyes. The birds were because of her. Owen patted her hand with a small smile, reassuring her that everything was okay and he saw the emotion in her eye as she stared at his tattoo before looking at her other brothers. Regardless of her not being in their life for years, her brothers had always thought about her, even though they were angry and tried to tell themselves they hated her, the rational and older brother part of them just wanted their baby sister to come home and babble her millions of stories as she chased the birds in the field. They would never have that sister come back home but were instead gifted with a mysterious girl who they couldn't wait to show her everything it meant to be a family. Owen looked at her face and poked her cheek to grab her attention, something was bothering her, and he wanted to find out what it was.

"Sup buttercup?" She wrinkled her nose at the new nickname in disgust to which he silently agreed to never use again, Lissy was the only nickname for her in his eyes. The door opened and Elisa watched Karson stroll in with trays of steaming hot coffee cups, his smile bright as he kicked at Finley who was still snoring soundly. He shot up with a yelp and groan of pain which created a domino effect of everyone else waking up and throwing their complaints of being woken up at a half-asleep Finley, who was still on the floor rubbing at his stomach.

"Lissy?" Owen prompted as he saw her eyes darken and unfocused momentarily, she shook her head and clenched her jaw before patting Owen's shoulder.

"Not yet." She simply said before she gave a small smile to everything else as they started to get ready for the day. Owen knew she was hiding something as per usual but this time he couldn't ignore it. He couldn't ignore the way she studied Karson out of the corner of her peripheral vision with a wary eye.

"Why on earth are we awake?" Roman spat as he walked out of the bathroom and grabbed a coffee cup, the smell calling him in and promising him a better mood and energy, something he desperately needed after his interrupted sleep; he had managed to wake up without crying out or screaming and had simply fallen asleep again when Elisa had stroked his hair, something their mother had done when they were younger and had bought them a sense of calm.

"I want to take you all out for the day since we've been cooped up. Besides, I wanted to surprise Elisa." Alexander said as he tidied away the blankets and pillows off the floor.

"Why do we have to get up for the brat? Why does she get a surprise?" He sneered in his usual Roman way without the heat behind his words, Sasha sent him a dirty look to which he sent a dirtier one back. Elisa didn't take his attitude to heart now knowing that that was just who Roman was. A moody child who didn't know what to do with feelings or where to direct them. She sent him a warm look to which his eyes softened slightly before rolling his eyes and messing up her hair. Their brother-sister bond was different from her bonds with her other brothers, but she loved it, nonetheless.

"She's not a brat. Go get ready guys." Sasha dragged a confused Elisa back to their room and began to get ready. Sasha wore dark blue jeans with a black knit jumper, black boots and a knee-length black trench coat, she had a black knitted hat pulled over her hair that had been braided back into a neat French plait and black gloves to match. Elisa wore thermal black leggings with a pastel blue jumper, black boots that Sasha lent her along with an extra pair of gloves, a ribbon pulling locks of her hair away from her face like normal.

"Where are we going?" Sasha looked over at Elisa with a small smile and made a zipping motion across her lips.

"Like your brother said. It's a surprise." She winked and hooked her arm through the West girls' arm before they went to join the others. One more fact about Elisa West, she despised surprises and so she couldn't help but glare at the back of her eldest brother's head. As they walked out of the building and through the streets of London. She was familiar with the hustle and bustle and felt at ease as they blended into the crowds, people dressed in similar warm clothing, their eyes and smiles full of excitement and joy, laughing and talking animatedly.

The boys were just as excited and pointed out various things to each other, the city thrill giving them a high. Alexander kept an eye on the younger humans making sure they were sticking together like a teacher watching her students on a school trip, Owen gently tugging Preston's arm whenever he stopped or tried to run off like a little child who had seen something wonderful. The group spent their day going through busy streets and into colourful and bright shops, music playing in speakers and the honking of cars and buses being used nearly every second. Her eyes jumped from stranger to stranger keeping an eye out for any danger or something that could pose a threat to them.

"Stop it, relax." Sasha whispered and rubbed her best friends arm reassuringly, they were okay, they weren't in any danger for the time being and Elisa needed a break from the paranoia.

As the day came to an end and the sky began to darken, Alexander became more hurried in his steps; too excited for what he knew Elisa hadn't experienced in a while.

They went to grab some fish and chips with hot drinks to help their bodies heat up, their cheeks flushing from the cold and noses numb, people gathered and chatted excitedly making Elisa confused as to what was happening. She shivered and wrapped her arms around herself regretting not wearing more layers, but before she could regret her decisions, even more, something suddenly smacked her in the face and covered her vision, nearly toppling her over her feet. Reaching up she pulled off the thick material only to realise that it was a white coat with fur trim on the hood. Her eyes met with chestnut brown eyes that seemed to radiate warmth and sent him a confused look. He rolled his eyes and bent to her level so she could hear him over the noise.

"Couldn't watch you shiver anymore... Alex would have scalped me for not attempting to do anything." He huffed and pulled back not meeting her surprised eyes. She pulled on the coat and giggled slightly at the way her hands were no longer visible; she felt like a little girl trying on her fathers' coat and the thought of it warmed her heart. Roman zipped her up quickly and made sure both girls were in front of him and the others, his action also making her smile whilst he tried to look away from her awe-filled eyes. He wasn't used to someone look up to him like that like he was their role model.

"Aren't you cold?" Elisa asked him after tugging at his jumper sleeve. He smirked at her obvious concern and shook his head but when her eyes only seemed to deepen with worry he huffed and snatched Andres knitted hat and scarf.

"OY YOU LITTLE-"

"See. All cosy and warm, happy?" Roman asked his little sister with a sneer to which she simply ignored and nodded with a smile of approval. Preston's excited eyes landed on Elisa and he burst out into laughter at the sight of her practically drowning in Romans' coat.

"You look like a polar bear!" She scowled making him and the others laugh harder, her supposed angry face not looking at all threatening. Sasha tightened her hold on Elisa's arm dragging her attention to the usually bubbly girl who now looked calm and had a content smile on her face.

"What's up?" Elisa said to her, they had to practically shout in each other's ears as the chattering and laughing around them was loud.

"I'm just so happy to find someone I can call my best friend." Elisa blinked in confusion and pointed questioningly at Quinton and Cyrus who were laughing with Preston and Andre, Sasha shook her head and threw her arms around her making her stumble slightly in surprise at the sudden affection.

"You are silly, you're my best friend." Sasha giggled as if the fact was so obvious; not realising how much those words truly meant to the other girl. Her eyes watered slightly for some reason and she slowly hugged the girl back, her eyes flickering everywhere as she felt a lump in her throat. She hadn't had a best friend in a long time, not a girl best friend, someone she could share her secrets with and giggle about things with, the only girl who was her best friend... had been her beautiful mother. But now she had this soft human holding onto her tightly.

Elisa lowered her face and buried it into Sasha's shoulder as she hid her happy smile, they pulled apart and Elisa laughed slightly as she wiped away a tear that had rolled down her cheek. Instead of making fun or teasing her, Sasha hooked their arms again and pointed towards the London Eye.

Suddenly a burst of colour shot into the sky and lit up the darkness, Elisa's eyes widened in awe, sure she had seen fireworks before, but she had never had friends and family to appreciate them with, she had never had the chance to simply watch them surrounded by happiness and light. The realisation hit her, and she looked over to Alexander who was already watching her with a softness in his eyes, she swallowed as she stared at her big brother who winked down at her with a straight face before he turned his face back to the colour bursts. It was November in England, Bonfire night. The wind blew gently around her, and sounds faded as she closed her eyes momentarily, her smile bright and the most genuine it had ever been.

Looking around Elisa took note of the people she had come to love.

Sasha clinging onto her arm and holding Cyrus hand with her free one, Quinton and Cyrus laughing with Preston and Andre, Finley and Owen pointing and making noises of wonder at the different shapes and colours painting the dark sky like the children they were, Roman had a small smile on his face as he was stuck in his head playing his daydreams and Alexander and Karson talked quietly whilst looking over their group now and then. She looked back up seeing bursts of blue, red, gold, white, green, pink, purple; the memory engraved in her brain and put into the chest of happiness that was slowly starting to fill with other memories of her family and friends.

Although her beloved parents weren't with them, she knew that despite their situation, they would be proud of Alexander for doing this. Although she wished they were here with them, she felt nothing but contentment.

Elisa West had never truly belonged anywhere.

But right there with her friends and her brothers, she couldn't imagine herself anywhere else.

16

Now

Preston West was a child; he had grown up being the youngest of the siblings and had never had the worries that his brothers were forced to carry at their young ages. He never worried about what they were going to eat for dinner and if they had all eaten, the burden of waking his siblings up and making sure they were ready for school was never sat on his shoulders, the stress of bills and food shopping was never his concern. Preston had lived the life of the youngest sibling not having any responsibilities except making sure he behaved and kept his grades up, he wasn't known to be one to flunk off school and neither did he hold a bad reputation. He was just the carefree prank-loving West.

However, Preston wasn't that boy anymore, he had responsibilities even if they weren't spoken, he had responsibilities as an older brother. He had never been an older brother to someone and as soon as he heard he had a younger sibling, a sister no less, he panicked. How was he supposed to treat her? Was he supposed to treat her like a princess, or would she be a tomboy? Did she complain all the time about everything, or would she be the most understanding and sweet girl to exist?

When Roman told him that she was the reason their mother left he felt fury. Hatred. The darkest of emotions all rolled up into one targeting at the sister he had yet to see. But even then he wanted to know her. The boy even researched what to say to her the moment they met! He had planned to tell her his name, how old he was, what he liked doing, but he should have known it wasn't easy when she had simply cut him off and acted as though their first meeting wasn't a huge deal.

It hurt him when she didn't seem to give him the time of day, it infuriated him when Owen and Alex became more insecure as they didn't know how to handle her, Roman angrier and more irritable. Nobody seemed to pay him attention, all the focus on their sister who kept herself away from them, Alex was insistent on finding out why she was the way she was, Owen wanted his Lissy back and Roman wanted to figure out her secrets.

Preston felt... forgotten in a sense.

It was an awful feeling that clawed at his heart while he sat alone in his room, wondering how his normal life had been tipped out of balance so quickly. When she had approached him in his room he felt mixed emotions. Annoyance that she had decided to finally make an effort but also nervous of speaking to her; she had changed all those feelings away with a gentle curve of her lips and the moment she smiled at him, her entire face changed. He didn't see an angry and cold stranger who had disrupted the peace of his family.

He saw a little innocent girl looking for a place to call home, he saw the way her eyes were unsure and her movements hesitant, her smile forced but he knew she wanted to relax and depend on them. He saw the lost look in her eyes and realised that she knew how it felt to be forgotten, perhaps she had felt that way for a long time too. At that moment, Preston wanted to hold her close and ruffle her hair while she giggled her heart out, he wanted to play pranks on his other siblings while she played along with him, he wanted to annoy her until she finally screamed at him to go away.

He wanted a little sister, his little sister.

Preston West had to grow up a bit the moment she stepped foot into the house. It was his job to protect her when she needed it, to be the ear she could talk off when she had words that needed to be heard. He had a job and that was to be a big brother to his 16-year-old sister who although seemed much more mature than all his siblings combined, was just a child.

When she had finally told them about their mum he had felt pain, pure pain knowing he would never meet his mother again, but that pain couldn't match the agony that engulfed his entire being when he saw the tears she shed, the memories she forced between her shaking lips and she way she clung to Alex like a baby. She had acted like she hadn't broken down in front of them the next day, but that night will always be stored away in his mind, the memory of his little sister looking so defeated as she poured her heart out for the world to see.

He thought she would have slipped back into her comatose state, her feelings hidden once more and her coldness biting, however, he saw the small changes she began to make, the way she began to talk more, initiate contact such as nudging and poking them playfully and start smiling. Her smile, he had decided, was his favourite thing about her. The rare radiant smile that made her glow like the little angel she was.

After bonfire night, Alex had said that it was time for them to go home, to send the phones off on different trains. Quintons' phone was slipped into the bag of a woman heading off to Paris if her thick accent was any indication whilst Finley's phone was dropped into a kid backpack who was heading up to Scotland. Two separate phones going in two completely different directions. Alexander had told the others to try to resist using their phone as much as they can for at least a week or so which had Roman, Preston, Cyrus and Andre in near tears. But the group knew that if they wanted to keep themselves safe and protected and drive the bad guys away from them for a while, then it was a sacrifice they had to make. They were lucky they lived in a small village where everyone knew everyone, they didn't have to worry much about not being able to see each other because chances are they would end up bumping into each other the minute they exited their houses. They were all aware that their little trick was only temporary, but they hoped it would buy them some time of peace until they figured out their next plan on how to get rid of them completely.

The journey back home had been quiet and oddly peaceful despite all the West siblings sitting in the same car. Owen had managed to persuade Alexander to sleep while he drove the car and so Alex was slouched in the back seat with his cheek leaning against the cool window, his hood covering his messy hair and arms crossed over his chest. Roman had taken the passenger seat and had his feet up on the dashboard, his sketchbook in his lap and pencil between his teeth as he smudged shadows into the paper, every so now and then he would engage in conversation with Owen about art or when they were going to stop at a service station. Elisa was silent in the car and her brows were furrowed, clearly in deep thought about something; she was too serious for his liking and so like the mischievous boy he was, Preston summoned his inner child that was always present and lifted his hand.

Elisa blinked as she felt a finger poke her cheek, she eyed her brother curiously to which he simple grinned at and stared at her with a look she can only describe as utterly creepy. Her attention went back to the memory playing in her mind's eye.

Going to London with people she could call friends and family had unearthed some memories of her first friend Levi. The boy who had cared for her like a little sister and played with her as they grew up, she had laughed with him and played adventure games in the sand pretending to be pirates. She was Eli Braveheart, the bravest pirate to sale the deep seas, he was Levy the Unseen, the mysterious pirate that nobody had laid eyes on. She didn't remember much about the boy, her memory only showing her the basics, his piercing jade green eyes and childish laughter. She wouldn't be able to recognise him if he sat next to her, he was simply a ghost, an echo from the past jumping around in her mind.

She felt another poke to her cheek and found herself feeling wound up by the simple and small action caused by her brother. For some reason, him poking her without a word was annoying her immensely and she didn't want to give in to what he so truly desired. A reaction.

For the next half an hour, Elisa sat stone still facing the front, no twitching, no sound as Preston continuously stuck his finger into her soft cheek that was slowly turning red from the number of times he had poked it, his grin slipping to one of boredom as he stared at her in disgust, what kind of person didn't get annoyed? How had she still not cracked? As he thought that, he barely registered the pain shooting through his hand.

Elisa had turned her head and chomped on his finger, her eyes blazing with revenge and evilness as she smirked, his finger still between her teeth. He slapped a hand over his mouth to stop himself from letting out a high-pitched scream that was trying to force its way out. He didn't want to startle Owen or wake up Alex who would no doubt pummel him instead of their younger sister.

Roman had been watching the exchange silently and snorted when his Shadow bit Preston, she was hilarious whether she realised it or not and very much like himself. Preston shot him a glare with his teary eyes and managed to get his finger free from the demon child next to him.

"Is anyone hungry?" Owen asked and Roman chuckled as he looked in the mirror to meet the amused eyes of Elisa.

"I think Elisa is." She nodded and patted her stomach.

"Yeah I could eat... what about you Pres?" He sent her a glare and elbowed her in the stomach to which she reciprocated with an even sharper nudge. He let out a wheeze and she shrugged.

"Don't dish out what you can't take bub." She hummed.

Preston was wrong, Elisa wasn't a little innocent angel; she was a little devil child.

Weeks went by with no unwanted shadows, no men in black, no black roses. Elisa should have felt relieved that perhaps they had believed their little phone trick, but the survivor in her knew it couldn't have been that easy. They were plotting something, making the little trick that would be sprung upon them when they least expected it. So while everyone else merged back into their lives of routine, while her friends went back to school and began studying for upcoming exams, while Roman went back into his artist funk and painted beautiful realistic paintings that people adopted into their lives, whilst her brothers and their friends went back to their jobs, Elisa watched.

She listened.

She observed.

She didn't let her guard down. She was the only one who had seen first-hand the damage these people could do, and she refused to watch anyone else go down.

Elisa had been keeping a close eye on Karson, she noticed things that she had never noticed before. His behaviour was strange, to say the least, and it worried her, no, frustrated her that she couldn't pinpoint exactly what it was about him that rubbed her the wrong way. Whenever he was in the house she noticed how he would casually look out the windows or check that black phone of his when he thought nobody was looking, how he would study her with those inquisitive grey eyes of his; searching for answers she didn't quite know. She saw the way his eyes would track them all one by one before he would relax and act somewhat normal again.

Maybe it was nothing, maybe that was just who he was, she found herself unconsciously finding excuses for him, defending him in hope that her gut was wrong for feeling odd about one of her brothers' childhood friends.

It grew increasingly harder when she would see him slip out of the house to take a call or whenever he would make an excuse to leaving early, he would disappear at different times, sometimes they didn't see him for two days which was a normal Karson thing to do. But it wasn't normal, she knew that. When she asked Karson where he was going one time he had said it was a small work business conference that took place in York, but what personal trainer had business conferences? Whatever he was hiding was big enough that he has to lie about his whereabouts.

Other than the Karson mystery and the West problem, Elisa thought life had been going pretty calm, she knew it was temporary like all things in her life and she knew she couldn't completely be content until she knew exactly why they were being watched and hunted down. There was something she was missing, her mother dead and father supposedly dead. What were they looking for? Why had they followed her to every foster family? What was it they wanted?

But instead of spending every minute obsessing over those questions and possible answers, she decided she could enjoy the moments of peace she had suddenly been rewarded. Christmas had arrived rather quickly, and she couldn't help the flurry of excitement that bubbled in her chest, Christmas.

She had spent it alone ever since her mother was taken from her. The first Christmas after her mother's passing was disorientating. She was in her first foster home with a couple and their daughter who encouraged her to sit with them and enjoy the holiday together. She had denied immediately and hidden in her given room ignoring the music and laughter from the family downstairs. It wasn't the same, her mother wasn't there to hold her close under a fluffy blanket as they sipped hot chocolate with marshmallows whilst watching a movie.

Her mother wasn't there.

That Christmas eve had been horrible for her, she felt so out of place as she sat on her bed holding the phone to her chest. The video of her mum laughing and humming on their last Christmas eve played in her ears, her mother's gorgeous green eyes sparkling with love and happiness as she stood her phone on the table and held out a hand to an 8-year-old Elisa.

They had been dancing to Christmas music and laughing the whole while, Levi and Leah laughing and dancing with Aunt Audrey in the background. That phone was the closest Elisa would ever be to her mother again and it wounded her; she couldn't smell the vanilla scent of her mum that would coax her to sleep, she couldn't feel the warm embrace as she chased away any fears and worries. Her first Christmas without her mother and friends was like stepping out of a storybook and into a world of grey and emptiness. She never joined in with all her other foster families, she never dressed up for the occasion or even acknowledged that it was Christmas. For Elisa, that holiday had died along with the colours, love and happiness that had stemmed from her mother.

This year, however, Elisa was with her family, her real family, and she wanted to feel that happiness again, she wanted to see the colours and joy in the world. The darkness that she had been stuck in most her life was slowly dissipating as the light of her brothers forced their way into her little cocoon of safety. She was ready to leave her haven and feel everything, she was excited to feel emotions other than guilt, grief and pain.

Preston was in his room gaming online when his door slammed open and Elisa shot in, his eyes widened when he saw her flushed cheeks and wide eyes and stared at her with his nose scrunched up. She looked nothing like the normal put together Elisa he had come to know and the look of her unnerved him.

"I need your help." She practically whispered as she shuffled over to the beanbag he was slouched lazily in; he put his controller on the floor and gave her his full attention wanting to know what could have caused her to look so dishevelled.

"Who are we killing?" He whispered back and she shook her head as she paced.

"Nobody yet but I need your help with something else. I've been trying to figure out what to get everyone since its Christmas in like two days and I made some stuff, but I want to get your guys amazing presents to make up for the years I wasn't here and-" He quickly stood and held her still by the shoulders, her hazel eyes flying up to meet his awed hazel ones that were so similar to her own.

"That's what you're stressing about? Eli its, not a big deal man, presents aren't everything you know? It's about love and..." She gave him an unimpressed look, but a smile teased at her lips as she listened in amusement.

"You forgot to get presents huh?" His shoulders dropped and he nodded furiously as he quickly grabbed his navy coat and pulled it over his white t-shirt, he ruffled his already messy hair and pulled a woolly hat over his head as the weather had dramatically changed to match with the season. She giggled at her brother's panicked face and followed him out of his room and down the stairs, both of them trying to be quiet and avoid being seen by their other brothers.

However, they should have known they wouldn't be able to slip out of the house unseen; the two youngest Wests froze as they heard a heavy sigh behind them.

Roman sat on the stairs watching with mirth as his siblings slowly turned around with wide eyes, looking like they had just been caught trying to cover up a murder, he knew if that was the case Elisa would have grabbed him and not Preston, that boy was way too squeamish for anything. His eyes danced between the two, Elisa had her usually indifferent expression whilst Preston chewed his lip; his nervous habit making Roman smirk as he zoomed his attention to focus only on his younger brother.

"So, Pres... where were you guys wandering off to?" Preston's eyes widened comically as he heard Romans toneless voice, the tone he used only when he wanted to get the truth out of Preston. Usually, Preston would cave and quickly tell Roman what he was doing as he didn't want to be tackled by his older brother for lying, however, he didn't want to let Elisa down. She had come to him in confidence, and he knew that she wanted to surprise everyone. The sacrifices one has to make, he thought. He straightened and stopped chewing his lip.

"Eli and I were going to hang out. That's all. I've hardly spent time with her since you three were always hovering over her and since this whole danger thing has been bought to light I haven't had any one-on-one time with my sister." It was a partial truth, and he felt the confidence seep through his lips and into the words he spoke making Roman frown in confusion. He was hoping his brother would lie to him just so he could get in a punch or something, but he couldn't tackle him without a reason. He huffed and went to leave but saw the flash of excitement in Preston's eyes making him stop and grin maniacally. Roman was a master at lying, he, of course, knew when someone else was unless they were 16, quiet and their nickname was Shadow.

"Ooooh, little brother is lying? Where did you learn that huh?" His tongue piercing darting out flashing Preston who made a disgusted face, he like Owen didn't like the tongue piercing, it completely grossed him out and as a brother, it was Roman's job to disgust them and annoy them as much as possible. Preston felt his confidence being sucked out of him and Elisa resisted the urge to roll her eyes at the dramatic people who were her brothers.

"We're going to get my lady things." She said bluntly hoping that he would get disgusted and move on without a word. However, he just stared at them with the same apprehensive look not at all believing them for their lies; he was also sort of worried that they could get taken but quickly dispelled that worry as soon as it entered his mind.

"Okay and?" He pressed and Elisa mentally cursed at the understanding and mature brother she possessed. She looked at him with her lips parted in surprise as he raised a brow daringly, she clenched her fist and quickly thought of something else to throw at him.

"And nothing. He's coming with me to get my stuff and since I don't know him as well as I've had the chance to get to know you, I asked him to come with me, okay?" Roman rolled his eyes and grabbed her coat before hurling it at her face making her splutter and yank it off her face with that face she makes when she thinks she's glaring. Adorable and comical for him to look at.

"It's bloody freezing knucklehead." He mumbled to which she simply stuck her tongue out at him and rushed out of the house with Preston hot on her heels, both siblings wanting to get away from their short-tempered brother who seemed surprised that she stuck her tongue out. Such a small childish act that made his heart feel lighter.

Roman smiled at their retreating figures that dashed down the driveway. Finley was right, it was fun to wind her up.

Preston and Elisa hunted for the best gifts they could find for each other, their siblings and friends. It was fun for them both to run around and search whilst also throwing ideas at each other. They would pick items up and show each other, sometimes they would pretend to be one of the others and put themselves in their shoes. Elisa didn't like buying things for herself, but she loved buying presents for others for one reason only; she loved surprising people and seeing smiles on their faces.

Preston enjoyed their little hangout, the little jokes they threw at each other and the pranks they played. She was his mini partner in crime, and he cherished every second they spent together. He took her to get fish and chips and they sat on a picnic table overlooking the sea, the breeze was even colder, but their food warmed them up. He looked over at Elisa who had a small content smile on her face, her cheeks and nose pink and eyes sparkling with childish innocence, she sipped at her tea that she held between her small hands and let out a heavy sigh.

"You happy with everything you bought?" He asked her wanting to fill up the silence they had settled into, he was naturally a talkative person and he just wanted to know her. She nodded and sent him a smile; his lips curling at the sight. Her smile made him happy, made him feel accomplished in some way. He and his brothers weren't always affectionate but showed their care and love for each other through simple acts of kindness or the odd side hug. With a little sister, it was different, they wanted to treat her like they treated each other but they also wanted to treat her like the princess she was when she was younger. He faltered for a moment and looked down at his steaming cup of tea as he realised something.

"I'm sorry." Elisa's brows knitted together in confusion and she looked up into his face wanting to know the reason for his sudden apology.

"What did you do?" She teased thinking he had pranked her without her realising but when he shook his head and the seriousness hadn't left his face, she felt her concern peak for him.

"When Roman first told me about you he said you took our mother away, I don't remember her. You guys all had her for a long while... I had five years. Five years I didn't and don't remember. I was so willing to push the blame on this so-called sister because I didn't know her but at the same time, I just wanted to know her, wanted to know you. I wanted to say that I'm sorry. I'm sorry."

His eyes closed as he felt tears well up in his eyes. He hadn't outright told anyone exactly how he felt about not knowing or remembering his mother. He always brushed it off as if it wasn't a big deal, as if it didn't bother him but it did, it bothered him so much. He heard a shuffle, and the tea was taken out of his hands, she placed them on the table behind them before she turned.

She hugged him.

She hugged him ever so tightly wanting to fill those cracks in his heart with all the love she could muster, her arms wrapped around his waist tightly and her face pressed into the side of his body. It took him only a moment to respond and his arms wrapped around her holding her closely, he buried his face in her soft hair breathing in the gentle smell of strawberries. She rubbed his back soothingly as her mother used to do to her and sighed softly, her heart feeling heavy knowing that her sibling was sad, that he was hurting.

"It's ok Pres... let it out." She whispered soothingly into his coat, so quiet, so tender; it was the key to opening the floodgates and his eyes involuntarily closed as the first tear escaped his eye, his lip trembling and his arms tightening around her. His little sister.

"Let it out."

17

Now

Christmas in England wasn't like a Christmas you see in the movies, the snow didn't fall from the sky like flakes of confetti at a party, children weren't giggling or singing as they walked by and the birds weren't singing like angels.

No, this was England, the land of bipolar weather. The view from her window was beautiful despite the fact there was no snowflake in sight, the dense soup-like mist covered the lavender field like a blanket, mysterious and magical in a way, the sun peeping through cracks in the grey clouds. Tears fell from the sky and slid down the glass window in a race to see who could reach the bottom first.

Elisa sat cross-legged on her bed wearing fluffy white pyjama bottoms and light blue polar bear pyjama top, her hair neatly brushed and braided into a loose plait with a ribbon holding it together, her eyes were wide and excited, and she kept glancing towards her bedroom door. She wasn't sure how Christmas worked at her childhood home and she didn't know what was expected of her. Were they early risers or did they sleep in till noon? Did they go to church or did they have special traditions?

As if hearing her inner turmoil, her bedroom door slowly creaked open and Preston peeked into her room. Upon seeing his little sister bright-eyed and awake, he ran in and quickly tackled her to her bed in a warm and loving hug. Elisa smiled brightly as she tried to push out of his arms but not completely trying, enjoying the contact she had avoided most her life.

"Merry Christmas Eli." He pressed a quick kiss to her forehead and stood up straight with his hands on his hips, his smile dropping into a face of determination, suddenly looking like a man on a mission.

"Now no questions! You are now my partner in my morning Christmas tricks and will be helping me with the three bears currently sleeping, understand?" She nodded as she stood up and saluted him making him grin and wave her towards the door. The two siblings tiptoed down the hallway to the eldest brother's room to execute their first trick.

Elisa wasn't sure if this was a normal thing to do but instead of feeling the hesitance, she thought she would feel, she was surprised at the excitement and rebelliousness jumping to life in her body; as if a shot of adrenaline had been injected directly into her system waking up all the childishness and mischief that had been buried long ago.

Alexander was laying on his stomach, sprawled out under his covers like a starfish, his mouth gaping open and an arm under his pillow. The room was dark due to the blackout blinds that covered his window, so Elisa flicked on his lamp so they could see the surprisingly neat room.

Her eyes lingered on a photo across one of his walls, she could easily figure out who was who, Roman wore all black and looked annoyed in the photo, his calculating eyes staring at the camera and his body leaning away from the boy holding him, Owen had a big grin on his face as he wrapped his arms around Roman in a hug. Alexander had his arms crossed with a small smile on his face, not happy but not exactly sad. Preston was making a face at the camera like the weirdo he was. But the man caught her attention, his hazel brown eyes that she saw every day in the mirror, ruffled brown hair and an infectious smile that made her lips curl involuntarily.

Before she could delve deep into her thoughts about the father she couldn't remember, Preston's waving arms caught her attention. Turning her head, she blushed sheepishly as she realised, he had been trying to grab her attention for however long she had zoned out.

"Jump on him." Preston mouthed to Elisa whose eyes widened comically.

"Are you kidding? I'll kill him!" She hissed back.

"Shut up and do it!"

"You do it!" She didn't want to accidentally break his back.

"Oh, for- don't worry! His highness is a freaking detective who is prepared for specific situations."

"What if he kills me?" The thought of her brother being so angry that he'll throttle her filled her mind but then she realised that Preston would get the blame and not her.

"Eli. You are currently my best friend right now so either do it or I'll tell everyone what you bought them." With that Elisa pinched his arm and slowly stood on Alexander's bed before jumping on top of his back. A loud grunt escaped his lips and he cursed out loudly making Elisa freeze. Alexander paused as he noted that the body on top of him wasn't heavy, it was the shock of something falling on him that woke him up and the hissing that he had thought was in his dream. His face was practically being suffocated by his pillow but if Elisa could see his face, she would have seen the elated look on his face and the beaming smile that stretched his lips as he realised who had jumped on him.

Without warning, Alexander turned around and grabbed the poor unsuspecting Elisa before tickling her mercilessly. After a moment both brothers realised, she was sat stone still looking slightly awkward as he tried to make her laugh, to hear that painfully innocent giggle they heard from time to time.

"The heck? Are you not ticklish?" Preston asked to which she shrugged and got off the bed with a pouting Alexander.

"Are you sure she's, our sister?" He joked earning a glare from Alexander and a smirk from the girl.

"Please tell me you're not roped into his Christmas pranks?" Her eyes twinkled and he groaned dramatically.

"I'll start breakfast." He resigned and pushed his younger siblings out of his room with a fond smile on his face.

Owen was curled up in his blanket with an arm thrown over his eyes, loud snoring coming from the man sounding like a wild beast. The prank Preston had lined up for Owen was pretty simple, and Elisa knew that this prank would have her rolling around on the floor laughing. She shook her head in a weak attempt of telling him not to do it, but Preston had already prepared for this moment and he couldn't not go through with it. Climbing onto the bed ever so slowly to not jostle the mother hen in any way, Preston carefully stood over Owen's head and made sure that Owen was under the blanket. He checked that Elisa was holding down the bottoms ends of the blanket before closing his eyes tightly.

It wasn't a small one no, Preston didn't pass gas quietly nor was it scentless, it sounded like a roar, she was pretty sure she saw the bed shake. The reaction was almost instant as Owens body tensed up and began thrashing around under the covers as he tried to find an exit from the dark cave Preston had so effortlessly made. He found the foot holding down one of the corners and pushed it away making Preston tumble to the ground.

"Merry Christmas bro, hope you liked your gift!" Preston cheered; Owen threw him an incredulous look as he gagged from the smell that he believed had taken permanent residence in his nose.

"Gift? What do you mean gift you abomination of nature?"

"You said last night that I couldn't leave the table unless I had eaten all my Brussel sprouts and despite me eating them you didn't believe that I had, so you made me eat more. You then asked for evidence that I had eaten them after I complained so... there's your evidence dear brother of mine."

"Guys do you want- oh lord have mercy what died in here?" Alexander plugged his nose and looked around as if expecting to see a rotting corpse somewhere. Elisa was red from laughing silently and tears rolling down her cheeks, her hands clutching her sides and legs crossed in fear that she would pee from laughing so hard.

"I think Owen may have." She managed to choke out as she pointed to the brother who had his head stuck out the window and his body leaning in an awkward angle. Alexander gagged like the other West had and quickly ran out of the room with Elisa following behind, her hands still pressing against her mouth as she laughed. Preston winked and grinned mischievously at her little sister before he grabbed her hand and pulled her over to Roman's door.

Roman was the easiest for Preston to trick as he knew all of his triggers and fears. Elisa watched as Preston pulled out a scary looking doll that made her smile drop and shivers travel up her spine as she stared into those soulless bright blue glass eyes. Its creepy painted red smile looked deadly, and she wondered if the maker of dolls were sane when they made their toys, they were empty vessels made for ghosts to take over.

She winced as Preston made a lot of noise as he tried to tiptoe around the room. She rolled her eyes and managed to navigate herself through the room at a much quieter level then Preston had managed it; sheepishly Preston handed the freaky doll over to Elisa who cautiously pulled back Roman's bed sheets and slipped the doll under them, the head eye level with his own. Preston slapped his hands over his mouth to smother the laugh that was threatening to appear, Elisa was fighting off her giggle.

"Roman? It's morning get your fat butt up." Preston called out making Roman groan and turn over in his bed to face the door, his eyes still closed but the moment he opened them he would see the creepy doll Elisa swore was possessed.

"My butt is fantastic. Bugger off." He mumbled before trying to slip back into the haze of sleep, for a moment Elisa felt a twinge of guilt knowing her brother had woken up at some point during the night and was probably exhausted, but on the other hand she wanted her Christmas to start.

"ROMAN!" Preston yelled.

"WHAT-" Roman let out a high-pitched scream as he quickly backed away from the doll, his body got caught in the sheets and he fell off his bed with a pained grunt, a second later his head popped up over the bed making Elisa dissolve into a fit of giggles.

"You two little-"

"MERRY CHRISTMAS RO!" Elisa cheered and tackled her brother back to the ground in a quick attempt to soothe his anger, which luckily in her case worked as he chuckled lowly and pushed her away teasingly.

"Ew don't be so sentimental you little muppet." She grinned and helped him stand before she skipped out of the room and down the stairs humming, her three brothers watching her with amused looks. Owen slowly turned to his brothers with a glare that could kill, Roman and Preston, lost their smile as they looked at their older brother warily.

"Mess up this day for her and I will slowly tear out your organs. No mercy." His voice came out sickeningly sweet and the two boys nodded quickly with the fear apparent in their eyes, the cold and dark expression slipped from Owen's face and was replaced with his usual happy one.

"Great! Hurry downstairs for breakfast!"

Elisa was practically a puppy jumping up and down, way too excited to sit still during breakfast. Owen and Alexander cleaned the kitchen while the other three grabbed pillows, blankets, the tray of biscuits Owen had insisted on baking the night before and hot chocolate just the way they liked it. Roman had explained that they had their own way of celebrating Christmas and had carried on celebrating it the way they had when their parents were there. They would stay in warm clothing all day whether it be pyjamas or loungewear, exchange presents after breakfast and sit down to watch movies for the rest of the day. They would then order take out before going outside onto the back porch to simply chill out for the rest of the evening and watch the sunset. To say that she was thrilled to be part of their traditions was an understatement.

Elisa sat on the beanbag watching her brothers attentively for instructions, Roman took up one sofa whilst Owen and Preston took up the other. Alexander knelt by the tree that they had set up the night of Christmas Eve and rubbed his hands together. Alexander and the boys had agreed to give their gifts to Elisa last and so they quickly exchanged gifts whilst Elisa clapped and grinned, simply happy to be there. They were pleasantly surprised when she skipped to her room and bought out a bag of gifts for them, something they weren't expecting her to do at all except for Preston who enjoyed the look of delight on her face as she handed them their gifts.

For Preston, she bought a pair of neon green headphones, new video games to play and a mug with a clown on the front because he was the joker of the family. She had also gifted him with a picture of their mum she had found in the red journal and slipped into a small frame, that was his favourite present and kept staring at the smiling face of his mother that was frozen in time.

Owen was given an apron with the saying 'How can you help?! Get out of my kitchen!', a recipe book and the best present he could ask for, a hug. Her arms wrapped around his neck tightly and he responded immediately with tears in his eyes as he hugged her back just as tightly.

Roman had been gifted some more paints and a frame that held a photo of him and his best friend who he had sadly lost. It was a present she was unsure about, but the small tilt of his lips showed that he was thankful and a bit emotional.

Alexanders present she said she had to give to him later to which he had responded with an 'I don't need anything from you Dove, you being here means the world'. Could the West family get any cheesier? The answer was yes!

"Okay Dove, we saved the best till last." Her smile disappeared; shock covered her face as she watched the brothers produce gifts that they had hidden behind the sofa. Preston, Owen and Roman had bought her various small gifts, books, hoodies which she couldn't wait to snuggle into and an adorable bird plush that she blushed at and put to the side. However, she knew that she would become overly attached to that plushie very soon. Alexander sat in front of her and smiled gingerly.

"This last present is from all of us... and mum and dad." Her eyes lit up with pure confusion as he pulled out a box from behind his back, her fingers slowly encased over the small matte black box and she began to open it. She pulled back the lid and a small gasp filled the room as she stared at the beautiful Rose Quartz necklace.

"It was mums... we wanted to get something for you to remind you of her and I remembered that dad had kept a box of her stuff under his bed so... I looked through it and found the necklace and a picture of them." He handed her a small picture of her mum and dad, they were young and smiling brightly in the worn-out photograph, her mothers' eyes slightly closed, and her lips parted in a laugh as her dad whispered something in her ear; a joke only they would ever know. There laying on her mothers' collarbone was a necklace, a rose quartz stone resting against her skin. Her finger gently stroked the stone that was cool beneath her fingertips.

"Please can you...?" She turned around as Alexander clasped the necklace around her neck. As soon as the stone touched her skin, she felt a weight on her chest that she hadn't felt in a long while and as she turned to look at her brothers it happened.

The first tear dropped, then the second, her lips trembling and her eyes darting between her brothers' faces that each held an emotional look. Her arms reached out for Alexander who held her in the safety of his arms. She felt safe, something she had yearned for since her mum passed. She felt cared for, protected and that word she hadn't seen or heard of.

Loved. She felt loved.

"Thank you, Xander, guys. Thank you." She whispered vulnerably, her eyes landed on each of her brothers, and she started to giggle when she saw Owen a blubbering mess on the sofa.

"Shut up you sissy." Roman hissed even though his own eyes were misty.

"This is just too cute!" Owen sobbed out and threw his arms over Alexander and Elisa, the former rolling his eyes in exasperation and the latter patting Owens head like an owner would her pet.

The rest of the day consisted of watching Christmas movies and a lot of junk food, their friends had come round, and the experience was something she had never had the chance to be involved in. The day was perfect in every way she could imagine, the joy and colour that had been sucked from the day was back and had filled the dark cloud that took residence above her. They were now scattered around the porch, the elder boys sipping at their alcoholic drinks, Quinton and Cyrus had managed to sneak a sip or two in before Owen caught them and scolded them like an angry mother catching out her mischievous children. Their drinks had been replaced with spiced hot chocolate, a bowl of marshmallow and a plate of cake had been placed on the small wooden table in the centre of the porch.

Elisa looked out over the Lavender field watching the sunset, a permanent smile on her face as she watched the day come to an end. The laughter and chatter echoed in her ears and she let out her laugh now and then. Sasha leaned against Elisa with a blanket draped over both their legs to give them a bit of warmth. The cold wind brushed over them teasingly making them all tug their blankets closer to them, their feet covered with fluffy socks and they all wore Christmas jumpers that Finley had gifted them with; they looked utterly ridiculous.

Elisa touched the stone sitting on the centre of her collarbone, the stone was smooth to the touch, cold. She imagined her mum wearing the necklace and little sigh escaped her lips which caught Sasha's attention.

"It's really pretty." She mumbled quietly making Elisa hum in agreement. She caught Alexander's eye and slipped out from under the blanket to join him on the bench next to the door. His brows were furrowed as he tried to figure out if something was wrong. She waited until everyone paid no attention to them and slipped her arms around his waist, an action he reciprocated by resting his arms around her shoulders.

"You alright Dove?" The concern was apparent in his voice making her smile and nod against his jumper that for some reason smelt like peppermint and chocolate.

"Thank you for taking me in and giving me a home. Mum said that one day I'll be able to see my knights and... here you are." He smiled.

"If I had known I would have bought you home the moment I gained custody over the other three... but I guess fate had things set out differently huh?" They sat in silence until finally, Elisa said the words she had wanted to say to him the moment she began to open up.

"I love you, Xander." His entire being tensed and he looked down at the little girl in his arms, he tightened his hold and pressed his lips to her head as he clenched his eyes shut. 13 years he had waited to hear those words again. She was only a baby when she first learned the words, I love you and even then, it was hard to understand her speech. But his biggest wish had come true, and he was hearing her soft voice. He didn't want to cry but he couldn't help the tear that slipped down his cheek.

"I love you too Elisa." His voice low and cracked slightly from the overwhelming emotions that were building up.

"Wanna bet?" She suddenly heard Roman snap and groaned when he tackled Preston, the two of them trying to get the upper hand in whatever squabble they had found themselves in once again. Owen began shrieking about wanting to last a day without them fighting while Finley, Andre, Cyrus and Quinton cheered them on. Karson shook their heads before grabbing the two boys to separate them; Alexander reluctantly unwrapped his arms from his little sister and ruffled her hair before going to help his best friend, her giggle almost musical.

"Pack it in you idiots." Karson bit out as they dragged them off the porch and onto the field. Elisa's laugh slowly faded as she looked over at Karson who threw his hands up in the air in defeat. The boys laughing and Sasha shouting at the boys to stop through her amusement. The sounds faded into the background and all she could hear was her heartbeat thundering in her ear, her hands felt clammy, and her throat clogged up all of a sudden.

On the outside, nobody would have guessed that she was slowly slipping into the darkness, her hands grasping out for something to hold onto to prevent her from falling into the abyss her brothers and friends had helped her climb out of. Her feet trying to find a ledge to stand on, but the ground kept breaking the longer she stared at Karson. She shouldn't have let herself get too carried away with this feeling of euphoria, her guard had been down lower than she realised.

Just one day, one day of being a normal 16-year-old girl. That's all she wished for, but wishes don't come true; reality swallowed her whole and she sat up straight as her survival instincts awoke once more.

Perhaps her first Christmas with her family could have ended with the contentment and joy she had been hoping for, perhaps she could have finished her day with a smile on her face as she drifted off to sleep, perhaps she could have stayed in her temporary happiness.

If only she hadn't seen the black rose peeking out from Karson coat pocket.

18

Now

Elisa was stressed. It had been an entire week since Christmas, New year's had come and gone and she was now sitting in January. The weather was unforgivingly cold, and roads had started to ice over, frost lining the windows. Her birthday was in a few days and she would be 17, but she couldn't feel that excitement she had experienced a week ago with her friends and family. Not after seeing the blasted rose that haunted her sleeping and waking thoughts. A nudge to her arm pulled her out of her thoughts and she shifted her eyes to face a concerned Cyrus.

"You good?" He whispered as he carried on writing not wanting the teacher to separate them for talking, Elisa copied his lead and her hair fell in front of her face slightly creating a curtain.

"Just something on my mind." Cyrus studied her face and noted how her eyes looked distant as if she was seeing something he couldn't, her hand clenched creating crescent moons in the palm of her hand. He had known Elisa long enough to know when something was bothering her no matter how hard she tried to hide it. He was a quiet person and never spoke unless he had something to say, he also noticed a lot more than people realised but it didn't surprise Elisa when he shook his head.

"You've been like this since Christmas. Did something happen that nobody is aware of?" She shook her head but stopped once seeing his stern expression. She needed to tell someone preferable her brothers, she just didn't know how to tell them that their best friend could quite possibly be working with the people who had hunted her for whatever reason.

"Karson. He had a black rose." Cyrus froze not at all expecting her to say what she had said. Elisa had told her three friends everything about her past, about the foster families she had before leaving them, how her mother died and how there was always a black rose resting on the corpses. They knew that her and Roman's accident wasn't an accident, that Romans first car crash was planned, that the people wanted something from her. Specifically, her because her brothers hadn't been targeted until they met her, except Roman's accident which seemed to be just pure chance.

"It doesn't mean that he could be... part of them, right? Maybe it was planted on him?" Cyrus tried to calm her nerves, but she shook her head slowly.

"That's not how they work. They kill the body and then leave the rose. The rose isn't meant to be a warning, it's a calling card. They don't leave warnings they just... kill." She lowered her voice when she saw her teacher looking their way and quickly ducked her head. They waited for a moment before Cyrus spoke again.

"Do you have any idea why these people are still after you?"

Elisa bit her lip, a habit she had picked up from her brothers and began to run through everything she did know. Her mother and father were scientists, they created something called Project Miracle which could help eliminate unhealthy cells in the host's body, there was a small group in the government who wanted to use the project for bad, they killed all the scientists involved including her mother, her father was missing, and she was being followed.

"I don't know." She mumbled and Cyrus shook his head.

"You know something Ellie, its why they're watching your every move. Did your mum say something important to you or did she give you something?" Surprisingly, Elisa wasn't annoyed with his pushing and found it helpful. She had spent all her life running not having the time to sit down and question why she was running. She was a child, she wasn't involved in Project miracle, she didn't know any of the scientists except her mother, she didn't-

Elisa stopped writing as her eyes widened in realisation, she wanted to facepalm and scream at herself for being so stupid. She didn't see what was right in front of her, what she had all along. The bell rang and she quickly gathered her belongings, glad that it was last period, and she could go home, her bag was slung over her shoulder and Elisa quickly rushed out of the room with Cyrus hot on her heels. Sasha was walking out of her class chatting animatedly to a bored-looking Quinton when she saw her best friend speeding her way through the halls. Cyrus grabbed her hand as he walked past, and the three teenagers chased their friend out of the school.

"Stop Ellie!" Sasha called out making Elisa stop in her tracks and turn just in time for Sasha to wrap her arms around her.

"Jeez woman who was chasing you?"

"Nobody I... Cyrus made me realise how stupid I am."

"I could have told you that." Quinton quipped and Elisa shot him a quick glare.

"What did he say?" Sasha asked slowly ready to beat up her boyfriend if he had something horrible to her best friend, Cyrus screwed up his nose and took a step away from his girlfriend who was sending him death glares.

"He made me realise that I must have something and that is why I'm being followed and watched. I have something they need and want desperately which is why they're still watching me." She began walking off again with her friends stumbling after her realising she needed to be somewhere, and she would do it with or without them.

"What do you have?" Quinton piped up as they ducked through the narrow streets and alleyways.

"The journal."

Elisa told her friends that she had to look through the journal alone and that she would update her friends the moment she found anything out. As soon as the West girl got home, she went straight to her bedroom and dived under her bed where the backpack was hidden in a box with her shoes. She placed the bag on her bed and changed into an oversized shirt with a mustard yellow sweatshirt on top; she was wasting time she knew it, but Elisa needed a moment before she immersed herself in her mothers' journal.

She climbed onto her bed and pulled out the red journal she had carried around with her since she was 8. The journal she wrote in from time to time to document everything that happened in her life, the journal that held pictures of her parents and letters from her father to her mother. Elisa had opened that journal many times before, completely ignoring the first half of the journal that her mother had written in. She had believed that the journal was her mothers' diary, and she didn't want to invade on the private thoughts her mother had written down. But what if it wasn't a diary of her thoughts? What if it held secrets to Project Miracle?

Her tongue darted out to wet her dry lips and she opened the journal holding her breathe. At first, she saw what she had thought the journal was, a diary entry of a woman who had been recruited for a project. She skimmed through the page until she found another entry with a name, she was familiar with. William West.

'This idiot had bumped into me and I was ready to turn around and smack some sense into him. The man had nearly blown my cover! When I turned and saw his hazel eyes, I knew I was stuck, but men are men, and I didn't want to ever become attached. Turns out he was a dork, a cheesy dork and within seconds I had somehow trusted him enough to tell him my concerns about Lawrence and those mysterious men. He's sweet, genuine and I don't know where I'm going with this... but he's normal... makes me feel normal. Can someone quickly slap me before my mind goes haywire?'

Elisa smiled at the entry of a woman who had fallen in love at first sight and skimmed other entries of the journal. Some made her blush and quickly skip pages, and some made her giggle at her mothers' description of her father. They weren't even married at that point and still argued like a married couple. Pictures were glued into the book and her thumb brushed against the face of her beautiful mother; some loose notes were different handwriting to her mother's; she mentally cooed when she realised they were little love notes from William with his name signed at the bottom.

She saw a drawing of rocks and a W that her mother had written in bold, along the side of the page there were numbers and dashes. Another drawing of a weird looking shape with a rectangle in the middle, the word SUB ROSA written in red. What was that? Something in the back of her mind whispered words that she didn't understand, for some reason she believed she knew what this all meant, that this was another clue her mother left her. But Elisa couldn't decipher it and so she turned the page.

Then she saw it and her heart dropped.

She sucked in a breath as she saw the words she never understood before but now understood what they were. Formulas, trials and failures. Experiment notes. Annotations covered the next pages and her breathing quickened as she realised what the journal held, what it had kept secret. The formula for Project Miracle.

"Oh, shitake mushrooms." She breathed and reached inside the back pulling out a black box, she opened it quickly to see the vial that contained a liquid that looked greenish black. It was sealed shut and had never been opened; her mother had instructed her that the black box in the bag was to never be touched and always stay hidden in the back pocket inside the rucksack. She lifted it to the light and her face paled realising what she was holding.

"Project Miracle."

This is what they were after. For the first time Elisa cursed her mother in her mind, why had she told her to look after the journal and vial? What had her mother hoped when she entrusted her daughter with information that could have her killed along with her brothers? It had been right under her nose this entire time! She could have just gotten rid of the book and vial and maybe she would have had a normal life.

Furiously, Elisa grabbed the two objects and rushed down the stairs to the living room. She turned the knob on the fireplace which started the flames so she could burn the journal that had been the cause of her family's pain. The stupid book that had put her in danger. Her cheeks became wet with angry tears and she opened it, ready to rip out the pages.

"Wait!" A panicked voice behind her shouted and she spun around, her anger dissolving into fear as she saw Karson stood in the doorway breathing hard, his hands held up in surrender when he saw the look on her face. He wore black cargo pants with a black shirt, a leather jacket on top of that. She saw the phone in his hand and clenched her jaw.

"Hey! It's me kiddo... Easy." His voice was calm and soothing, the way it normally was when he spoke to her. He slowly tried to approach the West girl but stopped when she stood up with the vial tightly tucked into her hand and the journal pressed against her chest. His eyes lingered on the objects that she held before looking back into her face.

"It's me Muffin."

"That's what scares me... Karson? You?" His brows furrowed slightly, and he took notice of the defensive stance she was in and the way her eyes had hardened considerably, the fear now hidden and replaced with coldness. He swallowed and slowly nodded not sure what she knew.

"Okay, okay. Let's calm down, and ta-" Elisa lunged and kicked out taking him by surprise, he doubled over when her boot landed a blow to his stomach but was quick to recover, he tried to grab the teenager, but Elisa had years of hiding, surviving; she quickly ducked and pushed him to the ground before rushing up the stairs. She didn't look behind her as she dived into her parents' room and locked the door behind her. Rationally, she knew that if Karson wanted to get in the room, he would, but she hoped that part of Karson did care about her and her brothers.

"Muffin open up, I don't think you understand what's going on." He tried from the other side of the door while Elisa's eyes flickered around the room. Her father must have had some sort of protection in their rooms but where would he hide it? She saw the closet and opened it, her parents' clothes, boxes on the floor of the closet and was that... yes! She knelt and moved one of the boxes which were heavier than she realised. She ignored Karson's sweet taking from outside the door and moved boxes and rubbish that hid a metal handle. There was a keypad under the handle, and she cursed, hoping that a passcode would come to mind. Her hand brushed the journal and she quickly opened it and scanned the pages for something, anything to stand out.

Her eyes stopped on a small square in the corner of one of the pages, a little box with four numbers and she huffed out a breath; clearly, her mother had thought of everything, maybe there was a reason she gave the journal to Elisa.

"Mum I don't know whether to scream at you or thank you for your subtle hints." She mumbled under her breath as she quickly pressed the numbers, a relieved sigh escaping her lips as she heard a quiet beep and soft creaking of metal; she roughly yanked the handle and gulped. A hatch opened and she saw guns, books and notebooks, sealed boxes. The weapons didn't scare her, weirdly they reassured her that her parents did have some form of protection against the evils of the world. She grabbed a gun, the name and model unknown to her, and glanced at the journal and vial as she made a decision. Elisa committed the password to memory and mumbled it over and over in her head hoping she didn't forget it. The journal and vial were shoved behind the boxes in the secret safe and she quickly shut the hatch door hearing the whirring of a lock slipping back into place. She paused suddenly and turned her head as dread engulfed her.

Silence.

She couldn't hear Karson outside the door anymore, no talking, no sounds. She frowned; he gave up? She quietly slipped the rubbish and boxes back where they were, so they covered the hatch once more, her nerves whispering to her that something was very wrong. Very wrong indeed.

There was a clatter downstairs making her freeze, was that Karson or was it her brothers? Her hands patted her pockets and she sighed in relief that she hadn't left her phone in her school bag, the phone she never used. She turned it on and clicked onto the family group chat Owen had forced her into despite never talking on it. She sent a text asking where her brothers were and wanted to cry out in both frustration and relief that they were all out. Her heart stuttered as she heard footsteps downstairs, more than one pair.

"Sure, bring the whole squad." She chuckled nervously as she eyed the phone in her hand that was now blowing up with text messages from her brothers. The footsteps were growing closer, and she heard the other bedroom doors being slammed open. Elisa hid her phone in one of the drawers under old clothes, she refused to have that phone in anyone hands except hers or her brothers. She didn't know what was going to happen, but she had a feeling she wouldn't be seeing her brothers for a while.

Her hands tightened on the cold metal of the gun, the object promising pain to whoever was on the receiving end. She tried not to think too much about the object she held, how her parents casually had them and how she hadn't wasted a moment to grab it. Had her world deformed so much that the simplicity of finding a weapon was normal?

The door burst open, and she lifted the gun at the men that poured into the room, her finger pulled against the trigger and satisfaction washed over her when she heard a yell of pain. She had never used a gun before and was glad her aim was completely rubbish, although she wanted to defend herself, she would never stoop low to kill someone. She wasn't going to become the very thing she hated. If they were going to take her, she wanted to make sure she dished out pain to these monsters whenever she could. Her arms were grabbed harshly, her legs kicked out trying to hit anything, to free her from the hell she was going to be placed in. The gun dropped to the floor and was put away into the pockets of one of the men. The men around her wore black with masks hiding the bottom half of their faces, goggle-like glasses over their eyes, exactly like that man who followed her in each foster home. One man approached her and gripped her chin roughly between his fingers; he lifted her face, and she felt a sharp pinch in the side of her neck. Elisa tried to bite at the fingers and the men around her chuckled at her.

"You're going to be a lot of fun huh kid?" He mused and she glared heatedly at the disgusting excuse of a human being, she gathered her saliva and spat at the man making him stiffen. It probably wasn't a good idea to antagonise a man who could kill her, but she didn't care, these men killed her mother. She felt pain radiating through her cheek and realised a little too late that the man had slapped her, her cheek tingling and warm.

"Behave." He growled before they began marching her out of the room, her eyes feeling heavy as the drug began working its way through her system. Elisa saw four bodies on the ground and her heart dropped, she needed to see who they were! But the drug decided to shut her down, her eyes closed, and her body went limp.

Please be okay, was her last thought.

A crawling sensation climbed up her arm and her eyes snapped open hoping it wasn't what she thought it was. She jumped and slapped her arm mercilessly; the small demon fell on the ground and Elisa's boot stomped multiple times on the cold, dirty concrete floor as she tried to get rid of it. She relaxed slightly when the spider was no more before she registered that she wasn't where she should be.

She blinked multiple times and her vision began to adjust to the darkness, only a few dim lights were on the ceiling meaning she could hardly see anything. But she could see what she was in, a cell. A small, dirty and putrid cell. She licked her lip and pinched her arms hoping this was a nightmare, that she would open her eyes and be wrapped up in a blanket on the sofa with her brothers watching a movie.

Her hands reached out and grabbed at the iron bars surrounding her, she couldn't hide it anymore, she was petrified. She couldn't hear any talking but could make out laboured breathing, snoring and soft crying. She wasn't the only one locked up in there, wherever there was. The air around her was filled with a metallic smell, a smell that was engraved in her brain. Blood. Blood mixed with sweat and possibly gunpowder. Elisa lowered herself to the ground still holding onto the bars in front of her. Was this it? Was she going to rot in this disgusting cell? Were those 4 months the only bit of normality she would ever taste?

It wasn't fair, it wasn't fair how she had to live 8 years of her life constantly looking over her shoulder wondering if she was going to die or if someone, she had shown the slightest amount of emotion to would be killed. But she knew that was the curse of being a West.

"Don't cry, child." A low rough voice said in the cell next to her, she sniffed and wiped her face with her sleeve before turning her head to try and find the person who had spoken. She saw a man with shoulder-length dirty hair, grime, blood and bruises covered his face making him indistinguishable. He held his arm close to his chest and she noticed it was bent slightly, his eyes facing the ceiling.

"Why are you here?" He asked with a note of sympathy in his cracked voice. When she didn't reply straight away, he shifted to face her.

"I... I don't know." Her voice came out weak and pathetic, she hated it, she hated how she felt so fragile and vulnerable. She was somewhere unknown and the fact that she was unconscious scared her to no end. Where had they taken her? Was she far away from home? At that last thought, she faltered. Home. Home was with the boys, where Xander would make sure that she had everything she needed, where Owen would call her down for breakfast and dinner, where Ro annoyed and messed about with her and Pres played pranks on her. Home was with the brothers she loved with all her heart.

She had been taken from the first place she could call home. A fresh set of tears rolled down her cheeks and all she wanted was for Alexander to run around the corner and gather her in his arms. Alexander was her haven; her brothers were her haven. The man on the bed sighed heavily and winced when he felt pain radiating through his body.

"Don't cry little one. I don't know why you're here and I can't lie to you saying it'll be okay because this is a real-life nightmare." He admitted sadly and slowly walked over to kneel next to her, the iron bars the only thing between them. Elisa shuffled back so she was out of his reach not trusting this prisoner but willing to listen to his words. He raised his hands in surrender and sat cross-legged on the grimy ground.

"But I know that you won't be here forever. Somehow, you'll be free and able to run back to your family, just stay strong." She nodded and stared at the man who spoke gently as if trying to coax a wild animal to stay calm. She swallowed the lump in her throat and rubbed her arms to warm herself up as she began feeling the cold seep into her bones.

"What's your name?" Elisa finally asked breaking the silence they had fallen in, the man let out a snort.

"My name? What do you want? The nicknames? The usual insulting ones? Mad hatter, nutter? Take your pick!" Elisa flinched at the detached tone he used; a feeling of pity tickled her heart towards the man who had been broken down. She gave a sincere smile trying to come off as unaffected of his tone.

"Your name." The man eyed the little girl who hid partially in the shadows, his body relaxing and eyes softening at the pure child in the cell. She wore black ankle boots, black jeans and a sweatshirt that he couldn't see the colour of her hair was messy with locks of her dark hair falling out of a bun. The curiosity was obvious in her eyes.

He nodded offering her a small minuscule smile, he cleared his throat and studied the girl who was too young to be in the place they were trapped in. The man sighed and rubbed the back of his neck as he spoke the name he didn't use or been called in years.

"William. William West."

19

Now

Roman sauntered down their driveway waving goodbye to Finley, his clothes covered in dry paint after helping Finley decorate his home as a surprise for his mother who was currently out of town. He ran his hand through his hair and groaned when he realised some paint had splashed into the strands making them stick together.

The living room lights were on and he could see Preston gaming, with Alex sitting on the sofa reading a book. He never understood Alex's love for reading, the only time he could sit still was when he was painting or drawing. But reading? That was a whole new level of patience that Roman didn't have; he had a habit of skipping right to the end if he ever did read a book. It was also a hobby Elisa had learned that she loved and sighed sometimes he would see her reading a book before passing it onto Alexander as soon as she was finished. It was their way of bonding as Alexander was most of the time working.

He walked into the house and saw Owen in the kitchen preparing dinner like he normally did. Roman loved Owen's cooking and he admired how Owen always tried to make new dishes, never stopping at a 'simple' meal and always going above and beyond. He had once come home to see loads of dishes covering the table. When Alexander had asked why Owen had made so much food Owen had simply explained, 'I was bored!'

"What we having?" Roman asked as he shrugged off his coat and slid onto the stool with a grunt. His arms aching from painting all day. Owen rubbed the back of his hand against his forehead and turned off the gas before he spoke.

"Cheesy pasta bake and freshly made garlic bread... where's Lissy?" He asked as he washed his hands with soap and turned to his artistic brother who wore a confused look.

"I dunno. I just got home." Owen nodded then paused. He looked over at Roman with a look that immediately had Roman sitting up straight. The two suddenly aware that something was wrong, like a deeply buried instinct that had finally become active.

"She wasn't with you." Owen more or else stated before he darted out of the kitchen and stood at the bottom of the stairs.

"Lissy?!" He shouted up the stairs but received no reply from his little sister, his gut-twisting as the instinct that something was wrong growing stronger.

"She's probably with Roman," Preston spoke from the living room hearing Owens panicked voice.

"She wasn't with me. I was out all day. She went to school... Preston, didn't you see her?" Roman asked as the brothers now discarded whatever they were doing and exchanged looks. Preston stood up and shook his head, his game long gone as he too realised that he was missing his partner in crime.

"I went down to the beach with some friends. I assumed she got a lift from one of her friends." Alexander frowned and pulled out his phone remembering she had texted him while he was still on duty.

"Well, she got home fine that's probably why she was asking where we all were."

"Any other messages?" Roman asked as they all pulled out their phones to check the last time she was active. Alexander had said that they were okay to use their phones normally as long as they kept an eye out and never dropped their guard. They had been doing fine, but now they weren't so sure. In the time they knew her, they had known that it wasn't normal for Elisa to go out without informing them. She always either texted them or left a note on the door, it was something she had started doing without them even asking her and Alexander was glad she was responsible.

"She didn't reply to the others we sent on the group chat." Owen realised and Alexander felt sick, his senses tingling telling him something was wrong just like the other three boys. He knew her disappearance had something to do with the men they had been hiding from, he just didn't want to accept it. Maybe she had her earphones in and couldn't hear them?

"Dove?" He yelled as he ran up the stairs to her room, taking two steps at a time. He knocked loudly on the door and listened for any movement. Maybe she had taken a nap? Ignoring the privacy rules, she had set up, Alex opened the door and scanned her room.

"She's not here." He whispered more to himself as he began to let his fear take over. Something had happened, something bad. Her room had always been empty as she never was one to decorate, but it had never felt quite so bare.

"I'm calling Quinton," Preston announced while Owen said he was going to call Finley. Roman pushed past Alex and swallowed as he noticed something his older brother didn't notice straight away. The bag. Her rucksack. The one their mother had given her. He stormed over to the bag and his face paled noticing the red journal Elisa had talked about was missing. They had never really looked inside it but they had seen Elisa write in it from time to time before she put it back in the bag. She wouldn't have put it elsewhere.

"Call her phone," Roman said and Alexander mentally berated himself for not doing that straight away. He held his phone up against his ear hoping that his sister had just gone out with her friends and forgotten to let him know. But when he heard a phone ringing, his heart dropped to his stomach.

"Guys!" Roman called out for his brothers to come upstairs, Alexander followed the ringing sound and frowned when he realised it was coming from their parents' room. Why on earth would her phone be in their room? The room they had all come to an unspoken agreement that it should never be entered. He scanned the usually dark room trying to see if anything was out of place if anything was amiss. If it weren't for Owens sharp eyes maybe he would have missed it. The speck of colour on the door, the burst of red that had been splashed like paint in the corner.

"Alex...." Preston said slowly and they turned to see him pull out an object from one of the drawers. The ringing stopped and he heard a curse spill from Romans lips, Elisa's phone.

The four brothers stopped, not quite sure what to say or do. Their sister was gone. They had accepted it. She wasn't here, her phone was here, the journal missing. Roman felt the fears return, the fear of his little sister being taken away again, but this time it was ten times worse as he knew she had been taken against her will. He couldn't lose her, they still had so much time to make up for.

"Guys?! Where are you??" They heard Andre from the bottom of the stairs.

"Dad's room!" Preston yelled and soon enough their friends and Elisa's friends poured into the room. It felt wrong for them to be in there, in the room that belonged to their mother and father but had been abandoned for years. It felt wrong.

"Where is she?" Sasha demanded angrily but upon seeing the brothers clueless looks she groaned knowing they were completely lost. She knew they were worried but she needed them to pull themselves together so they could start looking.

"What do we know so far?" Andre asked, always being the more level-headed member of the group. Even though the boy was quiet and reserved, he was very outspoken when need be and so they always took his words seriously.

"She sent us a text sometime after school asking where we all were. We replied but she never responded. Figured she went to see one of you guys." Preston shrugged as if the situation wasn't bothering him, but Owen could see that Preston was shaking.

"She was stressed about something after school not making a lot of sense. Talking about how stupid she was but-"

"Karson. She was stressed about Karson." At the familiar name, Alexander looked up at Cyrus who had interrupted Quinton, confused.

"Why was she stressed about Karson?" Owen asked and Cyrus paled, his eyes enlarging. He looked at everyone's muddled faces and felt the panic bubble in his chest as he realised how much Elisa still kept hidden to herself.

"She didn't tell you..." He whispered horrified which made everyone grow panicked.

"Didn't tell me what?" Alexander snapped, fed up with the boy who knew something he didn't. What had his sister hidden? He had thought they were past the secrets stage.

"She told me that Karson.... on Christmas she saw a Black Rose in his pocket. I said that it could have been a coincidence, but this is Elisa."

"She was watching him closely back when we went to London. I brushed it off, but she was watching him closely and her eyes would always trail back to him." Owen felt nauseous and sank onto the dusty bed.

"Guys... where is Karson?" Finley asked and they looked at each other in dread. Alexander couldn't bear the thought of his best friend not being who he said he was. Someone he had grown up with and saw as a brother.

"He's not picking up," Andre said as his phone rang out.

"Ok, are we going to talk about the bloodstain on the freaking door?!" Sasha stared at the stain and nearly died when she realised it was fresh. What the hell had her best friend been through? Was that her blood? The very thought made her want to cry.

"Someone was in the house with her." Quinton swallowed, a newfound feeling making itself known, he looked at the people around him seeing the lost expressions on their faces.

"But... Karson? Why would he do this? He's been our... I don't understand." Preston whispered in a small voice feeling like he was losing another role model. Owen wrapped his arm around his little brother, his thoughts turning on him and tearing into his heart. He couldn't help but think that this was all his fault, that this could have been avoided. Owen could see people's facades; he had always been able to suss them out and figure out whether their intentions were good or bad. Thinking about it, he had never really figured out what kind of vibe Karson gave off. He was just his older brothers' best friend who treated him like family. Maybe that was his downfall, Owen was too trusting; he should have been warier of Karson.

Alexander on the other hand was finding it difficult to believe that Karson was involved in Elisa's disappearance, he had known that boy since they were little kids. Surely, he hadn't been plotting the demise of his family when they were hiding under the bed as they played hide and seek. The timeline was all wrong, but the facts and evidence were right in front of him.

"What do we do?" Roman asked weakly and they turned to Alexander who shook his head. What could they do? The police weren't trustworthy, Karson and Elisa were missing, and they didn't know where they could be. Owen knew Alexander's answer before he even uttered them and sighed sadly.

"Nothing... we just have to keep a lookout, see if we can find any clues and just hope that... Elisa comes home." Sasha grew angry at the quiet words.

"Nothing??!? Do you think they're going to treat her to a nice cuppa with some jammy dodgers while she has a pedicure?! They may not kill her, but they want something from her, and they'll do anything to get whatever it is out of her." The boys winced at the truth spilling from the auburn-haired girl.

"Elisa is clever. She will have hidden the journal. There's no way she's kept it safe all these years only for it to get taken away so easily." Preston worked through his thoughts and nodded at his brothers. He looked around the room and smiled ever so slightly.

"I'll bet you it's here. She was in this room so it must be here."

"Then that's what we do. We look for the book, keep an eye out and don't put too much attention on ourselves. Preston's right. She's clever and she's survived a hell of a long time without anyone, we just need to figure out what it is they want before they get it." The group then dispersed to find clues.

William West was alive. No, his body was, but the personality of William seemed to have been erased, years of torture and mind games had stripped him to his core. He was never sure what was real and what was a nightmare, but then again there wasn't much of a difference between the two anymore. He couldn't tell the time of day or whether it was night, his life consisted of being shaken awake, being dragged away to the interrogation room, a daily beating that would last for hours until he lost consciousness, and then darkness, before he woke and was left in silence.

Those hours of silence were his favourite, those hours where he could close his eyes and pretend that he was home, he could pretend that his boys were running outside, his Lila humming in the kitchen with his daughter giggling in her highchair. Those hours he could forget that he would never see them again, that they lived only in his mind.

William had lost count of the time he had been in those cells, in the never-ending darkness. He even began to wonder if his family even existed, or if they had always been a figment of his imagination. Did he have four boys wondering where their father had disappeared to? Did he have a baby girl wanting to meet him? Did he have a beautiful wife who was desperate for him to come home?

In the first few years of being stuck in that hellhole, he would beg to hear his family, to at least see them, but they would never acknowledge them; the moment he began to doubt their existence, they quickly reminded him of his wife. They told him about her beauty and her smile, how clever she was to hide from them and hide their youngest child. They told him about how brave she had been... when they killed her. The horrifying reminder was enough to send William into a frenzy. His wife was dead.

His Lila. Was gone.

Life had only gone downhill for the man, his sons were safe, none of Their concern. But his baby girl, his little Miracle was their constant target. He never heard anything else about his family no matter how much he begged. But he knew that they were okay, he knew deep down that his children were stronger than him and his wife and he prayed every day that his daughter would find a life of safety and normality.

William remembered the last time he saw his boys, his little 10-year-old Preston who was such a little trickster, he remembered how he was supposed to have a heart to heart with Roman after school, he wondered if Roman hated him for not being able to be there for him. He knew that Owen and Alex would have no doubt slipped into the adult roles and taken care of their younger brothers despite their young ages.

He remembered the last time he saw his little girl, his baby Elisa. He remembered her soft round cheeks, her light hazel eyes that always sparkled with happiness. That little girls giggle was etched into his brain, echoing whenever he thought of her. She was such a loving and affectionate girl, and he couldn't wait to one day feel one of her amazing hugs again. Hopefully.

But those hopeful thoughts were only active in those few precious moments of silence, their childish laughter and twinkling eyes dancing around in his mind's eyes. When those hours were up, so was the hope. William West would unconsciously shut down, detaching himself from the thoughts that gave him hope or life.

When he would be yanked roughly into The Interrogation room, he would stay quiet, not willing to give any information or answers about what they wanted.

When he was thrown to the ground in the Treatment Room and he felt the blood escaping his wounds, he would think back to his children and fight to keep his eyes open.

When they threw him back in his cell, bleeding and exhausted, he would close his eyes with a weak smile, a hallucination of Lila lulling him to the darkness. But the darkness wouldn't last for very long before a nightmare would dig its claws into his body and drag him into a vivid alternative of life. Each one different from the last and shaking him to no end; sometimes they were memories, sometimes they were present events and the rest of the time it was unknown why he saw the graphic images in his head.

William West hadn't seen the other prisoners in the cells near him, they mostly kept to themselves; something he also did. He was too weak to save anyone else and he was determined to go home. He promised his boys he would come back, he had to. However, the little girl in the cell next to him threw him off. He couldn't leave her alone, the scared little mouse who had started hyperventilating the moment she had woken up. He didn't want them to break her as they did him, she was too young, way too young for that physical, emotional and psychological pain.

He didn't understand why she had frozen the moment he had told her his name; she had come closer to examine him and simply stared at him with an emotion he hadn't see on anyone other than Preston. Awe. Before he could ask her what the problem was, four men in masks came, two stormed into his cage and grabbed his arms. A scream caught his attention and his head whipped round to see two other men cruelly digging their fingers into the inside of her wrists as they made her stand.

"SHE'S A CHILD! STOP BEING ROUGH YOU DISGUSTING EXCUSES FOR HUMAN BEINGS!" He felt a harsh punch to his stomach and doubled over in pain before a hand gripped at his long dirty locks and roughly pulled his head up to look them in the eye.

"Speak to us like that again and we will shove a rose down her pretty little throat." At those words, William stopped fighting his guards and looked back at the girl whose eyes stared at him in fear. He gave her a reassuring smile and mouthed something to her which made her lips twitch regardless of her obvious distress.

Stay strong little one.

William was taken to The Interrogation room like every 'day', the smell of smoke filling the air making his sore throat burn. He was shoved into the cold metal chair and he winced as the movements jarred his bruises. They always beat him badly to the point of falling unconscious, but while he slept, he was fairly sure someone with medical experience would come to fix his wounds in time for the next session. They never gave him painkillers making sure he felt every bruise, scratch or burn that was gifted to him.

"Ahh, Dr West! It's been a while, hasn't it?" The man in the chair sniggered as he took in Williams ragged appearance, to which the West man simply stared back with an empty look in his brown eyes.

"Now will today be the day you tell me exactly what I need to know?" Silence greeted the man who sighed in disappointment.

"Come now Will. This is honestly getting boring. Delilah is dead, your kids forgot about you and your darling daughter will not be far behind her mother. You have nothing left to lose so why not... just tell me?"

"Sod off you maggot," William mumbled loud enough for the man's smirking expression to turn into a scowl; he slowly leaned over William with a shadow of demonic intent.

"You know, the men told me how you stood up for that little girl, how would you like me to give her your punishments instead? Give you a break?" He taunted and William's eyes widened, he shouldn't have spoken out of turn, but he couldn't watch that little girl shed a tear over the monsters that walked through the hallways of the place they were stuck in.

"I don't know who she is or what she's done but she is a child! I'll take her punishments too! But she's just a child, don't hurt her." The man looked at William with new interest, his eyes sparkling with glee.

"Ohhhhh, well this is just rich! You don't even know who she is, how beautifully perfect." He leered and said something to one of the guards who had bought him into the room before he turned back to William with a sigh.

"One last chance Will! I'm not a patient man so would you like to tell me everything I need to know about Project Miracle?" William spat at him and the man growled.

"TREATMENT ROOM! WE GO WITH PLAN C!"

His body was once again dragged like a rag doll through the dimly lit narrow hallways, faint buzzing from the yellow lights. His weal legs dragging behind him, too tired to walk down the steep staircase that went down to The Treatment room. It sounded great, treatment, but it was a posh misnomer for the torture chamber tucked away in the lower levels.

William knew the routine and lifted his arms for the guards to take off the decrepit shirt he had been wearing for god knows how many years. The moment his skin was visible he felt his skin tear viciously as the barbed whip was bought down hard on his back, a scream ripped painfully from his throat and his fists clenched as he felt the hot blood dripping steadily down his scarred back. Again, and again, the whip was bought down until he was almost numb from the pain in his back, he was pretty sure they had cut over old scars. Every day was a different method of punishment, whipping was bought out for 'special occasions' whilst stabbing, cuts and burns along with the usual punch were more of an everyday punishment.

It was part of his life.

His body flopped almost lifelessly onto the wet floor and his tired eyes closed momentarily as he tried to breathe through the pain, which gradually began to fade the less he thought about it. He wanted to fade into the shadows and become part of the darkness, invisible.

The laughing from the guards fading as a new voice was heard, one that grew closer and closer until it was right next to him. Hands grabbed his shoulders, and he was surprised when he didn't feel any pain, but that pain faded as he met light hazel eyes that glared into his own furiously. His little girls' eyes. He could never forget those eyes. Those beautiful hazel eyes.

"YOU LEFT THEM! YOU LEFT US! RIGHT WHEN WE NEEDED YOU THE MOST!" She said pushing against her father's chest with her tiny fists. He let her punch his chest as her eyes watered in anger and sadness; he didn't understand why she was acting like this and it hurt him worse than any whip or punishment could. He caught her arms and held her close to him, his eyes welled up with tears as he held onto his daughter's small form that thrashed in his arms, eager to get away from him. The guards near the doors parted as more guards walking in holding motionless bodies, bodies that he tried to ignore despite them being right next to him.

"I tried to come back! Believe me Miracle, I tried." He pleaded for her to understand, to see that he didn't want to leave any of them, he needed her to know that he was coming back to them. She sobbed against his chest and he felt his heartbreak in two as he listened to her choked words.

"You didn't try hard enough." Her soft broken voice whispered, and his eyes finally glanced at the bodies on the ground in a pool of his blood. He looked into the eyes of his sons, the once bright sparkly eyes, now dull and empty of life, his daughter's body shaking as she screamed in agony. The sound shattering his eardrums and stabbing its mark into his mind; her sobbing, screaming, and yelling merging into white noise, different frequencies pounding in his head until it all stopped.

William blinked and his body jerked, his arms tightening only to realise the small body in his arms was no longer there. His body was no longer laying in a pool of blood, but he could feel the ache in his back.

His heavy eyes scanned the cell he recognised as his home for the past years, and he exhaled as he climbed onto his bed, leaning his head against the wall of his disgusting cell. The cell next to him empty making him wonder if that girl even existed. Or if she like every pure thing in his life was a figment of his imagination.

He sighed heavily as he curled in the corner of his bed. The image of his lifeless sons scarring his mind, but he believed that it wasn't real. He was finding it harder to differentiate reality from dreams. The dreams so vivid as lifelike it confused his battered mind. However, he knew that the screaming of his baby girl, the lifeless eyes of his sons, wasn't real.

It was only a dream.

20

Now

Having a father was one of her wishes as a child. She wished to know her father, what he was like, did he love her? Delilah would tell Elisa that she was her father's little girl, his whole world. When she was younger, she would read books and watch movies, most of them included a happy family, a mother, father and their children. She would memorise how a father was supposed to act, she learned that a father was the protector of the family, the one who shielded them from the darkness of the world. Elisa had grown up hoping that she would one day find her way back to her father so that he may protect her from the wickedness of the world.

She recalled the distant and empty look in his eyes as he spoke indifferently to her, the way his body was slumped from exhaustion and pain. He didn't look like the father she had seen in pictures. There was no sign of the dazzling smile that used to radiate happiness, there was no trace of the twinkle of mischief in his hazel eyes. There was no recognition when he looked at her and even though it was dark and it had been years, Elisa couldn't help but feel the stinging in her cracked heart. She had dreamed of meeting her father once more, dreamed that they would hold each other tightly and smile brightly with happiness, their near-identical hazel eyes sparkling with love. But life wasn't a fairy-tale no matter how much she wished it.

Elisa had been shoved into a wooden chair for over an hour, her hands tied behind her back and her ankles tied to the chair legs. The new room was much brighter than the cells and hallways and her eyes winced from the sudden onslaught of brightness that enveloped the room. The concrete floors were wet with blood, old and new and she shivered nervously wondering what was next in store for her. She knew that these people were the same people she had been running from her whole life. The man who killed her mother could be any of the men standing in the room with her, their backs pressed to the walls. They had found her and now she was dreading what was to come. She knew how they wanted the journal and her parents work, she had to simply deny its existence. Her throat was sore, and she craved desperately for the cold relief of water, the fresh air and not the musty blood scented air she was breathing in.

Her head snapped towards the metal door that opened slowly, a man in a mask like the other men in the room, strolled towards the desk in front of her, his pace unhurried and leisurely as if he had all the time in the world. He sank into a leather chair with a soft grunt and lifted his feet to rest on the desk, he didn't pay her any attention as he shuffled through some paper and sipped at a bottle of water that the young West began to gaze at.

"Want some?" A honeyed voice with a hint of an American accent said making her eyes jump to the man in front of her, she made a slight face and the man chuckled lowly as he tapped the plastic skeleton mask covering the bottom half of his face; the black goggle-like glasses hiding his eyes.

"Not a fan of the mask Little Doll?" She flinched at the nickname, repulsion flooding through her veins. The man noticed of course and under the skeleton mask, his lips stretched in pure amusement at the fear and disgust she tried to conceal. She stared at him wanting to know who the monster under the mask was, she wanted to know who the head of all her troubles was. He shook the bottle in her face, and she leaned away from it though her mind was telling her to accept his offer; however, the more logical part of her knew that she had to stay strong and not take anything they offer her until they started talking. The man groaned in annoyance and slammed the bottle down on the desk.

"God your just like your parents, stubborn as anything. Let's see if you're smarter than them." He leaned forward in his seat, his feet falling to the ground as he clasped his hands and rested them on the table. She could feel his eyes raking her small form and she fought the urge to spit at him, she had a feeling he wouldn't appreciate it.

"Where is it?' He asked bluntly and she furrowed her brows as she slipped into an act. She tilted her head slightly and blinked innocently.

"Where is what, sir?" Her voice coming out as puzzled and meek, he kissed his teeth in dissatisfaction before clicking his fingers. A sharp pain radiated through Elisa's cheek as her head snapped to the side. She froze in shock and looked up at one of the guards who had smacked her.

"Let's try again, where is it?" She sighed heavily completely ignoring the fact that these men could kill her. Her mother had kept the book away from these men for years, she wasn't about to give up the one thing her mother died for.

"I honestly don't know what you're talking about!" Another smack. The man repeated the same question over and over and she would reply the same answer resulting in another smack each time. Her cheeks growing numb from the number of times she had been hit, silent tears tracking down the redness offering a bit of coolness to the warmth under her skin.

"FOR GOD'S SAKE TELL ME WHERE IT IS YOU, STUPID LITTLE GIRL! YOU HAVE NO IDEA WHO YOU ARE DEALING WITH!" He roared down at her, spit flying everywhere and the veins in his neck bulging.

"A man-baby?" She mused under her breathe making some of the guards in the room snicker in surprise at her retort, they hadn't expected her to stay strong and had thought she would have caved after the first slap. The man pulled out a gun and pointed it at her head, yet strangely, Elisa didn't feel fear.

"You'll do well to remember that your life is in our hands Little Doll. We know about your little playmates, your pathetic siblings. One call and its bye-bye." She swallowed her panic and held her head high.

"You won't do anything, you need me." A slight smirk on her face as she spoke, irritation flooding the man's body, his finger moved away from the trigger and he eyed her, studied her as if the answers were written on her face. He lifted a finger to his ear and tapped his thigh with the gun.

"Bring him in." The door opened once more and a person was being dragged by two guards, they pushed him into the chair next to Elisa and turned their chairs to face one another. The person's wrists and ankles were tied like her own and the brown canvas sack that was over their head was yanked off roughly.

"You might want to wash that I think I threw up a little, it stank so bad." A male voice she didn't recognise mumbled. She looked at him confused and he stared at her with the same look, they scanned one another trying to figure out who the other one was. They clearly weren't the same age as the boy looked slightly older than her, but he wasn't that old, the youth present in his eyes and face; the way he held himself that of a boy but also a man.

"Who is she?" He asked slowly and looked at the men around them. Elisa looked up at the man in charge and frowned.

"I don't know him..." The man looked between the two seeing the genuine bewilderment and let out an angry yell.

"CAN YOU NOT DO ONE THING, RIGHT? I SAID BRING ME SOMEONE SHE WAS CLOSE TO!" The two teenagers grimaced at the loudness and looked down as they saw the gun being raised. Two gunshots went off and for a horrifying moment, Elisa had thought her life had ended. But when she could still feel the thundering in her chest, she looked around to see two of the guards on the ground in a puddle of blood. A bullet wound between their eyebrows. Her eyes widened and she looked at the man holding the gun breathing hard.

"Damn man, you need an inhaler?" She looked at the teenage boy incredulously; he looked far too relaxed in his seat, he didn't look like he had given up, however, more like he had decided he was going to make their lives a misery and annoy them any chance he got.

"Shut up." A guard slapped the back of the boy's head and he hissed.

"Seriously? You all need anger management therapy! Violence isn't the answer! Besides my question was out of concern which is more than I can say for you." He retorted and glared at the guard who had slapped him.

"Shut up... or I'll put a bullet in your head." The teenager made a face.

"Look if your gonna kill me, make it more creative yeah? I mean if I'm going to die then I want to be on one of those documentaries where people try to figure out what happened to me and why. I've been kidnapped for an unknown reason, taken hostage and-" He stopped immediately when the gun was pressed to Elisa's head, god why did she have to be pulled into this? This boy had nothing to do with her so why the hell was she being threatening for his foolishness? She stared at the boy whose face suddenly blanked, and his eyes became dark with anger.

"If you don't shut up I will honest to god shoot her right in front of you." Silence. The teenager glared at the man holding the gun to my head and his lips pressed together, his eyes met Elisa and she saw concern and confusion swimming in his irises.

"What now sir?" A guard asked and the man sighed before going to kneel in front of Elisa, her eyes not sure where to settle.

"Where is it?" He asked in a softer tone, trying to earn some sort of trust with her.

"Just tell me Little Doll, and you can go home. Home to your brothers and those lovely friends of yours. You can have a normal life, we won't come after you, we will leave you be, and you won't ever have to look over your shoulder again. You have my word. Tell me. Where. It is."

A normal life.

That's all she had ever wanted her whole life, something this monster behind the mask was offering. She could have a normal life with her brothers and friends. She could grow up and be the girl she used to be, the happy and carefree Elisa West.

Was this all worth it?

She was just a pawn in a much bigger game, she was only a 16-year-old girl trying to get through her last year of high school. She had no idea what she wanted to be in the future, no idea what she liked doing. She suppressed the frown that wanted to slip onto her face as she realised, she didn't even know who she was. She was a stranger to herself; like her brothers and friends had once been a stranger to her. She didn't know her hobbies or the food she disliked, she didn't know what her favourite book or movie was. Running from danger, protecting people she met in her life and keeping the journal safe was all she knew. It was all she remembered doing and although she hadn't had a normal life, that was normal for her.

"Tell you where what is?" She said again and the man sighed heavily in disappointment. He nodded and stood up, rounding his desk before sinking into the leather chair he had occupied earlier, he lifted his feet and rested them on the table as he began writing.

"Take them back to the cells." Two hands grabbed her upper arms, and she was hauled to her feet once her ankles had been untied. She saw the other teenager in the same position as her and soon they were walking back through the dimly lit hallways, sweat and body odour clinging to the air making her want to vomit.

Another guard opened a cell door and soon she felt her body being shoved in. She groaned in pain from the bruises she had acquired already and rolled onto her back, her eyes staring at the ceiling. She heard a curse and suddenly the view of the ceiling was blocked by a mop of blonde hair and a sheepish smile. His hands either side of her head to stop his weight from completely crushing the younger teen, he gave an awkward chuckle and clicked his tongue.

"Well, hello there." The boy said and she scoffed in distaste as she pushed the boy away from her, she sat up and watched as the cell door was locked and the guards walked off laughing, stupid oafs. The boy landed on the ground with a hiss, and he sent her a slight glare before leaning his back against the wall, one leg bent at the knee with the other laying straight on the ground. His elbow resting on his knee and hand cupping his chin as he stared at the girl thoughtfully.

"You ok kid?" A voice said gruffly, and her head whipped around to spot the man in the cell next to her, her father. She squinted as she tried to figure out where he sat in the dark and felt her heart drop as she heard him groan in what she knew was pain.

"Are- are you okay?" She asked hesitantly and she was answered with another grunt and a small curse.

"Just a little scratch, nothing I can't handle huh?" He chuckled but she knew that he was hiding a lot of pain behind his laugh. She glanced at the teenager behind her and startled when she realised, he was examining her with narrowed eyes.

"Who are you?" He asked stiffly as he tried to figure out why she was in this situation.

"Who are you?" She parroted back and he tilted his head looking like a puppy.

"Okay as much as I like playing Guess who I'd like to know if you're okay. You too." Her heart warmed; he was concerned for her even though he didn't know who she was. Her father was a good man no matter what and it made her proud.

"I'm okay." William shifted and slid off his cot onto the dirty floor, he shuffled his way over to the iron bars and peered at her from under his straggly hair. They stared at each other for a moment, Elisa feeling the emotions in her rise, all she wanted to do was to make herself known. For the first time, Elisa didn't want to be invisible, she didn't want to hide who she was. She sat straighter and pushed the lump in her throat away.

"Your name is William West?" The man nodded with a slight wince as he settled onto the ground more comfortably.

"Why are you here?" The teenager piped up and Elisa wanted to strangle him, who even was he? Why was he locked in the same awful cell as hers? Why couldn't he have had his own for god's sake! William chuckled slightly.

"They want me for the things I can create, they want something my wife had, and they want to know our biggest secret." The boy scoffed.

"If I were you, I would just give it up and give them what they want man, it's not worth staying here for something like that."

" That something is the only thing that can kill people off without a person even realising it until it's too late." Her lips pressed together as soon as she said those words, William whirled to look at the girl with wide and suspicious eyes.

"Damn..." The boy whistled and Elisa couldn't help but ask him one of the questions that had been on her mind since he was thrown in the room with her.

"I'm sorry but who are you? Why are you here?"

"Who I am is a secret." He winked teasingly and she made a face as she looked him up and down showing her distaste. He rolled his eyes at her and carried on.

"But I'm here because they found me and are keeping me as a hostage..." He shrugged as if it was nothing but like Owen, Elisa could see the emotions he tried to hide. The fear and frustration of not knowing where he was or why he was there.

"How did you know? About that something?" William piped up and Elisa simply stared at him, words escaping her and her heart hoping he would make the connection.

She saw the realisation finally flood into his eyes and watched as he shuffled closer to her, the bars separating them from truly being together.

His shaky hand lifted and cupped the side of her cold yet red cheek as his eyes searched her own; she swallowed the lump in her throat and smiled slightly trying not to let the tears fall. His thumb gently stroked the soft irritated skin just under her eye, the mere action made a tear fall and her lips tremble as her composure broke. The pain that had been tingling faintly in her cheeks completely fading as he brushed her skin. His own eyes teared up as his other hand reached up to wipe her tears away, tears that slid down her cheek and onto the floor.

Elisa stared up at her father who nodded to himself, reassuring himself that this was real, that his baby girl was in front of him. He smiled softly at her, his lips trembling and hands shaking slightly as he stroked her cheek.

"Hey, munchkin." He whispered softly and she let out a shaky laugh as the emotions overrode her senses.

"Hi, daddy." She whispered just as quietly ignoring how childish she sounded by calling her father that, her voice barely audible but he heard it, he heard her soft and delicate voice, the voice he had dreamed to hear for years. Elisa felt like a little girl all over again as she stared up at the man, she had been away from for 13 years.

This moment may not have been the way she had dreamed she would meet her father. But she cherished it anyways, she cherished the way they studied each other, memorising each other, she cherished their first greeting and the way his eyes lit up upon realising who she was. Elisa stored the memory in one of the new chests she had created in her mind. The chest that contained every happy and unforgettable moment between her and the people she loved most. Her brothers, her mother, her friends and now her father.

She lifted her small hand and wiped her father's cheek, both of them laughing slightly at her attempt to reassure him that everything was okay, that this was happening, and it wasn't one of Williams dreams or Elisa's wishes. They had truly found each other.

"Are you really... you're my little girl. You're my little Elisa" He laughed in disbelief but overjoyed as he studied the little girl before him who grinned brightly, a sight that made his heart explode.

"It's really me dad... I thought you were... I thought I would never see you again." She sobbed softly and he yearned to hold her close to him, the bars only wide enough for him to fight his hands through. William looked over her shoulder and saw the teenage boy frozen and sat wide-eyed as he gawked at his daughter, eyes wide in shock and relief.

"Eli?" Her body tensed and she weakly looked over at the boy confused as to why he called her by one of her nicknames. She didn't move as he shuffled over to sit next to her, he poked her nose and watched as she scrunched her nose up, glaring at the offending finger with teary eyes. The small familiar action bought a smile to his face and he gave her a cheeky grin.

"Wow, I didn't think you would forget me so easily. I get that I'm Unseen and nobody knows who I am, but I'm hurt you don't recognise me." He pouted slightly as he teased her and watched in amusement as her eyes widened. She shook her head and pushed him away gently.

"One person at a time you idiot! Let me finish my moment with my dad." She said in a cracked voice before giving him a shove he didn't expect and toppled to the ground.

"Wow, tossed away like garbage, thanks for that Elisa." His tone snarky and bought a smile to her face. She looked up into William's warm eyes and held his hands tightly.

"I've missed you so much, there's so much to tell you and so much to explain, everything's been so hard dad I..." Her voice trailed off and he lifted her chin to look at him.

"Oh, sweetheart I never expected... This wasn't the plan. You were supposed to stay with your mother, safe and away from the danger after us. You were supposed to come home when I had prepared everything with your brothers. You were never meant to shoulder this burden alone."

"It's all well and good saying that it wasn't meant to be that way, but it happened dad, I haven't had a life and I fear I never will. Everything is still so secretive, I'm still so stuck in the dark. I explained everything to the boys and yet I'm still the one responsible. I have to protect that journal, but I don't understand what mum wanted to do with it."

His eyes lit up when she spoke of the journal and pleased that she had looked after it. But he felt the depression envelop him like a blanket, choking him slightly as he realised his little girl didn't have the chance to be a little girl. She was the youngest out of his children and he now realised she was mentally and emotionally older than them all. He opened his mouth to tell her what the men were after when suddenly they heard heavy footsteps walking towards their cells. Immediately, the three separated and sat in different corners of their cells, making it look like they had nothing to do with each other.

The man stood in front of their cells and she could feel his eyes on her before moving to the next person despite not being able to see who it was. He hummed and pulled a rose from behind his back and throwing it through the bars at Elisa. She jumped away and stared at the black rose in pure fear, memories of her old homes, her foster parents flashing through her mind.

The fire, the blood, the running, the death. It all merged into one and she couldn't contain the whimper that escaped her lips. The man chuckled coldly and made a cooing sound as a parent would to a baby.

"It's amazing really, how the mind works. How the mind makes connections between objects, events and people and makes a human react differently. A black rose can mean different things, it can mean rebirth and rejuvenation... but to you... it means death. All the deaths that surrounded you, the blood and the horrors all caused by YOU!" He spat the last word and she flinched.

Stay strong Elisa, he's only human. Be strong, find everything you need to know. Beat them at their own game. She steeled her mind from his words and looked at him with a blank face.

"What's your plan here? You take me, assuming I know something about my parents. I know nothing except the obvious. If you think I'm going to just hand over that journal, you must be dumber than I thought. Where's Karson? Why can't that twit show himself?" He chuckled at her fiery words and shook his head.

"Little Doll I know you know something else other than that journal; I know you think you're being the hero of this story but truthfully your just a silly little girl playing pretend." Her eye twitched at his sneering and demeaning tone, stupid man assuming she was just a little girl, he had no idea what she was capable of.

"Who are you and how did you get Karson to work with you?"

He slowly took off his mask and Elisa's eyes widened slightly not expecting him to show his identity so easily. She settled back slightly as she looked over his features. He looked a few years older than her father. His hair was jet black with a few grey eyes showing, his eyes were an ice-cold blue, almost silver, full of knowledge and malice. A dangerous couple. He ran his tongue over his teeth and put his arms behind his back.

"The name is Hamish Little Doll." There was a twinkle of pride in his eyes as he introduced himself which shattered when the boy let out a snort. They turned to look at the boy who had his hands over his mouth trying to hide the laughter leaking between his fingers.

"HAMISH! HAHAHAHA OH MY GOD WHAT A NAME! I THOUGHT FOR SOME REASON YOU WOULD HAVE A BADASS NAME BUT YOU GOT STUCK WITH HAMISH!" He howled and Elisa had to hide her smile behind her hand. Hamish glared at the insolent boy before ignoring him altogether.

"Last time Little Doll or things are about to get a whole lot worse for you."

"I Don't know what you're talking about! My mother didn't tell me anything else... you killed her remember." She added as an afterthought making her two cellmates look at her, one looking like the news was a blow to his stomach and the other in sorrow. Hamish scowled at her words.

"That wasn't meant to happen, the man who killed her was killed immediately after Little Doll, she had so much knowledge that we had hoped to obtain from her. We didn't realise you existed and when we came to know about you, we were always watching, trying to get you somewhere alone so we could grab you. But my idiot partner decided that it was better to simply watch you, that you probably didn't know anything." He threw his head back in a sudden cackle making them jump.

"How wrong he was! You were harbouring the very thing that could solve our little issue! Then it got better when daddy dearest here mentioned that his little project was hidden elsewhere. Only thing was that he didn't know where it was, said that his scientist wife was the only one with the knowledge of the whereabouts of this project. But by then his wife was long gone. But she told you didn't she. She must have told you." He searched the girls confused and scared face hoping she would finally give in.

"Who is your partner?" He growled like the monster he was at her question.

"Someone I regret putting my trust into, then again he had proven useful occasionally. You'll meet him at some point. Probably."

"Is it Karson?"

"Who is this Karson person? I wasn't aware you had a friend by that name... Get here! is there a Karson on that list?" He asked a man nearby who held a file in his arms. Her heart leapt into her throat as she realised, they had a file on her and her friends and family. Holy hell, they knew things about her! Then what he said hit her, Karson wasn't on the list of friends, why?

"Sir? He's here." Hamish groaned and sent a seething look towards Elisa.

"Sit tight Little Doll, I'll be back." The three sat in silence as they heard the footsteps gradually walk away, the silence only broken by another comment.

"You know I keep imagining him as Hamish from Alice in Wonderland, I can't stop seeing it." He snickered and she shook her head before focusing on him.

"You became The Unseen Pirate. I hardly recognise you."

"Is it because of my devilish good looks?" She rolled her eyes and sent an affectionate smile to the boy who had been locked away in one of her mind chests but had now managed to escape.

"Despite the circumstances, it's good to see you again Elisa. I missed your letters." She remembered the letters she used to send him until she hit 13 and truly understood the risks, she was taking by sending him letters. She had stopped immediately and pushed his existence to the back of her mind, not allowing herself to remember and miss him.

Now he was here and although it wasn't the best situation, she couldn't help but be thankful that she had been allowed to see him before she died; an outcome that was becoming more and more inevitable the longer they stayed in that grimy cell.

"It's good to see you too Levi."

21

Now

"I guess Paige decided to look over my file again on my family and realised I had siblings. I remembered seeing her look angry and she picked up the phone to call you, she was also angry that she didn't realise I had siblings before and said that it looked like their existence was hidden. I was surprised when she said Xander was going to have guardianship over me, confused that you didn't pick up the phone. Paige was excited for me and I was less, it was confusing you know? I knew I'd see my brothers again one day I just didn't you weren't going to be there."

Elisa finished her explanation of everything she had been through in the past few years. She explained the deaths she had to watch, how she grew attached to people only for her to push them away for their safety. She even explained why she had stopped writing to Levi who was quite hurt when he realised, he wasn't going to receive any more letters from his best friend. He also felt the ache in his chest when he realised the hell she went through.

William felt pure guilt as he listened to the way his daughter lived, what she had to go through because of her parents. It was unavoidable, they had hoped that after they had run away, they wouldn't be found out. Their identities had been erased from the Project system and so nobody should have known who exactly was on that project. Nor should they have been able to find them.

"So, these guys have been stalking you trying to figure out if you knew something?" Levi asked from his spot on the cot, his brows knitted together feeling a wave of protectiveness wash over him as he turned to look at the girl sat on the floor holding her father's hand tightly. She refused to move from his side and admittedly, William was in the same boat. He had just got his daughter back and he wanted to spend every moment he could with her. She nodded and sighed, a small smile coming onto her face as she remembered her London trip.

"Two bodies washed up on the beach last year and it scared Xander, so we made a plan to escape the village for a bit. He took us to London, and we spent Bonfire night watching the fireworks over the River Thames, dad it was magical." She giggled and William's smile widened at her soft giggle.

"What... what do your brothers do now? I've missed out on so much." She hesitated at his question. She wanted her brothers to have their moment with their father, she wanted them to be able to have the chance to update their father on what they had each gotten up to.

"I'll tell you the basics. Pres is in his last year of 6th form and will be leaving in July, Roman is an artist! You should see his work dad, they're amazing! Owen works in a Cafe that he owns; I didn't realise he owned it but yeah, he works there but also works at the library in the evening. Xander is a police detective and-"

"He's what?" William sat up straight ignoring the pain in his body. Elisa winced knowing her father was running through all the risks and possible dangers his eldest child could have gone through.

"Dad he's an amazing detective and protects the village and everyone in it. He knows how to stay low and the reason we went to London was to get us away from these people. We made a distraction and we believed they followed our bait, but they must have come after me when they realised we were completely aware of who they were and what they wanted. Or well I did in a way."

"Speaking of who are these people?" Levi asked and William sighed.

"I'm a scientist, well I was. My wife and I worked on a project together and made a breakthrough. We made a serum of a sort that would erase any diseases, any dangerous cells and would make that person healthy and strong. It wasn't something that would prevent them from ever getting sick, we didn't make it for that reason. We made it to help fight cancer, to help a young child who hadn't even had a chance to live. That was our goal. To make sure that everyone had a fair chance at life before nature took its course." He sighed and shook his head remembering the day they realised that their honest work could have been used for something worse.

"We ran, all of the scientists ran. The moment we realised that our work was going to be in someone else's hands. There are better scientists than me and they could easily use the serum to make it do the opposite. I wasn't sure how they planned to do that exactly, but I know from the whispers I hear through the walls that they planned to distribute the serum, make it into a drug that would be injected into the bloodstream and kill off the host in the most painful of ways." The teenagers shivered involuntarily, and Elisa realised just how dangerous the game she was playing was. She swallowed and tugged at her father's fingers to get his attention, his slightly darker hazel eyes meeting her lighter ones.

"Why are they still after me dad? What else did you and mum hide?" William swallowed his nerves and nodded before he spoke in a hushed voice.

"The journal was your mothers' diary, I've never read it, but I know it contained a lot of our findings, every failed test and god knows what else. She kept the small vial of the serum, Project Miracle. She was supposed to destroy it, but she grew too comfortable in the new life we made. But there was something else. Something she started and kept hidden. It was our private space whenever we weren't at the lab. We've always lived in Robin Hoods Bay munchkin. Well, we lived in York for a bit and I'm pretty sure we were on the road for the first few years of being on the run. But Robin Hoods Bay was always our to-go place. Your mother fell in love with the village itself, and I'll admit so did I. It was like something out of a storybook Lila used to read to me."

Although their lives were currently at risk, Elisa couldn't help but stare up at her father with awe twinkling in her eyes. She had always heard the stories from her mother's perspective but knew she left a lot of stories out. Hearing about her parents' lives from her father's side was exciting and new. Even Levi found himself leaning forward slightly in curiosity, he had also heard his aunt Delilah's stories and had always wanted to meet his best friend's knights and father.

"Mummy used to read to you?" Her voice was sweet and timid, and he couldn't help the low chuckle that slipped between his lips. He cradled her small hand in his own and rubbed his thumb across the back of her hand, he could feel the small scars that littered her knuckles and fingers.

"Yeah, she did. We used to have picnics in the lavender fields, cucumber and cheese sandwiches with pink lemonade. She would wear this white sundress with a sunflower print. She hated being a 'stereotypical girl' as she used to say but she loved dressing up and pretending to be a queen. She was one anyways." Elisa giggled whilst Levi gagged, the older West man smiled at the two before carrying on a wistful smile on his face as a memory of a gorgeous woman with an angelic smile played in his mind. Her green eyes shining in the sunlight and her hair dancing in the breeze.

"We would sit there for hours talking before she would pull out one of her books and start reading her book out loud to me. It became a small tradition that we carried on when Alex was born. Then Owen, Roman, Preston and finally you."

Another moment of her life she had no recollection of; her heart stung knowing she would never have moments like that again, moments with her entire family in one place smiling. She completely ignored the fact that he was meant to be telling her the big secret her parents kept hidden, all she wanted to do was hear the stories of her parents and what her family once was.

"I'm sorry but what's the secret?" Levi finally asked, sick of the tiptoeing around the subject, he wanted to know what these people were after and what he could do to help get them out of there. Elisa's smile slipped, and she lowered her eyes to her hand clasped within her fathers. She wanted this all over and done with, she just wanted to be able to sit and listen to the stories of William and Delilah West. William saw his daughters dejected look and swore that he would get her out of there, tell her story after story and hold her closely. He would never let her sit under a cloud of pain ever again.

"There's a secret Lab. Your mother said that we needed to find a secure location to hide anything important including Project Miracle. She didn't want to destroy it and hoped she could hide the project until the bad guys had been found out. But I vaguely remember her saying that there was an escape route, there was a way to destroy all the data and research once and for all. I do not remember where the lab is. She thought it would be best if only one of us knew and since she had moved to Cali with you, she decided that she should be the only one to know its location. Honestly, I think leaving with you was always her plan, to keep us all safe and separate until the time was right for us to all come home."

Silence.

Once again Elisa found herself mentally screaming at her mother. Why did she feel the need to be the world's saviour? Why couldn't she have just destroyed the data then and there? Why prolong it for so long? But she knew that those questions will never be answered. Her mother was long gone and whatever reasoning to why she hid the research instead of destroying it was buried with her.

"I need to find the lab, right? This is what mum wanted me to do, find the lab... any clue dad?" William sighed and shook his head regretfully.

"Whenever she took me there, she would blindfold me and put headphones on. We've only been once together, and I think she went before you guys left. I have no clue munchkin." Her shoulders dropped with the heaviness that pressed down on her.

"Maybe this is a good thing? They won't be able to find it, the secret stays with your mum." Levi tried to look at the positive side, but Elisa shook her head.

"They will never let us go... we have to get out of here and find that lab. It has to be close to home." William shook his head.

"Baby it's impossible to get out of here! These people are Scotland Yard and I'm pretty sure there must be some CIA agents from their base in America. These guys aren't normal policemen or anything. There's a lot of retired hitmen, trainee agents. These people are everywhere, we can't get away!" Elisa sat up straight and held her father's hand in her own firmly, determination blazing hot in her eyes making William smile internally. She looked so much like Delilah it almost hurt, the way their brows knitted together, and their noses scrunched up, the way their eyes would shine brighter when they were determined to do something.

"We can do this dad. We need to fight back, a distraction, something. I was knocked out when I first got here."

"Same." The men said in unison and she rolled her eyes. Some help they would be.

"Well clearly we're underground, I haven't seen one window in my time here and there are areas of the wall that are dirt," Levi said and she looked over at one of the walls he was pointing at, an entire wall made of dirt.

"So, we need to figure out which way is the surface. Do you have any idea how big this place is?"

"This is the only place they hold prisoners I think, there's an interrogation room and the treatment room-"

"Treatment?" William sighed at Levi's question and tried to avoid looking into his daughters' eyes.

"It's where they force information out of people." He stopped but Elisa didn't need him to continue to know how they forced information out of people, she knew it the moment he spoke up. Her father was in pain, a lot of pain and he had been for a very long time. She needed to get them out of here, she had to be the one in control for just a bit longer and then once they were safe and sound she could relax.

"We need to watch and listen. One small distraction and then we can get out of here." Elisa settled back onto the floor leaning her back against the tiles, her hand holding her father's which was still sat between the iron bars.

"Sleep munchkin, you'll need it." He said softly and with a resigned sigh and nodded and closed her eyes, she only hoped that they could somehow get out soon. She felt his hand stroking the back of her hand and with the low rumbling of Levi and her father talking, she soon drifted off.

"Elisa..." The voice broke through the darkness of her dream state, the clouds that surrounded her head began to part for the person trying to bring her back down to reality.

"Elisa!" Her eyes snapped open, and her hand shot out to slap the person in front of her, her hand connecting with cold flesh.

"JEEZ WOMAN!" Levi glared at the girl and rubbed his cheek.

"Next time don't get in my face when I'm asleep then you crackhead." She hissed back with a glare and a huff as she crossed her arms over her chest.

"Why did you wake me up anyway?"

"Your dad." Her head whipped around only to realise the cell next to her was empty, no blood, the cell door shut. Millions of scenarios rushed into her head and she felt her chest tighten as she only focused on the worst.

"Hey! I'm sorry calm down! He's gonna be okay? They took him an hour ago and-"

"Why didn't you wake me up?!" Her voice a deathly whisper causing him to shiver and take a small step away from the girl whose anger was simmering on the surface. One wrong word and she would probably rip his throat out. He swallowed and held his hands up in surrender, palms up.

"He told me to keep an eye on you, to not let you worry about him. They took him away without a fight which is probably why you didn't wake up." She studied his face that held nothing but sincerity, her head nodded, and she swallowed, gripping onto the iron bars as she pulled herself to a standing position. Her feet glided over to the cot Levi sat on and she perched herself next to him, her eyes trained on the spot her father had been before she had slept.

"He held your hand while he slept. He didn't want to let go until he had to." Levi's voice held a bit of sadness, something she didn't quite understand why. He breathed in and nodded as if he was accepting something.

"We're getting out of this, okay?"

"How can you be so sure?" He smiled at her softly spoken question, her eyes held so much pain that he just wanted to whisk her back to the time they would play tag on the beach, he wanted to take her back to the times where her and Leah would giggle as they hid from Levi in a game of hide and seek.

"Because your dad was sure of it, and you Wests sure are stubborn." A small laugh escaped her lips and she nodded in agreement. They sure were. The two sat in silence as they slipped into their thoughts, Levi wondering if his mother and sister had been notified that he hadn't turned up to his classes in a while. He had been walking to his morning College class when he had suddenly felt a sharp pain in his neck before darkness took him, and when he opened his eyes, he was in the musty old cell. Elisa's thoughts were on her brothers, wondering if they had figured out that she had been taken, that they were never safe despite their little distraction. She had wondered if they were safe and if escaping was the best thing to do. Maye this was her end?

BANG
CRASH
A fire alarm went off and pierced their ears.

Their head whipped towards the empty hallway which was now filling with yelling and shouting from one side. Men cursing and running away from what sounded like glass falling, smoke filled the hallways and they stood up in alert. What on earth was going on? Four guards came to the cell and grabbed the teens who struggled.

"Behave." One growled and Levi sent Elisa a warning look to listen until they figured out what was going on. They were led through the hall through another door, the room was another cell room except instead of bars separating them it was glass. Levi and Elisa were shoved into the free glass cell with William lying weakly on the ground in his glass cell next to them. She knelt on the ground and studied him with worry apparent in her eyes.

"What happened?" She demanded and watched as his head slowly turned to face her, his eyes bloodshot and drooping, bruising on his cheek and blood dripping from his nose and a cut on his lip.

"Just had a trip to The Treatment Room. Nothing to worry about Munchkin." He tried to send her a reassuring smile, but pain registered in his brain the moment he tried to lift his lips. Levi leaned against the glass wall and nodded, he felt sympathy for the weak man in front of him and admired him for the way he had carried on fighting.

"What's changed? Somethings happened for them to be panicking and rushing us here. This seems more secure."

William hummed in confirmation and shifted his body, so he was closer to the glass wall, his daughter on the other side with pained eyes.

"I know there's an experimentation room somewhere, I believe they thought they had managed to crack the serum, but it turned out to be a failure. Then one of the men had managed to drop a few chemicals and started a fire which they're currently having trouble dealing with. This is quite a small base so if they can't get the fire under control then we will be moved elsewhere, or maybe they'll leave us here..." The doors opened and two men walked in, their feet parted as they stood in front of their cell doors. Levi strolled up to talk to annoy the man in front of their cell.

"Were we bought here to die?" The guard scoffed.

"Obviously." He mumbled and Levi raised a brow as he made a face at the guards back.

"I can't tell if you're being sarcastic or not." He finally admitted and the guard huffed.

"Shut up."

"Do you know any other words?"

"Shut. Up." He had turned around to glare at the teen that matched his height.

"Okay so if you don't, you say No. N-O. Yeah? Bless ya man if we get out of here, I'll gift you a dictionary and direct you to the nearest school yeah?" The guard opened the cell door and pulled Levi by his shirt.

"Maybe I should cut out your tongue and replace it with a rose."

"What's your obsession with the rose? I'm genuinely really curious about-" He was cut off by the hand moving around his throat, squeezing hard to the point that his hands were slapping at the mans.

Elisa was up and ready, she kicked the back of his knees in making him buckle and fall, his hold on Levi loosening enough for him to quickly escape. She then delivered a sharp strike downward to hit the vagus nerve. She remembered reading about different techniques on how to knock someone out, something she thought she may need due to her dangerous life. A sharp strike on the vagus nerve can result in dizziness, disorientation, or even unconsciousness, she could faintly see the words directions showing in her mind and smirked proudly when the man's eyes rolled back, and he fell to the group in a heap.

"Nice one! When did you realise I was trying to rile him up as a distraction?" Her eyes widened slightly at her words and she flushed as she bit her lip and rubbed her arm up and down. He looked at her unamused and shook his head.

"You didn't did you- oh dear god not only are you Wests stubborn but also reckless." He looked angry and sounded angry for putting herself in harm's way, but she could also see the pride gleaming in his green eyes.

"Very reckless." A low voice said making them freeze. Two guards, there had been two in the room and now one was unconscious. Levi immediately stood in front of Elisa who rolled her eyes and stood next to him as she glared down at the man in the mask. She could feel his gaze lingering on her before turning to her father whose breathing was laboured.

"Now I'll be escorting you out of these cells and to a more secure place, you must obey my every instruction of else Dr West will die." Her eyes burned, and she nodded quickly offering her hands out for them to be tied. He grabbed her wrist harshly and took Levi's wrist also, another man entered the room and spared no glance towards the knocked-out giant on the ground; he then walked over to Williams curled up bruised body and somehow managed to help him stand on his weak legs.

They left the cells and marched through the halls once more. Levi frowned as he noticed that the shouting and yelling were louder, and the dark grey smoke had thickened. William began coughing as his lungs were weaker than everyone there due to his condition.

"WHERE ARE THOSE BRATS?! WHERE THE BLOODY HELL IS THAT USELESS DOCTOR?" A Man yelled, his voice thundering down the hallway, the guard mumbled something under his breath and quickened his steps causing alarm bells to ring in Elisa's head. She dug her heels into the ground and yanked on the man's arm which he wasn't expecting, Levi, caught on and elbowed him in the stomach before preparing to throw a punch. However, a hand caught it and the man wheezed as he rubbed his stomach.

"Call off your guard dog Muffin." He croaked; Levi huffed in annoyance at being called a dog. Elisa however tensed and she peered up at the man. His goggles had a black rim, but the lenses were clear whereas every other guard they had encountered had black lenses. Her eyes locked with dark grey eyes that looked cold and calculating but she knew that they could melt into snow.

"Who are you calling dog you son of a-"

"Karson?" The man's eyes lightened, and the corners crinkled indicating that he was smiling underneath the skeleton mask, although she was still unsure about who he was, she knew he was a better option than the men who had kidnapped her. There was a high chance that Karson was working with them but there were a lot of signs that pointed in the opposite direction.

Hamish was confused about a Karson and wasn't even aware she knew someone by that name.

Karson hadn't shown his face and she remembered seeing the twitch of curiosity wherever she mentioned his name.

Finally, if Karson was working for Hamish, then he would have stepped in and stopped her and Levi from knocking out the other guard, also the fact that people were now wondering where they had disappeared off to meant that this wasn't part of whatever Hamish had planned. She nodded slowly and sighed in resignation.

"I swear to all things holy Karson if you give me any reason to not trust you then I'll sike my guard dog on you." He chuckled at the serious look on her face and the way her eyes assessed him; he nodded holding out his large hand for her to shake, his movements urgent while still trying to stay calm, the other man watched in amusement and made sure William was still conscious.

"I promise I'll do everything to get you guys out of here and safe, I won't betray your trust. No need to set your dog on me." Levi sneered at the older man and crossed his arms over his chest.

"I'll bite your head off if you hurt her or Uncle Will." Karson blinked in surprise at the title he gave to William West but nodded in respect. Elise giggled and patted Levi's chest fondly.

"Down boy let's get out of here!" He mocked her behind her back but followed Karson who began to lead the teenagers further down the long hallway.

"Karson, we need to pick up speed the second explosive I planted in the lab is set to go off any minute."

"EXPLOSIVE?" They shouted in unison, horror on their faces. Karson and his partner rolled their eyes and ignored the dramatic teens and carried on pushing them along.

"HEY!" They looked behind them and saw four men rushing out of a room with their guns pointed their way.

"Okay... RUN!" They didn't waste a moment longer as they heard bullets shooting through the air. Karson and his partner wore bulletproof vests under their disguise and felt the bullets hitting the material, they were aware that they would most likely be covered in bruises, but their main priority was the two West family members and the young 18-year-old boy. Karson made sure he shielded the teens as much as he could whilst shooting back at the men and his partner rolled a small ball towards them.

"Cover your mouths kiddiwinks." He teased and they immediately covered their mouth and nose with their shirt or sleeves. She heard a small bang and hissing, a small glance behind showed the men coughing as they breathed into the red smoke leaking from the small ball. Elisa saw a staircase up ahead with two men guarding it, their guns ready and pointed directly at them. Karson tugged Elisa behind him and pulled two guns from his belt sending two bullets directly into the foreheads of the men who dropped within seconds, blood pooling under their heads making the girl look away not wanting her memories to make an appearance. Levi tucked her shaking hand into his and pulled her to his side as he notices her lag a bit.

"SHUT DOWN THE NEST!" Hamish's voice reached their ears and they pumped their legs to go faster as they heard another alarm go off and red lights start flashing.

"DOOR 2 SECURELY LOCKED." A computerised voice was heard, the door behind them shut closed but two guards managed to get through. There was a door slowly closing just before the staircase and Karson let out a determined growl as he practically shoved the teens through the door that was closing. Elisa heard a pained cry and turned to look back in the hallway, her heart pounding as she saw her father bleeding from a bullet wound in his arm, Karson and his partner quickly shot at the two guards left killing them instantly.

"COME ON!" The girl yelled as Karson quickly slid through the gap that was growing smaller and smaller, panic welling in her chest as she realised the inevitable.

"DOOR 1 SECURELY LOCKED."

"NO!" The glass door closed between them and Elisa looked around desperately for a control panel or button. Anything that would open the barrier between her and her father. Karson was rapidly talking to his partner with a walkie talkie while Elisa pounded her small fists against the thick glass. Levi felt his eyes sting as he watched his childhood best friend whimper and cry out for the door to open. She grabbed Karson's gun from his belt holster and tried to shoot at the glass, hoping she could crack it and break it. But the bullets merely bounced off and Karson snatched the gun away from her trying to get her to calm down. But she wouldn't.

"No, no, no, no, DADDY!" She screamed as she tried to get to him. She dropped to her knees in front of the glass doors, William managed to move his body in front of the glass door, his heart breaking as he saw the physical agony. Her hair was messy and sweaty, her clothes ripped and bloody, but she was still his beautiful baby girl. She was trembling and crying, her hands gripping her hair tightly.

"Elisa." His voice croaked over the blaring alarm. He called her name again and again louder and louder until he realised, she couldn't hear him. God, he couldn't talk to her, he couldn't reassure her that everything was going to be okay. He had honest faith that if he was meant to survive, he would. If not, then his story had simply come to an end.

Elisa heard a soft knock and after the second knock, she looked up. Her dad smiled at her softly and held a bloody hand up to the glass, she pressed her own bruised and dirty palm above his, studying the way his hand would have practically engulfed hers. She remembered not long ago how he held her hand and reassured her that everything would be okay. Her throat was clogged with emotion and she let out small whined of pain. Pain that hurt so much more than a physical wound. She looked into her father's hazel eyes, she memorised the everlasting love, she saw the pain and guilt in his eyes along with the regret and sadness. She had seen her father for the first and last time since she had left with her mum. This was how it was going to end?

He swallowed and pointed to himself, his index finger pointing to the centre of his chest before he covered the area above his heart with both hands, he then pointed at her and sobs escaped her lips as she understood what he was saying,

She could hardly see as she lifted her hand to point to herself, she covered her heart with both hands, her whole body shaking. She then lifted her finger and pointed at him, wails escaping her chapped lips and her arms pushing away Karson and Levi who were trying to pull her up the staircase.

William smiled sadly at the daughter he just met for the first time in years, the smoke beginning to fill the area around him. The man next to him helped him stand as he tried to speak to the West man. But William couldn't take his eyes off of his baby girl who was breaking in front of him. Karson gave a sad look to his partner and finally scooped Elisa into his arms ignoring her screaming and yelling that ripped his heart. Her arms reaching out towards the door where William stood with a soft smile, accepting the end of his story.

Levi rushed to the top and found a metal latch that he quickly opened, he pushed against the hatch door and welcomed the fresh air. Karson helped him push the hatch door open and they quickly rushed out onto a grassy field, the whole base had been underground and hidden from civilisation.

"WE NEED TO GO BACK. DADDY NO! DADDY!" She yelled out to the night sky.

Elisa managed to get out of Karson's grip and tried to go back, she needed to go back, she couldn't leave her dad down there, she could save him; she knew she could. Levi quickly grabbed her waist and pulled her into a tight hug, her arms trapped between his arms and her chest. They managed to pull her away before there were a great rumble and an explosion that shot out from the ground like a volcano. They were luckily at a safe distance meaning they weren't affected.

But as Elisa watched the flames reach for the sky, she let out a single ear piercing and heart-wrenching scream as she called out for her father.

This wasn't how she wanted to meet her father.

This wasn't how she wanted his story to end.

But this was reality, and boy was it cold.

22

Now

Death.

It comes to everyone eventually, wraps its icy arms around the people whose time had come to a halt. It envelopes them in the darkness... takes them away from the land of the living. Elisa had seen death, had brushed hands with it multiple times. She had stared into its eyes sometimes begging for the sweet release of life, but death had always rejected her, it wasn't time for her eyes to dim and her heart to freeze. It wasn't time and yet for some reason, everyone else around her was accepted into the dark embrace. A cruel joke played only on her.

The car ride was silent, her sniffles the only thing being heard over the soft rhythm of the car. Her cheek pressed against the cold window and she immediately felt a sense of deja vu, it wasn't that long ago since she was first bought to her childhood home, it wasn't that long ago that she had started a new page in her book and yet she had already gone through multiple chapters, multiple tragedies to get to where she was now. She had witnessed another life end so soon, too soon. Karson glanced at her now and then as he kept his eyes on the road and made sure they weren't being followed. Concern radiating from his calculating eyes that had momentarily melted. She still didn't know who Karson was, why he helped or how he knew where she was. But at that moment in time, she stopped caring. She wanted to care that millions of people could die if the bad guys found Project Miracle. She wanted to care that her brothers would miss her and feel lost if she never came home.

Yet she felt nothing but numbness, emptiness, distant and detached from the world. She didn't feel like she was living, that she had survived. Was this how she lived before her brothers? Had she once felt like this every day? The answer was yes, the moment her mother died she began hiding inside her mind, away from reality, safe and sound within the confines of her daydreams. She felt as though she was drifting through life again, she was going through the motions of blinking and breathing not seeing or feeling.

There are 7 stages of grief, 7 levels that a person unconsciously goes through, each level either harder than the one before or easier. She had gone through those stages' multiple times, but she had never really reached the final stage, perhaps that's what made her turn out the way she was. She was stuck permanently in one of those stages, one of those levels.

Whenever something good happens in her life, it was like she was seeing a preview of the next juncture, of what could be if she managed to overcome those challenging feelings. She was no longer in shock of the event that had just taken place, the numbness was slowly being overtaken by the fire that spread over her heart. The pain flowing through her body like the warm blood that swam through her veins; no the pain isn't what she focused on. It was the guilt. The guilt that she couldn't save her father when he was within her grasp, guilt that she got to see him one last time, guilt that her brothers would never see him again.

Guilt that she was alive.

Her eyes focused on the blur of the world outside her window, the rain pelting against the car lulling her into an almost trance as she listened to the calmness it bought. Her mind still focused on the memory she had of her father. Her fists clenched and her nails dug unforgivingly into her palm, words echoing in her mind, shouting at her as she mentally beat herself up.

Selfish. Idiot. Your fault. They'll never forgive you. Murderer.

Murderer.

Murderer.

A hand enclosed over hers and gently pried her fingers away from digging into her skin. She felt the distressed looks piercing the side of her face, but she refused to bathe in it, refused to acknowledge the sympathy and pity. It was her fault her mother died, her fault her father died. Why didn't she do more to help them?

"Muffin..." Karson called out gently afraid that a single word could tip her even further off the edge, what they didn't realise was that she was already holding onto the ledge of sanity and was willing to let go. She wanted to fall into the inky pits of regret, guilt, and sorrow. Levi held onto the girl's hand, somehow knowing that despite her acceptance of falling off the deep end, she needed someone to hold onto her tightly. Like she had been doing her whole life to every person she had met, she wanted, no, needed someone to save her for once.

"It's ok." Her childhood best friend mumbled as she turned her palm over, their fingers twining together as she gave him a broken smile, a single crystal tear slipping down her bruised and dirty face as she shook her head and spoke through trembling lips.

"No, it's not." Her voice emanating so much agony it wounded the boy's hearts.

Alexander sat cross-legged on the floor of his parent's bedroom. It had been three days since his dove went missing, three days of looking for clues and disposing of small cameras and microphones they had found littering the house. His hair was mussed up and dark bags hung from beneath his eyes carrying the weight of his worries and fears. Every day his friends would come round and help him brainstorm, they would search the town without making it too obvious that they knew something was wrong. They didn't know how many people were watching them or how many cameras and microphones they could have missed. They stopped talking in the house and would instead pace the long stretch of beach as they tried to figure out their next action.

He didn't want to ever lose hope this time, he knew his baby sister would come home to him with or without his help, and when she did, he would never let her go, never let her wander into the darkness of the world again. They had searched their home for anything she may have left, anything that could help them, he didn't expect to find a hidden safe. They had hunted for anything that could tell them the passcode, but when they were running out of ideas, Alexander suddenly remembered he was a police detective with skills that could prove useful. He scrambled off the floor and rushed into the main bathroom, looking through the drawers and cupboards until he found the objects he was looking for. His feet pounded across the carpeted floor as he rushed back to his parents' room attracting the attention of Preston who finally peeked out of his darkroom. They had all been handling Elisa's disappearance differently and Preston had been the first one to hide his face from everyone.

He shuffled after Alexander and took the time to properly observe the room he used to find comfort in. When he had a nightmare, he would climb into the bed with his father who would stroke his hair and talk in a low whisper until Preston had fallen asleep. He could hardly remember his fathers' voice but smiled slightly at the loving memory his father had left him with. He looked over and saw Alexander sat on the ground looking at something behind their parents' clothes and boxes. They hadn't touched anything in this room and since Elisa's disappearance, they had all been in the room a few times.

"What are you doing?" His little brothers voice questions meekly and Alexander ushered him over.

"Mum and dad were scientist's, had loads of secrets. They had to have had a place for hiding things and Elisa probably knew that and went looking for their hiding space. When I was looking around, I saw these boxes had been shifted and the door was open slightly, so I looked myself. They had this hatch door hidden behind all these boxes and I'll bet the journal is in here." He lifted a makeup brush that he had dipped in talcum powder and lightly dusted it across the keypad, he then blew gently across the metal and a proud smirk lifted his lips as he saw four numbers had powder attached to them more than the other numbers.

"Is that...?"

"Our dear little sisters' fingerprints, now we know which numbers were used we just have to figure out the order." Preston rushed to his room and came back with a notepad and pen. He wrote down the numbers.

1480

"Have you found anything?" Owen's voice interrupted the youngest and eldest boys thinking as Roman and he took their places on the floor next to their brothers.

"Found a safe, just trying to figure out the sequence. 1480. It's trial and error." Preston shrugged and handed the notepad to Roman who began writing different orders of the numbers.

"Okay, let's try this. we could have 1084. 4801, 8130, 0183, 30-"

"1-8-0-4. It's 1804 I'm sure of it." Alexander interrupted with a hesitant but determined expression. His parents were sentimental people and everything they said or chose always had a meaning behind it. His fingers pressed against the cold metal, powder transferring onto his finger as he typed in the combination, 1-8-0-4. 18th of April. His birthday. A small smile lit up his face as he heard a promising beep and the whirring of metal. He turned the handle, and he faintly heard his brothers cheering and slapping his back in pride.

Inside the safe he saw the red journal sat among files and boxes; guns also stacked neatly along with other notebooks. He took everything out and spread them in front of him and his brothers. Owen went to say something but Roman slapped a hand over his lips with a warning glare to not speak. Alexander frowned confused and went to ask Roman what his problem was when he heard it. Gravel crunching as the wheels of a car rolled over the gravel outside, they hadn't called anyone over. The West boys jumped into action and quickly stuffed the books into a bag, Preston threw the rucksack over his back while roman and Owen held two carrier bags between them, The small boxes in each of them. Alexander held the journal to his chest along with the vial, a gun in each of their hands as they crept to the hallways.

"Okay... plan. We need to get downstairs and out the backdoor, my keys are on the kitchen table and I'll grab it as we go through there, then we drive around a bit hopefully lose them and if need be we call the others to meet us elsewhere got it?" They nodded at their older brothers plan and began to move. They heard a car door slam shut as they got to the kitchen door; they paused as they listened carefully for any indication as to what the mystery person was doing. Alexander grabbed the keys, and they opened the door only to freeze at the gun pointed at them. The West boys immediately pointed their guns at the person in front of them but none of them made a move to pull the trigger and end a life. Alexander clenched his jaw as he glared at the man before him.

"Where is she?" Karson lowered his gun and sighed at his best friend; he hated the way things had turned out. Karson had grown up with Alexander, knew practically everything about him and been part of their family like Andre and Finley had been. The three of them had rough home lives and William and Delilah West had loved and cared for them as their sons did. Karson had been there when Delilah left with the little muffin, he had watched his friends curl in on themselves and look for answers as to why their mother left, he had held Alex in a hug when they discovered that William West wasn't coming home. He had backed up Alex in arguments and watched him protect his younger brothers from bullies in school, he had clapped his hands in pride when his best friend had graduated and become their villages Police Detective.

Karson and Alexander had been through thick and thin together and just as Karson had been there for Alex, it was the same the other way round. They trusted each other with their life and had never been aggressive towards each other. Alexander's eyes were filled with so much pain and betrayal, it stabbed at his heart. This is what happens when you keep secrets from the people you love and care about most; they don't know what to believe other than the facts or evidence someone else may have shown them. Karson had lost a lot in his life, his parents, close friends, a mentor. He refused to lose the West siblings, his chosen family.

"Alex man I need you t-"

"Where did you go? You didn't answer your phone and obviously, you weren't at home otherwise you would have answered the door when we went to check. Three days..." Roman piped up as he scrutinised the man before him. He was still hesitant to believe that someone they had trusted and loved for years could be behind their sisters' disappearance and helping the people who killed their parents. But the facts were there in front of them; he was missing the moment Elisa went missing, hadn't picked up his phone and the fact that Elisa had suddenly become wary of him meant that he had done something or was hiding something that the rest of them had overlooked. Karson rubbed the back of his neck and pocketed his gun.

"I can explain I promise, I know this looks bad but... we need to move somewhere safer than this place. They'll be back-" The click of the safety being turned off made him pause in his ramblings.

"Who will be back? Huh? What do you know mate?" Alexander's voice was slow and steady and if they didn't know him better, they would have thought he was completely unaffected by the turn of events. The sky rumbled and droplets of cold rain splattered harder around them sounding loud in the sudden silence as eyes flickered from one person to another.

"Bloody hell Alex, it's me! Just calm down and think about this you know me! Do you think I'm here to hurt you? Any of you?" He felt hurt but knew Alexander was simply scared and confused, he didn't know who he could trust, and his brotherly instincts were mixing with the fatherly instincts he had acquired when he turned 18; the eldest West didn't know what to think but his main priority was his youngest siblings and getting rid of any threats.

"WHERE IS MY BABY SISTER!" Steam coming out of his ears as he pointed a gun to the centre of his best friends' forehead. He swallowed and took a step out of his house, his stare unwavering. Preston was gently pushed behind Roman to protect him from anything gut-wrenching they may see.

"Alex bro, please it isn't what you think, hear me out-"

"HEAR YOU OUT?! WHY THE HECK SHOULD I LISTEN TO YOU?" Karson shushed him and looked around nervously, hoping that none of the enemies was close by. He didn't blame Alex in the least, he would be surprised if they didn't wonder where he had vanished to at the same time their sister had disappeared.

"Stop shouting, Muffin is okay I just left her-"

"With whom? The same people who killed my parents?" A cold and pain-filled laugh escaped his lips; Owen quickly intervened and stepped in front of his older brother whose face had gradually become red with anger and frustration, his words angry and filled with venom as he spat back at the man, they all saw as their chosen brother. Although Alexander felt the hatred rising in his throat, the tremble of his hand betrayed his true feelings.

"No, she's safe from them, I... I found her and saved her from them. Alex please just come with me. I don't want them to come for you as they did with Elisa and your parents." Owen looked at his brother with a soft and gentle look, trying to bring back the soft and understanding man they all knew.

"Maybe we should hear him out bro, he knows where Elisa is, and we do know him! If he was truly on the bad side, then he would have killed us years ago whenever we were vulnerable." He tried to reason with Alex who paused as he thought something over, his head tilting slightly the way Elisa did whenever she was confused or thinking of something.

"Did you know?"

"Did I know what?" Karson swallowed at the question, immediately knowing what Alex was asking. Alexander's nostrils flared, his tongue darting out to wet his chapped lips as his eyes roamed his friends face, patches of dirt and spots of blood on his skin that he had missed.

"Did you know how... were you aware before Elisa... Did you know when my mother died?" Karson simply bowed his head and his shoulders dropped giving the West boys the answer they didn't want to hear, he nodded, and his sweaty hand tightened on the gun.

"I should kill you." His voice cracking, Karson smiled sadly and stepped closer so that the metal of the gun pressed against his warm skin.

"Then do it. Don't hesitate, do what you always do. Trust your gut."

The two stared each other down steadily, unwavering. He wanted to hurt his best friend, hurt his best friend the way he hurt him. But after a moment Alex let out a hiss and lowered the weapon, his shoulder heaving and jaw clenching. He bit down on his lip and groaned in frustration, Karson slowly placed his hand on top of the gun and embraced the West man who hugged him back.

"I promise I'm going to explain everything to you. I will never let anyone get hurt, I swear on my life that I will always put Muffin and the boys first." Alexander nodded and pulled back, his eyes trailing over his brothers.

"Can we go see Lissy? I think I deserve a hug after she gave me a heart attack. I'm too young and beautiful to get grey hairs." Owen tried to lift the atmosphere and it briefly made their lips twitch, however, the rigid countenance on Karson made them pause and their protective instincts rise.

Nobody tells you how you must feel after someone you love dies, nobody tells you how you should prepare yourself, how the world seems so dull. She had only just reunited with her father before he was viciously ripped away from her. Instead of her leaving him again, he left her, maybe she just wasn't destined to have a family, maybe her brothers would be taken away from her soon too. She had lowered her guard way too much and all those emotions she had denied herself of, were making a rushing appearance. She had never fully recovered or mourned the death of her mother and now she would have to mourn the death of her dear father. Two parents' death she had seen first-hand, and her mind wanted to shut down forever.

Alexander didn't speak to anyone as they got out of Karson's car and made his way to the little cottage that was hidden in the treeline. He opened the unlocked door and faintly heard Karson yell that she was in the living room; his feet hurried across the carpeted floor and into the living room. It was a simple room with cream walls that were empty of any pictures, the carpet was an off-white with a fluffy grey rug in the middle, a small table on top of the rug which held three cups. The sofas were cream and looked like they had hardly ever been used, the whole room looked like it hadn't been lived in and gave the room a desolate feeling. The only thing giving it warmth was the fireplace that currently had a fire burning, crackling in the silence.

Elisa sat on the ground in front of the fire with Levi sat next to her holding her hand, he would squeeze her hand, so she knew he was there for her when she was ready to breakdown on the outside and not hold those feelings to herself. Although she was his childhood friend, he hadn't been there for her when everything first went downhill, he didn't know the extent of her torment, or how much it had damaged her. Her eyes looked dull and empty of life as she watched the flames lick the coal and dance to an unspoken tune. Her mind a million miles away and heart being beaten down by her feelings.

"Elisa?" A familiar voice broke through her fog, but she refused to meet his eyes and carried on staring into the flames, Levi subtly moved away towards Karson who led him out of the living room. He knew they needed to talk, that Elisa had to tell them what happened, and it was a private family matter. They deserved that much at least.

Roman frowned as his eyes latched onto a discolouration on her wrist, he stormed over and knelt next to his little sister who had been the cause of the sleepless nights he and the others had been experiencing the past few days. He wanted to scold her for her recklessness and for not telling them straight away of her concerns, they would have helped her figure it out together, he thought they got through to her that she wasn't alone anymore. Now he wondered just how much she kept to herself and if she had ever trusted them.

Looking at her face made him freeze, and the anger immediately left his body. He looked up at his brother and shook his head slightly feeling hopeless, he wasn't in his element. Sure, he loved his sister, he had seen the secretive side of her, the happy side, the sad side, the annoying side but this?

This side was one he had never seen and wished to never see again.

"Elisa? Hey, talk to me." Alexander finally said trying to get her to look at him. He kept calling her name feeling the concern and irritation mix.

"For crying out loud Elisa LOOK AT ME PLEASE!" If he wasn't feeling anger before, he sure felt it now, like a volcano erupting over a secluded island. Her cheek was bruised on one side in what looked like a handprint, her lip red and slightly swollen, a cut on her hairline. Her hair was wet as if she just showered, and he swore that the shirt she was wearing looked familiar. Her eyes drifted to his chest and he shook his head, it was like he was meeting her all over again, except she looked more detached than when he first met her.

"What did they do to you?" She couldn't find the words she wanted to say as her brother began throwing questions at her, each one becoming more desperate than the last as the worry ate him up. Preston looked scared for her and Owen looked like he had seen a ghost while Roman looked like he was ready to kill someone. Someone had hurt their sister and they were out for blood.

"Who were they?"
"Did you see their face?"
"Who is the boy?"
"Who the heck hurt you?"
"Are you okay?!"
"Damn it to hell talk to me, Elisa!"
"Did you see anything?"
"Do you know what they're planning or after?
"ELISA JUST TELL ME PLEASE!"

"IM SORRY!" She yelled at him, her voice hoarse and croaky. She stood up letting the blanket that had been draped over her shoulders pool at her bare feet. Her eyes wild and erratic, like a caged animal seeking to escape.

"Elisa what-"

"You want to know what they did right now? Just leave me be for a moment Xander, let me BREATH! Just let me process what the hell happened and how I can tell you. Let me try to figure out how I'm supposed to look you all in the eye after what I had seen! JUST LEAVE ME BE FOR ONCE I JUST WANT TO BREATH!" Her hands slid into her hair and tugged harshly at the wet locks, her chest heaving as she felt her composure slip. The tell-tale signs of a panic attack had Alexander take a step forward, but Karson finally stepped in.

"I've just got her out of there man give her space to process, god, knows she needs it after-"

"I may not have killed you at that moment but if you don't get out of my face and let me talk to MY sister then I won't hesitate to end you." He growled and Karson shook his head having about enough. Sometimes his friend could be so thick to what was going on right in front of him. She may not be his blood sister, but he loved her just as much as her brothers did.

"Look at her Alex. Get off your royal high horse and think that hang on maybe something horrible happened to her while she was in the hands of your mothers' murderer. Think that maybe, just maybe you need to calm down and watch your tone as you try to understand what happened to her." He stared at Karson wide-eyed, he knew he was right, he needed to calm himself.

Karson rubbed his arm reassuringly.

"She needs you more than ever. You need each other."

Elisa looked up when Alex took a step towards her, his eyes searching her red-rimmed eyed.

"It's alright, I'm here." She let out a shaky breath.

"I'm so sorry... He was there. Daddy was there and he, he wanted to come home he missed and loved you so much." Their faces paled at her words and Preston sank into the sofa next to him, Alexander wanted to cry and immediately reached out to his baby sister. Once again, he found her sobbing into his chest, however, it wasn't like the last time, this was fresh pain, this was pure heartbreak as she clung onto his shirt.

"I tried to save him I did, I didn't want to leave him I'm sorry, I tried I promise Xander, I wanted to bring him home and I didn't. They hurt us but I'm okay, they hurt him badly every day, they kept asking us questions and they wouldn't stop. Oh, it was dark so dark, I thought I'd never see the light again, I couldn't breathe down there! Then he was gone. He was there one moment and the next it was just fresh air and a boom, and I felt like I was dying. But I wasn't, I couldn't have been otherwise I wouldn't have felt the pain right here! I couldn't save him and now... now I'm gonna lose you. I don't want to lose you too Xander."

Owen gently took her into his arms and sank to the ground, his hand rubbing her back and his lips pressed against her head. Her body shaking violently as she blurted out her trauma. He felt his heart cry for the girl who continuously had her heart smashed, when would she be at peace?

"You're not losing any of us Lissy sweetheart, shhh, it's okay. It'll all be okay. Its wasn't your fault and if we have to convince you forever, we will. Darling you're just a child, this isn't your job. You can stop fighting for us Lissy, let us fight for us."

His voice soothing and loving, he didn't bother hiding the devastation in his voice and instead let it seep through his words. They were allowed to feel, allowed to cry and he believed it would help her if she saw that they were all in the same bought and wouldn't shun her. They were all hurting, and they would all be there to help each other breathe a little easier.

"I can't do this anymore." Her voice a broken whisper that clutched Roman's heart in an iron grip, words he had said once to Owen not long ago not realising the effect it had on his older brother until he felt it himself. He felt like a failure, Alexander feeling the same way while Preston just wanted to hold her and offer his shoulder as they cried together. She was so strong, so strong but they were reminded that she was just a little girl, she was just a child who hadn't lived the way she should have.

Once upon a time, the thought of her was a burden in the back of their minds, but within a short while, she had quickly regained what was hers, to begin with. She had their whole attention and hearts; she was their world and would always be. Elisa vaguely noted how her brothers all sat around her and Owen, their arms winding around each other in a protective cocoon, as they sobbed and held each other tightly.

Grief had many levels, many methods of showing itself. It all poured out of her as she cried for all her losses, all her challenges and sacrifices. She just wanted her mother to brush her hair to the side and press a kiss to her forehead. She wanted her father to hold her hand and stroked the skin, but this, this with her brothers was the only thing keeping her together; they were the only family she had left. She tasted salt on her lips and let out a shuddering breath as she repeated the only words that ran through her head.

"I'm sorry."

23

Now

Karson Hughes grew up as a single child with absent parents. His mother and father loved him dearly there was no doubt about that, but they never made the time for their son. They were never there for his first day of school, they weren't the ones to clean his bloody nose after he and Alex got into a fight, they weren't the ones to hold him tightly when he shed tears. So when his parents one day never returned home and a man turned up this door telling him that his parents had passed on, he ran straight to the Wests home seeking comfort.

Delilah and William West were his chosen parents, the West siblings his chosen brothers and sister. He loved them all dearly and despite not sharing the same blood, they were his family no matter what. His aunt had moved in to look after him but he hardly spent his time at home, choosing instead to stay with his friend at every waking hour. When Elisa and Delilah left, he was the one to listen to Alex weep and question whether it was his fault; he held his best friend and brother tightly as he cried into his arms not allowing himself to shed any tears. But Karson felt it the way his best friend did. He felt the heartbreak and loss of Delilah and Elisa, in his heart they were also his mother and sister. They had gone and Karson felt just as lost as the Wests.

When the two female Wests had left, the remaining family members changed. Alexander grew up and slipped into his rightful role as big brother, Owen became softer and more understanding as he wanted to help them all smile, Roman became an angry little boy who would snap at everyone as he hoped for his best friend to come home, whilst little Preston would innocently ask when his mummy was going to come home with baby Eli; until he began to slowly forget about baby Eli and what his mother looked like. The other boys were partly grateful and jealous that he didn't feel the same pain as them, 'blissfully unaware' Owen would sometimes joke but would feel the sting of reminder.

Life as always carried on, the boys slowly growing into men, their personalities hidden under a facade that only Karson, Andre, Finley and William were able to bypass. Of course, there was the odd person that would jump into their lives and were able to catch a glint of the real West Boys; those people never really stuck around and would jump back out of their lives voluntarily or sometimes unwillingly.

Of course, life seemed to have it out for this specific family and so when Alexander and Karson were in their last year of 6th form, they came home to an empty house. No sign of William, no note, his phone still on charge. They waited for hours, waiting for William to come home and make them dinner. Karson, Alexander and Owen were capable of cooking small meals and had taken it upon themselves to feed the younger boys.

Karson remembered that night like it was yesterday. He remembered waving goodbye to Andre and Finley who were picked up by their parents. Alexander was arguing with a stubborn Roman who refused to go to bed until their father came home while Owen was silently cleaning the kitchen and living room with a distant look in his eyes.

Little 10-year-old Preston was scared and confused, they had never stayed up that late and he didn't understand why his daddy wasn't home to tuck him into bed. Karson took it upon himself to gently guide the smaller boy up to his bedroom and like so many times growing up, helped him get ready for bed. Preston watched Karson's worried face the entire time, wondering when someone was going to tell him what was going on. The Hughes boy said a quiet goodnight and stood up to go and help his best friend with Roman who was now raising his voice slightly.

"He's not coming back... is he?" The quiet and vulnerable voice made him stumble and he didn't want to meet those light brown eyes that he knew was staring up at him in hope, hope that he was wrong. Karson swallowed thickly and sighed.

"I don't know little man, but I know he loves you so so much." Preston nodded and turned in his bed to face his window, the clouds hiding the stars and the moon peeking out every so often. A small tear tracked down his cheek as a feeling of abandonment settled in his chest.

"I love you, daddy." He whispered into his pillow and squeezed his eyes shut, hoping that when he woke in the morning, that entire night had been a bad dream and his father would come to tickle him awake.

Karson remembered that morning when Preston's shining and happy smile faded as he saw the policemen sat in the living room, he remembered how the 10-year-old shuffled over to a crying Owen and hugged him tightly, Romans face void of emotion and Alexander talking with the policemen and social services about living arrangements. Karson watched his best friend grow up once again in a matter of seconds as he chose to protect and keep his family close to him.

The West family had never had it easy; they had lost their mother, father, sister and childhood; Karson Hughes was present to see it all.

When he finished 6th form, he applied for a Police Force Apprenticeship, Alexander sharing the same dream of becoming a hero to their family and others, they never wanted to lose anyone they loved and cared about ever again. They both studied and trained, showing their dedication and loyalty. They were together through it all... until Karson was noticed. Why they picked him only, he never understood until a year later. They had always had their eyes set on Karson, especially since his parents also worked for the same people he would soon work for before they passed away.

Alexander was proud that his friend had been recruited by a Police Force out of town and was going to carry out his career elsewhere. What nobody but Karson knew was that it was a cover. He hadn't been recruited by a police force out of town, no he had been noticed by an agency he never would have dreamed of working for. He went through training and lessons; he shadowed other people and learnt the gist of his new job and life. Within a year Karson had worked his way through the ranks of his new job. Alexander and the others knew nothing of his job as they weren't allowed to for their safety and protection, and so MI5, Agent 839, was simply known as Sergeant K Hughes.

The West family was a known cold case within the agency and the moment Karson found out everything his chosen family was hiding without them realising it, made up his mind. This was how he could protect his chosen family. He would protect the West boys from any upcoming dangers whilst looking for William West who they believed wasn't dead. He would go undercover whilst having the advantage of being near them to make sure nobody hurts or takes them away.

He was doing well, he managed to track down the people who attempted to kill Roman in the first car accident; he had pulled an unconscious Roman out of the car and left him in the safe hands of one of his teammates before he drove after the black car. Karson had successfully taken down the small base that was located in Robin Hoods Bay and even found a map of where other bases would be. He sent his teammates to the closest bases, going to some himself to try and get rid of the threat. Of course, some bases were hidden too well, and he couldn't get to them which kept him on his toes, but everything was still going well.

Until Elisa West came back home, her eyes full of the darkness of trauma and knowledge that was too heavy, for a child her age, to hold. One look in her eyes, one moment of observation told him that she was aware. That she knew exactly what skeletons her parents had tried to hide from them; Elisa knew things that nobody else did and Karson knew that he would have to slowly gain her trust and get the information he needed to protect her and the others.

He was doing well, until Christmas. Karson had always managed to sweep their rooms of the house not to be nosey but to make sure that nothing was amiss and that no monster would jump out at them. Everything was normally okay but, on that day, he saw something lying in the centre of Elisa's bed, her window wide open and curtains billowing in the wind. He quietly shut her bedroom door behind him and scanned her room to make sure there were no microphones or cameras; once he was sure, he shut her window, locked it, attached a small flush mount alarm to the bottom of the window frame which would alert him if her window was opened; the weather was freezing and he knew for a fact that no matter the weather, Elisa always kept the windows closed as she hated the cold.

He picked up the black rose from her bed with a gloved hand and his muscles tensed as he realised that if he hadn't noticed the window and rose, she could have been gone the moment she closed her door behind her. He swallowed and left the room as he heard Preston rush upstairs, he quickly shoved the rose in his back trouser pocket hoping he hadn't just crushed his first physical clue in a long time, he wanted to see if there were any blood or skin cells leftover on the stem or petals. He casually left the room once Preston walked into his bedroom and made it sound and look like he had left the bathroom.

"You good man?" Alexander teased and he rolled his eyes as he joined his friends and family in the living room. He smiles softly and allowed himself to relax as he enjoyed the moment they were given. But he knew he would have to figure out how to save his family without breaking cover soon, especially as he saw Elisa's eyes harden and her body tense as she saw the rose no doubt peeking from his coat pocket. He tried to hide it by casually shoving his hands in his pockets, but he knew that the youngest West was also probably the cleverest. She was no doubt thinking the worst and he was trying to fabricate a story. He had a job to do, protect his family undercover, he couldn't afford to lose their trust too soon. He hoped he had enough time before everything went downhill.

Elisa sat on the sofa with Owens' arm around her shoulder, his fingers absently playing with her hair as he listened to Karson tell his side of life. Preston was on the other side of Elisa, his head laying on her lap with her hand in his hair covering as much comfort she could whilst in her fragile state. Levi, Sasha and Cyrus were in a heated glare down for a reason Elisa didn't understand yet, Andre and Quinton sat on another sofa as they watched Alexander pacing the room shooting incredulous looks every so now and then to Karson. Roman casually walked back into the room and took a huge gulp from an orange juice carton.

"You knew this entire time that our little sister was in danger?" Roman clicked on and his eyes burned into the side of Karson's head.

"NO! I knew your mother died and how she died but I was under the impression that she would be safe hidden away in the system. We weren't aware that she was being followed as the people who would foster her never mentioned anything out of the ordinary, just that they couldn't look after her." He defended himself.

"Look okay it's fine. We can put it all behind us now. She's here now and we know what's going on. It's fine." Alexander tried to defuse the situation but didn't realise that his words had done the exact opposite, making the small flame of anger that was hidden under all the fear and sadness in her heart, burn brighter as if suddenly remembering she was allowed to feel that emotion. She hated it, hated how they disregarded everything she went through and that everything was perfect now they were here.

"Fine? What do you mean its fine now? None of this is fine. Nothing has been fine since I told you guys everything. It's only got worse." Elisa piped up making Alexander sigh and looked at her from the corner of his eye.

"Dove just rest. Don't worry about it we're here now." Her eye twitched at his obvious dismissal and she sat up straight. Were here now, no. That wasn't the answer. A scoff escaped her and she shook her head fighting the urge to punch something.

"So, what, you're here now. You are only here now because Paige found out about you. Otherwise, we would probably have never met again! You would all be blissfully unaware, growing up and living out your life while I handled all this by myself." Her voice raised in pitch and everyone focused on the girl they realised was no longer trapped in the shock.

"Lissy girl, calm down its oka-" She ripped out of Owens hold and glared at him, not caring at how his eyes lost its sparkle and he looked up at her with a sad look. She needed to get everything out, she needed them to understand. They had never really talked about their differences growing up, sure they forgave each other and pretended everything was okay. But they hadn't spoken about their feelings and it wasn't okay. They didn't understand what she went through, they forgot that she was alone and was used to doing things by herself. There were things her brothers would say or do that made her fingers clench, 'we're here now' being one of them. As if the past didn't matter.

"It's not Owen. We all know that I was practically forced on you and if you had a choice then you wouldn't have given me a second thought. I was a burden remember. You hated the thought of me."

Quinton felt sympathy flash through his heart as he realised why she suddenly sounded and looked like a madwoman. She was overwhelmed from the death of her father, she was mourning the death of her parents alone as she was the only one to have seen them both die first-hand, she had never gotten the closure of her brothers' childish thoughts and he knew that they had never really talked about everything they felt growing up. It was pouring out of her now in a jumbled mess that made no sense, but he knew exactly what was happening which was why he gently tugged Sasha, Cyrus and Levi into the kitchen. Finley and Andre following but staying close to the West family in case they had to interfere.

"We didn't hate you, Elisa, we just didn't know... we didn't know what to believe or..." Alexander tried to defend himself but even he could not think of anything. The moment he saw his little sister, all negative thoughts escaped his mind and now that she was calling him out on the once felt emotions, he couldn't get past the guilt.

"YOU HATED WHAT YOU DIDN'T UNDERSTAND! YOU HATED ME... because you didn't understand. You can't excuse yourselves that you didn't hate me and that it was just childish processing. You can't just pretend you never felt those things and that suddenly everything in the past doesn't matter because WHOOP DE DOO 'You're here now'. You did hate me. Even if it was just a slither of hate that was hidden beneath all that confusion and anger... the hate was still there."

"For god's sake Elisa what are you crying about now? We have more important things to talk about." Roman asked, all of them tired and not paying attention to their words. She sent him a glare as her anger peaked, matching the anger of her hot-headed brother. She stepped closer to him making his back straighten as he looked down at her.

"Are our thoughts of each other not important enough for you? Is the pain I went through meant to stay hidden while you guys act like the heroes of my story? You don't know what it's like because your life wasn't as painful as you think it is," Alexander ran his hands through his hair letting out a frustrated breath knowing that Roman was triggered, and his defence mechanism was kicking into place. Preston frowned at her words and looked at the floor not sure whether he should join in on the shouting match about to take place or stay out of it.

Owen clicked onto the same thing Quinton had and relaxed in his seat. His brothers needed this wakeup call since they were the ones harbouring those ill feelings growing up. Owen had never once blamed his sister but the two of them know that deep down, the other three, well probably just Alexander and Roman, may still have those feelings of hatred. Feelings they had to get rid of before it festered into something bigger. Karson nodded at Owen knowing that this had to happen now before they made a plan that could put them all in danger, the cards had to be laid out, so they had no regrets if things went wrong.

"So, hang on PRINCESS. Are you saying that the pain we went through wasn't bad? Are you saying that because you're the youngest that we should hide our pain and fix you? Are you saying-'

"IM SAYING IT WAS BETTER THAN WHAT I WENT THROUGH BECAUSE I WAS ALONE! I WAS ALONE BUT YOU HAD EACH OTHER. I WAS FIGHTING FOR US ALL BY MYSELF." Roman still towered over her but his glare wasn't as heated as before as he listens to her words. They had never heard her talk this much at once except when she first broke down. They were once again unsettled by her words and slapped with the reality that she was only a 16-year-old. Her eyes blurred as she tried to stay strong in front of her big brothers, to carry on holding that iron facade she had always had. She had been fighting for her family for years, never complaining or demanding the world to give her a reason on why it should be her.

"I'm sorry for crying. God, I'm so, so sorry for crying, it's all I can do now that I'm here and I'm not alone. But I still feel alone, how is that? I'm sick of crying because nobody understands the pain I'm feeling. None of you understand the pain in my head and chest as I'm holding back tears every time I'm reminded of something that once made me happy. I'm sick of crying and feeling alone, I just want someone to pull me close and hug me and chase away this awful pain! But at the same time, I want everyone to go away and let me cry so that I don't have to feel this angry sea inside me, battering my heart and making it so hard to breathe!"

Her voice came out hoarse and weak, exhaustion clear in the way she spoke her heart out. Nobody dared breathe as they watched her gather her thoughts and try to calm herself; sniffles and little gasps from the girl filled the silence. Roman stared at his younger sibling with a wounded look, sure he had seen death, he had seen the body of his friend, but he hadn't watched the life drain from her eyes. He had a support system of friends and family to slowly help him get out of his depression and even though he wasn't completely better and maybe would never be, he had still been saved before he had fallen off the edge. Elisa didn't have anyone, and he wondered if they were too late to save her from the unforgiving darkness of misery. She wiped her cheeks with her hands and let out a shaky broken laugh.

"You know what sucks? Is that I know that nobody can make me feel better, nobody can physically take away the hurt. I have to just slowly get over it, figure it out and settle it in my head until the thought of it doesn't make me cry. I have to get over everything alone despite there being people around me. People can talk to me and help me understand but it's me who has to unloosen the tightness in my chest. I have to unknot that rope around my organs by myself. That's what sucks the most." Roman nodded and gave her a small smile as he took her hands in his own.

"Your right. Of course, you are. I know only a fraction of what you feel, and I know you aren't pushing aside my feelings and past. You've been there in our vulnerable moments more than we have been there for you in yours. We can never explain how sorry we are-" He was stopped by Elisa hugging his waist tightly with her face buried into his shirt.

"I don't want your apologies. I just want you to stop pretending that my past is nothing to do with you, I don't like to be cast aside and treated like I'm weak because I'm not. I've been through so much more than you've ever gone through and I want to prevent you from getting hurt." Preston tugged her into his arms and nuzzled his cheek against hers. A smile breaking out on her face as she held onto her brother, glad that she could always count on him to make her smile.

"AWWWW SHES SO CUTE!" He said in a high-pitched voice immediately easing the tension and causing them to smile. The Wests relaxed, everything was out there, there was no need for apologies, just the mutual understanding that they were there for each other. They were all they had left, and it was something they needed to work on, communication. Levi popped his head into the room with a grin.

"Are we done kiddies? It's time for dinner!"

Elisa was given one of Alexander's shirts to wear since her body was still quite sore from injuries she had received, small scratches and gashes than had been wrapped up and needed to heal. Sasha gently brushed out all the knots in her best friend's hair trying not to laugh every time Elisa let out a whine of pain. The boys, excluding the three eldest, were already fast asleep in the living room.

"You ok Ellie?" Elisa gave her a look and Sasha laughed as she hugged her tightly.

"You, my friend are my role model. Don't be surprised if I call you to yell at Cyrus for me." Elisa rolled her eyes and ran her fingers through her now soft locks.

"Thanks, Sash." The green-eyed girl softened and smiled.

"Any time. Get some sleep, okay?" She didn't respond as she watched her best friend leave the room. The day had been stressful, to say the least, and wasn't at all mad for her brothers forgetting.

"Knock knock, can I come in?' Alexander murmured.

"Why say the sound while your knocking?" She teased and Alexander stuck his tongue out playfully, glad that their argument hadn't caused them to take two steps back.

"I forget you're a 16-year-old sometimes, you make me feel so small." She giggled but let her smile slip slightly.

"17... it's 12:05." Her brother nodded with a bright smile and showed her the hand that had been hidden behind his bag. A wooden box.

"I know Dove. Happy birthday!" He sat on the be cross-legged next to her and gently placed the box in between them. Her fingers traced the edges, and she squinted her eyes as she felt a groove in the wood. Alexander turned on the lamp and a small gasp left her lips as she traced her name that had been burned into the wood. Birds and swirly patterns surrounding the name.

"I found it in the safe along with boxes for the others. I figured mum and dad made them for us so..." She nodded and gently lifted the lid. Inside were small polaroid photographs of a little smiley girl, she lifted a picture out, it was her beautiful mother wearing a pale lilac dress, her hair in a braid and her lips pressed against the baby forehead. She swallowed the emotion and Alexander wiped the tear that rolled down her cheek.

"It's mummy." He nodded and sniffed as he looked at the photo. He wanted to stay and look through the photographs and memories with her but knew that it was her moment.

"I love you." He whispered and pressed a kiss to her forehead making her lips tremble and eyes water.

"Love you too Xander." She held him tightly and he stroked her hair. He pressed another kiss to the crown of her head and left the room to talk with Karson and Owen about their options. Elisa looked through each photograph, her smile shaky but genuine and happy as she saw pictures with her and her mother, her father, and brothers. The box also contained small flower pressings and pieces of paper that had childish drawings scribbled over them, her drawings, and right at the bottom was a discoloured envelop. Her brows furrowed in curiosity as she gently took the envelope out. Her fingers dipped into the envelope and pulled out a letter than had been bent and crumbled. She unfolded the letter and noted the familiar strokes of her mothers' handwriting.

'Oh, my Little Miracle. I love you so much it hurts that I've had to put this job into your hands. If you're reading this note and neither I nor your father has given you this, then I fear that something terrible has happened to us. I'm sorry for whatever you've had to endure my love, for whatever your brothers have had to endure, but I believe in you. I know this isn't fair darling and I'm so sorry this falls to you. But you must do what I couldn't all those years ago. The red journal will hold all the answers, you just have to look at my writing and drawings properly, you'll understand the meanings they hold and will be able to finish this. We were wrong Elisa, Project Miracle should never have been made, the world should go by its natural course, people should use their time wisely and not cheat life with some miracle drug. It's not our choice to play Executioner and all our work should never have existed. Yes, the world is filling up, many diseases are being discovered, but it's the way of life. If we are meant to live, we will. Stay safe as always, my darling, never give up and never lose sight of who you are. You are stronger than anyone including yourself realise. I love you.'

She realised that the envelope was slightly heavy and tipped it over onto her bed, a single metal key falling into her lap feeling cold against her skin. She held the key between her fingers confused before reaching over her bed and pulling up the rucksack that held the journal. Alexander had given it to her saying that she's kept it safe all these years and was the only one equipped to keep it that way.

She scanned the book until she crossed a familiar page. A drawing of rocks with a bold W, numbers along the page and a rectangle inside a squiggly shape. The word SUB ROSA written in red pen in bold writing. Elisa was quite smart for her age and excelled in several subjects mostly out of boredom and wanting to keep ahead of the enemies.

Latin was something she had studied but wasn't especially good at. She was pretty sure Rosa meant rose and sub was a prefix meaning under, so it meant under the rose. She bit her lip as she racked her brain as to what is meant by 'under the rose'. Roses were usually associated with love and romance, and she knew that different coloured roses symbolised different things. Her eyes lit up with a sudden thought and she thought about it before smiling at her conclusion.

Roses can also symbolise confidentiality or... secrets! Under the rose, Sub Rosa, secrecy. Looking at the drawing she realises what her mother had drawn, what the numbers could signify and what the shapes were showing.

It was the location of the secret Lab.

24

Now

"I'm sorry but who are you again?"

"Someone who hasn't got time for unimportant people such as yourself."

"You are as insignificant as the K in Knife!"

"Great comeback Red, did it take you long to search it up?"

"Oh, just bugger off muppet."

"Sorry I don't speak British, what did you say little princess?"

"Don't call me princess you little-" Cyrus hugged a livid Sasha to his chest as he tried to keep a straight face, she was so close to pouncing on Levi who sent her a smirk and stuck his tongue out childishly, his eyes bright as he taunted her.

Elisa frowned at the scene as she came to a stop next to Quinton who was shaking his head in amusement at the argument that had erupted between Sasha and Levi. His eyes flickering between the two who kept throwing insults, Finley and Andre were stood on the other side of the kitchen with their hands covering their mouths with their shirts. Levi had told them how he grew up with Elisa as a child and hadn't heard from her in just over 4 years; their heart stung as he told them stopped talking to her only friend to protect him and his family.

"What happened? Are they angry about this whole situation?" Elisa spoke softly causing Quinton to jump slightly at how she had managed to appear out of nowhere. He gave her a small glare with no real heat behind them and rolled his eyes at her quiet spoken words.

She still thought that everyone would suddenly blame her for everything and that she would lose everyone if she said anything. He didn't blame her of course and it frustrated him and the others whenever she tried to keep things to herself thinking it would make sure they were safe, she had so little concern over her life that it had begun to worry him. He shook his head at her question and saw the way she physically relaxed before peering up at him with a curious look; like a meerkat peeking out to see if the coast was clear before making an appearance.

"They're arguing over who is your best friend." Her eyes widened comically, and a light flush covered her cheeks making the corner of his lip tilt up at how astonished she looked at the fact. Her brothers were in the living room while Karson was telling them about William; Owen had gently nudged Elisa into the kitchen so that she didn't have to listen how her father had died all over again.

"Over me?" Her quiet voice mumbled in curiosity; Cyrus, Finley and Andre looked over at the West girl with small smiles while Sasha and Levi carried on insulting each other.

"Of course, over you Muffin! You're such a cutie pie and they don't wanna share... I would argue that I'm your best friend, but I don't want Sasha to hurt me." Finley sent a slightly scared expression in the other girls' direction just in time to see her bare her teeth at Levi who glared back.

"Bite me Mongrel." She spat making Elisa snort at how seriously they were taking the role of being her best friend. The small sound made the two teenagers whip their heads round to face her with almost desperate and sweetly innocent faces, Elisa bit her lip realising she may have made a mistake bringing attention to herself. Sasha bounded up to Elisa like a puppy and threw her arms around Elisa's neck while Levi simply poked her cheek over and over making her smile.

"Ellie?'

"Yes, Sash?' She asked slowly and hesitantly as she saw the sickly-sweet smile on her face.

"I'm your bestest friend ever, right?" Her eyes widened as she understood the predicament she had fallen into, a predicament she didn't expect to ever be in and didn't know how to settle without causing bloodshed which was bound to happen if she didn't say that right thing.

"It's ok Elisa, you don't have to worry about she-devil's feelings because I'm pretty sure she doesn't have any... Just tell her the truth. I am and always will be your best friend." Her brown eyes darted to the amused faces of her other friends around the kitchen, all with grins and trying not to laugh at the deer in the headlights look Elisa sported. She bit her lip nervously as her eyes darted between the two children in the room who looked at her with bright innocent smiles.

"Well, I love you both the same-"

"Nope, none of that Elisa... me... or the Tasmanian devil?" Without looking away from Elisa's face, Sasha's leg shot out and Levi groaned in pain, doubling over while cursing under his breath. Elisa winced as she looked at Levi and tried to avoid looking at Sasha. Her eyes landed on ocean blue that seemed to have soft waves flowing gently and contently in his eyes, a smirk on his face as he watched the little fight in front of him.

"Who is it, Ellie?" Sasha whined and Elisa said the first person who popped into her head.

"Quinton!" The ocean blue eyes darkened as a storm passed over the once calm waves, his smirk dropped instantly, and he looked at the two frozen teenagers warily. Sasha let out a scary giggle as she let go of Elisa who bit her lip and backed away.

"This twit?" Sasha asked incredulously and Levi sized Quinton up like he was his prey, and he was the predator. Quinton spared a glance at Elisa and glared at her with the promise of death dancing in his blue orbs.

"Sorry, but what does this Quilt have that I don't?" Andre slapped a hand over his mouth as he tried not to laugh at the name Levi had dubbed Quinton. The two stood up straight and advanced on Quinton who watched them blank-faced and edged away from them.

"C'mon," Cyrus whispered as he gently tugged Elisa away from the trio and into the back garden where Andre and Finley had also slipped out, there they let their laughter loose and Elisa smiled brightly at the people she was with. Even in times of darkness and uncertainty, they always managed to make her smile in some way, she knew that her friends had acted this way to see her smile. She couldn't help but love these people even more than she already did.

Alexander ran his hand through his chocolate brown hair before taking a sip of the steaming hot tea that Owen had made them all. The house was silent, rain running down the windows, but that didn't seem to stop the laughing teenagers in the back garden. He could hear his little sisters loud and genuine laugh, so different from her usual low chuckle and quiet sweet giggle.

She was full-on belly laughing, he could see her gripping the sides of her stomach as she lightly leaned against Cyrus, her other three friends were still in the kitchen arguing but he knew there was no real hatred behind their words. He believed they found humour in the situation and were simply putting the small show on for his sister.

His brothers looked out the window and he could see Owen smiling warmly, Romans shoulders relaxed and Preston grinning, no trace of the anger and hatred they once had but simply pure adoration. How far they had come, he thought. Yes, they had arguments, yelled at each other, but she didn't regret anything that had been said he knew that it needed to be out there. He needed to have that awakening in the form of his little sister verbally slapping them all to the same reality. That there were no heroes in this story, they were all players reaching for the same goal.

A normal life. Or as normal life they can after what they've had to endure, especially Elisa.

Everything was okay for now, they were okay. Karson wasn't bad, he was looking out for Elisa and the family, for all of them. His brothers were safe in front of him along with their friends, new and old. Things weren't bad right at that moment, they weren't okay either. They were just living in the state of in-between. They knew they would constantly have the dark cloud of danger following them until they figured out how to escape it.

"I've been on this case for a while along with some other agents I work with, they're posted all around the town taking up random jobs and lives to blend in. We even had some moles who faked their allegiance to the people who followed Hamish-"

"Hamish." Preston snorted and roman sniggered along with him making Karson roll his eyes at their childishness before ignoring them.

"We won't be able to keep gathering information since the base was blown up with Hamish and whatever they had down there." They paused as the unspoken name floated in the air between them.

William West.

"There are other bases, I know that, and it'll take us a while to find them all and get rid of them. But my job and main assignment are to protect you while finding all of the masterminds. Hamish was the direct leader, a weak one at that and I'm sure there was someone else we have no idea about that is higher up."

"There's also someone Hamish was working with," Elisa spoke up as she walked into the room. Karson casually walked to one of the cupboards in the hallway and pulled out four towels which he gave to the four that had been outside. Elisa rested in front of the fire, Owen sat behind her on the sofa who casually took the towel off her and began to dry her hair for her. She sent him a grateful smile as he ran his fingers through her wet hair trying to get any knots out of the locks; her eyes fluttering closed at the familiar feeling of someone playing with her hair, something her mother used to do.

"Yeah, he mentioned his partner, didn't seem too fond of him if I'm honest and it sounded like he only kept him around because maybe he knew something or had something nobody else could get their hands on." Levi piped up as he remembered the animosity Hamish showed when speaking of his supposed partner. Her brows furrowed as she strained to remember everything whilst blocking out the soft soul that had been in the cells with them. Karson sighed heavily and rubbed his face with a groan exhaustion creeping upon him and he practically downed the cup of scalding green tea.

"My cover is probably exposed; I can't sneak into any more bases without them knowing of me and my connection to you guys. These... people have made a name for themselves, call themselves The Council of Thorns. TCT for short. Whoever their leader is, clearly loves symbolism." Karson chuckled humourlessly.

"So, they leave black roses after they've killed someone, and they're called The Council of Thorns... sorry what's the symbolism here?" Andre asked feeling his cheeks heat thinking he was missing the point. One look around the room made his shoulder drop in relief as he saw the bewildered looks on nearly everyone's face except Elisa, Karson and surprisingly Roman's face.

"Black roses symbolise death and despair, all things dark. A complete contrast to what a flower would represent, the colour makes a huge difference when it comes to sentimentality and symbolism." Roman commented as he thought the way an artist and reader would, he looked past the object and thought about the other meanings it could hold. Elisa nodded in agreement.

"Thorns are sharp, prickly. I'm assuming that means after all the hardships and troubles you are rewarded with the actual flower which is beautiful despite the colour. They make themselves sound like Saviours of the world." Levi blinked at what his friend had said before letting out a chuckle causing eyes to jump to him.

"See you can tell this is an evil British Organisation with your need to make everything sound Shakespearean. Like why can't it be called The Council of Thorns because it sounds cool?"

"Because it doesn't sound cool?" Finley mumbled around the rim of his cup.

"No, I mean like why does there need to be a load of symbolism behind the thorn and rose? You Brits are way too poetical." Sasha gave him a dirty look and rolled her eyes.

"Well excuse us for talking and thinking the way we were raised and taught to, you plonker." She sneered and Levi looked around clueless his eyes jumping around until they landed on a grinning Andre.

"What is Little Red Riding hood calling me?"

"She's calling you an idiot but normally we would just say you're an idiot. Seems as though you've made Sash want to call you every single British insult she can remember." Andre said in amusement.

"So, you don't normally say plonker?" His face a mask of confusion.

"Not really... I mean some people might, but we usually just say idiot or insult you behind your back." Preston shrugged as if it was common knowledge and Levi looked as though he was swallowing a large pill.

"Movies do exaggerate you guys huh?" More eye rolls.

"Anyway, back to the matter at hand. There's not much I can offer you at the moment, but it seems as though I will have to bring the main solution earlier than expected. At this time, it's probably best we put you into Witness Protection... let us handle this issue while you guys start up a new life." Immediately, the West boys began to argue along with the others, Elisa's eyes large at the words spoken by her brother's best friend.

"I'm sorry but we've seemed to uncover and figure out more than you and your poor excuse of employers! The only reason you know half of what you know now is because of my sister!" Roman snapped angrily, he refused to have them shoved into hiding when they were so close to figuring a way out of their problem. Alexander hesitated, although he didn't want to be hidden away under a new identity or lose his job, he thought about his family and knew that being put into Witness Protection would ensure his younger siblings' safety, that was all that mattered to him right now and he was more than willing to give all the knowledge he had to his best friend.

"Yes, but how do we know that the people you're working with aren't part of TCT?" Owen argued completely ignoring the way Elisa tensed. Karson sighed heavily as he tried to make them see that his offer was the best one, they had.

"Because the division I work for has committed their lives to stop crimes and problems like this. I've lost so many people who have given their lives just to find a bit of evidence for whatever we are trying to fix. My parents were in that organisation... It was their whole life and they've protected many innocent people. I'm following in their footsteps and making sure my family is safe." Alexander stood and gave Karson a tight hug, Romans eyes shifted to Elisa whose eyes were trained on the flames from the fireplace, her fingers gently rubbing her cheek as she was deep in thought.

"We have evidence that I and my team have collected of some other bases we have found but not been able to expose yet, Alex you've found the safe in your parents' room, they must have all sorts of evidence of who is behind everything or we can piece what they do know together. Elisa's past and everything she's learnt will also help with us ending TCT once and for all."

"But what about Hamish's partner? Project Miracle that wasn't contaminated? The vial in the bag and the red journal? Are we not going to find out who the other mastermind is? Are we not going to-" Karson knelt in front of Elisa with a small smile, his grey eyes studying her small face.

"Muffin it's ok... you've done so well! My team were trained to track people down, to get information out of people. You need to rest and live life as a normal teenage girl." He praised her and hoped that she would trust him to take control.

"But what if you don't have enough clues and evidence to find everyone from TCT? What about ending Project Miracle once and for all?"

"The vial and journal will be with MI5 so nobody can get their hands on it ever again, it'll be safe with them." She gave him a gentle smile, her eyes lowered back to the flames and he ruffled her hair glad that she had agreed. Roman and Sasha sat straight when they saw her give in so easily, something they knew she would never do, not without doing what she needed to do first.

"Alex, you have connections in the police force, people you trust. How about we set up a plan..." Elisa zoned out of the conversation and closed her eyes as she began to think. She had to be the one to finish this, this was her job and she had waited so long for it to finally be over with. The West girl wasn't just going to let someone else take it on. She smiled up at her brother and mumbled that she was going to change. Sasha followed her into the bedroom Elisa had been sleeping in and spoke up.

"You're going to leave aren't you?" Elisa paused in braiding her hair not uttering a word, but Sasha knew the decision had been made the moment she agreed to Karson. Elisa West never gave up on what she believed in. Once she was set on something she wouldn't budge.

"We're in, me, Cyrus, Quinton and even that butthead of an idiot you call a friend. We can help you get out of here, wherever you need to go, babe... I can drive." Elisa chuckled lightly and walked to her best friend to hug her tightly.

"Thanks, Sash."

"Always sis... we'll be here always. As soon as they're asleep we leave, okay?"

"How do we do that? I'm sure Karson has every door and window bugged so that if they're opened, he'll know." Sasha grinned mischievously.

"Oh, sweetheart Karson may be an MI5 agent, but he isn't Cyrus. Karson has that door next to the staircase which no doubt goes into a basement. The car wasn't outside when we looked earlier meaning he has an underground garage somewhere. He won't expect us to try and leave so Cyrus can lock pick the door, we grab the right keys and voila! We go down, get in the car and drive away to wherever you need to go." Elisa hugged her tightly again mumbling a thank you over and over until Sasha slapped her arm.

"Get a bag packed with anything you need." Elisa felt her shoulder lift as one of her problems were solved.

She knelt next to the rucksack her mother had entrusted her with all those years ago, the journal and vial sat inside snug, unaware of how much trouble, pain and death they had caused. She wiped her cheek when she realised a lone tear had escaped her eye, she knew what she had to do, what she always had to do.

Elisa thought about her plan. She was going to take the rucksack with her, she was going to find the lab and destroy Project Miracle so that nobody would have it. It should never have been created, what gave humans the right to decide who lives and dies? When everyone's time was right then they would end their story.

Hamish was gone but the knowledge that he had a partner who he kept around for a reason she didn't quite know yet lingered in the back of her head. She had a feeling that she would be seeing this person real soon and that it wouldn't have been the first time they met. The way that Hamish had said it made her think that perhaps this person and she had already crossed paths before, maybe she knew them quite well or perhaps they've been aware of her for a while. She knows this partner; she just doesn't know who it is yet and that worried her immensely.

"You've got a plan huh?" Her head snapped up to the doorway where Roman watched her with a blank face, her mouth opened and closed but she didn't say anything as she took note of the way he casually leaned against the door with his arms crossed over his chest. She couldn't and didn't want to say anything to them and it made her lips tremble as she knew she was holding things from them despite all their arguments and promises. Had he heard them? Did Sasha tell him?

Roman made his way over to sit on the floor beside her leaning against the bed, his eyes trained on the blank wall in front of them. He felt her eyes looking from her twiddling hands to his face multiple times; jaw clenching as he figured out what to say to her.

"Your so brave Shadow, I honestly wish I could be like you, facing your demons head-on. You've protected us longer than we even knew what our parents had kept hidden. You know I prepared for this. The day we had that accident and you told us everything, the day you finally let us in I tried to prepare myself. Deep down I knew that... I would lose you again whether it was your choice or not. I just didn't think it would be this soon you know? You haven't even been home for 6 months and yet I have to be ready to say goodbye."

She swallowed the lump in her throat and her hand reached out to hold her big brothers, her small shaking hand holding onto his larger warm ones. It hadn't been long at all and yet it felt as though she had never left them to begin with. He didn't know what she was planning, didn't know what was running through her head but he knew that whatever it was, was something she had to do alone. He would help in any way needed, even if that meant letting her go. His tongue darted out to wet his chapped lips, his teeth biting his top lip as he held in the sadness threatening to make an appearance. He sucked his teeth as he rubbed her hand, the small scars bumpy against his thumb.

"I need to do this Ro. Mum... she would want me to do this." He nodded and let out a shaky breath; without a word Elisa ducked her head under his arm and he immediately pulled her closer as he buried his face in her soft damp hair. His shoulders shaking as he let out silent sobs feeling as though he was losing his best friend all over again. Except for this time, she was aware of what was happening, she was aware that she was leaving them again to protect them and what was left of their family. Her tears slipped down her cheeks and she clutched at his shirt wanting to stay in the bubble her brothers had cornered her in.

"I love you Shadow." He whispered in a choked voice and his eyes closed as he held his baby sister closer, she vaguely smelt of vanilla and he wanted to never let her go to the wolves that no doubt waited for her.

"I love you more than anything Ro, you'll always be my first best friend."

No matter how hard he tried to tell himself that it was okay and that she was going to come back to him, he couldn't help but feel as though she was saying goodbye.

25

Now

Elisa West had grown up intending to protect her brothers from the danger and evil that threatened to take them away one by one. She had lost a lot of her childhood consistently looking over her shoulder wondering if those after her were close or far away. Now she felt as though her running was coming to an end, that perhaps she may get to finish her teenage years living like a teenager. She wanted to be lazy and eat junk food simply because she was bored, she wanted to hang out with her friends without thinking that she was going to be watched and killed on sight.

"You ok?" Quinton mumbled from the backseat, Levi and Cyrus had fallen asleep while Sasha was driving them through backstreets. Karson's house was quite a distance from the village. There were hardly any streetlamps, and the sky was still dark with it being around 2 am.

Elisa nodded without a word not wanting to delve into her thoughts. They had left after Alexander and Karson had fallen asleep, Sasha had made sure they all had rucksacks with cereal bars and water, cash if they needed it and a change of clothes just in case. Cyrus had picked the lock of the basement door after a lot of swearing and insults at Karson, they had descended the dark staircase until they came out into an open garage.

Two cars parked up with petrol cans on the side along with guns. It didn't scare them as much as it should have done however if they ever saw those weapons in action, there is no doubt a few of them would wet their pants in fear. Hearing and watching guns in movies are completely different from seeing them in person. Levi had grabbed a small handgun anyways just in case it came to it. Although Elisa had used a gun before, she didn't think she could use one against another person again.

Sasha had found the car keys and soon they had jumped into the car and drove out of the garage which went in an underground tunnel. The underground tunnel slowly ascended onto the surface and they found themselves on the road within minutes. They didn't know how long they had to drive and get away before the boys realised, they were gone, but Elisa wanted them to be far enough so she can figure things out.

"Do you have a plan?" Sasha murmured and Elisa licked her lips before letting out a slow breath.

"I don't... I'm kind of making it up as we go along." Quinton scoffed.

"Have you ever seen Scooby-Doo? They don't make things up on the spot. They gotta plan and still they go wrong before they find out who the bad guy is." Elisa pulled out the journal from her back and opened it to the page completely ignoring Quinton who pouted when he didn't get a reaction out of her.

"What's that?"

"What, Scooby-Doo?" Quinton asked incredulously as he looked at Sasha in disgust, eyes wide and scanning her as if he was seeing her for the first time. Both girls rolled their eyes while

Cyrus playfully slapped him round the head, earning a cold glare from the 'bad boy'. Levi raised his hand as if to ask what he was talking about but before he could blurt out the question, Cyrus slapped a hand over his mouth and Elisa quickly spoke up.

"Coordinates for my mother's secret lab. It's in Robin Hoods Bay, somewhere hidden but I'm pretty sure I'll know where it is the moment I see something." Sasha nodded not worried by Elisa's uncertainty at all, she trusted her best friend to know what she was doing and would help in any way they can.

Elisa looked out the window and watched the sky lighten from a dark navy blue to a gentle burnt orange, birds flying in flocks making her lips twitch as she watched them chase one another. The freedom they had as they played around in the open sky, dancing with the wind and conversing with the other birds passing.

Sasha rolled down Elisa's window, and immediately the West girl stuck her hand out feeling the wind push against her palm; the air nipping at her cheeks waking her up and making sure the call of sleep was overpowered by the sounds of the outside world. Her eyes momentarily closed as she pretended that she wasn't on a search for a secret lab, she pretended she was on a road trip with her friends and they weren't on a time limit, that they could enjoy the peace they had as they drove. Maybe one day she would be rewarded with something as simple as a road trip.

They parked up in one of the public car parks, Elisa didn't wait for her friends as she began walking down the street towards the village. Her back straightened and steps quickened as she felt stares on her body, her gut was telling her to find density or somewhere to hide. Her backpack flung over her shoulders with the weight of its contents reminding her that she was holding the very thing that could be the reason the world didn't have the chance to live before its time was up.

The teenagers rushed after her not willing to let her out of their sight in fear that she would easily get kidnapped the moment they couldn't see her. Levi fell into step with the girl who reached up to his shoulders and grinned down at her. He hadn't spoken much to her and he wanted to see if his childhood friend knew him as well as she used to. Elisa rolled her eyes as she felt the mocking gaze on her and nudged him with her elbow earning a soft grunt.

"Shut up."

"Dude I didn't even say anything?!"

"You were thinking about it."

"Oh, so now you can hear thoughts?" She looked up at him with a challenging look raising a single brow. Her eyes jumping around trying to see whose eyes were watching her unflinching, but when she saw nobody focused her attention on the boy.

"So, you weren't about to comment on my height?" He flushed slightly but shook his head as he stuck his hands in his pockets, his chin held high as they walked down the cobbled street keeping an eye out for anything dodgy. A cloud of happiness hung over his head when he realised, she could read him just like she was able to when they were younger.

"Nah..." She smiled slightly but felt it slip as memories rushed to the front of her mind. She peeked behind her and saw Cyrus and Quinton arguing while Sasha walked along beside them, her arms looping with her boyfriends. She sent Elisa a wink and mouthed the word talk, she smiled back at her gratefully as Elisa wanted to catch up with her childhood best friend in the short time they had. Although Sasha didn't really like Levi in a playfully and competitive way, she was excited for the girl she had befriended and smiled as she watched the two old friends converse quietly.

"How's Leah?" Levi blinked in surprise as if he completely forgot he had a younger sibling and he smiled radiantly as he remembered the last time he saw his younger sister. It was her 13th birthday and Levi had driven home from his apartment to surprise her, her blonde curly hair bouncing as she ran to greet her older brother. He remembered the way she clung onto him the whole evening since it's rare for him to come home with his busy schedule. Her mouth running too fast for her developing brain to understand what she was blurting out, but those rambling sessions meant the world to him.

He had always been close to his sister, he wanted to have the close relationship that a brother and sister should have and made sure she knew that he was her best friend and would always listen to her when she thought she was alone. As she grew older, he couldn't seem to get her to shut up, but he wouldn't trade her for anyone else.

"She was doing well the last time I saw her; mum had bought her a little puppy and that was it, the little rat was obsessed with this creature. She's a teenager now and I'm hoping she doesn't slip into a bratty stage." Elisa smiled as she saw and heard the love in his voice. A sight she had recognised in her own brother's eyes when they listened to her talk.

"Your mum?" Levi stopped walking and studied the girl before him, he heard the unspoken question that she didn't want to ask.

"She misses you, misses your mum. She always wondered what became of you after you stopped sending the letters." Regret lined her cold and lightly chapped lips as she thought about the woman who had looked after her mother and offered her the branch of friendship. She felt guilty for cutting contact, but she would rather grow up knowing she had protected them from the same fate everyone else who had looked over her had fallen for.

"I miss her too... I didn't think she would... or you." She shrugged as they carried on walking, her eyes darting to the alleyways they passed by trying to see if there was anything odd that would show her where the lab was. She was almost certain that the lab was hidden somewhere so obvious that it was easily overlooked. The feeling of being watched doubled and Elisa squirmed as she walked, her eyes now darting to look at windows and between trees.

Levi cleared his throat and sighed before pulling his wrist out of his pocket and shoving it in front of her. She looked down at his arm confused until he rolled up his sleeve a bit. Still a bit confused, the girl tilted her head to the side like a curious puppy making him grin albeit a bit nervously. Her fingers gently skimmed the blue ribbon around his wrist, frayed edges and the colour had faded drastically, but after a few moments she understood what was around his wrist and her hand darted to her hair which was tied up with a white ribbon.

"My ribbon..." He smiled and held his wrist with his other arm, his eyes looked slightly glazed as if he was remembering a time so long ago.

"It was the last time we saw each other; we were leaving the house and I stole your ribbon. I always did, I remember I would steal them and take them back home to try and tie them up in Leah's or mum's hair, but then mum would always force me to give them back to you because they were your favourite things." He clenched his jaw and scratched the side of his neck.

"I couldn't lose this one. It was the last ribbon of yours I had... I kept it under my pillow growing up but when the letters stopped, I started to take it everywhere with me. It would be in my pocket and I would hold onto it when I was walking through school hallways, I would sit in class and fiddle with it, sometimes when I was bullied or I felt extra lonely, mum would help me tie it to my wrist so that I had it in eyesight at all times... It bought me little comfort. It's stupid and I know you were too young, but you were my best and only friend for 6 years." Elisa felt tears prick her eyes at the sweet gesture but didn't allow the water to fall.

"I was there Elisa. I was standing in the driveway holding Leah who had woken up screaming for mum. I watched them bring Aunt Lilah out, I covered Leah's eyes and saw the blood dripping from the stretcher they carried your her in, I saw the open eyes that closed only because the paramedic closed them. I saw them carry your unconscious body in the ambulance and I vaguely remembered one of our neighbours trying to get me to go inside while mum gave her instructions. Then the doors closed, and the ambulance drove off with mum, Aunt Lilah and you. That was the last memory I had of you. I... Honest to god I thought you died the moment the letters stopped." He wrapped an arm around her shoulders tightly making her cheek press against his body and sent her a relieved smile.

"Boy am I glad that those bozos did get it right and kidnapped me." She couldn't help the laugh that bubbled out of her and Levi joined in with her amusement, glad that he managed to lift the sadness that had settled over them.

"STOP TALKING ABOUT ME!" Sasha called out making the two laugh harder and Levi stick his tongue out to antagonise her. Elisa grinned up at the boy in contentment.

"I'm glad too... though that does mean I'll have to save you now too." She sighed playfully and his eyes twinkled at the banter they shared. Despite there being a huge gap from the last time they saw each other, despite the fact they were older, and the childish innocence was long gone, it was as if they had never truly left each other. Perhaps that was because in their minds, even when they didn't mean to think about each other, they would wonder how the other was doing. They would think up scenarios of what the other could be doing until they next saw each other again. Perhaps it was because despite them getting on with their lives, they never truly forgot about each other.

"Sorry kiddies, would you like to share the conversation with the rest of the class yeah?" Quinton darted to walked alongside Elisa who simply poked his stomach at his lifeless words.

"You're too boring to converse with." She said and his jaw dropped before he not so gently shoved her into the oldest of the teens.

"Aww don't get so salty Quilt! I'm sure we can find someone to talk to you... how about that rock down there." Quinton huffed and grumbled under his breathe walking ahead, Levi giggled like a little kid on a sugar rush and skipped ahead to pester him. Elisa shook her head and carried on observing her surroundings, people had begun to fill the streets and some people had made their way down to the opening cafes for breakfast. The feeling of being watched still weighing on her shoulders.

Elisa only saw the village when she was going to school, shopping or on the beach with her friends since her home was just slightly out of the village in the fields. The sky had brightened considerably since they left Karson's' home and Elisa wouldn't be surprised if he was trying to track them.

Her lips lifted as she remembered that morning months ago when she was sat on the back porch without telling anyone, she remembered Owen practically ripping the door off its hinges as he rushed to pull her in his arms while crying about how much he missed her... a slow regretful sigh left her mouth. He was probably panicking a lot more now, she wouldn't be surprised if he started tipping furniture over just to have her in his arms again, her poor sweet brother.

Alexander would probably ground her for life and refuse her to exit with at least a tracking device planted on her somehow. Her being kidnapped and now running off would no doubt send his brotherly/ fatherly instincts off the rails. He would shout and scream at her, probably shake her demanding to know why she thought it best to run off. She should have told him before they left, she should have told him that he was doing well. That he was protecting them better than anyone could. She hoped he knew that, that he hadn't failed in any way and had made her feel like she had finally found a home.

Roman would probably shout at her like Alexander, his temper on an all-time high before he gives her the silent treatment and probably avoid her before he kills her himself. Then she would end up sitting next to him on the old swing set outside their home and they would swing in comfortable silence. She would apologise and he would give her a small smile reassuring her that everything was ok and that he wasn't going to abandon her. She smiled as she remembered the times in the past few months that had happened.

Preston was Preston. He would stare her down until she told him why she did what she did, then he would just hold her to him like the big brother he was. He would watch her and make sure she was okay, telling her not to do it again and if she did, to make sure she told him too so he could disappear with her. She had gotten to know her brothers so well that she could predict their behaviour and actions before they even did anything. Her fingers skimmed the rose quartz laying on her collarbone and tugged on it gently reminding herself that her brothers loved her more than anything. Just as they loved her, she loved them, and she would protect them despite them being older.

She felt a tear rolling down her cheek as she realised how much she was missing her brothers, how much she craved for the safety they provided. She couldn't shake the feeling that maybe she should have said she loved them all last night, that she should have hugged them extra tightly. She couldn't shake the feeling that this was it.

This was it.

"Ellie..." Cyrus said in a warning tone as he pointed to a man wearing all black with a skeleton mask covering his lower face and a pair of black tinted goggles. He stepped out from a shop with his finger pressed to his ear as he looked up and down the street. The teens quickly ducked into an alleyway, but Elisa felt his eyes land on her just as she turned away. The upwards tilt of his head made her eyes widen and heart pound.

"Run!" She hissed and pushed her friends through the gap between two buildings. Quinton and Cyrus took lead with Sasha behind them leading Levi and Elisa. They scurried through the cobble streets like mice trying not to cause too much attention to themselves. People raised their brows at the teens who weaved their way down different pathways.

"Okay I don't mean to rush you Weirdo, but you need to figure out where this lab is, this village ain't that big," Quinton said with a tone of urgency as they made their way back to the street they had been walking down, the shop the man had left from now in front of them with the man nowhere in sight. Elisa chewed her lip nervously looking around them and grabbed Sasha who was the closest to her.

"Okay, okay, okay." She mumbled as she tried to figure out where the lab could be. She felt overwhelmed and quite useless as her brain seemingly went blank and offered no ideas.

"Anytime babe," Sasha said nervously as they spied another man coming out of an alley. The teens cursed and Quinton led them to sit behind one of the shops, bushes hiding them from the street. Elisa pulled out the journal and skimmed the pages before landing on the familiar page where the drawings were. The strange squiggly shape with a rectangle in the centre and the words SUBROSA. Sweat beaded on her forehead and she wanted to cry from frustration. Quinton frowned and laid a hand on her shoulder that had begun to shake.

"Breathe idiot... breathe." His words insulting but the tone was soft and calming, breaching the panic barrier around her mind. She pressed a trembling hand to her face and let out a breath, she wiped her forehead with her sleeves and rubbed at her numb cheeks. She thought back to what her dad said that only her mother knew of its whereabouts, that she would blindfold him and give him headphones so that he couldn't guess where he was. That meant the place was obvious, that he could guess where they were because of the sounds. What was so obvious? What was it?

A squawking sound caught her attention and her eyes flickered to the street that she could see from the position she was crouching in. Chips on the cobbled ground from where a tourist must have dropped them and were now being devoured by seagulls... Seagulls.

Elisa's eyes widened in realisation and she looked back down at the journal in accomplishment.

"The beach..." They exchanged looks and Cyrus spoke up.

"Ellie there is no building close to the beach... nothing abandoned either so-" Her exciting tapping on the journal page cut him off, her hazel eyes twinkling in understanding and she let out a bright smile.

"It's a cliff! That's what this is! A secret door in the cliffs on the beach! The Lab is in the cliffs!" The journal was placed safely in the backpack before the West girl nodded confidently.

"I have an incredibly good idea of where this lab is too, we just need to navigate through the village down to the end of the beach, where we hung out that one time and it was empty. The day that body-" She stopped but the teens who had known the village like the back of their hands lit up in recognition.

"Okay, how are we doing this?" Levi asked seriously as they watched two more men in black rush down the street and Sasha grinned as she delivered a cliche line.

"Together." Elisa's eyes widened at the word that meant so much to her but was simply a word to everyone else. She heard the echo of her mother in her head.

"Together soon my love."

"Together soon mummy."

Elisa swallowed the lump and nodded with determination, Cyrus and Sasha stood at the front of their small group as they knew a quick, easy, and hidden way to get down to the part of the beach they needed to be at. Quinton grabbed her wrist in a tight grip forcing her to look at her friend who now had a hint of emotion in usually cold and distant eyes.

"Once we're on that beach we're exposed. Are you sure you know where it is?" He was not doubting her, it was a warning, that she had to be definite, that they only had one chance before they were possibly spotted. Levi rolled his eyes and ruffled Quintons already messy hair.

"Have a bit of faith in her Quilt!" Quinton sneered at him but gave Elisa a look letting her know he wanted to hear what she had to say.

"I'm sure." He nodded and sent her a rare smile that lit up his usually empty face, his eyes brightened, and Elisa couldn't help but respond in typical Elisa West fashion. She wrinkled her nose and gave him a disgusted face.

"Are you having a stroke, Quinton? Your face looks a bit weird." The scowl was back with death in his ocean blues, a satisfied smirk on Elisa's face and she patted his cheek not too softly. He shrugged her off grumbling under his breath and Levi secretly fist-bumping the girl.

"Now." Cyrus hissed and they darted out from their hiding spot across the narrow street and into an alleyway. They rushed after Cyrus and Sasha who held their hands up in a wait motion before they carried on. They had to duck or dive behind bins and walls whenever the couple spotted one of the people they were avoiding. They saw more and more of the people making the nerves in their body stand to attention, they knew they were here, they were searching for them, for her.

They quickly slid down the grassy hill that fell onto a path, Levi stumbled and nearly screamed when he fell over the next hill. Quinton grabbed him by the back of his shirt and yanked him under the dense tree they were all huddled under which shielded them from the path above them.

"Careful twinkle toes." Quinton spat and Levi made a face at him. They were on another main path; all it took was for one of the men to walk down the path from the top of the hill. They skid down the grassy hill and so made it there quicker. Elisa saw the cobble hill that went onto the beach, no trees and no coverage. She bit her lower lip and nodded to herself.

"You ready girl?" Sasha asked quietly as they all sized up the distance from where they were down to the beach.

"Nope." She said honestly with a wry grin. Then she was off, sprinting across the sandy path and onto the rocky path that became steep and slippery. Huge rocks lined the walls of the cliff and she stuck to them as much as she could, hoping that it would keep her hidden. Her friends followed her lead as they made their way down the beach to the one place Elisa had memorised the day they went there. Her eyes scanned the partially wet sand looking for a silver glint among the grains. Her heart thundered against her chest and she began to panic as she couldn't find it.

"Guys what are we looking f-" Levi was cut off as he fell to the ground with a curse. Elisa spun around and sighed in relief as she saw that Levi had tripped over a silver pipe that was deeply buried in the sand.

"That." She breathed and looked towards the cliffs, she tilted her head this way and that until a sparkle in the cliff face caught her eyes. Elisa ignored Levi's hand and ran towards the pile of rocks, using her strength and ignoring the stiffness and tiredness of her muscles she pulled herself onto the rocks, her eyes only leaving the sparkle in the cliff to make sure her foot does not slip into one of the many gaps between the rocks.

She noted how some of the rocks were placed discreetly like stairs which made climbing easier. She got to eye length with the sparkle and rubbed at the rock watching as sand and dirt fell off in a clump, revealing more of the silver that had been hidden. A giddy laugh escaping her lips and her throat clogging with emotion she did not completely understand. A metal W embedded in the rock face, rusted but she could still see the silver sparkling whenever the sun bounced against the foreign material. Her friends stood on rocks beneath and next to her staring at the W that had also been drawn in the journal.

"So where is it?" Sasha asked confused and Elisa rubbed her face. Somewhere close, it had to be here, this had to be it! This was a simple path to a lab. Down a hill, up a hidden rock stair structure and to the lab. But where was it? A thought came to her and she looked around the rocks she stood on, there had to be a gap... big enough for people to get down.

"Does anyone have a phone I can borrow? Or a torch?" Sasha turned Cyrus around and searched through the backpack he wore. She pulled out a torch and grinned.

"I raided Karson's spy gear before we left. Can you believe he had a whole box dedicated to torches?" She scoffed.

"He's not a spy Sash," Cyrus said tiredly as if they had already had multiple conversations about Karson's occupation. Elisa ignored their soft bickering and crouched near the gap, her hand against the wall supporting her as she pointed the flashlight down into the gap. She smiled when metal bars glinted in the light.

"Quinton, Levi." The boys climbed over and watched her curiously. She handed the rucksack to Quinton and made him hold the torch as she stuck one leg into the gap.

"WHOA!"

"THE HELL?"

"DUDE WAIT!"

"SPIDERS ELLIE SPIDERS!" Elisa shivered at Sasha's words but pushed her discomfort aside and her foot found the ladder.

"Elisa are-"

"Don't ask, or I'll think too much." She interrupted Quinton who pressed his lips together and nodded in understatement. Her eyes flashed in appreciation and she quickly but carefully climbed down the ladder until she felt sand beneath her feet.

Quinton dropped the rucksack into her awaiting arms and told her he was coming down. Elisa pulled the straps over her shoulders and lifted her torch, her eyes widening slightly as she saw a cave opening in the cliff face. One by one the teens came down and once again Elisa was off into the dark tunnel. A hand-pulled on the back of her jumper and she looked over her shoulder. Quinton and Levi glowered at her, Cyrus facepalmed and Sasha shook her head in disappointment. Elisa frowned confused.

"What?"

"Okay, babe do you seriously not think your parents placed security measures?" Her face relaxed and she acknowledged their concern with a small smile.

"Water got in here with the tide, there is a very small chance that there are any electrical measures in place." Yet her words didn't comfort them, and the two boys still gripped the back of her jumper, Sasha holding onto Quinton and Cyrus holding onto Levi in an attempt to stick together as they walked into the unknown. The cave opened and they heard the dripping of water, light from the torch lit up the cave room and landed on a door built into the rock. The teens felt a shiver as they stared at the ominous metal door.

Elisa couldn't believe it. This was, must be her mothers' secret lab. The lab that contained all the data and work her mother no doubt wanted her to destroy. This was it. This was the key and beginning to her normality. Quinton pressed his hand against the door and pushed as if it would just pop open for him. Cyrus and Sasha talked between themselves about how they could get into the room and Levi was frowning, his ears straining for some reason and he looked tense. He kept looking towards the entrance and Elisa felt bad that he was feeling the paranoia she felt.

"Does it need a key or something?" Cyrus mumbled as they looked for a lock of some sort.

"Or something." A voice that didn't belong to one of the teens called out. Yet a faintly familiar voice, one that Elisa hadn't heard enough of but recognised.

They spun around in fear and the blood drained from Elisa's cheeks as they looked at the small group of three men pointing guns at them, more men no doubt outside the cave and on the beach. The person smirked slightly and tilted his head innocently as he regarded the group of teenagers with a knowing expression. Elisa let out a pained sigh and her eyes briefly fluttered closed before she stared head-on.

"Hey, Little Princess! Ain't this a bit awkward?"

Awkward was an understatement.

26

Then

Dripping crimson liquid from the limp figure tied to an old wooden chair, dark hair matted with blood and eyes barely open. The darkness in the room played with his already weak vision making him see shadows he believed existed, light spots flickered in his eyes in what he hoped to be the beginning of an escape from the torturous life he had found himself trapped in.

Every muscle in his body felt like weights under his bruised skin, his body either too heavy to move or simply numb. He wasn't dead yet though, he knew that. Death would be a sweet release, too easy; death would mean he didn't have to feel and endure the amount of pain he had to take on.

"A nobody, that's what you are. Your death will mean next to nothing. I'll end you, right here and nobody would notice." He stated factually, cold eyes studying the broken man before him, his fingers tapped against his mahogany desk as thoughts whirred n his mind.

"I... I don't have anything to give you. Leave me be please." The man begged and the guards in the room lifted their gun to point at the trembling man.

"At ease..." The guards lowered their weapons after a moment but kept their eyes on the bloody man in the centre of the square room. Their boss ran his tongue along his teeth and a cruel smirk lit up behind the black mask he wore, his head nodding as he came to a decision and stood up. His footsteps only caused the anxiety in the man to rise, he wished for death quickly, no more torture, no more pain.

He knelt in front of the man and let out a slow sigh, his gun resting in his calloused palm making sure it was in his hostages' eyesight.

"See... you do have something I want. Or at least you know who has what I want. You, sir, are the least expected person, perfect for what I have planned." The man lifted his head and scowled at his captor, he didn't want to hear this disgusting man's plans, he had already had to listen to him rant over and over about some dumb project, something he wasn't interested in the least.

"I'm not taking part in whatever you have planned." The man chuckled gleefully and slapped a hand on the man's knee making him jerk away in pain and hiss loudly.

"OH! Do you think you have a choice? Oh, you poor thing... no when I want something, I get it. Whether I sent people out to do my dirty work or I do it myself. In this case, you are going to be my inside man." Inside man? Inside man for what? What was expected of him? Surely not death, he wouldn't kill anyone even if it meant saving his own life.

"I'm not killing anyone, not hurting anyone. Nothing of that sort."

"No, no, no! You've got me all wrong! Death and torture can easily be avoided if I have what I need, I don't care how you get the things I need, as long as you get them. Understand, Mr Nelson? You work for me now; you are my partner." The battered man closed his eyes in defeat knowing that he had no choice in the matter. His sore eyes watered in frustration; his life was no longer his own.

An entire 3 years it took for Mr Nelson to grow closer to William and Delilah West, he did so without rousing suspicion and hoped he could get whatever knowledge he needed to without killing the couple.

The married couple had been up and around England for the past three years, not stopping for too long before they moved again. They had moved to Robin Hoods Bay permanently with the hope they could start a permanent life away from whatever danger they had been running from. This was his chance to get the answers he needed. Those three years were hell, consistent beatings from his partner when he didn't have any information, stress when he couldn't hack into any devices owned by the couple and frustration when they began to grow suspicious of his constant wondering of their whereabouts. He knew it was Delilah he had to gain the trust of which had proven hard in the first few months of them properly knowing each other. Delilah, he knew, was a woman of perception, she could read people like a book and figure out their intentions with a single facial expression.

He sat in the West kitchen, Delilah humming as she baked cupcakes and William was watching the football match. Mr Nelson swallowed the nerves that bubbled in his throat. His assignment was simple, get them to trust him with their secrets, get the answers and then kill them.

His partner had given him all the necessary training and knowledge on how to kill without leaving a trace. He was ready if worst came to worst. His eyes landed on Delilah who had a soft smile on her face as she baked, her mind a million miles away as she daydreamed and had her back towards them; it had been 3 years of only talking over text or through letters, no personal information was shared, and his partner was getting angsty.

"You ok man?" William asked him curiously wondering why he was glaring at the table with hatred and looking at his wife hesitantly. Mr Nelson nodded slowly and rubbed a hand over his face, his stumble prickly against his palm reminding him he needed a good shave.

Delilah casually peeked at the man from under her lashes and studied his tense figure, there were times he had acted this way but both Delilah and William had brushed it off as him simply stressing about work. They hadn't been as close to the man and it was like they were just getting to know him. So much had happened in the past few years that all William and Delilah knew was that they could trust each other and nobody else; Mr Nelson being a close first. She placed a mug of tea in front of him earning a grateful smile from him.

"I'm just wondering something, and I'd like you to answer if that's okay?" William nodded slowly and sipped at his tea, his attention split between the man and the football match.

"Sup?"

"What do you do with your lives?" Delilah giggled at the strange question and slid the baking tin into the oven before turning to the man.

"What an odd question?" He sighed and wet his chapped lips with his tongue.

"I mean, I don't see or hear of you guys working now. So, what do you do now? I know you served in that Lab doing god knows what but, how are you able to live like this?" The West couple exchanged a look before shrugging.

"We got paid a lot whilst working in that lab, and when we... left... our employer managed to help out financially. Also, you know I work down at the diner and Lils works at the library." Mr Nelson nodded but shook his head.

"Yeah, but what do you do otherwise? Did you just give up on your scientist life? That's stupid if you ask me.

"Why the privacy breach?" Mr Nelson's eyes widened slightly before he sighed.

"Sophie and I are struggling, I'm just wondering how I can help make her life better than what it currently is... she also needs something to do with her life; said she's bored at home." He half lied, it was true what he said about his girlfriend Sophie, but they weren't in a lot of financial trouble, just enough for him to bring it up. Delilah immediately began looking for jobs available in their area and York while William studied his friend who seemed to be sweating a lot more then he should be for someone who was just talking to his friends.

"Are you hiding something from me?" He asked bluntly and Mr Nelson jumped. His heart pounding wondering how William had found out.

"Hiding what exactly?" He chuckled nervously.

"I dunno man... you're acting a bit strange lately." William's eyes bored into the man's head practically demanding the truth with his aura.

"I'm not I'm just stressed; I need something else to concentrate on which is why I asked about what you do in your spare time and if you were still scientists. It would be cool if you were." William spared a glance at his wife who had paused in her searching, her brows knitted together and her eyes on the nervous man in the kitchen. He could see her mind working fast as she studied him and no doubt trying to read his behaviour through his actions. William sucked his teeth but smiled.

"You know you can ask us for help anytime bro, just let me know." Mr Nelson nodded and sighed as he realised, he wasn't going to get anywhere by asking them nicely, he would have to use force. He didn't want to use the darker method, but he had no choice. As he pulled on his coat, William called out to him with a grin.

"Before you go... I've been trying to figure out how to say this to you and Lils said we should ask you straight away before anyone else finds out and begs us." Delilah chuckled at her husband's anxious rambling and walked over to slip her arm around his waist. She grinned up at him as he placed his arm around her shoulders and handed a card to Mr Nelson. The man frowned in confusion at the couple who grinned widely at him, his fingers turned to envelop over and opened it, his eyes widening as he saw the front of the card.

'Will you be my Godfather?'

His watery eyes lifted to the shiny brown and green ones that watched him in earnest hope, his heartbeat fast as he stared at the words he had never expected to see, especially not towards him.

"What do you say, mate?" William asked and Delilah tilted her head as she saw the genuine emotion on the trembling man, his hand covered his mouth as he nodded and let the tears fell. William whooped and hugged Mr Nelson who hugged him back, he then took Delilah into his arms and smiled when she rubbed his arm in reassurance.

"You'll be great." She mumbled and Mr Nelson could only hope he would be the best godfather to exist. But then came the problem... his partner. The dark abyss of depression and guilt grabbed hold of him again and he hid the emotions with a grin. His life was never going to be easy until he got rid of the men who were threatening his life.

"Tell them!" Sophie begged her fiancé who paced the living room, the ripped-up letter sat on the table between them along with the broken pieces of the teacup the man had thrown down. The letter that told him his time was running out and he had to give them some information that the Wests were hiding or else they would kill him and send someone else in his place. He shook his head before an idea came to him, he knelt in front of Sophie ignoring the sharp pieces that dug into his knees and searched her wide confused eyes.

"We can run." He breathed and his eyes lit up as if it were the most amazing idea, he had ever thought of. He would take his Sophie, they would run and hide, away from the man called Hamish, away from TCT who practically controlled his life. Sophie, however, shook her head in sympathy.

"We can't..." He groaned and took her small hands in his larger ones.

"Darling we can! I know how to erase our existence, we can hide under the radar, live in a small cottage that isn't on maps, we could live a life of peace away from all this and-"

"We would never officially be married. I would never see my family and friends again. Yes, I want to be with you and become Mrs Nelson but there are certain things I refuse to give up." She sank slowly onto the ground next to the defeated man. Her hand held his hands tightly as she willed him to understand.

"You need to tell William, tell Delilah. They have a little boy on the way, your godson! They're in so much danger and if they're in danger and whatever they've hidden is found? Nobody would be ever free. You have to warn them, help them stop this." He lifted his tired eyes to meet the light grey eyes of the woman he fell in love with. She wiped a tear from his cheek and gave him an encouraging smile.

"Save the Wests Harrison. You need to help save them."

"They found me." William jerked awake from his slumped position on the sofa and blinked away the sleep as he tried to focus on his best friend. Harrison held a bottle of beer in his hands making William screw up his nose. William and Harrison had ever been drinkers and would only drink when something was wrong or when they were celebrating something. There was nothing to celebrate, not that he was aware of anyways, and so his body straightened as he cleared his mind.

"Who found you?" Harrison met his best friend's eyes and watch the fear and horror enter them, he watched the panic settle in and the way he jumped up with his eyes jumping to the staircase that was visible through the doorway.

"They're not here! They don't know where you live." William relaxed before his best friends' word's registered in his mind, he took a step backwards and looked at his friend in disbelief.

"You... You're with them?" Harrison stood up and held his hands out in surrender.

"Not by choice! Damn never by choice! They somehow knew. They... god I don't know exactly but apparently, one of the street cameras had picked up on my car or face and since I didn't erase myself out of the system, they knew who I was. Where I lived. They didn't know you or any of the other scientists, but they knew I had a connection to you, that you guys trusted me. They clicked on that you were the missing scientists and that I helped hide you." William's stance was defensive, and Harrison blurted everything out, he spilt his partner/ bosses plan.

"They watched me, Will. They followed me, took pictures of me, then began sending me threatening letters just to stress me out. Then they caught me. They tortured me and covered my disappearance up-"

"How long were you gone? When was this?" William began feeling guilt as he realised that while he and Delilah had managed to get away, his best friend had taken the heat.

"About a year after we managed to get you away. It was before I met Sophie, I was at home when the doorbell rang, two guys grabbed me and threw me in a van, knocked me out and the next thing I knew I woke up in a room strapped to a chair. They started asking questions, demanding to know my connection to Project Miracle which of course I didn't even remember what the hell that was. They explained the group of scientists that had been recruited and stuff, and said they knew I was connected somehow as they caught my face on a street camera. I managed to erase you guys from all surrounding cameras and you guys ditched your car, right? So, I was the only lead they had." Harrison licked his dry lips and looked out the window making sure he wasn't being watched in any way, he couldn't believe he didn't erase his face from the cameras. How was he so clumsy?

"Long story short they made a deal with me after a while. I would get the information they needed but I wouldn't tell them your name or who you guys were. They agreed that if they got what they needed, they wouldn't resort to killing you guys or me. They would let us live in peace. I got rid of any cameras and microphones they had on me the moment they dropped me off home, but they would always stay in contact."

"Is this why you were insistent on knowing where we were all the time?" William felt his stomach clench and his eyes darted to the staircase. Delilah had talked to him a while back saying she felt weird about Harrison, that he was hiding something important from them. Like always, his wife was right.

"I needed to keep tabs on you, so I knew you were safe. I tried to get something out of you without losing your trust. I know you wanted to live a life away from what you were running from which is why I tried not to bring it up. But I need to tell you. You have a kid on the way and god... I want out Will. I want this to stop."

The room settled into silence as the two men had no clue what to say to each other. William was frozen in guilt and sadness; his best friend had been protecting them whilst trying to protect himself. Harrison was hunched over feeling a sense of relief. His best friend was aware, he wasn't hiding something that could alter their lives if he said one small thing. He wasn't alone in this game no more.

"We need to make a plan," Delilah spoke up from the doorway making the two men jump in surprise.

"Delilah I'm so-" She held up a hand with a gentle smile.

"This isn't your fault if anything it's ours so we're sorry. But we need to make a plan so that all of us are safe."

"We do that how?" Delilah walked around the room until a thought came to her.

"False information mixed with the truth. You can tell them that we are remaking the serum and that it is taking time, that we are driving all over England trying to stay under the radar whilst gathering equipment and materials needed. Keep them on their feet. That way they know you are complying with their orders and are giving them the info, they need." Harrison nodded slowly before letting a small smile light his face.

"That could work! They don't know your face and I didn't tell them that you're here, only that you're in a town close by. They're aware that you travel from my past reports. This could work!" Delilah relaxed into Williams side and he smiled at his best friend whose shoulders had slumped in relief.

"You said false information mixed with the truth... are you remaking the serum?" Delilah hesitated but slowly nodded before shaking her head.

"I have some leftover hidden someplace nobody else knows. Not even Will." William gave her a disapproving look to which she completely ignored. He knew she was hoping that one day they could make their Project Miracle a vaccine for people who needed it, hell even he had those dreams that they could make their project a worldwide reality. But they both knew deep down that it needed to stay hidden, away from governmental figures. Harrison saw the tension between his best friend and the woman he saw as a sister, the quicker this project miracle was out of the way, the better for everyone.

"PRESTON!" Roman ran down the stairs with Owen hot on his heels, both boys scowling as they searched for their youngest brother. Alexander didn't lift his head from his position on the sofa, a blanket wrapped around him as he watched TV. His two brothers ran into the room and looked at him questioningly. He sighed heavily and rolled his eyes as if he wasn't a childish 10 years old himself.

"No, he's not in here." He drawled and the two boys ran back out taking their eldest brother's words to heart. He listened to them run about the rest of the house and search through cupboards. The blanket wrapped around Alexander was tugged and pulled down making him laugh slightly as he saw two light brown eyes poke out from under the blanket.

"Gone?" 2-year-old Preston asked loudly from his hiding spot under the blanket making Alexander laugh and try to shush the giggly boy in his lap.

"Yeah, bud. Go find Uncle Harry." Preston's lips frowned and he clung onto his shirt.

"Stay?" He whimpered and Alexander groaned; gently he pulled his littlest brother away from him and placed him on the floor ignoring the way his brother began sucking his thumb and looking around a bit lost. He nudged Preston with his foot to gain his attention again.

"Quicky run before Roman, and Owen come and eat you!" Preston gasped horrified making Alexander grin mischievously and his little feet padded across the room and down the hallway in a rush to quickly seek 'safety'. He heard his godfather grunt and knew Preston had found him; now he could get back to watching his program.

Harrison finished cooking dinner for the boys just as a small body collided with his legs. Chuckling, he scooped up the small boy that clutched his jumper whilst looking around.

"What are you doing squirt?"

"Hide," Preston stated quietly and Harrison shook his head in amusement as he ushered the young boy behind the door just as Owen and Roman ran into the kitchen.

"Whoa, whoa, whoa! What's going on kiddos?" He managed to grab the 5-year-old Roman and 8-year-old Owen. The two boys stopped thrashing in his hold and looked up with their doe brown eyes.

"Preston sat on our playdough house!" Harrison snorted and composed himself to act serious.

"Oh, dear can't you fix it?" Roman stomped his foot angrily.

"NO! HE MIXED ALL THE COLOURS WITH HIS FAT BUM!" He yelled and Harrison sat him in the chair, Owen climbing onto one of the other chairs.

"Ok boys how about we stop the hunt for Preston, and I'll buy you some more playdough? Yeah? No more shouting. Mummy and daddy are coming soon." At that statement, Preston clapped his hands giving away his position and making Roman stick his tongue out at his little brother. Owen sulked at the mention of his parents knowing they weren't coming home alone.

"I don't want to see mummy and daddy," Owen whined and Harrison sighed. It had been a constant argument since Owen was told he was going to have a baby sister. Owen said girls were stinky except his mummy and that he didn't want a silly sister. Before he could reassure his godson that he would love his little sister, the door opened, and he watched Roman, Preston and Alexander rush to their parents.

"Mummy, mummy!" Preston giggled as he ran into his mothers' open arms. Delilah scooped her youngest son into her arms and kissed his small button nose eliciting a squeal.

"Hello, babies!" She cooed and hugged Alexander who held onto her waist. She stroked his hair back and pressed her lips to his forehead. She knelt back down to the ground so Preston could sit on her knee and held her hand out to a moody Roman. He shuffled towards his mother and let her tug him into her arms. She cupped his face and pressed multiple kisses to his cheek making him moan in annoyance and try and pull away, his cheeks red as he blushed embarrassed. Delilah smiled at her three boys who were all different, and she found amusement in their reactions. She frowned slightly when she noticed Owen in the kitchen doorway holding onto Harrison, refusing to look at her. Harrison gave her a soft smile and she relaxed knowing Owen was just being Owen and he would give in within seconds.

"Mummy where's-" Alexander stopped when their father walked through the door holding a baby seat that had a pink blanket sat inside. The boys were stood in silence as they followed their father into the living room, their eyes not leaving the car seat. Harrison carried a sulky Owen into the living room and felt his own eyes water as he watched William carefully scoop out the little pink bundle.

Delilah took her first daughter into her arms and sat on the floor, her sons sitting around her staring at their baby sister with wide eyes.

"This is your baby sister Elisa," Delilah whispered to the boys. Preston reached out and stroked the baby girls' hand-making her twitch before relaxing. Alexander looked at his mother for permission before stroking her cheek with his finger, his skin barely brushing hers afraid to make her cry. Roman simply stared.

Owen was put down and made his way towards his baby sister, her eyes cracked open momentarily and her lips tilted in a smile as she shifted in her mothers' arms; a bright smile lit up Owen's face and he was instantly in love. He wanted to hold his baby sister close and give her loads of hugs so that he would be her best brother. As if hearing his thoughts, Alexander announced that he would be her favourite brother before Roman interjected and said he would be, a small argument starting between the three as Preston simply sat there touching Elisa's hand every so now and then.

Harrison smiled down at his godchildren, the first West daughter making his already protective instincts go haywire. He needed to protect this pure family, he needed to save them.

"She's gone." William read the text on his phone and shared a worried look with his wife. Harrison's fiancée, Sophie, was gone. She wasn't ill, nor was she in some freak accident. They were aware that Harrison had been at a meeting with the man he was forced to work for, they had managed to keep their lives safe and away from the bad men, they had thought maybe they had given up. Sophie had been murdered in front of Harrison; Harrison had lost the person he loved most. They knew what was to come next.

Delilah swallowed and nodded to her husband who held onto her wrist. One look from her made him drop his arm and he watched her pull a rucksack from under their bed before going into a safe hidden behind boxes. She picked out a red journal, vial, and a few other small things before shoving them in the bag.

"We could run together..." William tried but stopped when he saw the tears on her face.

"We need to protect our children Will. I'm taking miracle. You protect our boys. I'm taking all the stuff with me and when it's time to come home, we will destroy everything once and for all."

"Why didn't we destroy everything now?" William asked and she paused, regret in her eyes.

"I... I don't know... I got caught up in our family. I pretended so much that everything was okay that I started to believe it. It's too late to destroy everything. But we will when everything calms down." He held his wife, his best friend tightly.

"Everything will work out; things will go okay... I'll keep you up to date, you keep me up to date. Don't stay away for too long... I want to have my family close to me." She smiled and the West couple held onto each other tightly.

Little did they know it would be the last time they would ever hold each other again. Harrison was done keeping them safe, the one person who loved him and the one person he loved was gone, all because he centred his life around the West family.

"Just promise me that. If anything goes wrong. You protect my children. You make sure they're not dragged into this. They don't know anything. They won't know of this stupid mistake we made. That I made. Promise me that you'll be the best godfather ever and that you'll love and protect them the same amount I would have?" William rasped between his bruised and bleeding lips, he leaned heavily against the cell bars looking up at the man he grew up with. He knew he had no right to ask a favour from his heartbroken best friend, but he was the only one who could look over his children.

Harrison looked down at him coldly, the reminder of his Sophies death fresh in his mind. However, he loved the West children like his own, he watched them grow into the perfect children they were today. He felt that familiar spark of sympathy and looked both ways of the hallway making sure they were alone.

"I promise Will." But in his head, Harrison prayed that his godchildren will never find out about their parent's past. Because he knows that if they knew something, he would have to break his promise.

"Okay let's get to introductions. This is Andre, Finley and Karson. They grew up with us and we are all practically siblings. And this is Harrison... Dads best friend." Harrisons' eyes landed on a small beautiful little girl with wavy brown hair. He had never seen this girl before but one look at her hazel eyes made a memory flash in his mind.

"You look just like your mother... but you have your father's eyes." A frown lit up her face and Harrison mentally berated himself. He didn't know exactly what this child had been through. After he sold his best friend out, TCT immediately began searching for Delilah West. He was aware they found her 8 years ago as they grabbed William around the same time.

He felt guilty when he thought about his best friend but like always, he pushed that feeling to the back of his mind. He was only around to care for his godchildren who assumed their parents had simply abandoned them. He wondered what happened to Elisa in the past 8 years, he hadn't been told of her life as another TCT shadow had been watching her.

"You just closed your only escape. Why?" Harrison asked as he stood still in the kitchen. His eyes could barely make out the small girl in the doorway.

"My brothers are in there. I won't let you hurt them." Her determined and strong voice echoed in the silence and in that moment, Harrison knew. The way she so confidently spoke out, the way she blocked the pathway to her brothers, the way she stood defensively and only relaxed once she saw him.

Harrison began trying to make conversation with the stoic and somewhat empty child, he managed to make her relax but as he walked away, the smile slipped from his face. He made his way to a guest room and laid in his bed; the promise he made all those years ago would have to be broken. Because at that moment, Harrison Nelson realised with a heavy heart.

Elisa West knew.

27

Now

"You."

"Me." Harrison shrugged his shoulders unapologetically and Elisa clenched her fists as she slowly nodded as if it all made sense. It made sense how her mother was found, it made sense why her father was taken, it made sense how TCT always had an eye on them and why they interfered more in her life. Her mind flashed back to the moment she met him, how curious he had been, how happy and welcoming he had seemed. After that evening, she didn't see much of him.

Now that she thought about it, she didn't know anything about him. Since Alexander was their legal guardian, they probably had no reason to question his life. They had no reason to wonder why he never visited or asked them about their day.

Harrison Nelson may have been their godfather, but he hadn't been around much after William was taken and Delilah died. Now she knew why, Harrison despite being the reason the West couple were gone, was guilty in some sense. Staying away from his godchildren was his way of apologising without telling them what he had done. Harrison had figured out she knew things that she shouldn't have and had information that they were probably trying to get out of her father. The information they killed her mother for.

Elisa's hand tightened on the straps of the bag, her feet taking a step back and eyes darting around as she tried to see some clue as to what she was going to do next. She couldn't believe that one of TCTs men who were in such a high position, was close to her family. He had literally been under their noses waiting for someone to show they knew something.

"You know him?" Cyrus asked confused at the familiarity shown between the two, Elisa nodded her head hesitantly and regretfully. An expression on her face that didn't escape Harrison. For some reason he didn't understand, his heart dropped at seeing the disgust and hatred in her hazel eyes.

"He was my father's best friend." Harrison nodded and pocketed the black gun he had been holding, he walked closer to the teens not paying attention to any of them except the West girl. He wanted to smile when he saw her straighten and stand in front of her friends in a sign of defence, her hazel eyes glaring into his own with no sign of betrayal or hurt in them. He guessed it was because she had the least amount of connection to him compared to the other boys, or maybe it was because she had never trusted him when they first met and had always held some sort of suspicion over him in the back of her head. He wished she didn't know anything, then he could have gotten to know the little princess.

"I was... I'm also a lot more involved in her life then you realise." Her friends frowned confused, and he chuckled as he laid a hand on Elisa's head, ignoring the way she tensed and glowered. She wanted to be far away from the man who reeked of desperation and betrayal.

"I'm her godfather." Quinton scoffed and stared at the man who was supposed to protect his friend and love her like his own, in hatred. Sasha reached forward and took Elisa's hand into her own silently offering her support while Cyrus observed the other men behind Elisa's so-called godfather. Levi was struggling between glaring and making a Star Wars reference.

"Of course. Of course, you're her godfather." The other teens felt a wave of sympathy for Elisa who stood as still as a statue. Would she ever get a break from the betrayal and lies? Although she wasn't as affected as her brothers might have been if they were in her position, she still felt the pinching in her heart as she felt sorry for her father. He had been deceived by his best friend. She felt disgusted that she shared a connection with the man before her. Harrison scoffed at the pitiful expression on his goddaughter and moved away shaking his head.

"Your father knew."

"Knew that you were going to probably kill me?" He rolled his eyes at the teenager and crossed his arms over his chest as he looked away from her, he didn't like looking at her and feeling bad.

"He knew who I worked for; he knew why I betrayed him. He and his 'perfect' wife ruined my life. It's their fault that... if they didn't involve me... if they got rid of it-" Elisa didn't care nor want to listen to the reasoning behind Harrison's betrayal. There was never a good enough reason to betray people you say you love and care about. She scoffed and shook her head at the man who clearly acted on his emotions, he didn't think of the consequences his actions would cause. She wondered if he truly understood what Project Miracle was, what TCT had planned to do with it.

"My dad didn't sit there and plan to ruin your life. Not like you did." Harrison Nelson shook his head wanting to get this over and done with. He wasn't here to tell his story and beg her to understand why he did what he did.

"Why didn't he tell me that... that you worked for TCT?"

Harrison sighed and felt a flash of guilt as he remembered his last promise to his best friend. He clenched his jaw remembering the way William looked at him through his bruised eyes, his body weak leaning against the iron bars on the ground. William West was once his best friend, his brother. But some bonds were meant to be severed. He looked down at the West girl looking slightly past her head, he didn't, couldn't look her in the eye.

"You led us here, to the lab which I'll thank you very much for! Good girl!" He sneered and ran his hands over the metal door, searching for a handle or something. He frowned and groaned in frustration as he saw a small box in the wall next to the door.

Using a knife from his belt sheath, he dug the sharp metal between the small gap where the cover would pop off. They heard a satisfying clink and Harrison's frustration deepened as he saw a scanner of some kind. He pressed his calloused hand against the pad and watched intently as a blue line lit up under his skin and scanned his hand. A moment later the pad turned red and sucked his teeth mentally cursing Delilah.

Elisa watched her so-called godfather curse and punch the rocky wall in anger, he called over one or two of his men to discuss ways they could open the door. She rubbed at her cheek and the side of her neck, completely lost. How had her life come to this? Standing in a cliff cave, her friends around her with her godfather trying to get into a secret lab that nobody but her family was meant to know about. Again, Elisa felt the relief and gratefulness that she wasn't alone, but she also couldn't help the guilt and worry that something could happen to her best friends.

Levi, the unseen pirate who had finally made himself known even if he didn't mean to. Her childhood best friend whom she grew up with and was the key to some of her childish happy memories. She never thought she would see him again, but it seemed as though everyone she had met in her life would always be entangled and stuck on her path until she changed direction.

Sasha, the bubbly girl who had taken her under her wing when she first started school. Her first girl friend who treated her like a human being, who didn't feel threatened by her once standoffish and cold personality. Sasha had simply danced into her life and refuse to dance out of it. A notion that Elisa would always hold dear to her heart. Sasha could have left the moment she realised that Elisa's life was dangerous, that people who knew Elisa always got hurt. But she didn't leave her.

Cyrus, the level-headed teen who acted as though he was the guardian of the group. He kept them all in line, let them fight but would put a stop to it if need be. He was kind and thoughtful and had a protective nature over his friends and girlfriend. Cyrus had helped her understand her thoughts when she couldn't understand them herself. He had been there for them all individually and she was grateful for his presence.

Quinton, the idiot boy who tried to act angry and mean. The boy who tried to intimidate her the moment they met but had instead backed down. The moment he backed down, it was as though they had an understanding between them, that he could see she wasn't fake, that she hid stuff to protect the people she loved. Elisa saw herself in Quinton, the way he was mysterious and quiet, how when he talked it was to insult or throw about sarcastic remarks. But there was a side to Quinton he tried to hide. The protective and caring nature, the boy simply tried not to care about people because he didn't want to lose them. Yet he had cared about them all in his own strange way.

"They can't get in," Sasha mumbled as she watched the men arguing and Levi rolled his eyes. It's not that he hated Sasha, he just enjoyed this frenemies banter they had going on. He also knew that the silent arguing helped distract everyone from their fears.

"No way? How did you come to that conclusion Red?" He snickered and Sasha rolled her eyes with a small smile. Cyrus gave him a grateful smile for trying to ease the tense and stressed atmosphere. Quinton looked towards the entrance and counted four other men standing guard, probably more on the actual beach surrounding the rock formation. He needed to help get his friends to safety, if Harrison couldn't open the door to the Lab, then they could run. They could get away and leave it to these men to figure out.

As if hearing his thoughts, Elisa looked over at him and shook her head, she then looked deep in thought before making her way over to Quinton who scrutinised her, trying to figure out what she was thinking.

"You could run. Go get help. You have a family Quinton, and you have a life that was perfectly fine before I came along." Quinton rolled his eyes at her words. They had all semi accepted that Elisa would always overthink, will always try and pin the blame on herself when in reality, she was as much of a victim as they were. As her friends, they silently agreed that no matter how long it took or if she never stopped blaming herself, they would always put her fears to rest and make sure she knew that they never have or will blame her.

"Okay, I don't want to listen to your sacrificial hero speech. If we run, we run together... but you don't want to run, do you?" She shook her head at his knowing face and the two sighed, both feeling protective instincts curling in frustration as they tried to figure out the best way to save their friends. Elisa turned to

Harrison with his shoulders tense and set, a bit of a plan formulating in her head.

"I can open the door." She said with an aura of certainty about her. Her friends looked at her confused at why she had said that while Harrison nodded slowly.

"Makes sense. Your mother told you everything for a reason..." Elisa nodded not correcting the fact that her mother didn't tell her everything, that she had to work things out herself and piece things together; she walked over to the man who stood next to the scanner. Taking a deep breathe she lifted her cold and slightly red hand, her hand shaking slightly from nerves. The West girl let out a trembling breathe before she placed her palm on the pad. Everyone's eyes on her hand and they all held their breath wondering if there would be a different outcome.

Green. It lit up green!

"Kiddo you're a godsend!" Harrison chuckled happily and they stepped back as they heard metal creaking in protest as the locks slid out of place. The door mechanism whirred as it opened, a slight breeze rushing out making Elisa frown slightly. How was there a breeze coming from inside a cave in a cliff... Unless there was an exit? Harrison grabbed her upper arm and dragged her into the small tunnel another door at the end. The small group marched towards the door which opened with a turn of the handle. Lights flickered on automatically and Elisa was in awe.

The entire room was enforced with concrete which was how everything had been safe from seawater that would no doubt crash against the door when the tide was high. They stood on a walkway that sloped down to a lower level, Elisa leaned against the black metal railing and looked over at the Lab belonging to her mother.

Lights hung from the ceiling, tables and cabinets against one wall. There was a large desk that had a no doubt dusty computer sat on top, black and white wires connecting to other monitors and laptops. There were quite a few cobwebs around the room. Pipes and beams ran across the walls reminding her of the pipe she found on the beach, why would pipes be running from the lab down to the beach? Surprisingly, it didn't look much like a lab, just a workspace.

The room itself was ice cold and Elisa wrapped her arms around her body as the cold seeped into her already cold skin. She suddenly wished she had stolen Roman's coat before they left both for the warmth and the comfort it emitted. Harrison began ordering his men to start looking through the lab and search for anything and everything regarding project miracle. It then hit her that they perhaps had no clue about the journal and vial currently in her bag, which meant she had to figure out how to get these people out of the Lab. Quinton strolled up beside Elisa and swallowed as he took in the room that was lit up by a warm yellowish light. He looked down at the West girl who, after a moment, looked up to meet his gaze.

"We need a plan soon weirdo." She nodded slowly and counted the number of people belonging to TCT, not many.

"We need to figure out how to get them out of this room."

"How do you propose that?" Levi joined the two and kept his eye on Harrison. The man made his lip curl up in distaste.

"We need to destroy everything here. There are two men with Harrison, 3 outside and god knows how many on the actual beach." Sasha piped up softly as she and Cyrus stood with their backs against the railing.

Elisa's eyes landed on the cabinet on the ground near the computers, she noticed something metal just behind the cabinet. Her mother wasn't stupid, she would have made sure there was another way out of the Lab for when the tide came in and she couldn't go out the way she came in. There was a hidden door behind the cabinet, that was their exit.

"Bring those kids down here! What are you whispering about?" Harrison narrowed his eyes in suspicion and his eyes jumped from face to face. They gave him blank looks back not giving away anything making him huff. Somehow the computer wasn't letting him hack around the password, everything was heavily encrypted, and he knew he would need an actual password to be able to see anything. He might have been one of the best hackers, but William and Delilah were scientists with their skills. He wouldn't be surprised if Delilah had managed to find someone to strengthen the security on the laptop. He needed the stupid password.

"How do I get into this computer?" He asked bored and Elisa gave a confused chuckle and tilted her head.

"I don't know. I didn't even know this existed until... until my dad told me." Harrison nodded slowly and looked down at his phone. His men had found a group of people looking around town for a certain West girl. He smirked suddenly and laughed loudly, making the teens cringe.

"Do your brothers know how to get onto the computer?" Before Elisa could respond that her brothers knew nothing and to leave them alone, she heard familiar voices echoing down the small tunnel getting closer to them. Her eyes fluttered closed as she sighed. Of course, these idiots decided to come looking for her. She didn't think they were dumb enough to be caught, however. Which means they probably did want to get caught. Idiots.

"GET OFF ME YOU DISGUSTING PIECE OF-"

"Ah, ah, ah! You know how your mother felt about swearing Alex." Elisa's eyes narrowed angrily as her brothers and their friends were shoved into the room. Her brothers' faces confused and hopeful when they recognised Harrison... until they realised where they were and what that meant. Alexanders face paled and he stood up straight his jaw clenching and he wanted to punch the smug look off his godfather.

"You." He stated and Elisa wanted to cry at the amount of pain she heard in the slightly higher pitch his voice had taken. Roman scowled hatefully wanting to burn holes into the side of Harrison's face and Owen was just as furious. Preston looked so done as if he expected someone close to him to betray them and the fact it was his godfather, the person who their father had trusted, made him want to dish out as much pain as he could to the man.

Harrison didn't understand why he felt his heart clench. These weren't his actual children, he owed them nothing, he had gone too far to just stop what he had been trying to help find for years. The damage was done, and his godchildren stared at him like he was the most despicable person to exist.

In their minds, he was.

28

Now

Owen saw his little sister and he yanked his arm away from one of the men before practically flying down the slope, his arms pulled Elisa towards him and he held her tightly. Her arms wound around his waist and he felt a bit of the tension in his body drop away. When he had woken that morning, he immediately knew she was gone, that she had run off on her own. Holding her, he realised how empty he felt, how angry he felt that she didn't ask him for help. His face buried in her messy hair and his arms wrapped around her body that had begun shaking slightly. He pulled back to hold her by her shoulders and roughly shook her.

"WHY DID YOU LEAVE? WHAT PART OF WE'RE IN THIS TOGETHER DO YOU NOT UNDERSTAND?!" Elisa didn't shout, she didn't cry, she simply hugged her brother tightly and rubbed his back in reassurance as he let the tears fall down his cheeks. He knew the answers to his questions, she didn't need to respond. Preston rushed over and ruffled her hair and punching her arm.

"Don't run off like that." He scolded lightly and she punched his stomach playfully. Roman didn't say anything, he simply pulled her into his arms and hugged her tightly, happy that he could see her again, that she hadn't left him forever.

"Why are you holding my sister hostage Harrison? Why are you even here?" Alexander demanded, his body language and tone shifting to his Police detective voice, as he tilted his sisters face to look at him; his eyes scanning for any injuries. She sent him a gentle smile and he breathed deeply through his nose trying to contain his anger.

"Long story short, William West is the reason the love of my life died, he's the reason I was tortured and forced to work for an organisation I knew nothing about, he's the reason I've never been able to live peacefully without someone watching me make sure I didn't run off. You know I promised your dad to look after you, to be the godfather who will love you the way your parents did." He shook his head with a cold smile and finally looked Elisa in her eyes; the hazel darkening until they looked almost black.

"See I was going through with my promise, I didn't tell them where your house was, I didn't tell them where you worked or the school you went to. But when little princess here came home, she accidentally showed her cards." The boys glared at him warningly as he took a step closer to Elisa.

"She knew everything. Your mother told her to be careful, that she had to protect you? Right? Don't get me wrong, your mother was lovely, sweet, you remind me of her a lot. But you both have one thing in common. Stubbornness." He sighed and shook his head 'sadly'.

"When the love of my life died, your parents somehow knew I would be... what was the word your father used? Corrupted? Tempted? Delilah left with you and William began watching me closely, only sharing things with me when he needed to. In those years after Delilah left TCT approached me more and more, convince me to join them for real. That I had skills they could use and that their purpose was the right thing for the world. At first, I refused.... but by time I realised how wrong I was." He leaned against the desk; his light blue eyes gleaming with a spark of malice.

"I joined TCT. I became Hamish's partner and my life revolved around finding Project Miracle. They told me that if I could get all the information on Project Miracle from your father, he didn't have to be killed or hurt. I would text your dad, warn him of the consequences, begged him to give in. Until finally I just gave up. TCT were right and your father needed to go. Although I had begun to hate your parents, I couldn't and didn't want to involve you guys when you knew nothing. Of course, until Elisa came." His grin grew and he bent slightly so he could be eye-level with her.

"Your father would be turning in his grave... oh wait... we didn't bury him." He added the last part in a mumble as if remembering that William was gone.

She looked even angrier at his bored statement and took a step towards him, her shoes kicking at a few small rocks. She hated the way he sounded unbothered. Harrison's light blue eyes no longer radiated the gentleness and calmness they held when she first met him, they were unfamiliar and indifferent, looking over her, through her, not looking directly at her. She hated it, feeling so insignificant. He spoke at her not to her, not worthy of his entire attention as his eyes scanned the rocky damp walls around them, looking for something she didn't know yet. Alexander held her by her shoulders stopping her from lunging at the man.

None of them knew what to say after Harrison's little speech, too shocked at the words and the amount of hatred that leaked from his voice. Elisa felt a lump in her throat, her mind replaying the same phrase over and over.

Until Elisa came. This was her fault... her brothers would be safe; her friends would have never been aware of anything. She had to fix this, no matter what. He had seen most of her cards, maybe she should show a few more.

"How many men outside?" She mumbled to Alexander who squinted down at her, Harrison back to ordering his men to do certain things.

"4 outside the door and about 20 on the actual beach," Karson spoke making her jump, she forgot he was with them. Nodding she began to formulate a plan, her eyes flicking around the room as she saw the plan in her mind.

"Do you have any backup on the way?" She asked slowly and hesitantly, Karson nodded slightly not wanting to call attention to them and she relaxed. The men on the beach would be easily apprehended and too busy to help anyone in the lab. Harrison slammed his hand on the table.

"I might know the password!" Elisa piped up making Harrison spin on his heel. He grabbed her harshly by the wrist and shoved her in front of the computer.

"Well then hurry up kid." She swallowed and nodded before quickly reaching into her rucksack and pulling out the red journal. Harrison's brows piqued interested in the book, he recognised Delilah's handwriting immediately and took note that he would have to grab the notebook too.

Elisa skimmed through the pages looking for something, anything that could be a password. Something memorable, something her mother had probably said over and over. Miracle? No, West? Her mind flashed back to the last words her mother said, words her mother had said before. Perhaps...

T-O-G-E-T-H-E-R

Accepted. Oh, she loved how sentimental her mother was.

Harrison rubbed his hands together and practically giggled as he began looking through files as if it was his birthday gift. Elisa on the other hand began working on the next part of the plan, she searched the desk with her eyes, looking for something that would help her figure out how to destroy everything. She walked around slowly and quietly aware that her brothers, friends and the guards were watching her with scrutinising eyes.

She could see cabinets full of paper files; she would have to destroy everything to end the nightmare. What else had her mother written, told her or left her? She paused in her steps and remembered the envelope from the box her mother left her. The box that Alexander had given her on her birthday. The key. It meant something; it had a purpose. But what? She made her way back between her friends and casually took Cyrus wrist to check the time. It was already nearing evening. They had spent the whole day, running, hiding, trying to figure things out.

"What are you planning shadow?" Roman hissed between his gritted teeth. She sent him a teasing smile trying to ease the tension.

"Something spontaneous I hope."

"You best not be hiding anything from us." He warned but Elisa didn't respond as her shoe caught on something on the ground. Her eyes lit up in realisation, she knew what she had to do.

She had found a hidden door behind a cabinet on wheels, pipes leading to the beach, she held a key in her bag that she knew probably didn't unlock something but was rather the key to turning something off... or on. Most of Project Miracle was on paper and the stuff on the computer could easily be destroyed. She also had the vial that contained project miracle. She thought about her science lessons on how to dilute solutions.

Normally you would add water to a chemical, however Project Miracle was more of a medicine. If that was the case, she needed some sort of powder to mix in the solution. The cabinet! Her mother surely had things ready for emergencies. Her eyes trailed back to the door they had entered from, there was a scanner on the inside as well as outside.

Harrison was still mumbling as he read files and the guards had slowly lost interest in her as they looked around the room themselves. Elisa locked eyes with Alexander and looked over at one of the guards. He caught on and elbowed Karson before muttering something to him under his breath. Sasha winced and shook her head as she realised the risk Elisa was about to take, these men had guns on them, they all knew they weren't afraid of shooting them if they did anything that wasn't part of their plans. Elisa ignored her and kept her eyes on the entrance.

Three.

Two.

One.

Elisa darted across the room and up the slope. Harrison heard the slapping of shoes against the concrete and sound around.

"Grab her." He said bored, knowing she would be caught either way and wouldn't be able to escape the cave. But what none of them realised was that they had wrongly thought of Elisa's plan, they didn't realise that Elisa wasn't going to leave and find the police, that she wasn't going to lead the MI5 agents who were no doubt on the beach fighting against the TCT men, down into the lab.

No.

Karson and Alexander tackled the two guards to the ground with Andre and Finley helping to restrain them. Alexander felt a punch to his gut and doubled over as his breath escape him. Andre threw his first at the guard and smirked as they heard a satisfying crack. The guard lay unconscious with blood pooling from his nose and the boy's fist-bumped proudly. Karson dodged a knife that had been inches from his neck and Roman hit the man's wrist making him drop the weapon. Finley then proceeded to kick the guard on the side of his head knocking him out cold.

Elisa slapped her hand on the scanner on the wall next to the door and the door slid closed. She had locked them all in with the enemy who laughed in amusement.

"So, you trapped us in here effectively cutting me off from my team outside? Good one... now be a good girl and open the damn door." He waved his hand over his shoulder not paying them much attention. Elisa relaxed slightly and walked back down the slope.

"Get away from the computer please." She said in a hard voice. Harrison faced her once more and the smile he gave her made even Quinton shiver.

"See sweetheart. I'm in charge here. Your little stunt of locking us here won't do anything. Now open the door." Her spine straightened and she shook her head. Harrison eyed her before making a face and shrugging. Faster then she could comprehend, he pulled out a gun and pointed it at her. Her eyes widened as she heard a bang echo loudly. Her name being yelled out by her brothers and friends.

But Elisa didn't feel any pain, she didn't sway or stumble because of a bullet. Instead, something heavy had pushed into her and they fell to the floor, the only pain she felt was in the back of her head from smacking into the concrete. When she opened her eyes she looked to the ceiling, her mind vaguely aware that someone had taken the bullet, that someone had jumped in front of her. She didn't want to look and see who the person was, but her head turned anyways.

She wanted to cry when she saw messy jet-black hair covering half of his face. His ocean blue eyes that usually glared her down were hidden under his eyelids. His face pale and his lips parted slightly. Shakily, Elisa pushed herself into a sitting position, her trembling hand hovering over the boy next to her, not knowing whether to shake him. She wished it was a bad dream, that he wasn't actually on the ground motionless.

"Q-Quinton?" She stammered breaking the spell everyone had frozen in. Alexander, Karson, Levi, Andre, Roman and Cyrus immediately attacked Harrison who was just as shocked as the rest of them.

Owen rushed over and checked Quinton over, relieved when Quinton was still breathing and quite strongly. Elisa could barely hear over the thundering of her heart. She could see her friends trying to figure out where Quinton was hurt, she could see her brothers and the boys disarming Harrison and beating him up. Blood pouring from his nose, a cut on his cheek and his lip busted. She stood up ignoring the way her head throbbed and pushed away Preston's concerned hands.

"Don't knock him out," She said loudly and clearly. Her brothers gave her an incredulous look. However, after seeing the murderous expression on her face, the boys understood. They knocked him down to the ground and made sure he was injured enough and had no weapons. Elisa approached him.

"I'm getting my family out of here. You are going to sit here and watch me destroy everything you've been searching for." Reaching into her bag she pulled out the vial making Harrison gape comically. She had it, the entire time she had the finished product and had managed to keep it hidden for years.

Elisa found that the cabinet drawers were open. Checking each one she saw files in some and equipment like test tubes in another. She checked the third drawer and saw a clear bottle, a light cream powder and another liquid. A note underneath them reading,

Just in case.

The girl laid everything on the main table and opened the nose. Instructions on getting rid of the one and only vial or project miracle.

Harrison begged her, pleaded with her to just let him go with the Project, he tried to bargain with her saying he would leave them be if she gave it up and let him go. But Elisa was far from listening to anyone.

She followed them and felt a weight lifting off her shoulder with each step. Pour project miracle into the clear bottle, pour in the clear liquid, and shake which made the solution turn a weird orange colour. She then put the powder in and shook the bottle making sure the powder was mixed in. Her eyes watched the mixture begin to fizzle and so she quickly put the lid over the bottle, tightening it to make sure nothing would come out.

The group watched the solution fizzle and bubble, the solution decreasing in volume and leaving a brown stain on the inside of the bottle. She realised with a jolt that she was effectively burning Project Miracle, but the ingredients she had used made sure that there was no toxic gas or anything; no residue, nothing to save. It had ceased to exist, and she smiled slightly before placing everything including the now non-existent Project Miracle, on the huge table.

She picked up a broken pipe piece leaning against the wall and smashed it against the computer screen, glass shattering and the computer crashing under the weight of the metal. All her anger, pain and fear were let out on all the computers that Harrison had been trying to get into; the monitors not spared from the beating. Harrison's yelling and cursing quietened as he realised it was done. There was nothing left of project miracle. The computer files were trapped in the destroyed computer. Sure, there were paper files, but he knew as well as Elisa that Delilah would have a procedure in place to erase the data. All Elisa had to do was trigger that procedure.

"ELISA STOP!" Owen grabbed her by the shoulders and winced at the manic look in her eyes. He cupped her face hoping to bring her out of the trance she had fallen into.

"Lissy girl, please. We need to get Quinton seen to right now." Her eyes flickered to the body that was cradled limply in Karson's arms. She nodded and ran over to the cabinet. Sasha rushed over and the two of them rolled the cabinet away, a fresh gust of wind hinting them in the face as they looked into another tunnel. The door had opened the moment she had locked the other one telling her that if one was open the other would close. Andre and Finley rushed out with Levi.

Elisa walked over to Karson and brushed the hair away from the boy who had become one of her closest friends, cheek. She swallowed the guilt that threatened to overwhelm her. She didn't like seeing him unconscious. She was used to him saying witty and sarcastic comments that would have her eyes rolling into the back of her head in annoyance.

"You'll be okay creeper." She whispered in his ear, sure of her words. She turned to Karson who studied her in curiosity before he rushed down the tunnel with Sasha and Cyrus hot on their heels.

"Come on Dove." Roman found a rope and with the help of Owen and Preston, the three tied him to one of the metal poles in the room. Harrison didn't fight them, not knowing what he could do now that the only reason he had been after the Wests was gone. Elisa let Alexander lead her towards the exit, her nose scrunching as she refused to let the water fall from her eyes. Her brothers hugged her as they walked past and went into the tunnel. Their relief was obvious in the way they talked and walked. Their only worry was Quinton.

"Dove?" Alexander blinked as she suddenly hugged him tightly; he hugged her back stroking her damp hair confused. She backed away into the room again holding her hand up for him to wait.

"Just give me a sec. Mum left me this key... It's the literal key to getting rid of this whole lab." Alexander sighed but nodded. The brothers stood in the tunnel watching their sister look around the desk before she found a small control panel, a keyhole caught her attention. She inserted the key and turned it. Immediately she heard clanging which caught her brother's attention and made them straighten up, Alexander had a bad feeling and held his hand out towards Elisa.

"Dove? Dove come here?" Elisa turned to go to her brothers when the door suddenly slammed shut.

"NO!" The boys yelled as the doors shut between them. Elisa gaped as she felt a sense of deja vu. Except for this time, her brothers would be safe. Their hands pounded on the door as they tried to get to their sister. Elisa placed her hand on the scanner but paled when the scanner had suddenly stopped working. She turned to the other door and frowned when she saw it open. Had turning the key reversed the open doors? Elisa ignored Harrisons confused look and searched the red journal that was sat on the desk.

SHUT DOWN PROCEDURE

<u>ONCE THE KEY IS TURNED, IMMEDIATELY EXIT THROUGH THE BEACH ENTRANCE, MAKE SURE THE KEY IS TURNED JUST BEFORE HIGH TIDE GIVING YOU ENOUGH TIME TO LEAVE THE LAB AND BEACH AS THE BACK ENTRANCE WILL AUTOMATICALLY LOCK.</u> SHUT DOWN PROCEDURE <u>WILL ERASE AND DESTROY ALL COMPUTERS AND PHYSICAL FILES.</u>

Stupid, she thought angrily. Why didn't she think to search the journal first?? She turned the key again hoping it would turn off the Procedure but with a heavy heart she realised it was not reversible.

A dripping sound caught Elisa's attention and she turned to the front entrance; the slope had water running down it onto the floor she stood on. She swallowed as the realisation hit her; Harrison coming to the same conclusion. Elisa quickly pulled out the wires from the power outlet next to the computers and turned off the power in the room. She immediately fell into darkness but was glad when she found the torch in her rucksack pocket. She didn't want her brothers to worry, but how much longer could she hide the inevitable from them?

"You're not getting out of here kid," Harrison stated, but it lacked the hostility she had been hearing from him earlier, he sounded sad, dejected.

"Yeah well... neither will you." Harrison could barely see in the darkness; her face being lit up by the torch she held. He saw her shoulders drop in defeat and he smiled sadly. It was as if realisation hit him that this child with him was a mini version of his ex-best friend and that this child wouldn't grow up, because of him... Elisa nodded to herself, this was it. This was the end of her story. She rubbed at her eyes that were beginning to mist over.

"I'm glad Paige bought me here, she thought it wouldn't work. I thought it wouldn't... but it did. I've never been so happy in my entire life. You guys are the best brothers anyone could ever ask for." She started as she walked back over to the door where her brothers were calling her. Alexander didn't like the way she was speaking, the finality in her tone making his skin crawl.

"ELISA WHAT ARE YOU DOING!" Alexander yelled through the door. She nearly whimpered when she felt cold water in her shoes, she didn't dare look behind her and see how much water had already flooded the room. She could hear it sloshing in the beach tunnel and knew the room would be quickly filling up. Her eyes searched around her, looking for something, anything that could ensure her survival. Her eyes landed on the control panel where she had turned the key, a button next to the keyhole. Her eyes flickered to the ground as she remembered something. She wondered if...

"The shutdown makes it so nobody can leave... I can't leave." Roman scoffed and shook his head, refusing to think the worst.

"Head back to the beach entrance and we will meet you there." He turned to leave but Preston shook his head as his eyes left his sisters face to look at the room behind her. He saw water pouring from the doorway and immediately checked his watch.

"She can't." He realised, his voice cracking.

"What do you mean she can't?"

Preston looked up with moisture gathering in his eyes. His partner in crime, his little sister simply smiled at him, telling him that everything would be okay.

"It's high tide.... the sea is coming in..." The boys realised the severity of the situation and how little control they had over it.

Elisa West was locked in a room; the only available exit was flooding with seawater.

Elisa understood what the shutdown procedure was, why most of Project Miracle was on paper files. The room would flood, the computer would be damaged beyond repair and within 20 minutes, any paper documents wouldn't exist. They would dissolve within that time and the formula for the serum would be gone forever. Even if she could stop the room flooding, she knew she had to let it happen, she couldn't wait for the tide to go down knowing that TCT knew where the lab was. That MI5 would know where the lab was. Project Miracle had to die at that very moment.

Contrary to what people may have thought of her, Elisa wasn't afraid of death. No. She was afraid of leaving behind the only family members she had left. She was afraid of their parent's burden falling on her brothers. She was afraid she would never make friends or taste happiness and freedom.

But she finally did, with her brothers. She got to taste and experience happiness. Even if it was temporary. She was happy with that temporary chapter and she was no longer afraid. Death was inevitable and when her time came, she would accept it. Yet she still felt that slither of fear trying to choke her.

There was no way for her to get out of the room. She knew there were risks when trying to destroy the lab, she knew it wouldn't be so easy and yet she did it. She had never really had a choice most of her life, everything was always decided for her; every decision made for her she felt disgusted, she felt like a coward and a pawn in a game. But standing there in that room, she felt at peace. That she had finally made her own decision that would greatly benefit others. She had done the one thing she swore to do ever since her mother died. She could live, there could be a chance that she survives. But just in case, she needed to say goodbye.

Elisa West had protected her brothers. The princess had saved her Knights in shining armour.

"I love you guys so much...." She let out a sob as she felt the water around her waist. The cold threatening to cut off the feeling in her legs. Her mind focused back on the boys and she saw them arguing and yelling as they tried to open the doors. Roman pulling out his phone and probably calling Karson or one of the others. Preston pushed his way to the front to talk to her, she needed them to be strong.

"You're gonna be ok Eli. You're my partner in crime and we're going to get you out of there." He said determinedly. The two staring at each other before he rushed off down the tunnel. He didn't want to see the inevitable, he wanted to remember her smiling and full of life.

Roman shook his head at the sudden turn of events. His eyes trailed over his Shadows tired face, but he could see something in her eyes that he hadn't seen before. Acceptance, peace. She smiled wobbly at him and he smiled just as shakily. He pressed his forehead to the window, and she pressed her own against the glass.

"We're going to go get Karson's team. Hang in there." He winked before rushing off after his younger brother. They wouldn't lose her. Never. Not now. But like his younger brother, he just wanted to remember her as she was.

Owen glared at the baby of their family.

"I swear when you get out here, I'm going to do a Roman and strangle you. Got it?" She giggled and nodded.

"Got it, Owen." He nodded and pointed a finger at her he sucked his bottom lip into his mouth as he tried not to let out a sob.

"You... you're...I want a hug. You're giving me too many grey hairs." He tried to joke when he saw the panic on her face as the water was up to her neck. She didn't check on Harrison, he wasn't her concern, and she didn't want to see him die like she had watched her mother and father. She could vaguely hear him struggling, but like herself, he had accepted his ending. He didn't bother to try and hold his breathe, he welcomed his ending like an old friend, it was time to see his Sophie. Elisa's eyes flickered over to Alexander. Owen began trying to find a way to get the door open, but due to the shutdown procedure, it seemed as though it were sealed shut.

Alexander didn't bother hiding his tears. The heartbreak clear on his face making Elisa cry. She wanted her big brother; her big brother wanted to hold his little sister. Her whimpers echoed and he laid his palm on the glass. She laid her much smaller one on the other side, lining up their hands the way she did with her father. Her lips quirked up and she looked into the gentle brown eyes that belonged to the man who had taken her in. The man who was her role model and her haven.

"I'm not scared." She said like she was trying to convince both him and her. He nodded with a proud smile, her eyes glittering from the torchlight.

"It's okay dove. It's ok. Keep looking at me, ok??" He begged and she nodded. The water reached her mouth and she kept bopping in the water so she could still breathe. She began gasping to breathe as the water rose higher. Alexander felt useless, he couldn't do anything. Here he was, watching her fight for her life like she had done many times before she came home. He had promised her that he would be there for her, but he failed.

"ALEX, I HAVE A TEAM GOING DOWN TO-" Karson stopped talking as he came to a stop behind his friend. His eyes wide as he saw the water filling up in the Lab. Quinton was stable and he had sent a team to make sure that everyone was out from the Lab. His heart dropped as he witnessed the sight in front of him. He couldn't do anything. If Alexander was simply standing there trying to calm her down, then it meant there wasn't anything he could do.

"Elisa?" Alexander choked as the water went above her head and her hand left the window. His fists pounded on the glass as he tried to see her torchlight in the dark. Owen was frozen and turned to Karson as if he could save her. The two eldest West siblings pleaded for anyone, someone to do something.

The water was almost touching the ceiling and Elisa made sure to tilt her head above the water surface, try and get her last breaths of air. She greedily sucked in the air before the water filled the room; her legs pushed against the ceiling and she swam back to the door with the torch in her hand. Sounds blurry and fuzzy, the pounding from the door sounding like mere tapping. Her hair floated in the water around her face, and she squinted in the dark. She grabbed onto the door ledge and her hand pressed against the window again. Alexander and Owen being the only two she could see, both sobbing their hearts out while hearts broke.

She wanted to hug them and tell them it was okay. That despite the tightening in her chest, the chill gripping her bones and crushing them into pieces, despite her head begging to shut down and her eyes stinging from the water. She wanted to tell them that despite that, she was okay. But instead, all she could do was smile brightly at them and mouth two words.

The water rushed into her mouth and she choked on the feeling of the ice forcing its way into her lungs. She watched Alexander and Owens mouths open in a scream that was silent to her ears. Karson grabbed them and dragged them away from the window; to not let them watch the next part.

Her body jerked now and then despite her giving in, her body wanted to fight but she had given up. Her lungs burning despite the coldness that trickled down her through, heart pumping desperately to keep her functioning. The torch floated away from her numb fingers and she could see the light dropping to the ground. Her eyes closed as she felt a blanket of clouds envelop her and hold her close. Promising a sleep of comfort.

Memories flashed through her mind like a movie, the smiles of her mum, her dad, aunt Dree Dree and Leah, Levi, Sasha, Quinton, Cyrus. Then her dear sweet brothers who had shown her what family was. Alexander, Owen, Roman and Preston. She clung onto those memories, the way their eyes spoke a thousand words and their smiles.

Together soon, she had whispered yet soon those words faded from Elisa West's mind. A surge of desperation pumped through her as she kicked her feet towards the control panel, hazel eyes searching for what she needed; her fingers grazing the key and button.

The last thing she heard and felt was a soft feather-like kiss on her forehead, warmth surrounding her and a voice she barely remembered whispering in her mind.

"Together soon, my love."

29

Then and Now
Then

Delilah sighed softly as she stared down at the computer, her eyes growing heavy from tiredness. She wanted, no needed sleep. She wished she were normal, that she didn't become a scientist. What would her life have become if she picked a different route? She could have been a teacher working with little children in a primary school or nursery. Maybe she would have been an artist, selling her interpretations of the world to others. But then again, she wouldn't be the woman she was, she wouldn't have married the kindest and goofiest man she had ever met, she would never have had her 5 beautiful children who made the darkness of her life, that much brighter.

Delilah shut everything down on the laptop and made sure all the security measures were in place. She double-checked the cabinet and made sure all the papers were placed in places she could easily grab and destroy when she came back. Taking all the files with her was a liability, she also still clung to that small bit of hope that she could come back and finished what she started one day. But the realistic and logical part of her yelled at her for her naivety. She had helped create this serum and instead of getting rid of it, she kept it.

"Mummy and Elisa see daddy?" A small voice tugged at her heartstrings and a smile immediately grew on her tired face. Elisa sat on the table where Delilah had placed her the moment they had gotten into the lab. Elisa was not at all interested in the room and instead played with the little teddy bear Delilah had bought for her new life, a little comfort buddy. Delilah laughed softly and strolled over to her littlest girl who made grabby hands at her approaching figure. She scooped her into her arms and the 3-year-old snuggled into her mother, trying to steal the warmth she emitted.

"We, my love, are going to go on a princess adventure." Elisa perked up with wide eyes and an awed expression on her face. Her doe eyes glittering in excitement and wonder as her mind whirred with all sorts of stories jumping to mind.

"With daddy and my... my"

"Your Knights?" Elisa nodded enthusiastically and not for the first time since they had to put their plan into action, Delilah was glad Elisa was only a little 3 years old. A little girl who would slowly forget how close she was to her brothers. She would never let Elisa forget her boys, of course, she would make sure she told stories of them every night so Elisa would grow up knowing about them.

"No miracle, daddy and your brothers are going on their adventure. But we will see them again soon, okay? You gotta trust mummy." She mumbled the last part to herself as she tried to reassure herself that she was doing the right thing. They were on their own, the government was corrupt, and she knew that if she tried to find some sort of help, she would be found by them.

With a sigh, Delilah closed the beach entrance with her palm on the scanner. She heard the entrance closing and the exit door opening, her hand tightened the strap of the rucksack over her chest and made sure it was secure. Her feet echoed as she walked along the concrete flooring of the tunnel, the material soon turning to dirt and the air much fresher. She slipped her body through the gap in the huge rocks that hid the exit, wind surrounding her and making her hair fly around frantically.

Her eyes scanned the area around her, and she looked over the cliff, the sea pounding against the rocks demanding to be let into the room she had just left. But she knew it would hold. After all, it had been there way before she discovered it, and it will be there way after she left it. She knew that the lab probably used to be an underground government bunker but had long since been abandoned. She had changed the hand scanner and gotten rid of anything that may attract anyone towards the lab whether that be governmental computers or any cameras and bugs. She 'cleansed' the hidden room and made it her personal space, the hiding space of Project Miracle.

A small sigh made her remember where she was, the sun was setting over the horizon and she smiled at the picture of melted colours painting the sky. How long until she would be able to stand here with her family and watch this same sunset? How long would she have to wait? Her feet carried her to the car that she had parked, clothing, cash, and food ready. She laid Elisa in her car seat and brushed her brown hair away from her baby face. She pressed a kissed to her cheek and grinned when Elisa's face smoothed into a small smile before settling back into a soundless sleep. Delilah slipped into the driver's seat and began her journey through the village, past her home and onto the long road.

She stopped only for petrol and making sure her daughters needs were met. She refused to give herself time to think, time to think about how everything was her fault, that if she had let go of her need to make the world a 'better' place, she would not be on the run with her family. But it is what it is, and what it was, was tragic. Painful. Before she knew it, hours had passed, the evening had closed over them and she was boarding a plane with her daughter still asleep.

Time was nothing to her, her mind not being able to focus on one thing and her hands shook as she felt the overwhelming urge to scream, and cry wash over her. Elisa woke up and her little self sucked her thumb as she saw the panicked version of her mother. Her eyes flickered over her mother who immediately masked her emotions the moment she realised her daughter was watching.

"Mummy?" Elisa spoke softly over the sounds of the plane and Delilah wrapped her arms around the small girl who wanted to explore her surroundings, her little hands tugging at the belt over her lap.

"Shhh my love, it's ok. Mummy's here. We are going on an adventure! We're flying in the sky!" She tried to make her tone sound exciting and soothing and mentally cheered when Elisa had a look of curiosity on her features. Her wonder only lasted for so long before uncertainty and a frown made residence.

"I want daddy." She whimpered, wanting the bear cuddles her father would gift her with. She didn't like this new place and wanted to be home with her daddy and brothers. Delilah swallowed the whine that wanted to escape and simply shifted her daughter into a position where she had her legs on her seat and head in her mother's lap. Her hand stroked Elisa's hair down and she leaned her head down so she can press soft kisses to her daughter's forehead.

"It's okay baby. It's okay. Do you want something to eat?" Elisa curled into a ball and sucked on her thumb for comfort.

This wasn't a good idea, she couldn't hold off the onslaught of negative yet true thoughts that had been banging on the walls of her mind the moment they found out Harrison worked for TCT, the group after her and her husband.

This was all her fault and now her family were paying the consequences of her actions and decisions. She should have destroyed everything all at once, she shouldn't have tried to be a hero, because now, just like Dr Lawrence once did, she had inevitably chosen her children's life for them whether they realised it or not. She had ruined her children's chance at a normal childhood, at having loving parents who would hold them close in their arms for however long they could. A tear rolled down her cheek to which she quickly wiped away before her daughter could see.

A body came to stand next to her in the aisle and she looked up to meet the bright green eyes of a beautiful woman who offered a small soft smile. Her presence was calming and immediately put her at ease.

"Hi there, I don't mean to sound nosy but... are you okay?" Her voice asked over the hum of the flying bird they rested inside. Delilah sighed and nodded slowly making the woman smile understandingly, Delilah wasn't okay, but she wasn't about to ask for help.

"I came to England for a holiday with my little one. He's just a few years older than your beautiful girl." Delilah smiled at the compliment and then looked over to where the woman was pointing out her child. A little boy sat in the seat across the aisle from them, headphones sitting on his head but since they were too big for him, his hands were holding them against his ears, his knees pulled up to his stomach as he watched a movie on the TV screen. He had curly light blonde hair and his eyes were bright green.

"What's his name?" Delilah asked in a quiet voice as she looked back at the kind woman.

"Levi. What's this one's name?"

"Elisa..." The woman smiled and sat back in her seat which was still near Delilah. They engaged in casual conversation talking about England and the best places to visit for a trip, where the tourist sites were, and their favourite places. Delilah hardly noticed when she had a genuine and relaxed smile painted on her face, nor did she realise that her body had stopped shaking, the cold and loud noises in her head had receded and the feeling of comfort took over. They had spoken through the night in soft hushed voices while their children along with many other passengers, slept.

"Morning ladies, Breakfast will be ready soon. Here are your menus and if you have any questions, please let me know." An air hostess said as she gently woke up passengers or handed out menus. The women gave shocked looks as they checked the time before laughing quietly. Delilah gently shook Elisa a few times until her pretty eyes fluttered open. She stared at her mother dazed for a few minutes and Delilah smiled as she simply stroked her cheek in a comforting gesture. Elisa took a while after waking up and she would take her time to figure out and remember where she was. Soon the youngest West lifted her hands towards her mother's face.

"Hungry." She pouted making her laugh as she undid her daughters' belt so she could move in her seat.

"Wow love! No good morning kisses?" She jumped up and hugged her mother tightly before pressing wet kisses to her mother's cheek.

"Food?" Elisa heard another voice asked and looked over her mother to the little boy sat on his mothers' lap. Feeling her gaze, Levi looked around before he noticed the little three-year-old girl watching him with wide eyes. His own eyes widened before he stuck his tongue out at her making her reciprocate the action.

Delilah scanned the menu before deciding for them both.

"Okay sweetie, you get food- what are you doing?" She frowned when she realised Elisa had her fingers on her face and she was making weird looks towards Levi who was doing the same. Both women chuckled at their children's antics before settling them down for their breakfast.

"So have you got family in California?" Delilah swallowed the orange juice and shook her head, her reality smacking her, and she frowned at the imprint it left behind.

"No... we just left our family..." She trailed off not wanted Elisa to hear but was glad when she watched her daughter mumble to herself as she inspected the fruit pieces and tasted them warily. The woman once again smiled understandingly and placed a hand on Delilah's arm.

"I get it... sometimes a fresh start is all we need to make things better than what they were."

Delilah felt more at ease the moment they managed to get through airport security, Elisa talking to her teddy bear while holding her mother's hand with the other. Delilah had her rucksack securely fastened and a suitcase with their clothes and any other essentials that they may not be able to replace. Little Elisa also had a pastel purple rucksack on her back, however, that was filled with snacks and some of her toys.

The two walked out of the airport with no idea what to do next. Perhaps they could find a cheap motel, of course, Delilah doesn't need to work since they had been saving up ever since they first became scientists, but she couldn't just rely on that money. She would need to find a job; she would surely need to change her identity? There was so much Delilah had to do to keep both her and her miracle safe. Yet her mind couldn't focus on what to do first.

"Mummy look." Delilah looked down at Elisa pointing at the little boy from the plane who was being dragged by his mother towards them with a grumpy look on his face. Delilah plastered on a fake smile as they approached.

"Look, you have no reason to say yes or trust me. You don't know me we just met. But I can see the signs of a woman needing help even though she is independent and strong. You need help, don't you?" Delilah blinked at the straight forward question and looked around nervously. Her gut wasn't telling her that this woman was dangerous. She felt that she should trust this woman. That this woman had nothing to do with the darkness of the world and was simply offering an act of kindness. Delilah looked down at her little girl who had slowly edged her way towards a pouty yet also curious Levi. She had to think of Elisa, what her child would have to face and prepare for. She nodded slowly and the woman smiled softly holding out a hand.

"Oh, I don't think I told you, my name. I'm Audrey."

"Delilah." Elisa waved at Levi who hid behind his mother slightly shy making Audrey laugh and kneel to his level. He buried his face in her shoulder and refused to look at the little girl in front of him.

"Alright mister, this is Elisa. Elisa my name is Audrey, and this is Levi." Elisa giggled and swayed her body as she held out the teddy bear towards Levi. His eyes were focused on his mother's shoulder, his fingers tracing the patterns in her shirt. He felt something furry touch his hand and looked over at the girl who was nearly the same height as him, her teddy in her outstretched arms. He took a step and quickly took the bear into his arms making Elisa give a toothy grin of happiness.

"Friend!" She cheered making Delilah stroke her daughter's hair in amusement. She knelt and gently held her daughter by her shoulders facing her.

"Shall we spend more time with Levi?' Her head bobbed up and down excitedly and she clapped her hands as she looked over at her new friend who looked like he didn't know whether to be excited or scared. Delilah and Audrey grabbed their suitcases and led their children towards a car. They got themselves settled in and began their journey.

"Will your husband-"

"He won't mind or question, okay? If he does, I'll just tell him that I'm helping out my friend."

"We're friends?" Audrey smiled slightly and spared a glance at Delilah.

"Not yet, but I hope we can be. I don't have many friends myself since I don't trust people but you... I have a good feeling about you." She winked and Delilah chuckled shaking her head.

"Honestly, we're running from something... some people are after us and trust is hard when you don't know exactly who those people are. We left to hide... and they shouldn't find us." Audrey nodded slowly and swallowed.

"Is it possible that they do find you?" Delilah thought back to her husband's best friend and sighed.

"Someone amazing at hacking. I won't be surprised if they find me one day. Luckily, we didn't tell him I was leaving. I just have to be careful when going out in public and working. I think I'll have Elisa home-schooled..."

"We'll figure it out together, okay? I'll help you get a house set up maybe under my husbands' name. Or mine. We can look for a house close by, if you don't want to work or you're finding it hard to find a job, then you can do jobs for me while I work my basic shifts at the hospital and stuff. You can be my baby sister for Levi when I'm out or I dunno." Delilah looked at the woman with a teary look.

"Why are you being so nice?"

"Because I was in a similar position, running from a horrible past and I had nobody to help me until I met my husband. Us women gotta stick together." They shared a smile, a bond of trust forming between them before they realised the car was quiet. Delilah investigated the back and she laughed quietly when she saw the two children fast asleep. Levi had his head leaning against the window with his lips parted, Elisa sat on the middle seat leaning against him with her thumb hanging out of her mouth, her teddy bear clutched tightly in Levi's arm with Elisa holding onto one of the bears' arms.

"Can't rip them apart now." Audrey shrugged with a grin and Delilah agreed. Maybe Elisa could have a few happy years, people who will become her second family until they could reunite with the rest of their family. They arrived at a house near a beach, the warm air pressing their clothes to their skin. The mothers carried their children to Levi's bedroom where they snuggled up, soft sighs escaping their lips.

"There's a guest room right here. Take a nap or come down. Whatever you want. There's a bathroom attached."

"Thanks, Audrey." The woman winked before she walked off to her room to unpack.

Delilah pulled out a phone from her rucksack and snapped a picture of the two kids in the backseat before placing it back in the rucksack. Her smile faded slightly when she noticed a white envelope peeking out from between her journal pages. She walked into the guest room Audrey had pointed out and shut the door quietly. A window seat caught her attention, the view of the sea reminding her so much of her own home that she left behind. She curled up in the pillows and opened the small envelope pulling out a slightly worn piece of paper.

Her lips turned up and her heart pinched when she recognised the handwriting as her husbands. Her eyes scanned the ink, small blotches indicating his sadness when he had written it making her own eyes well up as she could practically hear his voice in her head. Her fingers shook as she read the note and felt the weight lift off her chest as she acknowledges the words her dear husband had written.

Delilah held the note close to her chest and closed her eyes as she sobbed into the silence of the room. What's done is done, the mistakes she had made could never be undone but could be corrected. She just wanted to scream to the world that it wasn't fair that it would be her children should be the ones correcting her mistake.

"I'm sorry." Her voice cracked as she hugged herself, her husband wasn't here to hold her, her boys weren't here to make her laugh, her miracle was only a baby. Delilah was responsible for what was going to happen and as much as she dreamed, she knew that she wouldn't get her happy ending.

She wasn't going to have her forever with her beautiful family and that was okay, as long as her children and husband had theirs. As long as her miracle was reunited with her brothers. As long as William saw his daughter again. As long as her boys and girl made friends and happy memories. She would be happy and at peace.

Sometimes people do not get their happily ever after and unfortunately, Delilah West was one of them.

Now

People believe that the worst villains are the ones you read about in a book; the ones with a tragic background, a broken family and nobody to love them. These villains are evil for the sole reason that they believe if they couldn't be happy, then why should anyone else? They're stuck with this notion that the world is against them and they are against everyone else in the world, that every individual was somewhat responsible for their pain and must feel their wrath. Sometimes the villains don't stay villains in books and are simply shattered misunderstood people who had more power than your usual people.

Then you have your real-life villains. People who are supposed to protect the world but instead use their money and power for their own sake. Their greed takes them on a different path compared to the one promised to the world. These villains either target everyone or a group of people and they abuse their power simply because they can. Not because they've had a hard life or because they feel unloved.

However, both books, movies and real-life share one common enemy. Time. So subtle in its actions that a person wouldn't know it taken from them until it's too late. Time is the invisible enemy that creeps up slowly, killing silently and taking everything a person holds dear.

Clocks were a physical reminder that time was running fast, that soon the present would be the past and your future would be the present.

Tick, tock, tick, tock.

The man clenched his jaw as he listened to the sound over and over in the quiet hallway. The plain white walls somehow enhancing the worries in his head as he waited for the murmuring on the other side of the door to stop. His knee bounced up and down in agitation and he rubbed his fingers together to try and distract him from the emptiness he was sat in. A door opening caught his attention and he stood up quickly, the man in the doorway sighed and shook his head.

"I've told you before, not yet." He said as they walked down the corridor together.

"You said that yesterday-"

"And I'll tell you again. We've not been called in yet." They stared each other down, one glaring in determination and the other holding a sympathetic stare. They had formed a trusting bond during their escape and although he hated the rules, the man respected the agent overseeing him. The man didn't like hiding in the stupid safe house, he didn't like not knowing or being aware of what was happening.

"I know it's hard but-" A beeping from his phone caught his attention and he looked down at the message he received.

"What is it?" The anxious man demanded knowing that everything going on around him was his business. The other gentleman sighed and sucked his teeth.

"Karson called us for backup. We're heading down to the beach." The agent began walking away and the man hurried after him not wanting to be left behind. Other agents began grabbing guns and any equipment they may need before piling out of the safe house they had all been hiding in.

"I'm coming with you."

"With all due respect sir my boss-"

"I honestly don't care what your boss says!" The agent looked at the bruised man who despite looked weak with all his injuries, seemed determined and completely oblivious to all his wounds. He nodded after a moment and opened the back of the van. The vehicle immediately drove out of the wooded area and found the main road, Karson had sent the details of where they were, and they were all surprised when they found themselves on top of the cliffs near loads of rocks. They all piled out and half of the agents ran down to the beach while the others ran towards the rocks. The man's eyes scanned his surroundings and he watched as more MI5 agents came to a stop near him before jumping out and shouting orders. He didn't completely understand what was happening and his legs bought him over to where he could hear Karson yelling.

He saw a group of teenagers yelling at the agents, begging them to save her. Save who? He wanted to voice his question and ask what was going on when one of the kids turned to look at him. He froze in his footsteps as he looked at the young boys' eyes, a feeling of shock pinching at his nerves. Preston turned to look away from Karson who was holding onto Owen and Alex's arm tightly whilst trying to explain that they were trying to get into the lab. He didn't want to hear their plan; they were wasting time He wanted to help save his baby sister right that second and they were wasting precious time yelling. He turned to find someone who could take him to the beach when an approaching figure made him freeze.

"Dad?"

That single word made all the kids turn, nobody moved for a moment as they tried to understand what they were seeing. A man who looked older than what they had imagined. His hair looked freshly cut and washed, his clothes were baggy showing that he was severely malnourished, purple and green covered skin from the bruises healing, stitched across his head and lip and a few cuts spread out. He looked like nobody they had ever met before and yet, yet his hazel eyes that immediately teared up told them exactly who he was.

Surprisingly the one who made the first move was someone they didn't expect out of the boys. Roman charged forward and threw his arms around William West who held him just as tight. His son holding onto him as if he were the only thing anchoring William there. Preston followed and William pressed a kiss to both of his sons' heads, words not being spoken as they simply held each other tightly. Their shoulders shaking as they let out the tide of emotions overflowing the dam they had built throughout the years. The dam that had slowly began cracking when Elisa came into their lives and had now collapsed at the sight of their father.

"You came back." Preston choked out and their father wanted to cry in agony. These 'men' were still his little boys and his heart broke as he listened to their pain-filled cries. Roman pulled away and looked at the ground.

"I'm sorry about... that morning. We never got to-" William slung his arm around his neck and pulled him in for another hug.

"We're here now." Roman nodded and Owen smiled happily, the emotion in his eyes bright enough to make people want to look away. But nobody did as they watched the reunion.

"I don't think I told you I loved you when I left for school that morning so... I love you, dad." William chuckled and playfully ruffled Owen's hair.

"Love you too kid." Alexander stepped into view and simply stared at his father with a blank face. William matched his serious stand and the two nodded at each other with respect and pride in both their eyes. The eldest West child who had grown up quickly, the boy who had transitioned into a man overnight, the brother who had raised his younger brothers, let a tear loose. He reverted to his 18-year-old teenage self who had joked with his father before he went to school. Alexander let out a shuddering breath and the two embraced. William laid a hand on the back of Alexanders head in comfort and rubbed his back as he shook in his fathers' arms.

"I tried my best dad." William nodded and pulled back to give him a serious yet proud smile, his hand clasped behind his son's neck.

"And you did it perfectly." He looked at his sons before a sinking feeling overcame him, his eyes scanned the other teenagers who already understood who he was looking for.

"Elisa?" The boys lowered their heads, the shame hitting them and the fear running through William's veins. Karson was barking orders to the other agents and he understood why they had been called. He didn't want to accept anything his thoughts were whispering; his baby girl was perfectly fine!

"Dad I'm sorry-"

"I NEED AN AMBULANCE STAT!" Their heads snapped over to a group of agents who rushed out of the tunnel, a small body cradled in the arms of one of the men. A limp, motionless figure. Her arm hung limply at her side and her head drooped against his arm. She looked like a ragdoll with her body soaked, her skin tinted a sickly blue.

"Elisa?" William whispered as they all tried to get closer but were stopped by a fence of MI5 agents.

"Karson? How did-"

"Half the men went through the exit in the rocks which was closed so they opened it with force. Our tech guy managed to bypass the security scanner and they got in. Turns out there was a safety measure also in place that Delilah set up just in case she was ever trapped in there or something. Elisa must have clicked on it but didn't know if it was exactly what she thought it was, she took the risk anyway. She waited for the room to fill up which effectively destroyed the evidence. Water dissolves paper within 20 minutes. I imagine it took about 5 to 10 minutes for the room to fill, she held her breathe for as long as she could and when she couldn't hold it anymore, she pressed the button. The beach entrance door shut and there was a drainage system on the floor of the room. Pipes that led back to the ocean."

Alexander roughly pushed past his best friend who was explaining how Elisa had destroyed everything, he knew he was doing it to keep them distracted from what they were trying to do to Elisa, but Alexander had to be with her.

He fell to his knees next to her body, the men and women trying to save her life while they waited for an ambulance ignored him. He watched them perform CPR on her, her body moving only when they moved her, her eyes shut except when they would forcefully open them to check her eye activity and dilation. Alexander shakily took her small cold hand in his and rubbed her hand to share warmth.

"Pulse?"

"Negative."

The West boys and father stood behind Alexander peering down at the unconscious body in the grass. Sasha had her face buried in Cyrus' shoulder who tried to reassure her whilst trying not to cry. Levi kept rubbing his cheeks as he watched them try to bring life back into his childhood best friend whilst Quinton glared at her body, mentally promising to kill her if she didn't hurry and wake up. Tears rolling down their cheeks, not caring about how they looked.

"Pulse?"

"Negative."

Roman clenched his jaw in anger. She knew what they had all been through, she can't leave them too, not again. Preston did not know what to do, where to look, he just couldn't bear to see her in that state. Owen was planning on ways to protect her from the world, he didn't care if she hated him for the rest of his life, she needed his protection forever and always.

Rain began sprinkling over them sharing their sorrow as the minutes of shouting and yelling passed by, her body growing colder, further away from reality. She was bit by bit becoming a person of the past, time whisking her away to a land they couldn't follow just yet. Water droplets landing on her cheeks, running down her skin like the tears that ran down theirs.

"C'mon dove! Wake up please!" Alexander begged through the rain that began pelting down harder, angry grey clouds spread across the sky as they cried their tears of torment. Hands pressed against her chest, shouting as they tried to figure out where the ambulance was. A siren was soon heard, and they immediately jumped into action, her body picked up and placed into the vehicle, their feet running to jump into the ambulance with her. The others jumped into one of the other many cars around them.

"COME ON MISS WEST!" One of the paramedics should desperately, none of them wanting to see this bright spark disappear forever. They pulled out a defibrillator, not wanting to wait till the hospital to try and bring her back. There was still a chance they could save her from the tight grasp of time. They quickly pulled her wet clothing up and slapped the sticky pads onto the skin they dried off. They heard the machine start-up.

"CLEAR!" Her body jerked as a shock was pulsed through her scary light blue body.

"No pulse, again!"

"CLEAR!"

"No pulse..." William closed his eyes praying that his baby girl would open her eyes. The paramedics exchanged looks as they prepared for one last time, they couldn't lose this little girl, the family sitting with them couldn't afford to lose her. Alexander closed his eyes, don't go too Dove, he thought.

"CLEAR!" It seemed as though everyone held their breath as they watched her body, hoping to see the rise and fall of her chest, a flash of a grin or perhaps a sarcastic remark. However, their heart shattered when she stayed still. Roman sank onto the ground holding himself together with Preston holding onto him. Owen leaned his head against the seat with his eyes closed. Alexander stared at her, not understanding, or believing. It can't be real; they couldn't have been this close and too late... surely this wasn't... this wasn't her ending?

A twitch. That's all it took for the eldest West to grab her cold hand and press it against his cheek. The paramedics frowning at his actions but then zeroed in on her other hand that twitched. They pulled out equipment and began checking her over quickly, all the while Alexander never let go of her hand.

"There's a pulse!" Three words that had the Wests up, holding onto anything while they drove their way to the hospital.

"Elisa?" Alexander murmured as her lips parted and her brows scrunched up, an oxygen mask immediately put over her mouth as her chest began to rise and fall, breathing growing stronger as she fought against the claws of time. It wasn't her turn yet. Not yet.

Her eyes fluttered and slowly opened as an onslaught of light attacked her, her body gently being lifted by unfamiliar hands as they quickly wrapped her in a thick blanket. Voices were still hazy along with her vision. But the moment her sight cleared; her tears fell. There they were.

Preston.

Roman.

Owen.

Alexander.

Her father.

The boys immediately pulled her into a group hug, cautious of her tubing and any wires, the paramedics relaxing and smiling as they wrote things down and checked over her. Her body was laid back on the gurney, Preston sat on the end with Roman perched on the edge, Owen sat on one of the seats near her head. Alexander stood next to Owen and William sat on the only other free chair as he watched his children interact. He wanted them to relax in the presence of each other before she sees him and gets confused. He grinned at the way they laughed and joked; their eyes trained on her every move as she turned her attention to whoever was talking to her.

And for a moment, her eyes landed on him. Her beautiful hazel eyes which always bought everyone so much joy. His beautiful little girl who had grown into this stunning and brave woman. The little girl whose lips slowly curled into a radiant smile. Her honey pools glittered with a familiar sparkle that she had lost years ago.

Time had not captured her yet.

Epilogue

'What are stories? They are the adventures of people, the once upon a time of a persons' beginning and the happily ever after of their end. Stories can be made up of the past, present and future; everyone has a story, finished, ongoing or paused. We don't... refer to ourselves as characters, however, yet we are the main point of interest in our books.

This is life.

Life is a story full of monsters and evil that take the form of greed and selfishness. It contains nightmares and physical obstacles whether it be people or mundane activities that sometimes are too much for us to handle. Life is a maze with different paths leading in different directions, some a dead end and only one with the exit. Each dead-end could be an obstacle or big event in life that takes up a large portion of time. But in the end, you backtrack onto the main path, looking for the exit, reaching more and more dead ends with each turn until finally, the end is in sight. The exit of the maze took so long to find, welcoming the sweet escape from the confusion of life.

Life is never straight forward, there is always something that changes our paths, there's always one exit, just different paths to get there. The straight path, the long winding path, and the short quick path. It just depends on which one we choose...'

"It feels weird you know. I've never really dwelled on everything in the past, especially not when I was busy trying to figure out what I had to do. But now it's all over... it's all I can think about." I played with the orange beaded tassels on the cushion I hugged to my chest.

I avoided looking at Claire who was reading through one of my journal entries. She was the only one who I really allowed to read it but even then, she only read the ones she asked me to write about. She would ask me to think about a certain question and write how I felt about it. She ignored the entries I wrote from my past, from when I first met my brothers to when I finally saw my dad again.

Claire smiled sympathetically as she sat with her legs on her desk. She lowered my journal that had been bookmarked on the pages she had asked me to write, the one she had set for me as homework. Claire Whitely was an agent of MI5, a good friend of Karson's and now, it turned out, my therapist. She annoyed me at the beginning with her bright smile and happy nature. But as the months went by, I grew to like the gentle women who helped me figure out my feelings and thoughts. Her dark chocolate eyes were as warm as milk chocolate, no bitterness or boredom in her gaze. She was in her early 30s, newlywed and was an optimist.

"You're no longer feeling trapped, and you don't have a time limit. You have more time than you used to and now your brain is finally processing what you went through. It's normal-"

"But it wasn't. What I went through wasn't normal Claire. I feel like a broken record, so I apologise for bringing it up all the time. But what happened wasn't normal and I still sometimes don't know how to get out of the funk." Claire studied me for a second and although I didn't like the way her dark brown eyes would study me like a scientist would study their projects, I knew it was simply her way of trying to analyse me. To try and find a crack in the mask. The mask was just barely clinging on; what I didn't realise was that the mask was falling quickly.

"How are the nightmares?" I looked away from her and stared at the fish tank containing numerous colourful fish. Free yet trapped in a box, never truly going anywhere but always moving. We sat in silence for a moment, neither of us speaking or moving.

My nightmares were worse than any of us realised. I would wake up drenched in sweat, sometimes my brothers would find it hard to wake me up from my sleep; I would scream and scream, at times hurting myself or my brothers without knowing where I was. My dreams consisted of watching my mother die with her blaming me, her green eyes sparkled in hatred as she reached towards me. Sometimes it was about my old foster homes and the many warnings I received when living with the kind strangers. Black roses dancing in the air mocking me. But the most recurring nightmare was drowning. The cold holding me captive in that Lab; I would wake up disoriented after those nightmares and at times would be held over the toilet throwing up the contents of my stomach.

"They're still there. The homes, that family, mum, Quinton getting shot, the water... Sometimes the faces are replaced by others or I dream that its more than one person I lose. It is like I'm drowning all over again but this time I don't pass out. I'm stuck in this endless cycle of trying to find a way out of the cave, but the button isn't there and I'm choking on water." My arms itched and I twitched as though the water was enveloping me right then and there in the pale blue room. I remembered the feeling of the water flooding my lungs, the way it held me prisoner in my own body for a few seconds and despite my giving up, it still pushed me to fight.

"How is Quinton?" Her calm voice broke through my fogged mind and I sent her a grateful smile at the obvious way she changed the subject. I thought back to when I was stable laying in that surprisingly comfortable hospital bed, how I demanded over and over where Quinton and my friends were. I remember how he had rolled his eyes at me when I finally escaped my room to go search for him, he had yelled at me for being an idiot getting out of bed and Sasha and Cyrus joined in. In the end, the nurses discovered us passed out on the bed with the movie credits on the small tv rolling.

"Better. He's just started playing football with the boys again but now and then I can tell it hurts. He jumped in front and protected me; it kills me knowing one of my closest friends put themselves in the line of danger. I don't understand why-"

"Would you have done the same?" I looked at her as if she had lost her mind.

"Are you kidding me? Of course, I would! They're my family and the only people who didn't abandon me despite my numerous attempts at pushing them away or-"

"Exactly." I paused at her blunt answer. These people had told me the moment we met that they wouldn't give up on me. My brothers had told me, their friends had told me, and my small group told me. Repeatedly they told me that they would always be there for me, so why was I still surprised that they go through with their promises?

"It has only been a few months since everything happened, in your mind, you're still waiting for this calm chapter to end, you're waiting for someone to show up and tell you that people are after you. It's going to take a while for you to finally understand and believe that your safe, and that's okay. Your family and friends will continuously remind you, that's what a family does." Claire sighed and wheeled her chair over to the sofa I was curled into. Her finger tapped against the coffee cup she grasped between her hands. I didn't meet her eyes knowing she was right; I was waiting for someone to shake me by the shoulders and demand me to wake up. That I was still stuck in that cell with Levi and dad, or I was in that damned lab.

"Let's make a plan of action. What's your main worry?" I met her kind brown eyes and thought. What was my main worry? What was I scared of most?

"I'm scared I'm gonna lose my brothers, that we'll grow apart. I'm scared that my friends will up and leave me one day... I'm scared that this is temporary too..." I'm scared that I'm going to lose everything all over again.

"Everything is temporary sweetheart; you just have to make the most of everything life gives you. You can't live in the past Elisa, we can talk about it, remember people you've lost. But you can't stay there with them. It's time for you to think about yourself for once. I know, I know it's easier said than done, it's just something we need to work on, something we need to remind you about." She bit her lip as she thought and looked down at her phone before grinning at me.

"I understand it's hard to let go of the past, sometimes you need reassurance that its ok to move on and leave people in the past simply for your own sake." A knock was heard on the door and I frowned confused at the interruption. Claire called for them to come in and my eyes lit up. I was up and running into their open arms with Claire laughing in amusement, my heart bursting with joy.

"Hello, sweetheart." She said softly, I felt her hand stroke the back of my head as she hugged me close. My face buried in her shoulder and my arms tight around her waist; she let out a shuddering breath and I felt her kiss my head tenderly.

"Paige!" I croaked with emotion as the women who had looked over me most of my life held me. The one person in my childhood who had never given up on me and cared for me more than a social worker should. I revelled in the familiarity the women gave off, the one temporary person who always hoped for a better future for me.

"I missed you so much!" I looked up and saw her wide surprised eyes that held tears as she looked down at me, her soft features looking the most relaxed I'd ever seen her. She chuckled and stroked my cheek the way my mother used to, making me lean into her loving touch; my lips pulled up into a smile that was becoming more and more familiar as the months went by.

"Oh, sweetheart I missed you so much too! Look at you! Didn't think I'd live to see this beautiful smile you're so obviously sporting." Her happiness reflected in her smile. Claire motioned us towards the sofa and grinned at the ecstatic look on my face.

"We got in touch with Mrs Fields after we found out she was your social worker and had the most connection to you in those years. She knew you more than anyone despite not knowing your hidden agenda." My smile slipped slightly, and I looked over at Paige with wide eyes. Her hand squeezed mine in reassurance.

"I don't know everything, just the need to know. The fact you would make sure your foster parents didn't have you for long and you were running through the system so certain people didn't have an exact location of where you were. It makes sense now... why you were always such a closed-off girl."

She reached into her bag and pulled out a small object, soft and fluffy still despite its age. Her hands cradled the object with care and my eyes widened slightly in recognition.

"When we first met... you didn't talk to any of the other social workers. You didn't give them any indication that you heard them or would listen to them. Then they introduced you to me, this small baby-faced girl cuddling a little teddy bear in her arms. The one thing you refused to part with until after that one home..." She slipped the soft toy bear into my shaky hands and I stared into the glassy golden eyes, my fingers rubbing against the soft furry material and the frayed ribbon around one of its ears.

"I held onto her for you... carried her around until you asked for the last thing your mother gave you." I brought the stuffed bear up to my face, the scent of vanilla long gone along with the women who gave her to me. Paige pulled me into a hug and stroked my hair as she noticed the tell-tale signs that I was about to breakdown.

"You don't need to forget; you don't need to ignore everything that happened to you. You need to let it out, talk to the people you love and trust. It's time to let go sweetheart." I closed my eyes as the tears rolled down my cheeks, tension leaving my body and the sobs racked through me.

"It's going to get better."

⁂

"Alright, guys enjoy your holidays. I want this essay submitted by next Monday and I'll set you some more work."

"Seriously sir?" One of the girls towards the front of the class whines, her bleach blonde hair twirled around her finger as she chewed on a piece of gum.

"You're on a roll man." Another student commented over the groans and complaints of everyone else.

"Oh shush. A level isn't like GCSEs! A lot more work, you know this!" More groans and the teacher chuckled lowly as if he enjoyed our annoyance. I stood up packing away my notebooks and pens, my phone pulled out and I stuck my earphones in as I slung my rucksack over my shoulder.

The other students rushed out laughing and talking amongst themselves about their upcoming holiday plans. Plans that included leaving Robin Hoods Bay for day trips in London or perhaps a trip to Cornwall. People here were so desperate to leave the small town as much as they could, believing the world had so much more to offer. It was true to an extent but then again anyone in the world would probably think that about their home town or city. The truth is that the world itself is just a domain where humans create their opportunities and memories. Robin Hoods Bay offered as much as it could, it offered tranquillity, happiness, and stability. Normality. The town offered me what the world couldn't.

A home.

An arm looped through mine and a head leaned on my shoulder, her hair tickling my skin.

"Ugh please remind me why I decided to take Chemistry?" Sasha moaned tiredly from what I presume was a lesson of information overload. I leaned my cheek awkwardly against her head as we walked through the crowded corridors trying not to accidentally push over a small year 7 kid. Sasha didn't care as much as me and simply gave sheepish smiles when her bag would accidentally hit a student in the stomach.

"Probably the same reason why you chose Bio and Maths too." Cyrus rolled his eyes at his whining girlfriend and checked his phone. His hand ruffled his hair and he grinned over at us. We all studied similar subjects and at least one of us was in each other class.

Sasha took A level Biology, Chemistry and Maths, she was probably the hardest worker out of all of us taking the trickiest subjects. Cyrus was taking Maths, Geography and History, he constantly had his head in a book studying ahead of his classes. Quinton took Geography, Art and he was studying French. He wanted to travel the world and was studying different languages; he already knew Spanish along with Sasha and Cyrus and was planning on studying some more. My classes included Art, English and History; I've learnt that I loved writing. It also helped with... It helps me express myself when I am anxious or angry, it was another way for me to communicate with my family, friends and Claire without outright telling them what was bothering me. I shared Roman's love of art and surprisingly Preston would join us in our casual sketching sessions, Owen and I bonded over our love of books and Xander would listen to me whenever I learnt something new in History.

"Why aren't you two exhausted or anything?" She pouted and I grinned at the envy in her eyes as she realised, we still had a lot of energy.

"Maybe that's because Mr Chapman is practically asleep at the beginning of their classes and only remembers he has a class to teach like 10 minutes towards the end," Quinton stated as he joined us. We made our way out of the building and into the fresh air.

Sunshine and warmth were rare especially since we were near the coast. The wind was still present providing us with sweet cool relief from the beating we were receiving from the sun. I immediately rolled up the sleeves of the pale cream blouse I wore. Our 6th form, unfortunately, required us to wear formal wear and so instead of wearing pinafores or formal dresses like some of the other girls, I stuck to wearing black flared trousers with pastel-coloured blouses. My hair was pulled back into a neat low ponytail, small black studs in my ear lobes and the rose quartz necklace being my only form of accessory. Sasha hummed as she checked her phone for the time.

"So, what's the plan?" Quinton asked as he fist-bumped a guy from one of his classes, I exchanged a look with Sasha, and we rolled our eyes. The boys were revelling in their newfound popularity since a lot of new students had enrolled in our 6th form and a lot of the high schoolers had left for colleges out of Robin Hoods Bay; it was amusing watching their interactions with people they didn't even know. However, they didn't leave our little group and always showed that our friendship was our little family.

"Home, shower, and then meeting up later with the others for the sleepover. Is Levi coming tomorrow?" I shook my head at Cyrus's' question checking my phone on his whereabouts. I hadn't seen Levi in a few months, and it was the first time seeing him since THAT day. We kept in touch over facetime and texting though, so it felt like he never really left.

"He texted me a few hours ago saying they got an earlier flight so they should be on their way. I think Xander went to go pick them up from the airport."

"Oh great... that dumbo." I playfully whacked Sasha's arm, making her burst out laughing and raise her hands in surrender.

"Okay okay! I'll be nice... I baked him a welcome back cake!" She said, clapping her hands in excitement making my brows furrowed in suspicion.

"What kind of cake?" Cyrus asked slowly, sharing my suspicion for this supposedly nice act.

"A coffee and walnut cake." There it was, I shook my head trying not to laugh at the proud smirk she wore, and the drained look

Cyrus wore. Quinton smirked and the two fist-bumped at their obvious dislike for Levi.

"Levi is allergic to nuts." She looked at me with a pout trying to look innocent, as if she hadn't just admitted to planning his death.

"Oh, I know." Great, my best friend was a sadist. Cyrus pulled her into a headlock and tried to explain to her why they would not be poisoning my childhood friend, Quinton shook his head and looked over at me with a single eyebrow raised.

"Stop smiling. You look creepy." My smile dropped and I glared at the idiot boy who always loved making fun of me. My lips pressed together as we walked along the cobblestone paths.

"Stop breathing." I retorted.

"Stop living."

"Can't tell me to do that when I've already basically told you to drop dead."

"Doesn't mean I have to listen to you zombie."

"Fall in a hole!" I hissed as I finally looked over at him, my lips quirking up when I realised, he was already trying not to laugh. His ocean eyes brightened as he looked down at me. I allowed myself to grin and we laughed at the stupid banter we always seemed to fall into. My eyes fell onto his stomach and he playfully nudged me giving me a stern look. He had told me over and over that he didn't like the guilt I always seemed to carry and would immediately snap me out of the guilt train when he noticed it picking me up.

"Remind me we need to work on your insults." I huffed and crossed my arms as we made our way to Sasha's car, his loud laugh cutting off as I slammed the door. Like every Friday, I slipped into the front seat with my best friend in the driver's seat. The boys laughing and joking in the back, every so now and then pulling me and Sasha into their conversation.

However, like most times on a Friday after school, I simply stayed silent as I looked out the window, Sasha gently patting my knee from time to time, Cyrus handing me snacks and Quinton tugging on my hair as they talked. Not ignoring my presence but simply accepting my need for isolation without me physically being alone. These past few months had been hard, accepting that I needed to go to therapy, talking when I feel like my mind had reached its max occupants, writing down my past- our past. But they had been here for it all, supporting me when I felt low and helping me heal. My eyes met Sasha's and we shared a smile.

"You ok babe? Everything ok with Claire?" She asked softly when she saw the content smile on my face. I nodded at her question and grinned at her concern.

I adored these people.

"I didn't get to ask but how was your session yesterday?" Alexander asked me as I rushed over to help him get the food from the boot of his car. Roman ruffled my hair with a blank face as he carried the drinks over to our small picnic area. My friends grabbing food and games from their cars and setting up the area on top of the cliff away from the edge. It had become sort of a tradition to go on picnics, the cliff where the lab exit was hidden was our main spot, safe and overlooked the beach and village. It was the first time Levi, and his family were joining, however.

"I was able to see Paige again, I was able to say goodbye." I smiled wistfully at the memory, I looked up at my eldest brother who gave me a sad smile taking notice of the bit of sadness I was trying to hide from them.

"Yeah? How do you feel about saying bye?" I leaned against the side of the car holding the bag which contained different dishes Owen cooked up.

"I'm sad, I probably won't see her again and it's weird because before I came here, she was the only person I saw and heard from consistently. I feel a bit weird knowing that if something goes wrong, she won't be here to whisk me away... but at the same time I'm glad." We walked side by side towards the group.

"Yeah? What are you glad about?"

"This means this is it. This is my forever home." As soon as we got to the group, Xander placed everything down and took the bag from me placing it next to Aunt Dree Dree who was working alongside dad and Owen setting out the food. My brother pulled me into a huge hug and swayed us slightly making me giggle and hug him just as tightly.

"Women I can't breathe!" He wheezed jokingly and I let go. He pinched my cheek and I swatted him away like the annoying fly he was.

"Love you, Dove." He mumbled before walking off to shout at Roman and Preston who were currently wrestling in the grass with Finley, Andre and Quinton cheering them on. A pair of arms hugged my waist and a young girl I had only seen through a screen when I was talking to Levi beamed up at me. Her eyes a light grassy green and blonde hair curly, she looked like a beautiful little doll and despite only being 4 years younger than me, she held the innocence of a little child.

"You're even prettier in person! Why are you friends with my brother? He's an ugly troll." Leah said in disgust, her head flying back as Levi yanked on her plait.

"Watch it rat." He warned but I could see the playfulness in his eyes and the amusement when she glared up at him.

"Your right. He is ugly." I teased and she pointed her finger in his face with a triumphant smirk.

"HA! UGLY MCFUGLY!" Levi glared at me before staring at Leah. She let out a squeal and went running for her mother. Levi rolled his eyes and smiled at me genuinely.

"It's nice to see you again Elisa."

"Nice to see you too Levi." He pushed me slightly before chasing after his little sister who once again erupted into screams making me laugh. Aunt Audrey was shouting after them yelling at them to behave and act their age whilst dad was attempting to help Alexander separate my two arguing brothers. Sasha and Cyrus in their little world talking and sending me a bright smile when they caught my eye.

"How's it going?" Karson said as he came to a stop next to me, I eyed him but the suspicion and hesitance I felt towards him were long gone. Now I wondered what he knew about me and if he told my brothers whenever I would sneak out of the house with Sasha to watch the sunrise. He chuckled as if he could hear my thoughts and smirked.

"Your dad knows, not your brothers. Your dad was fine with it since we always have eyes on you guys. Your brothers? They'd skin me alive and then lock you away in your dads safe." Yup, that sounded accurate.

"I'm okay. I mean it. I'm feeling okay." His eyes ran over my face and he nodded at my words, his hand patted my head like I was an animal and I groaned pushing him away. I could see the questions in his eyes as well as the shock and amusement as if he couldn't believe I was okay. In his defence, a lot of people including my brothers were shocked at how I was handling things.

"You, Elisa West, really are a little mystery." I winked at his words and pulled out my journal as he walked off to join the others, the journal dad gave me, a black leather-bound journal with a blood red spine and gold accents. According to Claire, writing helps with people who have... post-traumatic stress disorder, something with which I have recently been diagnosed with. Dad gifted me the journal saying it was one of my mother's spare ones.

'It's amazing how everything started with a red journal, my mother's secrets, project miracle, the small moments and memories of my parents, all written inside the red leather-bound journal that I carried with me for nearly 8 years. I guess evil, chaos and disruption are never truly gone. It's never erased rather hidden in plain sight. There will always be some form of corruption in the world, I was just one of many to put a stop to one of them.

Sometimes we get too comfortable after something bad has happened. We believe that nothing could be worse after the hell we've had to endure. TCT, The Council of Thorns, still existed. It was never my intention to figure out how to bring down a hidden organisation that seemed to want to wreak havoc within the shadows.

Even when I found out who had been after me and my family, I didn't suddenly decide it was my job to end them once and for all. My job was to get rid of Project Miracle, the data and information gone forever, nobody could reproduce what my dear mother had created, and my father couldn't recollect what they had done. My family was safe, we held nothing TCT wanted, and we were under the protection of MI5. Of course, we didn't trust them with our lives but for now, we would embrace the safety we were given, we would bask in the protection Karson and his team offered. TCT was out there, and I wouldn't be surprised if they had their new target, their new obsession.

But that's another story, not for me and my silly brothers, not for my best friends who have become part of my family. That story isn't mine.'

I looked up from the pages, the pen resting between my fingers; laughing and yelling coming from behind me making me smile. It was surreal watching the genuine happiness radiating from not only Owen but from my other brothers too. It was like the sun was shining permanently on those I loved, showering them in warmth.

The wind tugged at my hair making it fly about wildly, freely, the ribbon I had tied into my hair slipping away and dancing with the wind. My hand reached out to try and grab the black silk, but the ribbon darted away cheekily, rising higher in the air, off the cliff, away from reach. My hand slowly lowered as I watched it with a tilt of my lips.

A heavy weight settled on my shoulders, dad kissed my head and held me closely, enjoying the peace we had finally achieved. This was all that mattered. My dad, my brothers, my friends, my grades, whether I'd fail an exam, sneaking around with my best friends. That was all that mattered. Normality, a mundane life, with a bit of excitement and rebellion. This was everything I've wished for and it made my eyes leak and a relived giggle slip through my lips. My father's eyes shone with pride as he looked down at me; Preston let out a scream and ran towards us grabbing me by the shoulders before hiding behind me like I was his shield. Roman charged towards us and we let out piercing screams as we ran around dad away from the angry bull.

"I DIDN'T DO ANYTHING!" I laughed out but Roman kept coming.

"YOUR GUILTY BY ASSOCIATION!" He lunged but I quickly ran towards Xander who had long since given up trying to parent Roman and Preston and was relaxing in the grass with Karson, Owen, Finley and Andre. I dived onto Alexander who caught me, dropping the plastic cup he was holding.

"DOVE!" He exclaimed.

"ROMANS CHASING ME!"

"ROM- OOF" I let out a grunt as Preston and Roman tumbled on top of me and Alexander. The others had managed to roll out of the way and laughed at the dogpile we had created.

"Get off you big fat dogs! You're squishing ME! And Elisa!" Xander groaned and pushed away Prestons' foot that had somehow managed to fall next to his head. We shifted and began to untangle ourselves when Owen being Owen decided he was being left out.

"CANNONBALL!" He yelled taking a running start. We froze in realisation and all turned our heads to where we could see Owen charging at full speed.

"OWEN NO!" Our voices mixed in a panic, trying to get away from each other.

"OWEN YES!" He yelled back in determination before he was airborne; we let out yells of pain as his body collided with ours, our whines turning into joy and laughter at the hilarious situation we had fallen into, Roman cursed and yelled at Owen and Alexander groaned in pain since he was underneath us all.

Rolling onto the grass I saw my friends doubled over in laughter, Aunt Audrey and dad taking pictures and shaking their heads at us. I was on a natural high, the moment we were in making me feel lightheaded.

"For god's sake Owen!" Alexander yelled, finally letting loose, and tackling the second oldest sibling into the ground. This was family, fighting, laughing, playing, insulting. This is what gave life meaning.

'Now I write, I write about my past, the nightmares and my dreams. I express the pain and nausea I experience when I recall a dark memory and don't want to talk about it with my family, in this black and gold journal. I write about my past, about a girl with light hazel eyes that contained flecks of gold and green. A girl who is the youngest of all her siblings and had been in the foster system since she was 8 years old after her mother was murdered. I write about a girl who was a mystery to all she met and hid inside a shell of herself, searching for her forever. I write about me.'

"Alright alright, truce! Come and eat!" Dad yelled through his amusement making us all run towards him cheering like the kids we were. Sandwiches, bowls of pasta salad and snacks were passed around. Hot chocolate was poured into travel cups, peppermint chocolate and marshmallow cookies handed out. Sweetness and warmth exploding in my mouth, the air gradually cooling down making the hot chocolate our only source of heat.

The flapping of wings caught my attention; sounds going faint and my focus only on the little bird that landed on a nearby rock. I sipped at the rich liquid watching the bird tilt its head this way and that.

A Robin.

I got my obsession with birds from my mother. She would tell me random facts whenever we were together, facts I hardly remembered now except the odd few. Robins were signs, they symbolised a new beginning and life, they were a symbol of a lost loved one visiting them. Of a loved one saying goodbye.

'It was time to listen to Claire, to forgive myself for the events I couldn't control. To accept help when it was offered. To live my life in the moment like a normal teenager would do. It was time to move on, to let go, to heal and finally be happy.'

I watched the bird flap its wings and lift off into the air, its tiny body circling us before travelling over the cliff where we could hear the sea crashing against the rocks, the sky painted orange and peach as the day came to an end.

Standing up, I ignored the curious glances being thrown my way as I walked towards the cliff edge, not too close but enough so that I could see the beach down below, the water shimmering like a sea of diamonds. It felt like a flood gate had been opened that day in the hospital, the relief, happiness, guilt, regret; all of it hit me at once. The last few months full of smiles, laughter, and tears of solace.

The talking from my friends and family was still quiet to my ears, but I swear, I swear I heard her. Soft musical laughter down by the beach, a squeal of surprise and the sounds of pure joy. I swear I could hear her shouting my name and if I concentrated hard enough, I'm sure I could feel phantom kisses across my cheeks.

'She would be happy, proud, at peace. This was what she wanted; it was all she ever wanted. For us to be together, for us to be home together.'

The Robin flew out of sight leaving behind a sense of contentment and closure. My eyes closed as her laughter faded and everyone's voices returned, Xander calling me over for a hot chocolate refill and Preston demanding we played a game of charades.

I turned towards the others slightly but kept my eyes focused on the small black dot of the robin flying further and further away from us, a single tear rolling down my cold red cheeks as I smiled.

"Goodbye, mum... I'll see you again soon."

Acknowledgments

Thank you so much to the amazing writers, Alana, Dominique, Saba, Rishika, Mirica, Shatha, Angie, and Victoria, who I had the honour of getting to know despite us being spread all over the world.

Hugs and kisses to my girls Biran and Tia for listening to my crazy ideas and the constant support.

Thank you to my best friend and partner in crime, Hawwa, who motivated me and helped me with the book's development.

Lots of love to my parents and siblings for putting up with my stress, and writers' block. Thank you for supporting my dream of becoming a writer and for encouraging me to finish Finding my Forever!

Printed in Great Britain
by Amazon